The Most Lovable Detective
You'll Ever Meet...

Heron Carvic's MISS SEETON

**Don't miss a single misadventure of
the marvelous mistress of mystery!**

PICTURE MISS SEETON
A night at the opera strikes a chord of danger when Miss
Seeton witnesses a murder...and paints a portrait of the
killer.

WITCH MISS SEETON
Double, double, toil and trouble sweep through the village when Miss Seeton goes undercover...to investigate a
local witches' coven!

MISS SEETON DRAWS THE LINE
Miss Seeton is enlisted by Scotland Yard when her paintings of a little girl turn the young subject into a model
for murder.

MISS SEETON SINGS
Miss Seeton boards the wrong plane and lands amidst a
gang of European counterfeiters. One false note, and her
new destination is deadly indeed.

ODDS ON MISS SEETON
Miss Seeton in diamonds and furs at the roulette table?
It's all a clever disguise for the high-rolling spinster...but
the game of money and murder is all too real.

Continued...

W9-AVR-270

ADVANTAGE MISS SEETON
Miss Seeton's summer outing to a tennis match serves up more than expected when Britain's up-and-coming female tennis star is hounded by mysterious death threats.

MISS SEETON BY APPOINTMENT
Miss Seeton is off to Buckingham Palace on a secret mission—but to foil a jewel heist, she must risk losing the queen's head...and her own neck!

MISS SEETON AT THE HELM
Miss Seeton takes a whirlwind cruise to the Mediterranean—bound for disaster. A murder on board leads the seafaring sleuth into some very stormy waters.

MISS SEETON CRACKS THE CASE
It's highway robbery for the innocent passengers of a motor coach tour. When Miss Seeton sketches the roadside bandits, she becomes a moving target herself.

MISS SEETON PAINTS THE TOWN
The Best Kept Village Competition inspires Miss Seeton's most unusual artwork—a burning cottage—and clears the smoke of suspicion in a series of local fires.

HANDS UP, MISS SEETON
The gentle Miss Seeton? A thief? A preposterous notion—until she's accused of helping a pickpocket...and stumbles into a nest of crime.

MISS SEETON BY MOONLIGHT

Scotland Yard borrows one of Miss Seeton's paintings to bait an art thief...when suddenly a *second* thief strikes.

MISS SEETON GOES TO BAT

Miss Seeton's in on the action when a cricket game leads to mayhem in the village of Plummergen...and gives her a shot at smashing Britain's most baffling burglary ring.

MISS SEETON PLANTS SUSPICION

Miss Seeton was tending her garden when a local youth was arrested for murder. Now she has to find out who's really at the root of the crime.

STARRING MISS SEETON

Miss Seeton's playing a backstage role in Plummergen's annual Christmas pageant. But when a murder takes place, she'll hand over the culprit—gift wrapped—to Scotland Yard, in her usual show-stopping style...

MISS SEETON ROCKS THE CRADLE

It takes all of Miss Seeton's best instincts—maternal and otherwise—to solve a crime that's hardly child's play.

Available from Berkley Prime Crime Books

MORE MYSTERIES FROM THE
BERKLEY PUBLISHING GROUP...

Heron Carvic's Miss Seeton

MISS SEETON UNDERCOVER
HAMILTON CRANE

BERKLEY PRIME CRIME, NEW YORK

This Berkley Prime Crime Book contains the
complete text of the original hardcover edition.

MISS SEETON UNDERCOVER

A Berkley Prime Crime Book / published by arrangement with
the author and the Estate of Heron Carvic

PRINTING HISTORY
Berkley Prime Crime hardcover edition / April 1994
Berkley Prime Crime paperback edition / October 1994

ISBN: 0-425-14405-4

Berkley Prime Crime Books are published
by The Berkley Publishing Group,
200 Madison Avenue, New York, New York 10016.
The name BERKLEY PRIME CRIME and the
BERKLEY PRIME CRIME
design are trademarks belonging to Berkley Publishing Corporation.

PRINTED IN THE UNITED STATES OF AMERICA

10 9 8 7 6 5 4 3 2 1

CHAPTER 1

"Mountains," said Amelita Forby, with a wistful sigh. "Snow and pine-trees and gambolling goats . . ."

There came no answer from the busy figure on the far side of the bedroom. After a moment, Miss Forby continued: "Ski-slopes and scenery and sparkling fresh air . . ."

"And avalanches—and glaciers—and another broken ankle or two—and frostbite to boot, I shouldn't wonder," retorted Thrudd Banner, continuing to throw things into his suitcase without pause. "If, in the midst of your excessive raptures, you'll—ahem!—excuse the pun, that is."

Mel, who had no intention of excusing anything, promptly switched off the pathetic look with which she'd planned to melt his hard heart if he'd turned round as she'd hoped—her undoubtedly beautiful eyes could, as other Fleet Street journalists knew to their cost, cope with whole icebergs if necessary—and substituted for pathos a decidedly accusing glare.

"So whose fault was it I broke my ankle? It takes two to tango, Banner, and don't you forget it!"

Her partner, still refusing to turn round, pressed on with the remainder of his packing. "It certainly does—and I don't." He permitted himself a lascivious chortle. "Fun, though, wasn't it?"

Despite herself, Mel had to smile. The particular—and peculiarly personal—variant of the tango in which she and

Thrudd Banner had been engaged just before she tumbled out of bed and ended up in plaster had, indeed, been enormous fun: but that was hardly the point.

"That," she said, "is hardly the point. Fun's all very well, in its place"—she couldn't help her gaze drifting briefly bedwards—"but this is *work* we're talking about, Banner—your work and mine—"

"Not yours," said Thrudd. "On this occasion, mine—*exclusively* mine." He snapped the locks on his suitcase, slipped the keys in his pocket, and seized his camera from the chest of drawers. "Talented though you may be, Mel—for a relative newcomer to journalism, that is—"

He ducked, dropping his case, as Mel hurled a shorthand notebook at his head. It missed. Mel cursed, and Thrudd straightened, with a broad grin on his face.

"Talented in many ways, Forby, but take my advice and stick to what you know—or think you do. Don't bother applying for the netball team, okay? Better not take up clay-pigeon shooting or darts, either—hey!"

"Bulls-eye," crowed Mel, as the passport found its target. "So now who's the one with the talent and know-how—when *you* don't even know enough to take the right paperwork with you? A fine thing for the star of World Wide Press to be turned back at the border. You know what the Swiss are like—tidy-minded, law-abiding . . . One look at you and they'd run you out of town, and I for one wouldn't blame them in the least."

"So why blame me?" Thrudd bent to retrieve the dark green card-covered document from the floor. "For not taking you along, I mean. As I started to say before, Forby, talented I'll grant you may be—*may* be," with insulting emphasis, "but even you can't work flat out for two organisations at the same time. If I'm the acknowledged star of World Wide Press—"

"Not by me you aren't!"

He ignored the interruption. "—then a judicious observer might just admit you could be called the twinkling candle of the *Daily Negative*—okay," as the glint in her eye showed him the joke had gone far enough, "the full-blown searchlight, if you prefer. But the *Negative* doesn't send its home-front crime reporters abroad if there's an international story breaking, and World Wide does. Which I would have thought," witheringly, "should have been obvious from the name, to a smart sleuth like you—just as it ought to have been equally obvious that I was leaving my passport for last so I could be sure it ended up where I could grab it easily."

So saying, he slipped the passport into the breast pocket of his jacket, and smoothed the fabric with a firm hand. "You know what the Swiss are like—efficiency's their middle name. Wouldn't want to keep the immigration officer waiting, would I?"

Mel—whose broken ankle had mended some months earlier—was tempted to kick at this remark, but restrained herself to a further scowl.

"How should I know what the Swiss are like? I've never been there, remember? All I know's what the travel pages tell me. Chalets, and mulled wine, and cheese fondue—"

"Alpenstocks and yodelling contests and cuckoo clocks—talking of which . . ." Thrudd glanced at his watch, nodded, and sat down on the edge of the bed. "Oh, and chocolate, of course. Ask nicely, and could be I'll bring you back the biggest box you ever saw—but in the meantime—"

"I don't need a consolation prize!" Mel tossed her head, and pointedly chose to ignore the way her paramour was patting the counterpane beside him. "You get to handle the biggest drugs story for years—and all *I* get's the kind offer of a box of lousy soft centres when you come back!"

"There's gratitude for you." Thrudd contrived to look wounded at his lady's ill humour. "Some of the best chocolate in the world, and you don't want it? I'll never understand the female mind—unless—hey, I get it!" He clicked his fingers, and grinned. A mischievous gleam danced in his eyes. "Of course! You're not a rotten loser after all, Forby. You'd just prefer me to bring back a few bottles of duty-free booze so we can mull our own wine, wouldn't you—or how about a fondue set, instead?"

Mel muttered that she would rather enjoy these products on their home territory; but Thrudd wasn't really listening.

The mischievous gleam remained.

"Talking of fondue sets, since it's obvious you're lost without me and absolutely determined to pine while I'm out of the country—if you're looking for ways to fill the long, lonely hours, how about you watch that television cookery series that's getting such good reviews? You might learn a trick or two about making gravy without lumps, or—hey, Mel, I didn't mean it!"

Thoughtfully, Mel weighed in her hand the heavy—and expensive—bedside lamp she'd just snatched up, and measured with a calculating eye the length of flex between the lamp and its attendant power socket. "If this," she enquired sweetly, "hits you before I unplug it, will you be electrocuted?"

"I don't know—but if I am, you don't get to collect on my insurance."

Mel choked. She could never—no matter how great the provocation—stay seriously cross with her swain for long, and it was a struggle not to let him see her laughing now. "But if the bad guys get you in the course of duty, you mean, I do? Great! How much?"

"Not nearly enough." He patted the bed again. "Not to make up for what you'd be missing, Mel . . . "

"What I'm *missing* is the chance to watch you being the ace investigator you're always telling me you are—"

"Plus the chance to see me at the scene of one of my greatest triumphs—I think." Thrudd's restless hand was stilled as, with vacant eyes, he gazed into the past. He frowned. "That was the first time I had any dealings with MissEss . . . "

"And the poor woman's never been the same since," came Mel's automatically acrimonious response. "Now, when *I* met Miss S. for the first time, the two of us got on like a house on fire . . . " She hesitated. Perhaps, given that there had been a later occasion when only the swift actions of Amelita Forby had prevented the lady in question from being burned to death in her bed, that wasn't the happiest of similes.

"Well, we got on fine, anyway. She was really helpful, right from the start. Friendly, too—of course, I didn't make her uneasy the way I bet you do, always thinking the worst of the poor little soul. She could tell I had a pure, unsuspicious mind, unlike—''

''Pure?'' And Thrudd leered in a meaningful manner.

''Unsuspicious,'' she repeated firmly, feeling her cheeks grow warm. ''Unlike some I could mention! I'm not—never have been—one of the evil-minded types like you. I *trusted* Miss S., from the word go—which I still do, no matter how many faces you make,'' as Thrudd rolled his eyes, and let out an exasperated sigh. ''I'm sure she can't help sensing you don't trust her—you know how she picks things up without realising—and that's why she's bound to feel a bit uncomfortable with you around.''

''So who's disagreeing with you?'' Thrudd gestured expansively, then subsided. ''Though I'm not sure *uncomfortable*'s exactly the word for the rest of us, with MissEss at full throttle . . . ''

He couldn't help it: the very mention of that name had been enough to set memory ablaze. He was back in Switzerland, those—how many?—three, four, five years ago, when he'd first encountered Miss Emily Dorothea Seeton at a press conference: a press conference over which she'd presided in such masterly fashion that she'd won his undying admiration. Mel might (after all these years!) try to tell him the old lady was just so honest she wouldn't know how to mislead—well, sometimes he could almost believe her, when he heard Miss Seeton burbling (was there a better word?) all injured innocence and honesty—honest as the day was long . . .

But this was October, for heaven's sake, and well past the longest day. As for Miss Seeton . . . if he thought back to that press conference, how could anyone seriously suppose her to be the innocent she seemed? Why, in verbal thrust and parry that sweet little spinster schoolma'am had matched—had outmatched—every reporter present, himself not excluded . . .

And the subsequent complexities of what turned out to be a major currency case, with murder and art theft thrown in, had left him—and the rest of the world's newshounds—gasping with admiration. How could he forget the night he'd been chased through the steep streets of Geneva Old Town, escorting Miss Seeton, pursued by members of an international gang—and Miss Seeton had emerged (as he, her escort, had likewise emerged) unscathed—although there had been others who hadn't—including one he'd killed himself . . .

"And look at the way she brought back that severed arm from Paris on a plate for Bob's wedding present," he murmured, so low Mel had to strain to hear him. He sighed, and shook his head: he knew he'd never really know, know with a reporter's certainty, whether Miss Seeton was what she seemed—or not. "What a woman . . . "

"You mean me?" Mel, too, had had her eye on the clock, and now put down the lamp, and was minded to preen herself. "Gee, thanks—though I can't be *so* much of one, if you're happy to hop off abroad and leave me behind without even trying to wangle me along on expenses—though I guess I might just be . . . persuaded to forgive you, this once." Her gaze drifted to the king-sized bed, and she allowed the hint of a smile to soften her expression. "Mind you, I still think it isn't fair you should get this chance for a scoop while I'm stuck here with nothing."

"With no Yours Truly, granted, but—seriously, with nothing? Come on, Mel, how many more scoops do you want? Aren't you still basking in the glory of having covered the Blondes in the Bag case?"

"That," Mel reminded him, "was last month—and even a week's a long time in Fleet Street. Besides, you were in on the Blonde Bagger business as well. Nobody who knows what's what could call that an exclusive—"

She clapped a hand to her mouth as she realised, from Thrudd's grin, that she'd fallen into his trap. He chuckled gleefully. "And no more would my Swiss Seasickness Scandal be an exclusive, either, if you came tagging along with me and started snooping on World Wide expenses for the *Negative*'s benefit!"

He chuckled again. "Be fair, Mel, admit you've been beaten to the scoop—if it turns out to be a scoop, and we can't be sure that it will—by a better man, and wish me luck without grudging it to me . . . and, who knows? Your luck might turn. The police may yet come up with something on this Ram Raiding story. Then it could be your byline on the front pages days before mine, because goodness knows how long it'll take to follow up my theory about the batch numbers being tied in with the account numbers. These Swiss banks're closer than oysters about their clients' affairs—and, talking of affairs . . . ''

He checked the bedside clock. ''Time to say a final, fond farewell, Miss Forby? Before I fly off in search of fame and fortune . . . ''

''Leaving me to the tender mercies of the Ram Raiders?'' Mel pursed her lips. ''I'm not so sure that's much of a bargain, Banner. You've got a lead in the drugs case—could be it's wrong, but at least it's a lead of sorts—whereas the police don't seem to know any more than when they started.'' She frowned. ''Or, if they do, they're not letting on—not even to me, with my personal hotline to high places!''

Thrudd watched, grinning, as the pursed lips and frown turned to a martial glare, and Mel muttered grimly, ''Wonder if I ought to be down at the Yard right now, bending the Oracle's ear? He can flannel till the cows come home on the telephone—but if I had the slightest suspicion he was holding out on me . . . ''

''He wouldn't dare.'' The grin turned to another chuckle. ''Your pet Scotland Yarder has a healthy respect for your talents, Mel. You know darn well *he* knows you'd eat him for breakfast if you ever caught him keeping you in the dark when there was a story breaking—which, I admit,'' as Mel looked slightly mollified by this tribute to her professional acuity, ''it doesn't seem to be doing, or sure as hell one of us would have heard a whisper. Which must mean the police *can't* have any leads in this Ram Raiding business, not that they've got them and they aren't sharing them . . . ''

His gaze was once more vacant as his thoughts, by what process of logic Mel could only guess, made him add:

''I wonder what Miss Seeton's doing now?''

"This," announced Detective Chief Superintendent Delphick, as he tossed a bulging buff folder across the room towards the desk of his startled subordinate, "brings the grand total, Bob, to eight in three weeks since they arrived on our patch. And"—he sat down grimly in his swivel chair, frowning—"I don't like it."

"Er—no, sir." Detective Sergeant Bob Ranger might have added, as his blotter skidded sideways and his in-tray wobbled, that for himself he didn't much like being bombarded with bumf from a distance by someone whose eye wasn't quite as keen as his inarguably brilliant brain; but Bob was not only—after more than seven years as the Oracle's sidekick—tactful, and mindful (being now a married man) of his pension: he was entirely in sympathy with the sentiments of his superior. It didn't surprise him in the least that his boss wanted to let off a little steam: and who better—Bob, even as his huge hands failed to stem the avalanche of paperwork now spilling all over the floor, suppressed a chuckle—than a chief super's sergeant to be his safety-valve?

"No, sir." Above the Oracle's apologies as the avalanche began, Bob scrambled from his desk to start collecting things. "Er—neither does Inspector Terling, sir, from what they're saying in the canteen."

Delphick, after a moment's silence, in his turn chuckled.

"And misery loves company? This, no doubt, is intended to encourage me, Sergeant Ranger. I have to inform you that it does not. In the present circumstances, the company of Inspector Terling and his colleagues of the Art Squad is better, in my opinion, avoided like the proverbial plague."

Bob, settling himself at his desk again, risked a quick grin as he opened the buff folder and began to study its contents. "That why you've been in hiding the last few days whenever he's rung, sir?"

"Hiding?" Delphick uttered the word in his chilliest tones, and raised an oracular eyebrow. Bob, unrepentant, glanced up from his reading and grinned again, allowing his pointed gaze to fall upon the telephone extension to one side of his desk, and its fellow—muffled behind a high-piled in-tray—on his superior's.

The eyebrow relaxed; the Oracle sighed, and grinned ruefully back. "On reflection, alas, I fear you may be right. It would seem useless to try to persuade you, of all people, that my, er, apparent reluctance to answer the telephone of recent times, and my unwonted willingness to allow you to take messages which I am regrettably slow to acknowledge, derive from any enthusiasm on my part for concentrating on clearing away my backlog of paperwork."

"Absolutely useless, sir." Bob's agreement came promptly: he was a realist. "No use at all trying to kid me, sir—you hate paperwork as much as I do." He scowled at his even higher-piled in-tray, and there was an undertone in his voice which made Delphick chuckle again.

"Every bit as much," he cheerfully confirmed. "But until, Sergeant Ranger, you achieve such exalted rank as mine—or even that of a mere inspector . . . Ouch."

"No getting away from him, is there, sir?" Bob turned a page. "From this, he certainly sounds in a bit of a tizz about what's been going on—Inspector Terling, I mean. I'd have thought it'd be right up your—our—street, what with . . . well, you know, sir."

"Indeed I do." Delphick pushed back his chair, rose, and headed for his sergeant's desk. "I also know, as I said earlier, that I don't like it." Pulling out the visitors' chair, he sat down, reaching across to tap with a warning finger the buff folder Bob still held. "It is extremely fortunate that no-one has as yet been hurt—as yet," he repeated, in the same grim tones he'd used before. "For how much longer this good fortune will hold, however, I hesitate to guess. Many antiques dealers sleep above their shops—it amazes me that none of them so far has woken in time to confront the robbers before they've made their escape. A healthy dislike of violence, in those not trained to it, is perfectly understandable, but I would have thought there was an even healthier sense of property among the English middle classes . . ."

Delphick stiffened. His voice tailed off, and his grey eyes darkened as he murmured absently: "Consider the example of the noted connoisseur Soames Forsyte, for one—though possibly we should in his particular case amend 'healthy' to '*un*healthy' . . ."

As the chief superintendent once more drifted to a halt, Bob scratched his head. Like most of the nation, his knowledge of the works of John Galsworthy was based on the television adaptation of *The Forsyte Saga* some half-dozen years previously, although—again, like most of the nation—he'd dipped into the paperback version. He couldn't really see much connection between an unlovable man with an overpowering possessive instinct, a beautiful woman with velvet-brown eyes and autumn-leaf hair, and the Ram Raiding thefts from West End antiques shops. Unless . . .

He turned back to the folder. Clipped to the inside cover was a lengthy typewritten list, which he scanned with renewed interest. He looked up, puzzled.

"Nobody seems to have pinched a portrait of Venus, sir, if that's what you're getting at. I mean—Irene, sir. Forsyte. You know how—how, er, beautiful she was supposed to be, in the book . . ." Delphick, himself puzzled, stared at his subordinate and saw him blush. "Anna Diomedes, sir," said poor Bob, blushing still more. "The kid thinks she's beautiful too, sir—his mother, I mean. Irene." Bob gulped. "Like—like Venus, sir, only the kid can't pronounce it properly, and his father—that'd be Young Jolyon, sir—he, well, he does." And the Oracle'd better not ask *him* to pronounce it, because no way was he going to make a fool of himself trying—he'd felt sorry for the kid in the book, and that's why that bit had stuck in his mind after all these years.

"Ah, yes, of course, Botticelli—*Venus Anadyomene*." It was pronounced perfectly: the Oracle, on occasion, could be a kindly man. "You have a good memory, Bob. I'd quite forgotten the scene until you reminded me—it wasn't shown on television, was it? But I didn't mean that. I think." The thoughtful look returned to the grey eyes. "It was—what might be called a slight change of focus, perhaps—the idea of a connoisseur... But no, it's surely ridiculous. Though coincidences, I won't deny, do happen... And in any case," shaking himself back to reality, "this has to be the work of experts, Bob. Whoever they are—and whoever they work for—they go straight to what they want. They ignore many more conveniently placed items in favour of the best—they have even ignored those items which, to the relatively expert eye, would appear the best, but which to the superlatively expert eye—or so the legitimate experts tell us—show signs of repair. Repair which makes those items less valuable, less collectible, to the connoisseur..."

Bob opened his mouth again. This time, Delphick nodded to him to speak. The sergeant cleared his throat. "That's—that's more or less what Inspector Terling says, sir. If you'd only heard him..."

"If I hadn't been avoiding him, you mean? Point taken, Sergeant Ranger. This office, however, only concerns itself with serious, that is to say generally violent, crime—which the inspector knows as well as you or I. And, I repeat, these Ram Raids—or at least those in London—have been—so far—remarkably blessed by an absence of violence... although we must question for how much longer the blessing will continue... but they are also the work of experts." He frowned. "Experts who, at a guess, could well be stealing the various items to order..."

Behind his desk, Bob wriggled, if the actions of anyone who stands six foot seven in his socks and is built accordingly can be described in so undignified a word. This time he did not even bother trying to speak. He gulped once or twice, and coughed. Delphick sighed.

"Inspector Terling is of the same mind, do I gather from your horrible grimaces?" Another gulp, and a nod. Delphick quirked an eyebrow. "Then, Sergeant Ranger, I am in excellent company—as likewise is the inspector." He leaned forward, and frowned once more. "In which case, since the two of us are so clearly theorising along almost identical lines, it passes my immediate comprehension why any opinions I might offer on the Ram Raiding should be of such interest to him that he persists in sending me up-dates of every single case report as he receives them . . ."

Bob, having gained his second wind, simply looked at his chief. His look spoke volumes.

Delphick looked right back at him—sighed—and sat up. "I said before that I did not like it. I was not referring merely to the criminal aspect of this case, Sergeant Ranger, but also to my dislike of the—the professional blackmail to which I am apparently being subjected by those who should know better." He watched Bob try to smother a sudden grin, and said, as if trying to convince himself:

"If I may just briefly jog your memory, Sergeant? There is nothing remotely . . . boreal about any of the items listed as stolen—that is," as Bob blinked, "nothing more wintry, either in subject or in title, than might be expected in an average haul of quality antiques."

"Er—no, sir." A light began to gleam at the back of Bob's eyes as he saw the Oracle building up a head of mental steam. Delphick, hardly hearing the words, noted the gleam, and his own eyes glittered as he went on:

"I won't deny the likelihood that these items are being stolen to order, Sergeant Ranger. Nor will I deny that, as the items have all been of the highest quality, it is equally likely that those persons ordering their—their appropriation from their legal owners are more than usually endowed with riches: the impecunious do not commission, as it were, gangs of knowledgeable criminals to commandeer powerful cars, send them at high speed into plate-glass windows, and thereafter help themselves to what we can only assume is a previously-listed selection of display goods . . ."

"Er—no, sir," said Bob, as Delphick appeared to run

out of steam, and stared at his subordinate for some moments in silent irritation before returning:

"The answer only prudence, presumably, has prevented you offering is surely 'Don't you mean *person* in the singular, sir?'" Delphick stopped steaming, and chuckled. "Confess, Bob. You don't believe in the—the plurality of the case, do you? You scorn the notion, logical though it may appear to the less, ah, romantic mind, of a syndicate of organised antiques thieves. You don't even believe the Ram Raids are so cleverly organised they may be, as has been suggested by more than one of our colleagues, the work of drug barons, hoping thereby both to finance their revolting trade and to launder their ill-gotten gains . . . "

He shook his head for his subordinate's wild imagination. "Admit it, Sergeant Ranger. You, like Inspector Terling, are convinced that we are once more up against our old friend Chrysander Bullian, aren't you?"

Bob, grinning, gave a shamefaced nod. Chrysander Bullian could certainly be regarded as an old acquaintance, if not quite a friend, by Scotland Yard, for their paths had indirectly crossed on more than one occasion. Bullian was an American-Armenian multi-millionaire recluse notorious for his acute paranoid delusions, which took the form of an intense fixation with low temperatures. He was believed to inhabit an underground bunker in northern Alaska, waiting for the nuclear winter of World War III: he was said to be furnishing this retreat with works of art—sometimes commissioned, more often than not stolen to order—depicting such subjects as ice, snow, hail and frost, although the most tenuous connection with winter could catch the fancy of Chrysander Bullian—if, indeed, it was Bullian who was behind the recent world-wide outbreak of art theft. It seemed very probable, however, that it was. Could there be two people with not only the same neurosis, but with similar flourishing financial assets to support it, no matter how extreme its manifestation? He—whoever he was—had once instructed his minions to steal a stuffed polar bear from the Bellshire County Museum and freight it laboriously across the Atlantic: he had been thwarted then, but there was always the next time . . .

"Chrysander Bullian." Delphick's tone was wary. "You are, I most devoutly trust, mistaken, Sergeant . . ." Now it was almost pleading. "Aren't you?"

"Er," said Bob, and blushed again. "Well, sir," as Delphick regarded him quizzically, "it's—it's always a possibility, sir. I mean—he's just about the richest man in the world—and quite barmy enough to organise a scam like this—and, well, we have come up against him before, sir. That is—coincidence, I know, but . . ."

Scarlet, he subsided. The Oracle favoured him with a long, thoughtful look; he frowned; he chuckled.

"I wonder," murmured Chief Superintendent Delphick, "what Miss Seeton's doing now?"

CHAPTER 3

What Miss Seeton was doing, while so many people wondered, was minding her own business.

There is nothing at all unusual in this. Miss Emily Dorothea Seeton is the most modest of English gentlewomen: she would feel it an impertinence on her part to display excessive interest in the doings, whereabouts, or business of anyone with whom she was not personally acquainted, whether in the social or professional sense. Similarly, she would feel it an impertinence on the part of anyone else to display such an interest in herself.

It would therefore seem the greatest of all possible impertinences that the doings of this elderly maiden lady should interest—among others—a pair of high-flying Fleet Street journalists and at least two detectives from Scotland Yard. Miss Seeton, should she ever stoop to eavesdropping on the conversations of strangers—than which almost nothing could be further from her thoughts—would (the casual observer must suppose) be justifiably annoyed at such an invasion of the privacy to which she considers herself entitled . . .

The casual observer would be wrong: Miss Seeton would be neither annoyed, nor even surprised, at such conversations—from the Fleet Street high-fliers and the detective duo, at any rate, for to Miss Seeton they are no strangers . . . And she herself, to an extent she cannot fully understand, would also be wrong. Entitled though in many ways she may be to privacy, she is hardly a private person in the way she so fondly believes. Her doings are news. Her escapades make headlines. Her name is known to few; her soubriquet of The Battling Brolly is known to millions.

Miss Seeton, in short, is one of Scotland Yard's most unexpected weapons in the constant fight against crime . . .

"It's criminal, so 'tis," said Stan Bloomer, as he and Miss Seeton stood in the latter's back garden and surveyed the damage wrought by the high winds and heavy rain of the previous night. "A regular crying shame!"

At least, that was what Miss Seeton *thought* he'd said. Long acquaintance with this hardy son of the Kentish soil—an acquaintance which had ripened, over the last seven years, into friendship—had not proved enough to conquer the richness of Stan's accent. There were times, as she knew only too well, when it was safer simply to nod, and to smile, and to guess at what he'd been saying from the tone in which he'd said it.

"A great pity," agreed Miss Seeton, with a sigh. "October can be such a—such an uncertain month, can it not?"

Stan chuckled. "Oh, well. Keeps us busy—and they worms've had a rare old time of it, anyhow. So long's they little black gennum devils don't hear of un's frolics, dare say we'll manage."

"Moles," murmured Miss Seeton, from what memory she couldn't have said, "eat worms *backwards,* I believe. They nip off their heads, and squeeze out the earth like—like toothpaste. So very clever—but, of course, one would far rather have worms than moles in one's garden any day, for the sake of the soil—not, of course," hastily, "that the quality of the soil in my garden is poor, by any means," in case she had hurt Stan's feelings.

Stan Bloomer has cared for the gardens at Sweetbriars, Miss Seeton's cottage, for twice as long as Miss Seeton has lived in Stan's birthplace, the village of Plummergen. Stan's wife Martha, a Londoner who came down to Kent every September for the hop-picking, met and married her farm-worker husband around fifteen years ago, and promptly undertook a new way of life as the local domestic paragon. Anyone having Martha to "do" for them during the week may rest assured that no microbe, germ, or particle of dust will remain in the vicinity once she has bustled through the house with duster, mop, and broom.

One of the first houses through which the new Mrs. Bloomer bustled was that of Old Mrs. Bannet, who lived almost directly across the lane from the Bloomers' little home. Old Mrs. Bannet was then approaching her tenth decade, and had come to the reluctant conclusion that housework must at last give way to health. She was growing deaf—which didn't matter; and arthritic—which did. She could not sweep and scour and polish as she used to . . .

Nor could she dig and mulch and prune; nor care for the chickens as she'd done in a more active past. Martha had been working at Sweetbriars a mere matter of days when she'd suggested to Flora Bannet that Stan might repair the Sweetbriars fowl-house, replace the stock, and supply the old lady with good, fresh eggs on a daily basis, the surplus to be sold by him in lieu of wages. Within weeks, the scheme had proved so beneficial to both parties that it had been extended to include flowers, fruit, and vegetables; and on Mrs. Bannet's death, her sole legatee, Miss Seeton—whose godmother the old lady, a cousin of young Emily Dorothea's mother, had been—was delighted to inherit not only Cousin Flora's dear cottage, but her domestic and horticultural arrangements as well.

"Moles," repeated Miss Seeton, in a regretful murmur. "Such attractive creatures—*The Wind in the Willows*—and yet, one cannot deny, so troublesome in the garden . . . "

"Caper spurge," said Stan, who had planted numerous sprigs of this hardy perennial around Miss Seeton's garden when, in the previous spring, the Plummergen area had suffered the attentions of an unusually large number of the little gentlemen in black velvet. Caper spurge, with its yellow flowers and distinctive scent, was a noted country remedy against the incursion of moles, and by both Stan and Miss Seeton was greatly preferred to the spring traps or noxious gases of the more dedicated mole-haters such as the disgraced official catcher, Jacob Chickney.

"And, I think, the wall, and the canal," ventured Miss Seeton politely. "They are not, I believe, fond of water—moles, I mean—and the foundations of the wall, perhaps, and the lane . . ."

The topography of Plummergen is simple. The village's main—indeed, virtually its only—thoroughfare is a long, wide, gently-curving street named, by the prosaic citizenry, The Street. The Street runs from north (where eventually it reaches Brettenden, at six miles distant the nearest town) to south, where it divides in two on a right-angled bend. The angled offshoot, calling itself Marsh Road, winds around and across the Levels and the Marsh until it, too, arrives in Brettenden, after dividing in Wittersham to ramble also towards Rye, five-and-a-half miles away. The Street proper narrows abruptly as Marsh Road saps its strength, and runs on as a mere lane between high walls and cottage gardens to the bridge over the Royal Military Canal, and thence, meandering again, over Walland and Romney marshes to the coast.

It is on the Marsh Road corner of The Street that Sweetbriars is situated, its front windows looking northwards up the long, gentle curve, its side wall—mellow brick, like that used to build the vicarage opposite—running down the narrow lane into which The Street is metamorphosed. In one of the cottages on the other side of the lane live Stan and Martha Bloomer; between their front garden and Miss Seeton's wall the foundations of the southbound lane lie deep enough, it seems, to keep out any number of tunnelling moles.

"Bin a fine ole dinner for 'em here," Stan said, "if they'd a dug their way unnerneath—which thanks be they've not done, seemingly. Better worm-putts nor mole-hills to be swept away, any day, I reckon . . ."

"Indeed, yes." Miss Seeton surveyed her leaf-strewn lawn, sparkling with raindrops, spotted with the brown curlicues of myriad worm-casts which, if left to the mercies of wind and weather, would stifle the grass beneath and leave dead patches among the green. "Yes, indeed." She sighed. "I suppose," she said humbly, "that it really is beyond repair? I know how clever you have been in the past at mending things—such a useful skill, and quite beyond me, in so many respects. If, perhaps, it is simply a matter of tightening the string, or winding it farther up—though you are the expert, Stan, of course . . . ''

Stan shook his head as he studied the jagged white cleft in the age-smoothed wooden handle of the birch broom his employer now held out to him. ''Bin worse nor trod on, so this has,'' he began, taking the broom from her and pointing with a stern finger. Miss Seeton turned pink, and hung her head. Stan ignored her guilty flutters, too preoccupied with his explanation to notice. ''No manner of binding'll hold this here crack from growing to splinters—blood poisoning an' lockjaw, iffen you're not careful, which even with gloves you can't be sure. Safer by far t'buy a new one . . .''

''Oh, dear.'' Miss Seeton looked more uncomfortable than ever. She had hoped—dear Stan had worked so many wonders, over the years, with her garden implements—not, of course, that she had been (she believed) unduly careless, always oiling them before putting them away—but the chuck, or was it chock?—anyway, the piece of wood which stopped the garden roller from, well, from rolling down the garden . . . not that she grudged the expense, of course, if it was necessary—but that her own (she blushed again) carelessness should have made it necessary—

''I'm afraid it caught, you see,'' she said. ''The handle—my umbrella, that is, not the broom.'' She blushed as Stan stared at her with a *might-have-known-it* look on his face. ''At least, not at first,'' she added, with another blush: one had no wish to mislead, but it was sometimes hard to remember everything at once. She sighed, and went on:

''I took a walk along the canal yesterday afternoon—there are a great many interesting waterfowl to be observed at this time of year, you know. Mrs. Ongar—'' Miss Seeton broke off as she recalled that this was no time to be speaking of her friend from the Wounded Wings Bird Sanctuary in Rye. ''But I fear I lingered rather longer than I had intended. Shovellers, and gadwall, for instance—and goldeneye, which have just begun to arrive from Scandinavia, and even a pintail or two, I believe. With their moult complete, they look splendid, even though one cannot, of course, reasonably expect to see them so well in the dusk, and, unfortunately, the clouds had been building up without my noticing them. And it began to rain. And I was, perhaps, in a little too much of a hurry to return home . . ." Miss Seeton sighed for her impetuosity. "I had a light raincoat, of course, as well as my umbrella, with the weather so uncertain—but I came in through the side gate—so much quicker, as you know, than going on round to the front, when it was really coming down rather heavily by then— the rain, I mean . . ."

Stan, who'd had to cycle home through the same down-pour, nodded without saying anything. Miss Seeton, encouraged by this silent sympathy, went on:

"Although, naturally, one knows exactly where the beds and bushes are, I fear that somehow—in the dark, I mean, despite my flashlight, which was rather awkward, in the circumstances—with the rain, and having it open in front of my face against the wind—my umbrella, that is—they seemed rather to—to shift about a bit and take me by surprise. So that when I stepped sideways, as it were, and slipped on the flagstones—so wet, with the rain—I dropped it. Most unfortunate—trying to save the bulb, you see, thinking it less likely to break, which of course it would be, not being made of glass—likely to, I mean." She paused. "Although if one could invent an *unbreakable* glass, which might be folded into a convenient shape . . . However." Miss Seeton coughed, and firmly deflected her wayward thoughts from the possible manufacture of trans-parent umbrellas, sensible though the idea—now it had oc-curred to her—seemed.

"However," she went on bravely, "I fear that somehow, as I tried to find it, the handle must have caught against the chock, and loosened it. I did think," she confessed, "that I felt something when I tugged, but it was raining so hard by then . . ."

Stan gazed at her, and then at the broken handle of the besom. "You weren't never brushing up leaves in all that rain, surely? Nor yet propping rollers with'n."

"Oh, dear—no." Miss Seeton coughed again, and the

pink flush returned to her cheeks. "Er—no, indeed. It was just that—this morning, when I noticed how many had come down in the night, and the number of worm-casts on the lawn—leaves, I mean—as soon as I had finished break-fast I fetched it from the shed, and then the telephone went—and I laid it down on the flagstones—the broom, I mean—and they were still a little damp—and . . . ''

Stan, who knew Miss Seeton of old, could guess the rest. "Ah, well, best buy new, like I said. You'll not sweep leaves nor worm-putts with that'n again—though it's never wasted," relieving her of the battered besom, "when 'em twigs'll make fine stringing for seedbeds next spring, and I judge the handle's long enough for staking, with new apple trees to be planted once the beds is ready."

Miss Seeton was greatly relieved to learn that her care-lessness, and its resulting damage, could be turned to good use. Black sewing-cotton cat's cradles over springtime beds were always an excellent method for keeping birds from seedlings, and she had watched Stan plant enough trees and bushes to realise that their stems needed support through the early stages. She wondered why such an invaluable wrinkle for the reuse of damaged garden implements was not, as far as she recalled, to be found among the pages of *Greenfinger Points the Way*—a book from which she had learned, over the years, so much—though perhaps this was not so remarkable after all, since Greenfinger (she'd noticed very soon after purchasing that invaluable tome) very often pointed in quite the opposite way from Stan, which could make things confusing. In fact, it was sometimes extremely difficult to know whose directions she should follow, and particularly so when Miss Treeves, or Lady Colveden, or other gardening friends might advise a different course of action altogether—and when, if one looked at their gardens, there seemed really very little to choose between them. One could not, of course, say so, for fear of hurting Stan's feel-ings . . .

"Monbretia," murmured Miss Seeton. Stan bristled, and waved the besom as he waxed eloquent.

"Be dug up, they should," he insisted. "Cold frames—never! Hang in a shed's what's best, till the leaves're browned down, then cut 'em off and in boxes—apples, too,'' he added, casting a proud eye towards the end of the garden as it sloped down to the canal, where the boughs of laden fruit trees bent low to the earth. "Make a grand display, they will, for the church. Vicar'll be pleased—and iffen I *was* to enter 'em in the Show, they'd win first prize easy. Save that with they Murreystone lot,'' rolling his eyes and gesturing expressively, "there's no knowing what tricks they won't be getting up to—and I'll not,'' Stan said grimly, "stoop to their level, no more'n I'll set meself up to be a mockery in their eyes, the devils!''

Stan was by no means the only gardener in Plummergen so determined to exhibit none of this year's produce in this year's Show. The decision was heart-breaking, but, to many honest souls, inevitable, in the circumstances. Since the parish hall of Murreystone—arch-rival village to Plummergen through the centuries—had been destroyed by fire the previous spring, the two communities—who already shared a vicar in the person of the Reverend Arthur Treeves—had been forced to enter into several joint enterprises they would normally never have dreamed of holding under the same roof: the Produce Show was just one of many. But it was one where opportunities for villainy, chicanery, and downright jiggery-pokery were legion—and confidently expected to be seized: and a large proportion of Plummergen's horticultural fraternity was resolved to have nothing at all to do with proceedings until the builders had been to Murreystone, and Plummergen's hall was once more its own.

"A grand year's work," said Stan, with a faint sigh of regret. "But there's allus next year—and 'tis maybe good for the soul to be humbled, once-a-while, and the church'll look a regular treat. A good month, October . . .''

And in celebration of the season, he raised his voice in the words of the well-loved Harvest Hymn:

> Come, ye thankful people, come!
> Raise the song of Harvest Home!
> All is safely gathered in,
> Ere the winter storms begin . . .

And Miss Seeton, catching his buoyant mood, joined in, warbling merrily—though not tunefully—beside him:

> God our Maker doth provide
> For our wants to be supplied—
> Come to God's own temple, come!
> Raise the song of Harvest Home!

CHAPTER 4

In Plummergen's little village school, Miss Maynard stood at the front of the classroom holding a stick of chalk. With her free hand, she pointed to a bright face beneath an eager waving arm. "Yes, Laura?"

"Michaelmas daisies, please, Miss."

"Good." Miss Maynard smiled, nodded, and turned to the blackboard. Under the neatly-printed heading *Flowers of Harvest Time,* she wrote the letter M, then paused.

"Who can spell Michaelmas daisy?"

A chorus of voices answered, most of them giving the correct answer.

"Very good." Alice Maynard filled in the rest, then asked if anyone knew why Michaelmas daisies were so called.

This was a poser. Unlined foreheads creased in frowns; treble voices chirped denial. Miss Maynard smiled again.

"It's because they first come into flower around the end of September, and Saint Michael's special day—*mass* is an old word for a church festival, or feast—is September the twenty-ninth. Now, who was Saint Michael?"

A louder chorus—Plummergen's youth prided itself on being very rarely caught napping twice—informed her that he was a saint. Young Gemma, after a pause, tentatively volunteered the additional information that he was the most important of the angels. At this, the chorus erupted into giggles; but Miss Maynard did not laugh.

"Certainly he was—in fact, he was an archangel, one of the five top angels, and their leader. Now, Gemma, do you happen to know who the others were?"

Gemma ventured the name of Gabriel, which was upheld by Miss Maynard as others sniggered. Raphael, Uriel, Zadkiel, and their lesser colleagues Chamuel and Jophiel were, however, unknown to any save Miss Maynard, who printed their names carefully to one side of her Harvest listings before continuing:

"And what is so special about Michaelmas? I imagine almost all of you must know the answer . . ."

"S'a Quarter Day," the classroom of farm-workers' children informed her, with one voice. No good trying to catch 'em out with that one: if they didn't know when the rent was due, it'd only be because their dads'd bin struck dumb and not able to moan about it over the past year, which none of 'em had.

"A Quarter Day," confirmed Miss Maynard. "And what are the other three?"

This caused a little confusion, with everyone shouting at once. Alice Maynard clapped her hands for silence, then instructed that they should call the name when she supplied the date. In this manner Lady Day, Midsummer, and Christmas Day were added to the blackboard, with Miss Maynard explaining to an argumentative few whose die-hard parents still held to the old ways in speech, at least, that the Old Style calendar had undergone its notorious—but necessary—eleven-day shift more than two hundred and twenty years ago, and that the final quarter of the twentieth century might be considered a good time to bow, at last, to change.

Having thrashed this matter out to the satisfaction of the majority, Miss Maynard returned to her original list, and asked for the names of more autumn flowers. Her pupils, country children all, promptly provided those of the chrysanthemum, sunflower, dahlia, purple crocus, and—another score for the argumentative element—the red-hot poker. Further argument seemed about to break out as the list then veered towards shrubs and their berries, but Alice Maynard decreed that these counted rather as Fruits of Harvest Time than Flowers, even if only birds and other wild creatures would eat them—this being the distinction between fruit and its earlier, decorative flower form . . .

From flowers to fruit—apples, pears, apricots, plums; from fruit to vegetables—onions, potatoes, beetroot, turnips, carrots: all chalked on the blackboard, all discussed, as points of interest arose, with enthusiasm by teacher and pupil alike. The discussion grew quite heated when marrows and tomatoes were mentioned, and Miss Maynard had recourse to the dictionary before the dissenters could be appeased with the printed definition of a fruit as opposed to a vegetable.

And then: "Other Foods," announced Miss Maynard, busily writing. The cereals: sun-ripened wheat, oats, and barley. A daring voice suggested nuts—which last raised not a few titters among the other children, while even Miss Maynard had to suppress a smile. For in Plummergen, "nuts" can have more than one meaning . . .

"Conkers, Miss!" The same daring voice was echoed by a dozen more, mostly male, as Miss Maynard's class recalled the forthcoming Grand Conker Contest against Murreystone, to be held on the same day as the Produce Show. There were mock-indignant groans when Miss Maynard refused to add the fruit of the horse chestnut tree to her list, ruling that other nuts—again she suppressed a smile—such as hazel (the renowned Kent cob), walnut and sweet chestnut—were truly useful to humans, while conkers—admirable sport though they might provide—were of greatest use to wild animals such as squirrels.

A brisk theological discussion then ensued, some of the die-hards insisting that squirrels were as much God's creatures as any human, and surely, therefore, equally entitled to give thanks. Someone wanted to know if squirrels and other wild animals went to Heaven, because when her cat had died she was told it had gone to join her granny, only cats lived with people and squirrels didn't, so . . .

Village schools are seldom the examination-geared hothouses suffered by urban children. Plummergen's fifty young share but two teachers between them: Headmaster Martin Jessyp instructs the Bigguns, as generations of children have labelled their eight-to-eleven-year-old colleagues, while Miss Maynard tends to the educational needs of the Tiddlers, who range in age from Almost Five to Over Seven. With such a range, it is vital to catch and maintain the interest of the class while, at the same time, encouraging some appreciation of the discipline pertaining later in life.

Impossible, in such circumstances, to stick to the absolute letter of the timetable. In one short lesson, Alice Maynard contrived to cover, in varying detail, aspects of botany, orthography, religious instruction, economics, history, astronomy, horticulture, agriculture, nutrition, and metaphysics. Her pupils had learned something, and the learning had been painless; Miss Maynard, too, had enjoyed the experience. But now . . .

"Now," she said, picking up the duster and rubbing it briskly across certain sections of the blackboard, "I should like Laura to hand out sheets of paper—one each for everybody, please. And Rachel, would you please distribute the coloured pencils? Just primary colours today—and who can remember what they are?"

A deafening chorus reminded her that they were red, yellow, and green. Someone who'd watched a programme on the family's new colour telly (acquired, to the ambivalent envy of their neighbours, on the costly never-never) about How It Worked smugly suggested blue, amid hoots of derision soon quashed by Miss Maynard: who confirmed that blue was indeed a primary *light* colour, but that until Kent County Council provided such things as light pencils for its pupils, she'd prefer them to keep to the ordinary sort. This part of the lesson was not Physics, but Art . . .

"And the best drawings," she said, as Rachel and Laura returned, their tasks completed, to their desks, "will be pinned up on the wall, so long as they're finished by break. Are there any questions?"

Fortunately, those that there were caused her no trouble in the answering. Alice Maynard's talents lay more towards the musical than the visual: Singing, Mime, and Dance were easier by far for her to teach than Drawing and Painting . . .

And as twenty industrious heads bent to the sheets of

paper on the desks before them, Miss Maynard wondered idly what Miss Seeton might be doing.

"What *have* you been doing? I was starting to think," said Lady Colveden, "that I must have made a mistake about which day it was, and you'd both gone off to market—and not taken me," she added, spooning vegetables on her husband's plate and passing it to her son.

"Which would," continued her ladyship, amid the subsequent deafening silence, "have been tremendously unfair, when you know how I enjoy pottering round the stalls and the shops while you two scratch pigs' backs and make noises at cows and brag to the other farmers about how well our crops are coming along."

Nigel, still busy trying to insinuate his father's lunch beneath the pages of *Farmers Weekly,* could only answer with a chuckle. Postman Bert had been late with that morning's delivery, and this was Sir George's first chance to catch up on the latest agricultural news, views, and theories. Nigel rustled paper, and coughed. Sir George, emitting a vague grunt of acknowledgement, moved *Farmers Weekly* three-quarters of an inch upward. Nigel relaxed as plate met place-mat in safety.

He turned back to his mother for his own serving, and a smile danced in his eyes as he accepted the plate, though it was in a solemn voice that he replied:

"Take you with us to Brettenden on market day? You're pushing your luck a little there, Mother darling. Do you seriously suppose Dad and I labour day after back-breaking day on the farm for you to spend the resulting all-too-meagre profits on folderols and bargains? Hats," he enlarged, as her ladyship's eyes widened. "Besides, if you really wanted to go, there's nothing to stop you going by yourself, in the Hillman."

Wide eyes looked hurt. "With petrol costing so much? And my egg-money's not enough to pay for even half a Monica Mary hat. Always assuming that's what I'd be going for, which of course it wouldn't, because your father never takes me anywhere, so what would be the point?"

Farmers Weekly danced a dry, rustling little jig as Sir

George turned a page: otherwise, a deafening silence continued to be the baronet's sole response to his wife's accusations of neglect.

"Of a new hat, I mean," went on Lady Colveden, as her son sprinkled pepper and murmured again of money. "I don't believe we've been anywhere smart together since the royal garden party, and goodness knows how long ago that was. Besides, why should you think I'm only interested in hats? I might have wanted to buy new saucepans—or cake tins—or something else equally useful."

Farmers Weekly rustled and jigged again as Sir George uttered a choking sound. Nigel's shoulders heaved as potato went down the wrong way.

Lady Colveden clattered knife and fork together on her plate. "I do wish the pair of you weren't always so—so disparaging about when I try to bake cakes. Everyone," said her ladyship in lofty tones, "has different talents. We may not all be Martha Bloomers, I know, but I'm sure my herbaceous borders are as good as any in the village . . ."

"Blooming good, in fact," gurgled Nigel. His father lowered *Farmers Weekly,* and coughed.

"Er—quite right, m'dear. Nigel," before his exasperated spouse could respond. "What we were talking about just now—might be worth giving winter barley a try after all, according to this. Seeing you've been keen for so long, I mean. How about Upper Cowdown? Seems the best bet, in the circumstances."

Nigel, beaming with pleasure, poured custard on treacle sponge with an abandon that set his mother's teeth on edge. "Twenty-two acres, and sheltered by the wood from the worst of the weather—yes, I agree, Upper Cowdown's by far the best place. If we *can* afford to take the risk I'd certainly like to try." His mother raised her eyebrows in silent query; the enthusiastic alumnus of Wye Agricultural College prepared to expound.

"We're talking about sowing one of the new continental winter strains of barley now, instead of waiting for spring as we usually do. Dad remembers, though I don't suppose you do, that I've suggested it several times before, but he's never been convinced the results other people have been getting are good enough—at least, he hasn't been, until now. But with everything I told him about last night—''

Sir George stroked a thoughtful moustache, above which his eyes danced. ''If you've told me *everything* about last night, I'd be surprised, at your age. I remember—ahem! That is—no, I don't,'' as he caught his wife's warning look, and huffed once or twice before hurriedly swapping *Farmers Weekly* for the local paper, which had larger pages.

''Really, George, I hardly think the Young Farmers are a hotbed of vice and iniquity—at least, not Nigel's crowd, I hope.'' Lady Colveden chinked her spoon against the rim of her bowl, and pushed treacle into abstract patterns. ''You two only ever humour me when I try to show an interest, but am I right if I guess that they had a talk at the meeting last night about this continental barley, and whoever it was thinks it works?''

''And,'' said Nigel, ''as I was about to say, before Dad began casting nasturtiums—it would seem that *Farmers Weekly* thinks so, too.'' He had picked up the discarded journal, and was scanning the pages which had caught the attention of his father. ''The evidence in favour is pretty strong—it's not just anecdotal, I mean. If the weather conditions are right, winter barley can out-yield the spring varieties in a big way—*and* you harvest it a good month before the other sort, and save yourself sowing-time in the spring, into the bargain.''

''It sounds marvellous,'' said her ladyship. ''But your father still has doubts—I can tell. Why, George?''

''Just so.'' Sir George coughed. ''Ah—why, indeed?'' He permitted himself a dry chuckle at this punning reference to Nigel's alma mater, then sobered. ''Boffins can't guarantee everything, y'know. Needs more fertiliser to establish than the spring sort, for one thing—and you heard what Nigel said about the right weather conditions. Dodgy and you'll have the lot going down with disease.''

''Rust,'' said Lady Colveden at once. ''Or smut, which I always thinks sounds rather silly.''

''Or mildew,'' admitted Nigel. ''Nobody says there aren't problems, but, as I said before, I'd certainly like to have a go. I must say I rather fancy the idea of a Rytham

Hall barley-sheaf or two at next year's Harvest Festival alongside the wheat . . . ''

"Talking of Harvest Festival—" said Lady Colveden; and then she said no more. Her words were drowned out by an indignant explosion from behind the august sheets of *The Brettenden Telegraph and Beacon (est. 1847, incorporating [1893] The Iverhurst Chronicle and Argus)* as Sir George turned another page.

"Good Gad!"

Lady Colveden blinked. Nigel enquired:

"Shock, horror? Scandal? Surely not in the *Beacon*, of all places . . . ''

His father, however, seemed too disturbed by what he was reading to accept this tempting invitation to explain. The future baronet looked at his mother, shrugged, then winked. "All right, Dad, don't tell me, let me guess. Mrs. Blaine's up on a charge of procuring? Miss Nuttel's been arrested for running an illicit still in the garden shed? Miss Seeton and Stan Bloomer have developed a strain of super-intelligent killer chickens?''

"Nigel," said his mother. "George, do stop popping like that, and put us out of our misery. What is it?''

"Whempstead," said Sir George, "poor chap. Loses his wife one week, next he's had burglars. Cleared the sitting-room completely,'' he added, above the expressions of shock and dismay from his wife and son. "Carpet, furniture, ornaments, the lot. Too much of that sort of thing going on in this part of the world recently— and he's only just the other side of Brettenden.'' There was a magisterial gravity in his voice as he lowered his newspaper to gaze, frowning, at his attentive family. "Can't say I really care for the idea of these blighters popping in and out of people's houses as if they owned them. Not the thing at all . . .

"Might not be such a bad idea if we revived the Village Watch," he said.

CHAPTER 5

Nigel put down his spoon, and groaned. "Oh, no, not the Night Watch Men! Not now, when the nights are growing longer every day—and we're all so busy at this time of year, with the end of the harvest and everything. If Dad has his wicked way, I confidently predict that half the village will soon be suffering from sleep deprivation and walking round in a daze—and staying in it for the foreseeable future, as well. Honestly, I had no idea there was such a strong element of sadism in my genetic makeup."

"Sadism?" Behind his moustache, Sir George bristled. "Plain common sense, that's all. Can't have complete strangers wandering where they please helping themselves to whatever they fancy without somebody trying to stop the scoundrels. No good blaming the police—impossible to be in half-a-dozen places at once," said the magistrate, with some feeling. "As I said, far too much of this sort of thing at the moment. Seems to be a fashion for it. Sitting-room antiques and furniture—sideboards, mostly. Hefty great things, some of 'em—get a good price, according to Szabo," he added, carelessly expert. "Chippendale—Hepplewhite—all those chaps . . ."

The "Szabo" to whom Sir George referred was an acquaintance of comparatively recent date, owner of a Bond Street establishment specialising in rare (and valuable) objets d'art. A naturalised Hungarian who had, for legal purposes, adopted the name of Frank Taylor, Ferencz Szabo was a plump, dandified exotic in a world of exotics, and one of the least likely people to dine with Sir George Colveden, most English of Englishmen, at his club on a regular basis: yet dine, and regularly, he did.

Rytham Hall boasted two of the finest William Morris rooms in the country. Cedric Benbow, noted society and fashion photographer, had used the rooms as background for super-model Marigold Naseby to display to best advantage the *Mode* magazine collection of high-class gowns. Marigold had worn, at Cedric's insistence, a selection of priceless Lalique jewellery, borrowed from museums in Lisbon and Paris. An attempt had been made to steal the jewels; and Ferencz, in his Frank Taylor persona, had been one of the persons instrumental in foiling that attempt—in commemoration of which foiling, Sir George had proposed that the principal foilers (except one, whose gender precluded her from participation) should meet at his club every so often for an evening of average food, better wine, and excellent company.

"Sheraton," added Sir George, then realised he'd run out of names, and hurried on: "But never mind that. Appreciate what you're saying, Nigel, but there comes a time when other things are more important than sleep. Has to be stopped."

"It's disgr-r-r-aceful," said Nigel, being Mr. Growser of Children's Radio fame. "It ought not to be allowed!"

His father eyed him sternly. "Quite right. Shouldn't be too much of a hardship for everyone if the rota's arranged properly—get Jessyp on it." Headmaster Martin Jessyp was by far the best paper-shuffler in Plummergen, even if Sir George, with his military training, was second to none in matters of general organisation. "Too busy on the farm m'self—but it won't do any harm at all to let the blackguards know we're on the lookout for 'em. Fire a warning shot or two across their blasted bows—sorry, m'dear."

Lady Colveden hid a smile. Since Rear Admiral Bernard "Buzzard" Leighton had moved into Ararat Cottage and made the acquaintance of Major-General Sir George, the baronet's language had, on occasion, acquired a decidedly nautical tinge. "I think," said her ladyship, "it's a perfectly splendid idea, George. In fact, as I started to say earlier—with Harvest Festival coming up, and the Produce Show the day before, not to mention the Conker Contest . . . "

"Murreystone," supplied Nigel, as his mother paused for breath, "are on the warpath again, and we ought to be ready for them—right?"

Lady Colveden nodded. "Your father will probably say I'm being unduly pessimistic, and you know I never listen to gossip, but—"

The snorts of mirth which erupted now from father and son were identical: it was like being insulted in stereo.

"But," persisted her ladyship loftily, "one can't help hearing things when people are talking in the shops . . . "

"Which is why, no doubt," broke in Nigel, as she paused for further breath, "you were so peeved to think you'd missed out on a trip to Brettenden. I should have thought the quality of tittle-tattle in the Plummergen post office was every bit as good as that in Brettenden market—if not better, with knowing everyone who's being talked about. Having a personal interest, so to speak. Speak no evil," he added, though not entirely sure why.

His father snorted a second time, and was heard to mutter of nuts. Lady Colveden said:

"That's exactly what I mean, George, because everyone else was saying it ages before the Nuts took it up, which proves it must be more true than most of the nonsense they talk. Because they didn't have time to invent it, I mean, before everyone else said it first . . . " She frowned. "Maybe that hasn't come out quite the way I intended—but I'm sure you both understand very well what I meant to say about Murreystone making—making noises, at least. And you know what's happened in the past," she added darkly.

"Making threats, you mean," amended Nigel, as Sir George huffed through his moustache and muttered that you couldn't trust the rascals as far as you could throw them.

"Which, in the case of the Murreystone mob," Nigel pointed out, "isn't very far—some of them are among the ugliest bunch of plug-ugly thugs I've ever come across. I say, that wasn't bad, was it? True, though—I wouldn't want to meet some of them alone on a dark night. We all know how they're still brooding about the cricket match—*and* the Best Kept Village Competition—though they hardly need an excuse for causing trouble, of course.''

Nigel was stating no more than the obvious. The rivalry between Plummergen and Murreystone, five miles to the east in the middle of Romney Marsh, is—as has already been said—of heroic proportions. The fifteenth-century Wars of the Roses are rumoured to have seen its inception: certainly the seventeenth-century Civil War saw it in full, well-documented swing. Plummergen was proud to favour King Charles; Murreystone marched to the support of Protector Cromwell. The Restoration saw Plummergen rejoiced, and Murreystone nursing a grudge which has never been allowed to lapse.

Plummergen's population is around the five hundred mark; Murreystone never rises much above three hundred and fifty. Plummergen plays more skilful cricket: Murreystone does better at darts. Both villages share a policeman: PC Potter lives in Plummergen. Both parishes—Murreystone has the larger church, which has always irked Plummergen—share a clergyman: the Reverend Arthur Treeves lives, with his sister Molly, in Plummergen. In earlier days, before he lost his faith, the Reverend Arthur frequently attempted a reconciliation between his two warring flocks: disillusioned in more ways than one, he has long since given up the unequal struggle. Plummergenites continue to glance sideways at Murreystoners whenever their paths cross, while Murreystoners continue to plot and scheme against their age-old enemies in a variety of ingenious ways. The recent cricket match and competition mentioned by Nigel were but two examples of the duplicity of the foe . . .

''I think,'' remarked Lady Colveden, beginning to stack dishes, ''that having people patrol The Street every hour, or whatever it was, would do more to show Murreystone we meant business—the burglars too, of course—than any amount of warnings PC Potter might give them—Murrey-

stone, that is, because of course he can't know who the
burglars are any more than anyone else. Assuming he's
heard the goss— the talk, I mean," as Nigel wagged a
reproving finger at her, and Sir George stifled a bark of
laughter. "Has heard enough to know to warn them to behave," explained Meg Colveden, on her dignity. "Which
I'm sure he will have done, because Mabel Potter shops in
the post office and she's very careful to let him know whatever's going on. You know," said Lady Colveden, "how
there's always so much *talk* . . . "

There is always talk in Plummergen's post office. Where
two or more villagers are met together, their tongues, invariably, wag—and never to more purpose, or with more
enthusiasm, than in Mr. Stillman's post-office-cum-general-
stores.

There are, of course, other places to shop in the Plummergen area, though none is more convenient than the post
office. The village has a draper's, run by the Welsted family, which stocks (besides fancy wools, sewing thread,
Manchester goods and clothes) china souvenirs and picture
postcards. Its range of the last two items has increased dra-
matically since Plummergen's second prize (to the inevitable wrath of disqualified Murreystone) in the Best Kept
Village Competition earlier in the year.

Like the post office and the draper, the grocer supplies
groceries, both green and otherwise; also (again like the
other two) sweets, tobacco, wines and spirits. The floor-
space in Mr. Takeley's little shop, however, is by far the
smallest of the three main emporia, and his deep-freeze,
though theoretically as well-stocked as the other two, is
more inclined to break down. Mr. Takeley is given (he has
a sense of humour) to frequent Liquidation Sales of goods
past their best, followed by periods of refrigerated famine
as first the electricians and then the wholesalers put matters
to rights: he does not, therefore, play too large a part in the
general life of the village, which in any case mistrusts a
bachelor with so pronounced a twinkle in his eye.

As well as its post office, draper's, and grocer's, the village has a butcher, whose splendid strings of sausages are

made to an old and secret family recipe; and a baker, who no longer has to bake his own bread, having become part of the county-wide Winesart chain. Mrs. Wyght, the baker's wife, is not kept so busy in the shop that she has no time to serve in the newly-opened tea-room, through the tiny bow windows of which one can gaze across The Street at the magnificent facade of Plummergen's favourite hostelry, the George and Dragon. The bakery is on the Marsh Road corner of The Street, near the village's one telephone box; farther up The Street, on the same side, is the blacksmith's double-doored forge, with its display cases outside for visitors and locals alike to admire . . .

And farther still up The Street, on the opposite side, is Mr. Stillman's post office, the clearing house for every rumour, slander, and supposition that village imagination can conceive.

" . . . a packet of sponge fingers, and a tin of peaches, please, Emmy love—oh, mustn't forget the custard powder, neither. Just a *small* tin," added Mrs. Henderson. It was her husband's birthday next day: he had dropped hints about trifle, and she was willing to oblige, but there was no need to spoil him.

Mrs. Skinner remarked, to nobody in particular, that when *she* made trifle she used Swiss roll with jam in it instead of sponge fingers—which were cheaper, goodness only knew, but didn't taste nothing like so good as Swiss roll no matter how much red jelly people might pour on trying to disguise them.

"And a bottle of sherry—a *large* bottle," Mrs. Henderson instructed, pretending to consult her shopping list. "That one'll do, ta," as Emmeline Putts, running a questing finger along the shelf, touched the price-label of the Phylloxera brand: cheap, cheerful, but undeniably alcoholic. "That's good and sweet for trifle, ain't it?"

Emmy's shrug suggested that she didn't know, and didn't much care. Mrs. Skinner's sniff suggested that anyone choosing to drink Quinta Phylloxera deserved everything they got.

"Weren't that the one," enquired Mrs. Skinner of the shop at large, "as them druggers in that gang used to poison the old folk and burgle their houses? Don't think I'd fancy giving that to any of *my* family, I must say.''

As Plummergen and Murreystone, so Mrs. Skinner and Mrs. Henderson. The feuding is equally intense, although in the latter case is of rather more recent date, and not so much political or ideological in origin as horticultural. The Church Flower Rota, as arranged by Miss Molly Treeves, is as fine an example of organised paperwork as anything drawn up by Mr. Jessyp or Sir George Colveden. In the case, however, of the Rota, the paper in question is pinned up just inside the church porch where it may be consulted when necessary, since Molly is often out of the house at meetings, and the Reverend Arthur cannot—it is generally accepted—answer the telephone or even give face-to-face messages with any degree of reliability. The porch system of consultation thus presents opportunities for abuse and double-dealing of the most dastardly kind: and Mrs. Henderson had, in Mrs. Skinner's opinion, abused the system to the uttermost when she took pencil and rubber to amend the Rota in her own favour, moving Mrs. Skinner's promised turn to a date three weeks in the future, when her peonies—on which she prided herself—would be past their prime. Even the repeated assurances of Miss Treeves that Mrs. Henderson had made the amendment on her authority had failed to convince Mrs. Skinner, in her secret soul, that she was not the victim of a gross miscarriage of justice; and matters had taken a still more serious turn after the choice of who should decorate the church for the coming Harvest Festival had finally been made.

Mrs. Henderson seized her purchases and stuffed them into her string bag with a defiant air. Emmy Putts held out a weary hand for the money, frowning over how much change she should give.

''I'll take two pound o' strong Cheddar, Emmeline, when you've quite finished,'' said Mrs. Skinner sharply. ''Begging your pardon if you'd already decided, Mrs. Flax,'' in hurried apology to the village Wise Woman, who had waived her right to be served first while she pondered the varying merits of Oxo cubes or a small jar of Bovril for tonight's stew. Mrs. Flax, frowning still in thought, after a nerve-racking pause nodded regally, accepting the apology as no more than her due. There are few in Plummergen who would willingly cross Mother Flax, and she is sensible of the need to maintain appearances at all times.

"And a large sliced white—and two pound of onions," gabbled Mrs. Skinner, eager to assemble all the ingredients for tonight's cheese pudding before the Wise Woman could change her mind and Overlook her. Curdled milk or addled eggs—Mrs. Skinner doubted even Mother Flax's ability to do much to a loaf of bread—would be the least of her worries, if the witch took it into her head to bear a grudge . . .

"Saving your onions for the Produce Show, Mrs. Skinner?" Young Mrs. Scillicough, whose respect for Mother Flax was minimal, cared nothing for the Produce Show, but enjoyed a good squabble as much as anyone in the village: the antics of her triplet toddlers, unsuppressed even by the most fearsome herbal remedies the Wise Woman could brew, had long since accustomed her to more disharmony and dispute than Mrs. Skinner and Mrs. Henderson could be expected to achieve in a lifetime. "Pity," said Mrs. Scillicough, "to waste a good crop on eating, I allus say."

"I've heard," remarked Mrs. Henderson to young Mrs. Newport, Mrs. Scillicough's sister, "as there's a regular plague of onion flies over to Murreystone. Costing 'em a fortune in sprays, I've heard—maggots everywhere, and the crop ruined—and o' course we've no way o' telling how far them flies can fly, have we? A fairish way, though, I shouldn't wonder."

"Shame if they've reached so far as here," agreed Mrs. Newport at once. "Especially for them as've bin saying all summer how they're sure to win, and now—"

"And now," broke in Mrs. Spice, who usually took sides but this afternoon felt her nerves weren't up to it, "it's Murreystone bound to win, if they're breeding them flies and sending 'em over here. Not as I'm saying I hold with entering the Show this year, meself, but for them as does it's a black day, make no mistake. If there's dirty tricks to be played,'' Mrs. Spice reminded the post office grimly, ''it's Murreystone as'll play 'em, no question.''

This ominous warning united—insofar as Plummergen can ever be united—the post office shoppers against the common foe. Forgotten were the Flower Rota, the failure of Mrs. Flax's nostrums to subdue the Scillicough triplets, the fact that young Mrs. Newport's quartet of under-fives was as much a village byword for good behaviour as their three cousins were for bad. The very idea of Murreystone could be enough, on occasion, to induce apoplexy in the most phlegmatic—and as most Plummergen emotions had a tendency to run high on the slightest provocation, those who managed to stay calm must be phlegmatic indeed.

''There's talk as how Sir George might be startin' up the Night Watch Men again,'' said Mrs. Flax, with a sniff. ''Could save hisself the bother, if he'd but ask me to send an ill wish across the Marsh—though 'tis tiring work, ill-wishing at a distance, and I've no mind to put meself forward and use my powers when there's clearly none with intent to be thankful after for what I might do for 'em.''

Since nobody was prepared to express gratitude for what she had not yet achieved, and everybody feared to be thought ungrateful, all eyes turned as one to the shelves of tinned baby-food, before which little Mrs. Hosigg had been hovering throughout the previous exchange. Lily Hosigg's husband Len being farm foreman at Rytham Hall, young Lil could be regarded as an authority on the Colvedens' future plans; but as she seldom spoke unless directly addressed, there was a moment's pause for someone to establish conversational pre-eminence . . .

When a sudden outcry brought eyes away from the blushing Lily towards Mrs. Henderson, now over by the door.

''Blooming cheek! Bold as brass, that Murreystone lot— see 'em marching down The Street as if they owns the place! At least''—as there came a concerted rush to the door and windows to obtain the best view—''driving down it. Stands to reason it's them, for the weather's not good enough for tourists today, and if there's an honest face in either o' them cars, then I'm Murreystone born and bred . . .''

"Strangers," said Mrs. Skinner, forced for once to agree with Mrs. Henderson.

"Spying out the land," said Mrs. Flax.

And the two unknown cars drove slowly down The Street, watched in silence by the post office shoppers.

CHAPTER 6

To Mrs. Henderson—she having been first to spot the strangers—fell the honour of scurrying out of the post office to stand, as if admiring the soaring beauties of the autumnal cloud-cover, on the edge of the paved footpath, staring down The Street.

"They've slowed," she reported to an enthralled audience with its ears as close to the open doorway as it could comfortably press them, given that almost everyone else—Lily Hosigg remained resolutely by the baby-foods, but Emmy Putts emerged from behind her counter to make up the numbers—was pressing likewise. "They've gone on again—past the forge—down to the end o' The Street, they've gone—and now turning in at the George, so far's I can tell."

She sighed, regretting, as did her eager listeners, the slight curve in the road which meant one could never be entirely sure. Still, it was near enough: where else would the strangers be going, except the George? Admittedly, the church stood beside the pub, and was well worth a visit, but it seemed unlikely that godless Murreystone would visit the rival place of worship unless there was a service on . . .

Lily made her final selection, paid for the tins, and hurried out to the infant Dulcie Rose, dreaming peacefully in the pram Mrs. Henderson hadn't quite summed up the courage to rock as she snooped.

With Lily's departure, the tongues could wag more freely—and did. The people in the cars had parked on the forecourt of the George *pretending* to visit the church: which was sacrilege, and Just What Murreystone Would Do. Or, they really planned to stay at the hotel: which was A Downright Nerve, being Right On The Spot—rather than drive too obviously back to perfidious Murreystone across the Marsh, taking the narrow lane between the high brick walls and the cottage gardens at the far end of The Street . . .

At which point, it was a mere matter of time before somebody said what everyone was thinking: and several bodies duly did.

"Near Old Mrs. Bannet's," cried a gleeful chorus: and nothing more was needed to make pleasure complete. They all knew who now lived in Old Mrs. Bannet's house—and they rejoiced that Lily Hosigg (who lived farther down the lane, in the old Dunnihoe cottage, and was known to be particularly fond of the inhabitant of Sweetbriars) was no longer present to prevent the seething cauldron of speculation and surmise from coming to the boil.

"Miss Seeton," breathed the chorus, in delight . . .

Exactly what Miss Seeton's fell purpose might be in encouraging the dark powers of Murreystone to do their worst was undecided. Had she, with Stan Bloomer, formed an alliance with the foe to wangle the (already unreliable) results at the Produce Show? Was there some plot afoot to sabotage the church decorations for Harvest Festival? This from Mrs. Henderson, seconded (to the amazement of all, herself included) by Mrs. Skinner. Did Miss Seeton plan to unleash some diabolical Murreystone contrivance upon the home team in the Grand Conker Contest?

An excellent time was had by all. Not a soul in the post office was making even a pretence at buying groceries, confectionery, or—the last resort—stamps. It was, perhaps, a pity that no one could be absolutely certain of what was going on, though they were confident they'd find out, in time. It only needed the bell over the door to ring, and the Ones Who Always Knew to enter . . .

And, right on cue, the doorbell *did* ring. And the Ones

Who Always Knew made their most welcome entrance: two eager female forms, one tall and equine of feature, one dumpy and bright-eyed with malice. The Nuts had arrived!

Miss Erica Nuttel, of the bony elbows, and Mrs. Norah Blaine, of the snapping blackcurrant eyes, are Plummergen's definitive information service. Rabid vegetarians (which rabidity in part explains their collective nickname), these ladies—there are those who would dispute their right to so courteous a title, but for now it will suffice—have lived in the village for upwards of a dozen years, in their little house with its plate-glass windows conveniently overlooking the post office and the garage next door, outside which the bus stop stands. Whatever happens, whoever travels, in and around Plummergen, the Nuts know the full facts before the happening is complete, the traveller arrived—and if (by any chance) they don't know, they invent.

Their powers of invention are remarkable, even for Plummergen, which prides itself on the general efficiency of its intelligence-gathering network. What the Nuts invent, however, always has a certain basis—no matter how distorted—in truth. It is, therefore, not often easy to be sure where Real Truth ends and Nutty Truth begins: indeed, since most people much prefer the latter, few trouble to make the distinction. If one Nut or other (though the pair usually work as a team) makes a pronouncement that Something Is So, then So, in the eyes of Plummergen, it will remain, carved on the stone tablets of collective memory and there stored for all eternity.

The Nuts, then, had arrived; but nobody, until their appearance at the post office door, had noticed their arrival. This meant that they could not have crossed The Street from plate-glassed Lilikot, but must instead have come along the pavement on the post office side of the road, where those inside could see nothing of them as they came. Which, in turn, meant that it was more than likely they had not come southwards down The Street, for there was little of interest north of the post office and its neighbouring bus stop apart from the nursing home (which the Nuts shunned as they would shun a visit to an abattoir), the police station, and the village hall. There was nothing happening at the village hall that day; PC Potter was known to be in league with Miss Seeton, and therefore suspect, and therefore (by the Nuts, at least) to be avoided . . .

Which left the inescapable conclusion that the Nuts had come northwards up The Street from the far end, where it narrowed to a lane between high brick walls and cottage gardens. Up from the end where Miss Seeton's house stood diagonally opposite the George and Dragon—where the mysterious Murreystone strangers had parked their cars and vanished.

Miss Nuttel, with a murmured greeting to the assembled audience, stationed herself by the revolving book-stand and made to consult *Master Hand-Loom Weaving in Thirty Minutes*. Mrs. Blaine, beaming about her, fumbled in her pocket for the back-of-an-envelope shopping list she didn't really need.

"Bit of a nip in the air this afternoon, Mrs. Blaine," said Mrs. Spice. "For all the sun's still so high—but not so cold a body can't enjoy a bit of a walk, though."

This was clever of Mrs. Spice. The Nuts never respond to any direct invitation to spill whatever beans they've discovered, preferring to weasel their way around the subject in what they fondly believe are frustrating circumlocutions. Plummergen, however, knows the Nuts of old, and refuses to grant them the satisfaction of such frustration by ignoring every circumlocution, hint, or lead-in, and by conversing quite naturally on everyday topics until, themselves frustrated, the Nuts crack wide open.

"Too bracing," agreed Mrs. Blaine, while Miss Nuttel turned a casual page and appeared oblivious to conversation. "Emmy"—Mrs. Blaine beamed round on the lingering shoppers, and received their tacit permission to jump the queue—"two packets of dates, please, and a lemon, and some digestives—better make it two packets, then I'll have enough over for a mock cheesecake base tomorrow."

Miss Nuttel stirred. "What's that, Bunny? Cheesecake? Told me to remind you we've run out of that seaweed stuff."

"Carrageen extract, Eric. Yes, thank you—but they don't stock it here, do you, Emmy? Only gelatine, which of course, being an animal product, we never use.''

"No. No seaweed, Mrs. Blaine.'' Emmy Putts wearily dropped the digestive biscuits on the counter from a height of some inches, reasoning that if Mrs. Blaine was going to crush them anyway, it wouldn't matter if a few broke now. "Do you some frozen spinach, if you like.''

Mrs. Blaine shuddered. "No, Emmy, as you know we grow most of our own vegetables''—Miss Nuttel preened herself and moved across from the book-stand—"but in any case spinach has no setting agent as carrageenin has, and a green cheesecake . . . Or agar-agar, perhaps, though if you have no carrageenin, I don't suppose you'll have that, either.''

Emmy added two sticky cellophane packages either side of the digestive cylinders, and said she'd never heard of such a thing. Mrs. Blaine nodded in triumph.

"Rather too specialised, I can see, though I've always said Mr. Stillman holds a surprising range, and one would have thought that for regular customers . . . but never mind, we can easily take the bus into Brettenden for the health food shop.''

"Bus?'' Miss Nuttel shot out a long arm and snatched at the lemon as Emmy rolled it casually from the bin end of the counter towards the rest of Mrs. Blaine's purchases. "No go today, old girl—early closing.''

"Early closing? Oh, and a tin of those delicious minced nut meatballs, please. Of course, the bus doesn't run when it's early closing, so that would explain the taxi. I did wonder. A box of cornflakes, I think—or would you prefer Wheaty Wonders, Eric? And don't say''—to Emmy— "that you don't stock those, either, or I'll start to wish— although one hates, naturally, to intrude—that we'd asked Miss Seeton to give us a lift in her taxi.''

Ears pricked. Eyes brightened. Bodies, oh so casually, crowded close. Mrs. Blaine, oblivious, continued to consult her envelope. Miss Nuttel said:

"Wouldn't have been any use, Bunny. With being early closing, I mean—can't have been going to Brettenden.''

"You're so right, Eric, too muddled of me not to think of that. No, thank you, Emmy, nothing more for now, since it seems we'll be going to Brettenden tomorrow and the market is really a great deal cheaper. How much will that be altogether?''

"Bus is cheaper, too," said Miss Nuttel. "Than a taxi, I mean." She frowned. "Hire car, rather—no sign." She frowned again. "Must have been going somewhere important, not to wait until tomorrow."

Mrs. Blaine was busy counting coins from her purse and could only reply in a murmur. This left the field wide open for everyone else.

"Miss Seeton gone off in a taxi, has she?" Mrs. Henderson, untroubled by the nice distinction, was all enthralled theory. "I'm surprised she never rode her bicycle, with no bus, to save money—"

"Except," flashed Mrs. Skinner automatically—that amazing alliance had been brief as well as fragile—"she'd be in a hurry, like Miss Nuttel said. You don't ride a bike when you're in a hurry, 'specially when it's uphill most o' the way to Brettenden, as anyone knows, though admittedly not steep, but all of six miles, which for someone her age, and the weather so uncertain this time o' year . . . ''

Everyone nodded: they'd seen Miss Seeton on her bicycle, pedalling against the wind from the Marsh, wobbling as she went, keeping herself fit and scaring other road users into a thousand nervous fits in the process.

"And this time o' year," Mrs. Spice pointed out, "there's the days growing shorter to worry about, too. Clocks go back in a week or so, remember, but even now the sun's down close on five, and the roads darkening—and you can't say a bicycle lamp's that good for seeing where you're going."

"Wherever," said Mrs. Flax, "that is." She wagged her head, preparing to pronounce. "A fair distance, though, stands to reason. She knows she'll not be back by nightfall—and that's why the bike's no good . . . ''

There was a moment's silence as speculation seethed in the post office. Mrs. Blaine swept her purchases into her string bag. "Of course, we aren't ones to gossip . . . ''

Heads nodded sagely, tongues murmured polite untruths.

"But it did strike us as rather odd," said Mrs. Blaine,

"too *furtive,* in fact, the way that taxi turned up just a few minutes after those people arrived at the George. Now, some people might call it a coincidence"—Mrs. Blaine looked round as if daring her audience to do so; there was nobody daring within earshot—"but I'm not so sure. I mean, we could hardly help noticing them as we came out of the church—the flowers for Harvest Festival, you know, Eric and I had gone in search of Inspiration"—plump hands, Inspired, made to clasp themselves, and tangled in string netting—"and as we came out of the lychgate, I noticed a stone in my shoe, so of course I had to bend down to take it off, and Eric had to bend as well, for me to lean on, so naturally none of the people in the cars could see us—but we could *distinctly* see them—and they were looking across the road straight at Sweetbriars before they went into the George—and not five minutes later Miss Seeton's hire car arrived!"

A chorus confirmed Norah Blaine's view that such concomitant events as the arrival of strangers and the prompt departure of Miss Seeton were more than coincidence. *Furtive,* some said, was insufficiently strong: *sinister* was surely more to the point . . .

"Especially," said Mrs. Blaine, producing her trump card, "as it wasn't Crabbe's taxi she went in!"

Sensation. Generations of Crabbes have fulfilled the transport requirements of Plummergen's carless for as long as anyone can remember. Old Crabbe, founding father of the garage beside the post office, lost his son (Young Crabbe) in the War, but had a grandson, Very Young Crabbe, to take his place once the boy had done his National Service. By the time Old Crabbe had grown rather too Old for driving buses and clambering down into inspection pits on a regular basis, Jack, son and heir of Lance-Corporal Crabbe, had conveniently come to years of discretion. Jack now not only drives the twice-weekly bus into Brettenden on days when the county service doesn't run, but will act as a taxi service when his father is busy and his great-grandfather otherwise engaged. Crabbe's taxis are a village byword for reliability—and for cheapness . . .

"Course," said Mrs. Flax, "we never noticed him driving past down The Street, which by rights we did ought to have done—but then, we wouldn't, would we? Seeing how she never had him. Suspicious, I calls it.''

"And it wasn't Mr. Baxter from Brettenden, either," said Mrs. Blaine. "Which simply *proves* she didn't want anyone to know where she was going, doesn't it?"

This argument, though having undeniable merit, was not the bombshell Mrs. Blaine had expected. Anyone who had ever taken aged Mr. Baxter's equally aged taxi from Brettenden to Plummergen—to anywhere else, for that matter—knew that the car was unreliable, to say the least. Miss Seeton, in planning the escape she'd undoubtedly taken, would have been less than wise to rely on catching a train (an express, of course, to go farther faster) if she'd booked Mr. Baxter to take her to catch it . . .

"If it wasn't one o' the Crabbes," mused Mrs. Skinner, "and it wasn't Mr. Baxter, then who . . . ?"

"That's just what we were saying!" Mrs. Blaine's little black eyes snapped with excitement. "*Who?* We certainly didn't recognise the man *at all,* did we, Eric?"

Miss Nuttel nodded; then shook her head. "Never seen him before in my life," she said.

Mrs. Henderson pounced. "Like the people gone to the George, you mean?"

"Strangers," said Mrs. Flax, in hollow tones.

"*Murreystone,*" said Mrs. Spice, thrilling to the thought.

"Certainly came from that direction," said Miss Nuttel. "Across the Marsh, now I think of it." She frowned again. "Must mean . . . either he's in league with them, or . . . ''

"Or," cried Bunny, "Miss Seeton was frightened they'd see him drive past the George to fetch her, and told him to come the back way where they couldn't—oh, Eric, you're so right! He's too obviously On the Other Side, and he's taken her into hiding so they shan't see her!"

Erica Nuttel looked at her friend. She shook her head for Bunny's innocence. "Or," said Miss Nuttel, "he's taken her somewhere else—for Further Instructions . . . ''

Which everyone realised at once must be the truth: and a delicious shudder ran at once around the post office.

CHAPTER 7

Detective Chief Superintendent Delphick smiled, and held out a hand in welcome. "Miss Seeton, good afternoon. It really is kind of you to have come up to Town at such short notice. I do hope, though, that you didn't let us disturb you in the middle of anything important."

Miss Seeton, courteous as ever, hurried to reassure him. "Oh, no, only the garden—which is there all the time, of course. Except that after last night's rain it needs rather a lot of tidying to suit dear Stan . . . "

Bob politely relieved her of her handbag and umbrella; Delphick took her light tweed coat and hung it on the stand. Miss Seeton's eyes held a shamefaced twinkle as she went on: "He is a little vexed with me, I fear, for having allowed the garden roller to split the handle of my besom so that we have nothing with which to sweep away the worms—when the telephone rang—or rather their casts, all over the lawn, as well as the leaves. Such surprisingly high winds, for October, though one can always make compost with them, and the earth is of great benefit—and the worms, of course."

Delphick ushered her to the most comfortable of the visitors' chairs, and she sat down, still trying to explain the unimportance of her doings that afternoon when duty called her elsewhere. "To the compost. Of course, it was an accident—the telephone—and naturally I have promised to take greater care in future. Besides, it can always be used for stakes, and to stop the birds eating the seeds, so it won't be as much of a waste as I had at first feared—and he will not be coming again until the day after tomorrow, which gives me plenty of time to buy a new one, since you did, I believe, say''—she paused, her head slightly to one side, a questioning note in her voice—"that it would be merely a matter of this afternoon when you required my services."

"Just this afternoon," Delphick agreed, crossing mental fingers as he added the silent rider *Deo volente*. With Miss Seeton, he knew, you could never be sure . . .

Miss Emily Dorothea Seeton stands five foot nothing in her stockinged feet, weighs no more than seven stone fully clothed, and is in her mid-sixties. With her grey hair, sensible shoes, and restrained (apart from her hats) attire, she is the epitome of the English spinster pensioner, having taken early retirement some seven years ago from the post of art teacher at Mrs. Benn's little school in Hampstead. There is, clearly, nothing in her appearance or general demeanour to explain why even experienced police officers such as Scotland Yard's own Oracle are apt to view any dealings they might have with Miss Seeton with a degree of circumspection. Who, after all, could be supposed more circumspect in her behaviour than a retired teacher of art?

She was, perhaps, not (Miss Seeton will regretfully admit) the most inspirational of instructors. Her enthusiasm for her subject she will never be so foolish as to deny; but her ability to impart to her pupils both her enthusiasm and the skill necessary to express their own were—and indeed, when she emerges from retirement to help out from time to time in Plummergen's little school, still are—sadly (she will sigh) *limited*. One did, of course, one's best to help people to look at things properly: to *see* things, and then to express what they saw on paper so that the seeing might be communicated to, and enjoyed by, all . . .

Miss Seeton, even judged by the exacting standards of an English gentlewoman, is too modest: she was, and is, a very good teacher. She will coax and encourage the most unobservant pupils to produce work of a standard far higher than anyone would suppose possible. She is a very good teacher, but she is not, in this respect, unique; and it is for Miss Seeton's unique talent for communication that she is so very highly regarded by the police—her ability to See, and to show in her work what she has Seen in so unique a fashion.

This unique ability she does her very best to suppress. She has the strongest possible feeling that one should only draw what is really there: she is always embarrassed when what she has drawn, or sketched, or painted proves her to have noticed far more than that—to have seen what, in philosophical terms, might be regarded as *really* there: the Ultimate Truth of that which has been painted, sketched, or drawn. She would blush to be considered psychic: she would think it not quite right; and perhaps, indeed, it is too strong a word, though it is hard to find another which will adequately sum up Miss Seeton's qualities. Her vision of life is . . . different. It is clear, and uncluttered; it is instinctive, and cannot be explained—but it can, by those who understand something of its value, be harnessed. And harnessed it has been: by the police.

When Miss Seeton, walking through Covent Garden one evening after enjoying a performance of *Carmen,* remonstrated with a young man behaving in an unacceptable manner towards his female companion, she did so by applying the ferrule of her umbrella to the small of the young man's back. She had no idea, as she did so, that she had interrupted the notorious Cesar Lebel, drug dealer and thug, in the act of knifing to death a prostitute—had no idea that such a person as Lebel existed, and certainly knew nothing of his name. But his name was only too well known to Superintendent (as he had then been) Delphick of Scotland Yard, and his face, when at Delphick's request Miss Seeton sketched it, was instantly recogniseable.

At Delphick's further request, Miss Seeton sketched again—and again: faces, scenery, impressions. All showed aspects of the case which had not previously occurred to any of those involved in the investigation: it was as if a new light, a new vision, had appeared in the drugs-riddled darkness. With Miss Seeton's help, Scotland Yard had managed to curtail the activities of certain of the drugging

fraternity, arresting Lebel, among others, and leaving the
air of London a little sweeter for those arrests. Miss Seeton,
in recognition of her contribution to that sweetness, to her
delighted surprise received the gift of a gold-handled black
silk umbrella from Superintendent Delphick as a token of
his gratitude and esteem. Seven years later, Chief Superintendent Delphick had lost count of the number of reasons
he had for being grateful to Miss Seeton, the number of
cases her remarkable insights had helped him (and his colleagues both at the Yard and in other forces) to solve. So
grateful were they for her efforts that they had officially
retained Miss Seeton, on a modest salary, as an art consultant . . .

A pity, though, that so much of what happened in the
vicinity of Miss Seeton wasn't always as clear and uncluttered as her invaluable insights. Was often anything but
clear and uncluttered. Could be (to say the least) confused
. . . exasperating . . . bewildering . . . exhausting.

"Just this afternoon," agreed Delphick, feeling exhausted at the very idea of trying to work out what she'd
been trying to tell him about the garden roller, the besom,
the worms, the stakes, and the compost. Worn out when
they'd barely begun—their official business yet to come—
and he wanted to see her safely on the homeward train well
before midnight, if remotely possible.

He cleared his throat. "Yes, just this afternoon, with
luck, and once we've had tea and biscuits—be a good chap,
Bob, and chivvy the canteen, will you?—we'll be off on
our guided tour, as I explained on the phone. And afterwards, a proper tea—at the Ritz, if you'd like it, or the
Savoy—no," as Miss Seeton seemed about to protest at
this lavish invitation, "you must allow Scotland Yard to
treat you, please, without questioning our motives too
closely." He smiled. "Although I'm sure you, of all people, will understand those motives only too well, and realise
that we expect you to sing—or rather, draw—for your supper. You have, of course, brought your sketchpad with
you."

It was not a question. Miss Seeton smiled back at him,
nodded, and reached down for the enormous handbag Bob

had placed by the foot of her chair. "And my pencils, and my eraser—plain, I thought, rather than coloured—the pencils, I mean. Autumn in the country," said Miss Seeton, turning a little pink, "is undoubtedly gold and copper and fading red, but in London, I always feel . . . except, that is, in the parks, of course, with the trees in silhouette, and the reappearance of form and line—my favourite season, and of course one notices such things so much better in the country, where there are so many more—and certainly more than we are likely to see today, of course, as you said we should be visiting only the shops and galleries which have been so disgracefully robbed. Trees, I mean. And although one appreciates that antiques and objets d'art are certainly not without colour, and the patina of the years"— the pink returned to her cheeks at this fanciful notion—"it is perhaps more—more rich than I feel mere pencils could in any case do justice to. And a paintbox," said Miss Seeton, recovering herself with a twinkle, "would be somewhat out of place at the Ritz or the Savoy, don't you think?"

Delphick said that he certainly did, adding that he was pleased she'd decided to accept his, or rather the Yard's, hospitality without worrying about it any more. It would, he reminded her, be on expenses—

"And fully deserved, I've no doubt," he added, as there came a tap at the door, and a uniformed constable appeared with a tray in his hands, a look of awe on his face as he gazed at the renowned Battling Brolly, maker of headlines, solver of crimes, sitting just like anyone ordinary—apart from the hat—in the Oracle's chair. Could almost be someone's old auntie up for the day, except that people's aunts didn't drop in on top-notch Yarders for a gossip over tea and buns the way everyone knew MissEss did.

"Thank you, Constable." Delphick, divining something of the new arrival's emotion, waved at Bob to grab the tray before it tilted to disaster and soaked MissEss sitting so unknowing underneath. MissEss! A quiet smile quirked Delphick's mouth as he recalled the argument he'd had with the Yard's basement computer, which considered itself infallible—how it had insisted that Miss Seeton, misheard, was first of all Delphick's Missus (the imagination boggled) and then, after much wearisome explanation, Delphick's MissEss, which seemed the best anyone was ever going to manage.

Bob reached for the tray. Shining buttons, their wearer still staring with fascination at the living legend in front of the Oracle's desk, moved forward to effect the handover. A booted foot caught—tripped—stumbled. The tray leaped, cups clattering, and was caught just in time by big Bob Ranger, stalwart of the police football eleven. Breathing heavily, he swooped the tray past Miss Seeton's innocent nose by just half an inch to set it, with shaking hands, on top of Delphick's blotter.

Miss Seeton, bending to retrieve her umbrella, babbled apologies, oblivious to the recent risk of boiling tea or falling china. Blushing, babbling his own apologies, the bobby beat a hasty retreat. Delphick said:

"Shall I pour, Miss Seeton, or will you?" No point in asking Bob: his hands were still visibly shaking as he sat down, without invitation, on the other visitors' chair: Miss Seeton, his dear adopted Aunt Em, had rattled his normal composure. Come to think of it, Delphick didn't think his own voice sounded too steady, either . . .

"I know you like it weak." He forced himself to pour as Miss Seeton fumbled with the clasp of her handbag, settled her tumbled umbrella safely—*was* there ever such a word, if you were dealing with the Battling Brolly's brolly?—across her knees, automatically adjusted that incredible hat, and dutifully prepared to be given her latest assignment.

"You'll have read more details than we had time for on the phone in the press, I expect." Not that Miss Seeton was known to pore over Fleet Street's daily output with particular interest, for all it so often featured her activities in blazing headlines, but she had, he knew, the local paper once a week, and the milkman delivered a daily *Times* (if it arrived from London at the Brettenden distributors before he left on his rounds) or—since acquaintance had blossomed with Amelita Forby—the occasional *Daily Negative*, out of loyalty to a friend.

Miss Seeton, sipping tea, sighed, and nodded. "A great pity that so much intelligence—for such, from the little one reads, it appears is used to plan these . . . these raids—could not be put to better use; and a real tragedy for so many works of art and pieces of genuine historical interest to be lost to the nation if, as one has been led to understand, the items in question are being . . . being stolen to order on behalf of someone who lives abroad. Although even if he lives in this country, of course, the fact that he will have to keep them hidden in future means that they are, to all intents and purposes, still lost. If they are of such a size as to fit inside a car, it will be regrettably easy for him to do so. And very selfish . . ."

She sighed again. "And very callous, too, as well as thoroughly dishonest—that someone with more money than, I fear, moral responsibility should, so to speak, simply write out a—a shopping list, and hire people to fulfil his requirements. In other words"—Miss Seeton sat upright, the cockscomb ribbon above her right eye bristling—"deliberately encouraging those who might originally be merely *weak* to become true criminals. Not just stealing the pictures and the porcelain, but even the cars with which to—to ram their way through the shop windows—and it is, as I understand it, no more than good fortune that so far nobody has been hurt in these disgraceful robberies . . ."

She looked at Delphick in sudden dismay. "Oh, dear—am I to understand that the reason you have asked me to—"

"No, no, Miss Seeton." Delphick forgot courtesy and interrupted before she could distress herself further. "No, you're right in your understanding—nobody's been hurt in any of the Ram Raids, not even the one early this morning." He paused; he met her eye with a look as knowing as her own.

"Nobody," he emphasised, "has been hurt—yet. But I have the feeling, Miss Seeton, as does Inspector Terling of the Art Squad, that it may only be a matter of time . . ."

CHAPTER 8

Delphick put down his empty cup. "Will you excuse me for one moment, Miss Seeton?" He swivelled his chair to face the window, and contemplated the view from the umpteenth floor of New Scotland Yard. Though smoky grey clouds were moving across the sky at some speed, patches of blue appeared between the smoke often enough for him to hope that it would keep fine for the next couple of hours, at any rate.

He turned back to his visitor with a smile. "There's no tremendous hurry, but when you've finished your tea, I'll phone for a car to Mayfair. And then, weather permitting—Miss Seeton?" Her expression brought him up with a start. "Miss Seeton, you seem somewhat troubled. Was it something I said? Or would you rather not go, after all? Believe me, there's no . . ." He was about to say *danger,* then thought better of it and, as he searched for a more suitable word, was forestalled by Miss Seeton herself.

"Of course, Chief Superintendent, I appreciate the kindness, but I can easily walk, or go by public transport. The expense of a taxi—unless, of course, you are anxious to see my sketches as soon as possible . . ." Miss Seeton blushed for her presumption in daring to suggest that Scotland Yard should rank her little scribbles so highly, then blushed still more as she recollected that time, in business, was considered to be money, and that her relationship with dear Mr. Delphick was (although undoubtedly, after so many years, deserving, she hoped, of the name of friendship) in many respects still a business, or at least professional, relationship; and her proposal to walk, or to travel by bus or tube, while cheaper in the short term, could perhaps work out more costly in the long. Which might not, in the circumstances, be sensible, although . . . a police car—when it was, after all, the second time today, which did seem perhaps . . .

Delphick made a praiseworthy effort, and kept his face absolutely straight as she flustered through her explanation, then smiled kindly on her.

"I think, Miss Seeton, that official funds could stretch to a car for you—or, failing a suitable unmarked vehicle, a taxi—without too much difficulty: we must take care of our experts, you know, for fear of offending them. We cannot run the slightest risk that they might fail to renew their contracts when the time came. We *need* our retained art consultant, believe me—and, if you don't, then let me assure you that it would be completely beneath the dignity of a Scotland Yard chief superintendent to arrive in Mayfair on foot, or from a bus, or by underground."

Miss Seeton brightened. "You're coming with me?"

"Of course I am. Did you think we'd let you out of our sight now we'd got you safely up to Town? Anyway, I can't think when I last took tea at the Ritz. Your visit is the perfect excuse for me to indulge myself at the same time as treating you—and," with a twinkling look for Bob, "to give your long-suffering nephew an uninterrupted hour or so for tackling this office's tame mountain of paperwork, which seems to grow ever higher each time we return to our desks."

Bob forced a grin—for himself, he'd never taken tea at the Ritz, but then Anne had been making remarks about his waistline recently, so perhaps it was as well he hadn't been asked to join the party—and agreed with his chief. Miss Seeton, who, like her adopted nephew, knew nothing of the pleasures of a Piccadilly tea—apart from the occasional treat in Fortnum's, farther down the road—in due course allowed herself to be convinced. A few minutes later, the expedition set out for wildest Mayfair.

The traffic was surprisingly heavy, and it was hard to find a convenient place to pull in. At last, however, the unmarked police car set them down on the north side of Piccadilly, and vanished, with a cheerful tootle on the horn, in the direction of Eros. Miss Seeton, smothering a sigh, resolutely turned her eyes from the tempting gateway of the Royal Academy, and wondered for a brief moment whether the superintendent might suggest they begin their little stroll along the Burlington Arcade—not that she could afford to buy anything, but it was always agreeable to look, and so peaceful, with the prohibitions on whistling, hurrying, and unseemly behaviour—before sternly reminding herself that the disgracefully destructive tactics used by the thieves hardly lent themselves to a covered row of Regency shop-fronts barely one car's length apart.

"Certainly no room to build up speed," she murmured, as Delphick, her escort, moved politely to the outside of the pavement. "Especially going backwards . . ."

Delphick had intended heading for Sackville Street to give Miss Seeton time to attune herself again to London: while she might have lived and worked there for most of her life, she'd been a country-dweller for some years now, and wasn't growing any younger. He caught her final words and stopped. "Back? You'd rather go the other way? I'd planned to come round to Bond Street from Burlington Gardens, but if you'd prefer going straight there . . ."

Miss Seeton, not realising she'd spoken so loudly, and now supposing this to be the chief superintendent's own preference, politely agreed that she would. Together they turned back, passing the Royal Academy again, past—Miss Seeton sighed once more—the Burlington Arcade, and headed for the corner of Old Bond Street, most exclusive, most expensive of London's shopping thoroughfares.

Delphick blinked in disbelief, snatched a quick look at Miss Seeton walking quietly beside him, stared ahead, and blinked again. Déjà vu? A small, slight, grey-haired woman in a light tweed coat, an enormous handbag over one arm, an umbrella in her hand, was trotting towards him down the middle of the pavement . . . with—Delphick almost rubbed his eyes, but stopped himself in time—a crocodile of twenty or so small children, wearing grey-and-maroon uniforms, in her wake. As the apparition approached, the voice of the handbagged one could clearly be heard above the mighty roar of London's traffic:

" . . . remind you once more that you are not allowed to eat sweets in the galleries, and there is to be no giggling, no raised voices, no horseplay of any kind. If there is sufficient time once our tour of the exhibition is over, you may be allowed . . ."

The head of the crocodile, intent on its harangue, seemed not to notice that it had forced a passage between the still-startled Delphick and Miss Seeton. Meekly following its head came the crocodile's forty pattering feet, brought up at the tail by a bored-looking younger woman with spectacles and straight, fringed brown hair.

Delphick, who had paused politely to let the little procession pass, stole a look at Miss Seeton as she emerged from behind the body of the crocodile. She turned, with a smile, to watch its retreat. She shook her head—

"Oof!"

"Oh! Oh, dear, I'm so sorry . . ." Miss Seeton bent to pick up her umbrella from the paving stone on which it had fallen after jabbing the waistcoat now being rubbed so tenderly by the man inside it.

"Oh, I'm so very sorry—I'm afraid I was a little distracted, you see, and—oh. Good gracious." Miss Seeton, straightening, had raised her eyes from the topmost button of the waistcoat to the face above the ashes-of-roses silk cravat around the plump, self-satisfied neck. "Mr. Szabo!"

"Mr.—Szabo, good afternoon." Delphick, recovering from his surprise, hailed the newcomer with only the slight hesitation of one who has interviewed a murder suspect under his legal name, yet knows him to be professionally recognised under another. Writers—especially married female writers—could cause similar confusion, the chief superintendent reflected as the two men shook hands; but if Taylor-Szabo wasn't on his own professional territory here, within two or three stones' throw of his gallery, then where, if anywhere, was he?

Ferencz Szabo bowed to Miss Seeton, who had finished readjusting her umbrella over her arm and had settled her hat and handbag to their former stations. She had been busily apologising the entire time she did so, but Ferencz knew her of old, and contrived to smile his understanding, acknowledge Delphick's greeting, and register Miss Seeton's murmurs for the babble they undoubtedly were without losing his composure for an instant.

"This is indeed a delightful encounter, Miss Seeton," he managed to slip in at last, as she ran out of steam and her blushes began to subside. His quick gaze fastened thoughtfully on the little spinster's tall, distinguished escort; Delphick gazed calmly back; and Ferencz Szabo, forgetting the cultivated dignity of his public persona, winked.

"I take it," he remarked, in a meaningful tone, "that your visit to Town is not entirely for pleasure, Miss Seeton." Absently, he rubbed his midriff; then, as she started to blush again, and spoke of meeting old friends, he swiftly changed the gesture to a hand-on-waistcoat bow, in his most florid continental manner. Delphick could almost hear him wondering whether or not to kiss Miss Seeton's hand: or was such a salute only warranted by people actually on the premises buying something?

"And in view of the lamentable occurrence only this morning at the establishment of one of my colleagues," continued the Bond Street dealer, with another wink, "may I venture to presume that—unless, of course, your steps have already taken you that way—you will shortly be heading in his direction?"

Miss Seeton looked doubtfully at Delphick. The matter to which Mr. Szabo referred could only, she supposed, be the Ram Raid—which was both foolish and ridiculous, giving so melodramatic a name to an obviously illegal activity, which surely only served to encourage them—that raid the chief superintendent had already discussed with her. And the unfortunate person whose property had been stolen was, so Mr. Szabo said, a colleague, which must mean that he himself was in a privileged position, especially since he seemed to have guessed that one was not—Miss Seeton sighed—in the district for pleasure, but on official business;

and the raids had been—Miss Seeton sighed again—written about in the newspapers. But . . .

Delphick came to the rescue. "An apt turn of phrase, Mr. Szabo—a lamentable occurrence, indeed. And may I say at once that the presence of an expert such as yourself, on our stroll along Bond Street, would be more than welcome, should you care to join us?"

Ferencz pursed his lips and creased his forehead in an artistic frown. His plump hand slipped once more to his midriff, although this time for the purposes of retrieval rather than massage as he made great play of consulting the gold half-hunter watch in his waistcoat pocket. He smiled, and bowed. "I should be charmed," he said, and courteously offered Miss Seeton his arm.

" . . . a Bilbao looking-glass, among other things," he said, as the little party approached the gallery. "A real tragedy—although," twinkling, "we might ask ourselves whose is the greater tragedy. My poor friend, for having lost such a wonderful piece—the carving! Such delicacy and ornamentation, even in marble!" He contrived to kiss the tips of his fingers in an expansive gesture which did not, for some reason, nauseate the amused chief superintendent. "The original oak frame as well, I believe—but never mind, it's gone, alas, though I'm sure your, ah, colleagues, Mr. Delphick, will do all they can . . ."

He turned to wink at Delphick before addressing himself earnestly to the lady on his arm. "But we must ask ourselves, Miss Seeton—if breaking a mirror can lead to seven years' bad luck, how much worse could the luck be for one who has dared to steal such an exquisite item?"

Miss Seeton echoed Delphick's quiet chuckle, and said she really had no idea.

Ferencz sighed. "An ever greater tragedy, to my mind, is the theft of the golden statue. A rare—a unique—figure of the Egyptian cat-goddess Pasht, or Bast—Bubastis, if you prefer the Greek." With a little bow, he implied that Miss Seeton was fluent in several ancient languages and could take her pick. "Solid gold, flawlessly modelled—one only hopes, Miss Seeton, that the rogues do not melt her down. That would be the greatest crime of all . . ."

And Miss Seeton, her aesthetic sense outraged by the very idea, had to agree that it would.

Miss Seeton had so clearly enjoyed the company of Ferencz Szabo, who put her entirely at her ease during their stroll, regaling her with selected titbits of gossip about various dealers of his acquaintance as each individual establishment was passed, that Delphick invited the other to join the Ritz party when the time duly came. Mr. Szabo professed himself, as ever, charmed. The little group settled themselves at a discreet table, where Miss Seeton could peep out at the many tea-taking celebrities, and could admire the golden statuary in the centre of the pink-and-white room, with no fear of herself being recognised or even noticed. It was also, reflected Delphick, the ideal place for her to whip out her sketchbook from her bag without even the haughtiest of waiters raising an eyebrow in surprise . . .

The tiny sandwiches, shorn of their crusts; the dainty cakes, brought round on their enormous silver platter; the elegant stand, laden with pastries; the delicate porcelain, the snow-white napkins, the fragrant tea—not too strong, the milk rich and creamy . . . all combined to make Miss Seeton feel shockingly spoiled, and more than a little guilty. Delphick once again reminded her that this was the Yard's treat, and she was to consider it, if it worried her, as the best they could legally do by way of a bribe. Szabo, with a twinkle, said that everyone was surely allowed some luxury in their lives. It wasn't as if she'd been whisked about the London streets in a Bentley, was it? She had walked on her own two feet, and deserved a cup of tea, at the very least . . .

He and Delphick chatted quietly together as Miss Seeton, delving into her bag for her pencils and small sketchpad, finally began to frown over the task for which Scotland Yard had summoned her to Town. Neither man wished to embarrass her by paying any attention to what she was doing: nothing must be allowed to interrupt her. When a hovering waiter caught Delphick's eye, and made questioning table-clearing gestures, he was glared away.

"Ahem." It was a quiet cough, barely audible above

the elegant clatter and chink of silver-plated cutlery
against bone china. Miss Seeton had waited politely for a
convenient pause in the conversation before venturing to
intervene. She now blushed as her companions turned towards her. "I'm—I'm so sorry, Chief Superintendent.
I'm not at all sure that this can possibly be what you
want, but I'm afraid . . . "

With another blush, she handed her sketchpad to the tall
man sitting beside her, then murmured of powdered noses,
and slipped discreetly away. Delphick and Szabo resumed
their seats, the Hungarian trying hard not to show his curiosity as the detective turned back the cover to gaze at the
doodle on the top page.

"Ah. Mm, yes. I see what she means . . . " He flipped
over two or three more sheets, in case—as sometimes happened when Miss Seeton was unhappy with her preliminary
effort—she had scribbled something on another page.

She had not. He turned back to the first drawing and
stared at it again. Szabo, with a chuckle, after a few curious
moments held out a plump hand. "May I?"

Delphick shrugged. "Why not?" It was unlikely that the
dealer was the brains behind the Ram Raids: he might just
have an insight into what was going on . . .

"Oh, dear." Damn. He hadn't.

"Now I'm the one," said Szabo, "who should apologise,
Chief Superintendent. If I hadn't wished myself upon you
both, and chattered away in such a fashion, you might have
thought the whole expedition worthwhile—but now . . . "

Miss Seeton had, with evidently loving care, drawn a
looking-glass. A Bilbao looking-glass? The frame was certainly most ornate. The glass, still in place on the wall,
showed the room—its walls picture-hung—reflected in its
distant depths. In close-up, the sleek and noble form of a
watching cat watched itself as it perched on the shelf beneath, with, ranged either side of the watcher, a selection
of porcelain vases and ornaments.

The overmantel cat was by no means the only form of
animal life in the sketch. On the floor, stately and shining,
stood a Rolls-Royce; and its bonnet decoration was not the
silver Spirit of Ecstasy known around the world, but a

large, proud-shouldered ram with curled, heavy horns held high, their points towards the looking-glass. And as a passenger in the Royce rode an unmistakeable Ferencz Szabo, his mouth open in a stentorian bellow—in much the same manner as Ferencz, in Frank Taylor mode, had bellowed at the Lalique jewellery thief . . .

Delphick had been an amused observer of that earlier episode in Miss Seeton's history, and had to supress a chuckle at the sight. He heard another. He looked up. Ferencz Szabo was laughing aloud.

Delphick joined in the laughter, then sighed. "Oh, well. She's done her best, of course—she always does. But I haven't the least idea what it all means . . . so we'll simply have to wait and see. The way," he added, with another sigh, "we so often have to do . . . ."

CHAPTER 9

In Ashford police station, in the county of Kent, the telephone rang on the desk of Superintendent Chris Brinton.

Brinton was out of his office, but the call did not go unanswered. His sidekick, Detective Constable Foxon of the flamboyant wardrobe and earlobe-length hair—which Brinton suspected almost as much as Foxon's previous shoulder-skimming locks—picked up the extension to a torrent of gloomy tidings from Police Constable Buckland.

"The minute His Nibs gets back," Foxon promised his unhappy friend, in the first available pause. Frowning, he studied his notes. "From the way it sounds, I'd say he'll want to be in on this one, so it's no use me charging over there on my own, because I'll only have to turn round again to fetch him." He paused. "Of course, whatever it's all about, she's on her way to hospital, isn't she?"

The telephone squawked indignantly in his ear. Foxon was quick to apologise, but added that it was bound to be one of the first things Old Brimstone'd want to know when he came in. "He's been expecting 'em to start taking a few risks, sooner or later," he reminded the telephone grimly. "Just a matter of time before they turn nasty, he's kept saying, though I must admit I thought—well," as the telephone squawked again, "let's say I hoped. Still, looks as if Brimmers was right all along, and they're starting to play rough—it would be on our patch, of course, but there isn't much we can do about it . . . We'll be with you as soon as we can—just carry on as usual till we get there.''

Foxon had hardly rung off when there came a clatter at the door, and Brinton appeared, carrying a small tin tray with two cups of canteen coffee on it, and with a lugubrious expression in his eyes.

''I should never have said I needed the change of scene,'' he grumbled, before Foxon could speak. ''I should've pulled rank—I worked hard enough for it, Lord knows—and sent you instead, as anyone else would've done. I should've just opened the window and taken a few good deep breaths of fresh air and saved myself a blasted lecture on the evils of artificial stimulants from that Bible-thumping idiot on the front desk who—Foxon. What is it?''

The superintendent forgot his own woes as his subordinate, who had given up trying to break into the flow of lamentation, had risen from his desk and was shrugging himself into his leather jacket. Brinton at once dumped the tray on his desk and demanded: ''Business?''

Even as Foxon nodded, his chief was patting his own jacket pockets, automatically checking the presence of routine investigative paraphernalia while he waited for the younger man's explanation.

''Sounds as if you were right after all, sir—it's the Swipers again, or at least it looks remarkably like them, from what Buckland just phoned in—and this time they've got physical.'' Foxon paused to allow his chief's explosive *I knew it!* to scorch his eardrums, then went on: ''You did keep saying it wouldn't be long before they turned to the rough stuff, sir—and I admit I thought you were being, er, unduly pessimistic in saying it would be on our patch—but you weren't, I'm sorry to say.'' Foxon grimaced. ''If it's them—and there's certainly a sideboard missing, along with a load of smaller sitting-room stuff, then this time they've hit an old lady over the head, and she's on her way to hospital with a suspected fractured skull. Just this side of Brettenden,'' he added. ''Not that it really matters, sir, does it? Who or where, I mean, because they still bashed and robbed her, poor old girl—she's the one whose sister died recently of some unpronounceable illness, and she's setting up a charity in her memory. I told Buckland we'd be there as soon as we could—''

"Then let's get going, laddie!" Brinton abandoned the coffee without regret and strode out of the office, beckoning to Foxon to follow him in double-quick time. He'd been afraid all along this might—would—happen: it had never been so much a question of *when* as *where*, when he'd thought about it, although—like Foxon—he'd hoped he was being unduly pessimistic. But now he definitely knew differently, and he didn't like it. It wasn't just a matter of honest thieving, if you could ever call it that, any longer: the Sideboard Swipers had turned nasty . . .

The Sideboard Swipers was the fanciful name given by the more sensational of the daily papers to a gang of discriminating furniture thieves. It wasn't that they simply stole sideboards. They denuded whole rooms of their ornaments, knick-knacks, and small, portable valuables; sometimes they might remove a display cabinet, or an occasional table, as well; but the tabloid press enjoys alliteration, and Sideboard Swipers has a good ring to it.

The Swipers' method of operation was to concentrate, for a few weeks at a time, on different parts of the country, chosen (apparently) at random, before moving on to another area to repeat the process. In each case, they would break into selected houses—their method of selection, one theory had it, would be an excellent clue to nailing them, if only anyone could work out what it was—and, starting in the sitting-room, parlour, or lounge, would remove therefrom not necessarily the most costly items, but the most saleable: *saleable* being in this instance an unfortunate (for those investigating the robberies, as well as the victims) euphemism for *easily disguised and thereafter disposed of*. With only a little intelligent "distressing" of a solid piece of work, it could be fenced—or even sold through a legitimate outlet—before anyone had realised what was going on: there was only a small chance that any of those robbed by the Sideboard Swipers would ever see their property again—or that they would recognise it, if they did. Certainly, none of them had as yet done so . . .

"But they've always played it canny before," grumbled

Brinton, as the police car sped on its way to the scene of the Swipers' latest (if suppositious) offence. "It's not like them to go hitting people, let alone old ladies, over the head. They've always waited till the house was empty, even with old Whempstead, and he's practically a recluse. Wonder what made 'em change their minds this time?"

"If, sir, it *is* them." Foxon sometimes drove his superior mad with his mischievous Devil's Advocating, although in this case the young man was genuinely trying for the balanced point of view. "Could be it's just somebody else who's pinched the basic idea, but this time it's gone a bit wrong. I mean, never mind them bashing the poor old girl, sir, but they do seem to be rather—rather bobbing around the countryside a bit, if it's them, and why should they turn up here rather than somewhere else? I mean, from the Midlands to Kent in one fell swoop . . ."

"And the West Country before that, and Lord knows where before *that*." Brinton sighed. "Stranger things have happened, laddie. And I know, I'm probably overreacting—getting paranoid—but can you honestly blame me? Some pretty crazy things happen around here, Foxon, you can't deny." Foxon (who understood the superintendent's hidden meaning very well) did not attempt to deny it, though his silence was eloquent. Brinton went on: "So why not the Swipers, turned violent, to add to the list? We've had plenty enough gangs of various types hit these parts over the past few years, remember . . ."

There was a further silence, while Foxon, keeping his eye on the road, digested the truth of this. A fair-minded young man, he might have added that there had been gangs in Kent even before the arrival of Miss Seeton—but he didn't. He simply said:

"Oh, and Potter rang just before Buckland, sir, to say they're, er, thinking of reviving the Village Watch." No need to say in which of the several villages under PC Potter's care: the superintendent's grunt was sufficient proof that he'd understood. "Seems old man Whempstead was a pal of the Colvedens in the old days, sir, before his wife was taken ill and he started, er, hibernating. Sir George read about what happened in the *Beacon,* and thought the Watch might be a good idea . . . ''

Brinton's reply surprised his sidekick, who'd half expected the usual groans, oaths, or even frantic clutchings of the superintendent's hair, though the seat-belt might be a hindrance in the latter case; but Old Brimstone's voice was not so much calm as resigned as he remarked that the Village Watch could indeed be a good idea. ''Sir George has a head on his shoulders,'' he pointed out. ''And they didn't do so badly last time he had 'em on parade, did they? He won't let 'em get carried away and start blasting off with shotguns at folk they don't know in the middle of the night—but they could just get a good look at the blighters if, by any chance, they turn up in Plummergen.'' He snorted. ''If! Seeing as we've already had dealings with one of the natives today, if you can call Miss Seeton a native when she wasn't born there, then chance doesn't enter into it. They might as well be prepared for the worst before it happens, which knowing Miss Seeton it will, sooner or later.'' Foxon, with an effort—he was very fond of Miss Seeton—said nothing, and concentrated on his driving.

Brinton suddenly chuckled. ''You know, I feel almost sorry for the poor devils—the Swipers, I mean, or whoever they are. They don't know what they're letting themselves in for. For a start, they'll have to sneak past the Nuts and the rest of that goggle-eyed gang if they want to try anything in daytime—I wish 'em the best of luck, knowing how strangers stick out like a sore thumb in Plummergen even at the best of times . . . ''

Emmy Putts of Plummergen was born, she believed, for great things—the films, perhaps, or the telly. Anything to get her out of the dump where she'd lived all her life and bin stuck working since school. A grocery counter in the post office! Why, her mum had a better job nor that, over to Brettenden in the biscuit factory—not that it was exactly the bright lights, but at least in Brettenden there was usually *summat* going on. Nothing ever happened in Plummergen: nobody *interesting* ever came there, just tourists and that—

by which poor Emmy meant no producers, no film stars who would instantly recognise the bone structure (if not the long blonde wig) of one who had twice been crowned Miss Plummergen. *Emmeline,* she'd call herself, once she'd hit the big time. Just the one name, like Sabrina, or Capucine. Look real classy up in lights, and not as if she'd have to invent it, the way some of 'em did . . .

Emmy was not alone in dreaming of stardom. Maureen, her best friend, waitress and part-time barmaid at the George and Dragon, also had visions of Discovery by Hollywood, the stage, or television. She viewed each new hotel guest, especially those who smoked cigars, with considerable interest until she'd managed to find out what their real jobs might be: whereupon, brooding, she would lapse into her habitual state of near-suspended animation. But, like Emmy, Maureen never gave up hope . . .

It was late afternoon. Emmy was surreptitiously checking the official clock behind the grille to see if there was really an hour to go before they shut, when the door of the post office burst open, and Maureen came running in.

Maureen? Running? This was unheard-of. Conversations stopped, heads turned, mouths gaped in much the same manner Maureen's so often did as she yawned and slouched her weary way through her daily round.

"Guess what?" breathed Maureen, ignoring the rest of her audience and concentrating on Emmy. "Go on—you'll never guess, not in a million years you won't!"

Emmy shot a glance at Maureen's left hand, then frowned. If Wayne hadn't popped the question, what else could possibly make her friend so excited? "Your Wayne's bought himself a car?" she suggested, though she didn't really think it very likely. Wayne was proud of his Kawasaki motorbike, and Maureen, in a confidential mood, had once confessed to having a bit of a Thing about black leather.

"Car? Wayne?" From Maureen's stare, it seemed that the meaning of neither word was recogniseable in her present state of mind. "Oh, no," with great scorn, "nothing like that—it's them at the George, come this dinner-time and bin mooching about the place ever since . . ."

Emmy's nod and quickening interest were accompanied by a chorus of curious murmurs as everyone else in the post office, ears flapping, pressed closer. Maureen, oblivious to all except Emmy, leaned across the counter and whispered, in thrilling tones:

"They're from the telly—*and* the newspapers—and they want to make a film about *us*!"

The resulting sensation was all that she could have wanted. After a double-take lasting just three seconds, the entire shop erupted into a babble of questions, exclamations, and high-pitched—the only male present, Mr. Stillman, remained silent behind his grille—demands to know more.

Maureen had dreamed all her life of being the centre of attention with every word she spoke, and at last her dream was fulfilled. She drew in a deep breath, tossed her head, and cleared her throat.

"It's that cooking programme on the telly, you know, *Not All Roast Beef*." Everyone nodded: they knew it well. For a subject-matter potentially so esoteric, the series had, by its unique method of presentation, garnered a surprisingly large audience across the entire country. "Looking to make a second series, they are," gloated Maureen, "and using Plummergen as a base while they does their research." She simpered. "Extras, they say they'll be wanting—and paying 'em, what's more."

She smirked, and tossed her head again, casting a scornful glance at Emmy's short dark hair, pleased with her own longer, wavy, genuinely—well, helped just a bit from a bottle, as if that counted, which o'course there was no need to mention, really—blonde locks. "Filming in a few weeks, they'll be, once they've found the right locations." Maureen brought out the jargon as if to the manner born.

"Gardens mostly, so they said," she went on, enjoying the sight of the whole shop holding its breath, wide-eyed, eager for every syllable. "People in 'em, o'course, and in costume—crinolines and top hats and feather bonnets and all sorts, if they find what they want, and mebbe in houses too, if there's the right . . . " The manner wavered, though only for an instant. "The right setting," said Maureen, recovering herself, the village's expert on all matters televisual. She frowned. Had the research team—or that reporter; he'd had a look in his eye—been having her on? "Looking for an apple tree, they said . . . ''

That second hesitation lost Maureen her place centre-stage. Once more babbling, questioning, and exclaiming, the shoppers of Plummergen hurled themselves at once into arguments as to the wisdom or otherwise of exposing one's house and garden (and possibly person) to the public gaze; and, if the attendant risks were deemed worth taking, whose houses, whose persons might be found worthy of appearing in a television series . . .

And when the first of the mothers with school-age children arrived with *their* titbit of news, they had to shout to make themselves heard above the din—while Mr. Stillman, for once bending the law and not caring in the least, pulled down the metal shutter, thus separating the post office from the rest of the shop, and put ear-plugs in his ears.

CHAPTER 10

After tea, there was a brief skirmish (which Miss Seeton eventually lost) over whether or not Scotland Yard should pay for her taxi to Charing Cross. So expensive, and so difficult to find one, at the start of the rush hour. She could (she insisted) walk the distance very well: living in the country as she did . . .

Delphick having won that round by speaking over her protests and asking Ferencz Szabo to slip outside, there's a good chap, and whistle up a cab, Miss Seeton firmly, though politely, refused the chief superintendent's offer to telephone Ashford and arrange for a plainclothes officer to meet her from Brettenden station. She had, she said, felt rather guilty at letting anyone collect her from home earlier on, even though Mr. Brinton—according to the charming young man who had so kindly driven her to catch the London train—had been most persuasive that he, that was the young man, had had official business in the neighbourhood in any case, so that she hadn't really been taking him out of his way, or at least—if she had—not too much. But going home, now that her assignment—Miss Seeton stuttered over the word, and blushed for the melodrama of it all—now that her little task was complete, there was no particular hurry, was there? She would see if Mr. Baxter's car was there when she arrived, or, failing that, she would ring Jack Crabbe, who would be sure to come for her. Or his father, if Jack was busy . . .

An afternoon in Town is not, no matter how pleasant the company, the most refreshing of occasions. Miss Seeton had much enjoyed her tea, and meeting Mr. Szabo again— so very knowledgeable, so amusing in his conversation, so complimentary about her foolish doodles—and the Ritz, of course, had been magnificent. But, once one's little excursion was over, it was even more pleasant to be driven down The Street and see one's own dear, peaceful cottage at the end; to find a kettle full and waiting in the kitchen, a cake in the larder, chocolate biscuits in the tin . . .

And Martha Bloomer, to Miss Seeton's surprise, on the doorstep.

"Why, Martha, how nice to see you. Do come in—I was just about to make myself a cup of tea, though it would in any case have been easy enough to add another spoonful before it has been standing too long. Or two," she added, remembering that Martha preferred her tea far stronger than did her employer—which, Miss Seeton knew only too well, was not an uncommon preference. "One forgets how very *dusty* a day in London can make one feel, even though Mr. Delphick was kind enough to treat me to tea, you know, at the Ritz. Such delicious sandwiches—though the cakes, of course," in a hurry, "were nowhere near as delicious as yours."

Martha's eyes twinkled as she followed Miss Seeton along the hall. Good cook though she knew herself to be, she doubted if even her tarts and pastries could equal the lavish concoctions served, as she'd seen on the telly and read about in the papers, at establishments like the Ritz.

"Kind of you to say so, dear—but anyway, I'm glad you had a good time. The Ritz, eh? Nothing but the best for you, and I'm glad Mr. Delphick's got the sense to know it." Mrs. Bloomer watched as boiling water was poured into the pot, swirled round, and tipped away before two-and-a-half spoons of tea were added. Not that you couldn't trust Miss Emily to make a proper cuppa, because of course you could, but it never did any harm to make certain . . .

"Been keeping an eye out for you," Martha continued, "with not being sure when you'd be back, and I was afraid you'd miss the message, for all I left it where I thought you'd see it on the table—which I couldn't help but notice,'' as Miss Seeton gave a little start, and looked guilty, ''you'd popped your hat and bag right on top of, dear, so it's lucky I come over after all, though I suppose you'd've spotted it when you went up later. Except it might have been a bit too late for ringing back, or else he'd've rung you first and you not knowing what it was about, and couldn't say no even if you wanted, caught on the hop like that. Though you might not want to, of course, so long as you're not too tired after today—it's Mr. Jessyp,'' she said, as Miss Seeton looked rather bewildered. ''He rang and asked me to make sure you knew, and would you ring and tell him once you'd had a chance to think about it—''

''Oh, dear.'' Miss Seeton understood at once what Martha meant. ''Not poor Miss Maynard's mother again? How dreadful—and so very unfortunate that nothing ever seems to help her for very long, although I, naturally, will be only too happy to assist in any way I can.''

''I knew you would—but no, it isn't her, it's young Alice in the wars, Mr. Jessyp said. Put her back out something cruel, poor Miss Maynard, fell off a ladder pinning pictures on the walls—Harvest Flowers and things she'd got the kiddies drawing on and off all day to keep 'em quiet, seeing as they're starting to get worked up about this Grand Conker Contest with Murreystone, and a lot of foolish talk,'' with a disapproving sniff, ''from their parents egging them on, I don't doubt—which won't bother you, of course, dear, them always behaving beautiful whenever you teach them.''

Indeed they do. Miss Seeton's control over the Junior Mixed Infants of Plummergen's village school is regarded, by the parents and families of these high-spirited juveniles, as nothing less than miraculous. Sinister, some say, while others applaud it: for, though the children rarely misbehave for headmaster Martin Jessyp, and only on occasion let rip in the presence of Alice Maynard, when Miss Seeton is their instructor they can never be faulted for courtesy, punctuality, or willingness to learn. Half the parents, mistrusting Miss Seeton's influence, insist that such enthusiasm for school isn't natural, that Miss Seeton—as everyone knows, a witch—must be casting a spell on the kiddies to keep 'em quiet, or else she'd not be paid for her teaching, and stands to reason she needs money to keep that cottage of hers going, for all the police pay her for her drawings and there's the times she's written about in the papers, you can't tell anyone she'll not be getting good money for that, no matter what Other People say . . .

Other People included, of course, the Bloomers. Stan once came to blows with someone casting aspersions upon his employer's character; Martha was noted for her temper whenever Miss Emily's reputation was besmirched. Mrs. Bloomer in a Grand Slam was a sight—and sound—best avoided, and there were those who still shuddered when they recalled the tongue-lashing she'd given them for believing the story, put about by the Nuts, that Miss Seeton sacrificed babies, strung them up, and collected their blood in a bowl for purposes of sorcery. If it wouldn't have been a waste of good, honest bramble jelly, Martha was sorely tempted to rub the noses of the worsted Nuts in their humiliation by presenting them publicly with a jar of the product of eight pounds of blackberries strained overnight through muslin . . .

"Behave beautiful," said Martha, as Miss Seeton, leaving the tea to brew, hurried back down the hall to retrieve the note her henchwoman had placed where she'd thought it couldn't be missed. And if Miss Seeton hadn't been just a little weary from her afternoon out, she wouldn't have missed it—but how fortunate that dear Martha took such good care of her that she had come across in person to make sure she knew of Mr. Jessyp's urgent wish to speak with her.

"Poor Miss Maynard," said Miss Seeton, and clicked her tongue. "To fall from a ladder—so precarious, I would think, if one leans over too far—angles, and centres of gravity, and balance—though I myself have only ever been on a ladder once in my life, that I recall, and then it was climbing straight upwards—which is far safer, I imagine, than leaning, which I had no occasion to do . . ." Whether Miss Seeton's pursuer on that occasion, he having been struck by her falling handbag and brolly as she climbed, would have considered that going straight upwards on a ladder was safer than leaning sideways must be left unanswered: he had been hoping to kill her, and she had ended by—inadvertently, but effectively—despatching him.

"Which is why," went on Miss Seeton, pondering Mr. Jessyp's note as Martha fetched an extra cup and the biscuit-tin, "I never had any great wish to become a sculptor rather than an artist." She sighed: she doubted, even after hearing dear Mr. Delphick's kind words this afternoon, whether one could dare to call oneself an artist, with so limited a talent. "Ladders, you see—one can never be entirely sure that the base is firmly fixed, and to slip—as poor Miss Maynard has done . . ."

"By all accounts," said Martha, pouring milk into cups, "it was the steps, and the hinge going—wooden, you see, and riddled with worms that nobody'd noticed, and the screws loosening over the years until, well, it was just a matter of time. Lucky it was her and not you, dear, with being that much younger and healing fast—not," as Miss Seeton looked shocked, "as she's broken any bones, but very badly bruised, Mr. Jessyp said, and Dr. Knight's told her to rest up the next few days, and I've rearranged my mornings for the rest o' the week to pop in every so often and keep an eye on her—see what she wants doing, living alone like she does. So if I'm not here when you expect me, well, if you're up at the school, it won't matter too much, will it, dear? Which if you ring Mr. Jessyp now, while I pour the tea, you can get fixed up and then nothing to worry about except the lessons, and there's books for them, after all, save drawing, which you don't need. Put your feet up," said Martha, carrying the tray into the sitting-room, "and maybe watch a bit of telly—there, now! Be forgetting my own name next—but never mind, you just give Mr. Jessyp a ring first and sort yourselves out, then I can tell you all about it." Gently, Martha pushed Miss Seeton towards the telephone, and, while her employer dialled the well-known number, occupied herself with the tea-tray.

"You know that telly programme about food, dear?"

Miss Seeton, now thankfully sipping tea, nodded, and smiled. "Entertaining as well as educational," she said. "I confess that the finer points of the cookery have tended to escape me, Martha dear, but I'm sure that you find them most interesting—the history too, of course, as I do, and the costumes are delightful. The Colvedens, you know, with their new colour set, have been kind enough to invite me to supper once or twice. And it is remarkable," said Miss Seeton, with a puzzled frown, "how it makes one's old black-and-white set seem rather, well, dingy—colour television, I mean, by comparison. So very strange, when you consider that one of my favourite mediums is charcoal—and most of the old films I so enjoy watching were made in black and white anyway."

"We've thought about getting one on the never-never," Martha said, "but I don't know: me and Stan, we're not ones for liking to be in debt—still, that's not what I was saying, was it? About the programme, you'll never guess—Emmy Putts's mother told me, and I popped into the George on my way home from the shops for a chat with Doris, and she says it's true. They're here, dear, in Plummergen. Now, what do you think of that?"

Miss Seeton set down her cup. "The television people? Of course, since the Best Kept Village Competition we have become accustomed to visitors—and Mr. Mountfitchet is bound to be pleased if they should feature his hotel in one of the programmes, although which traditional dish it would be, I am not altogether sure . . ."

The premise upon which *Not All Roast Beef* was based had been simple, but effective. The British Isles are famous, in culinary terms, for far more than bangers and mash, fish and chips, or beans on toast, traditional though these may be. *Not All Roast Beef* not only gave recipes, it gave a history lesson at the same time, with costumed actors—regional accents a speciality—bringing to life the birth of such temptations as Cheddar Cheese (much Somerset *oh aar, me dear*-ing and an abundance of be-smocked cider drinkers); Melton Mowbray Pork Pie (shots of contented Tamworth pigs feeding on the whey from the making of Stilton Cheese, and dedicated cooks raising hot-water pas-

try crusts by hand); Dundee Cake (kilts, bagpipes, marmalade, and gingerbread); York Ham (Middle White pigs
in a Keighley sty); Lancashire Hot Pot (clog-dancing mill
girls); and Bakewell Tart and Pudding (a crinoline-clad
Mrs. Greaves remonstrating with the incompetent cook at
her coaching inn for having baked an almond topping over
jam on puff pastry instead of the strawberry tart she'd been
asked to produce).

"Course, we enjoyed that Bakewell Tart programme special, me and Stan," said Martha, twinkling at Miss Seeton,
who smiled and nodded. One of the later characters involved in the development of the well-known Derbyshire
dish had been one George Bloomer, a baker, whose family
had acquired the secret of the recipe for a bottle of whisky
a week. Martha had been much amused when her stock
among the rest of the village rose appreciably after the
transmission of that particular episode, until Stan let slip—
she'd kept mum on purpose—that he was, as far as he
knew, no relation to the Midlands family. Emmy Putts had
stopped presenting her best profile whenever Martha
popped in for a pound or two of cheese, Maureen had gone
back to her yawning, Miss Nuttel and Mrs. Blaine had
stopped putting their hair so obviously in curlers . . .

"Dear, dear," said Martha, chuckling at the memory.
"Oh dear oh dear oh dear—these telly people, they've got
no idea, have they?" She glanced at Miss Seeton, still smiling politely at a joke she couldn't quite understand. "Nor
more have you, dear, so never mind me, it's just my nonsense."

But she couldn't help reflecting that the production team
of *Not All Roast Beef* might just have bitten off more than
they could chew when they'd turned up in Plummergen . . .

CHAPTER 11

Information is disseminated around Plummergen in a variety of ways. It is generally accepted that most people inform themselves through gossip, whether face-to-face—which can have the ambivalent advantage of involving others at the same time—or on the telephone—which has the definite advantage of privacy, on such occasions as this should be required, but which costs money. Experienced Plummergen gossips know very well that it is not always necessary, when visiting the village shops, to purchase anything . . .

Less dedicated shoppers, or people with better things to do with their time than run the gauntlet of clacking tongues whenever they wish for a bar of chocolate or a packet of soap flakes, infinitely prefer the personal touch—or the local paper, though this comes out only once a week, and stale news is no fun—or, in the evenings, the pub.

"A heavy night last night, Nigel?" Lady Colveden passed her son his coffee with a sympathetic smile, as he shook his head when she gestured with the milk, and motioned towards the sugar. "I wouldn't have said you came in late—and you certainly didn't start singing sea-shanties at two in the morning the way your father sometimes does."

The Times quivered indignantly in the baronet's hands, but he said nothing; as did Nigel, who stirred three spoons absently into his cup as if in a trance.

"Goodness, you must be sickening for something." It was all her ladyship could do not to reach across and feel her son's forehead. "This isn't like you, Nigel—missing a chance to tease your father, I mean. Not, of course," as *The Times* rustled in a threatening manner, "that I'd ever *encourage* you to be—to be disrespectful to either of us, but when you think how often the admiral flies his gin pennant, and how often your father just happens to be passing by to find out there's a party that evening, and how much everyone seems to—to enjoy themselves," she amended, as a pointed harrumphing erupted from behind Sir George's paper to drown out any reference to drink. "Well, it's not like you," Lady Colveden concluded, buttering a puzzled slice of toast.

Nigel watched her for a moment, and then said dreamily, "If you had cheese on top of that, you'd have Welsh Rabbit, of a sort. Did you know," as his mother stared, startled at the very idea of mustard-flavoured cheese, cooked in ale and spread on toast, for breakfast, "you shouldn't call it Rarebit? It's a common mistake," he enlarged, in tones of great authority. "But it *is* a mistake. Everyone who knows what they're talking about will always say Rabbit. The Welsh part's the same in either case, though . . ."

Lady Colveden's eyes narrowed as she studied her son, whose own eyes were wide, gazing—presumably—across the hills and valleys of Wales, following who knew what spectre of cheese-eating Celt towards a loaf of bread, a toasting-fork, and a waiting fire.

A loaf of bread . . . Lady Colveden sat up. It wasn't *a toasting-fork* that came next, as far as she recalled—but the next words rang a very loud bell as she looked at Nigel—at his absent expression as he drank his coffee, at the way his egg was congealing, half-eaten, on his plate . . .

"What else did she tell you?" she enquired, returning to her toast as if nothing was further from her mind than finding out what manner of female—Welsh, presumably—had made such a sudden and vivid impression on her ever-susceptible son. "You're not usually so interested in cookery, any more than your father is."

"Don't bring me into it," muttered the major-general, as he turned a page. "Good plain food's enough for a working farmer. Can't be bothered with anything fancy."

"But that," said Nigel, blushing, "is the whole point—that British food's not fancy, it's good, plain, wholesome nourishment with just a few frills to stop it being boring, the way people who don't know suppose it is. At least, so Bethan says." He blushed still more, spearing cold yellow yolk with an embarrassed fork. "That it's what people who don't know always think, I mean. And she wants—they want—to change the way they do it—think, I mean. It's very—very educational."

"Educational?" Sir George lowered his paper. "Thinking of going back to college? Can't be done. Busy time of year—need every man we've got."

"Is it ever anything else? But I think, George," his wife went on gently, as Nigel swallowed poached egg and rendered himself thankfully dumb, "that what Nigel's saying is—what *are* you saying, Nigel? Is Bethan someone you've met at the Young Farmers? I don't believe I've heard you mention her before."

Nigel emerged from his egg and affected a careless front which fooled nobody. "Oh, didn't I tell you? I, er, met her in the George last night—they're staying there for a few days while they research another programme for the new series. *Not All Roast Beef*—you've watched one or two of them, haven't you, Mother? Bethan—Broomfield," he added, savouring the name, "is the director's research and personal assistant—chap called Jeremy Froste. With an e." Nigel's pleasant features twisted in a grimace. "He wears a corduroy jacket, and a perfectly ghastly shirt, with the most hideous cravat you've ever seen." He sighed. "Bethan says he's brilliant, though. I suppose he'd have to be, to get away with an outfit like that."

Lady Colveden, who had nodded her recognition of Jeremy Froste's name from the end-of-programme credits, frowned. "What great British food do they expect to find in Plummergen? I mean, we do have a lot of great British *cooks*, but—don't snigger like that, Nigel. George, there's no need," as *The Times* scrunched and writhed in her husband's hands, "to be so—so—"

"Realistic?" Nigel, having broken the news of his most recent infatuation, had at last relaxed. "A good roast, or a casserole, yes, we'll grant you those, and if Martha keeps a *very* close eye on you our kitchen has, occasionally, been known to produce an edible fruit cake—but you must accept your limitations, Mother darling. As we do. We cannot, in all honesty, call you great—and anyway," as his mother feinted at him with the coffee pot, "they aren't looking for food, they're looking for fruit. An apple, actually."

"If apples aren't food," retorted Lady Colveden, "then I should very much like to know what is. I think your Bethan has been having you on—unless you're trying to bamboozle us, which at this hour of the morning . . ."

"No bamboozlement," Nigel assured her, as she paused to think of a suitably aggrieved conclusion. "Old English Apples, they're making a whole programme about—you'd never believe the numbers there used to be. Local varieties just in one village, perhaps, and never grown elsewhere. As you might say, peculiar to the place—and that's what they're looking for, the Plummergen Peculier." Nigel chuckled. "Also with an e, I'm told. And judging by some of the other names Bethan came up with as examples, I'd call Plummergen Peculier pretty tame."

The Times was lowered once more. Sir George's wayward fancy had obviously been caught. "Such as?"

"Ah. Yes." Nigel had clearly been paying more attention to Miss Broomfield herself than to what she'd told him about her work. "Pig's Snout, I remember that one—better warn the admiral about letting the bees loose on the blossom next spring, if they find any of those. Goodness knows how the honey would taste with a name like that. It'd certainly be different." Nigel frowned. "Fair Maid was another, and Marriage Maker—and," as his parents exchanged amused glances, "Morgan Sweet, and Dick's Favourite—and Bottle Stopper—and something about Jerusalem, as well."

"Goodness, I shouldn't fancy going all the way to Jerusalem, just for an apple." Lady Colveden began to stack plates. "Do they know what these Peculier apples look like? I can just imagine how half the village will be convinced they have one of the trees in the back garden, and if your Bethan and her Mr. Froste aren't careful, they'll be dragged into every house in The Street to check."

"Not coming here, I hope," muttered Sir George, hastily joining the ranks of those who did not care to worship the great goddess Television, and who would prefer to see no strangers in their homes, Plummergen Peculier or not.

Nigel was undismayed by the reaction of his sire: it was no more than his own had been, as Bethan discoursed on her mission, though he had acknowledged at the time that not everyone would feel the same way. "Oh, there'll be dozens of places they can visit, without the Hall," he said. "The more the merrier, Bethan says. She really takes an interest in her work. She's very thorough . . . "

He sighed. "She says this Froste is one of the up-and-coming television Turks, and she's privileged to be helping him right at the start of his career—and," said Nigel, sounding puzzled, "she's not the only one. There's some kind of reporter following them—him—around wherever he goes for this series, so that he can feature him in a lead article in one of the glossies, and Bethan says he, that's the reporter, thinks it will help *his* career, too, if he turns himself into the expert on Jeremy Froste."

He sighed, still puzzled: there was no accounting for taste, although from his appearance reporter Roy Roydon didn't have much to begin with. His clothes were even less to Nigel's liking than those of Jeremy Froste.

"Fool," said Sir George, loudly.

Nigel jumped, then decided that his father surely couldn't be referring to his son and heir. He brightened. "I'd no idea you'd ever met the chap, but I'm jolly glad to have my unbiased opinion shared," he began; then stopped, as Sir George shook his head.

"Fool—I remember now." He glared over the top of *The Times* towards his wife, who had stopped stacking and was on the point of rising to her feet. "Thought I'd sleep all the way through it, as I recall. I didn't."

Lady Colveden sat down again. "Didn't you? Oh! No,

of course, you didn't.'' She glanced at her spouse in some surprise, then at her son. ''Your father's right, Nigel. You were out, so you didn't see it, but the programme last week—or was it the week before? Anyway, it was called *Capital Food*—London, you know. Boodle's Fool, although why your father should remember when Boodle's isn't his club, I don't know—but it sounded delicious. Orange and lemon juice, and whipped cream and sponge cake—and Boodle's Cake, too, if it comes to that. And Omelette Arnold Bennett, at the Savoy—they showed him writing part of *The Old Wives' Tale*—and Bismarck drinking Black Velvet at Brooks's, because until the First World War it was named after him—Guinness in champagne, I mean, not Brooks's,'' as Nigel raised an eye-brow at the notion of one of London's most exclusive gentlemen's clubs being named for the German chancellor.

''Sounds fascinating,'' he said, not being merely polite. If he could impress Bethan that he knew what she was talking about . . . ''Anything else?''

Lady Colveden giggled. ''There was some terrible music called Bubble and Squeak—that's what woke your father up in time to see the fool.''

''Wow wow,'' said Sir George, surfacing again.

Nigel blinked. ''Er—you want me to feed the dogs this morning? You only have to say the word. Just pass me the tin opener and the Chummy Chunks, and—''

''Nigel, really.'' His mother stifled another giggle. ''Not bow-wow, Wow Wow Sauce—that's what went with Bubble and Squeak—they showed Dr. Kitchiner brewing it, if that's the right word. Mustard, and red wine, and mushroom ketchup, and pickled walnuts—they would have been rather tough, I should think, after soaking in the other things, but Bubble and Squeak's not terribly exciting, so I suppose every little helps.''

''So where does the music come in? I thought,'' Nigel said, thinking of boarding-school mealtimes, ''that the cabbage bubbled in the pot, and the potatoes squeaked in the frying-pan, but I wouldn't call either noise particularly tuneful. Or not, as the case may be.''

''That,'' said Lady Colveden, ''is because you know

nothing of history. Not that I did,'' she added honestly,
"until the programme, but I must say they did it well, or
your friend Jeremy Froste did. It was originally cabbage
and beef, not cabbage and potatoes—they showed a World
War One housewife, poor thing, having to make do on rations—but you can spell them out on the scale, and Dr.
Kitchiner did, in eighteen-hundred-and-something, and
that's what they played. B, E, E, F, C, A, B, B, A, G, E.
See?''

"Tonic,'' remarked Sir George, without warning. Nigel,
startled but ever willing, gazed about him for the bottle,
while making a mental note not to let his father drive the
tractor until later. "Solfa,'' added his father, after a pause;
and Nigel relaxed.

"Tonic or fool or pickled walnuts,'' said Lady Colveden,
once more making to leave her chair, "I'm sure there are
more important things to think about this morning. Or,''
she added, thoughtfully, "apples . . . ''

CHAPTER 12

Martin Jessyp, efficient as ever, had confirmed yesterday evening's telephone conversation by leaving a neatly-typed timetable on Miss Maynard's—temporarily Miss Seeton's—desk. After General Assembly, the Bigguns and Tiddlers would divide for their separate classes. For the Tiddlers, the first lesson was Nature Study . . .

A great pity (mused Miss Seeton as the school, Assembly over, prepared to settle to its lessons) that it was still raining. The children were unusually restless this morning: one could, had the day been fine, have taken them out for a Nature Study ramble. There would be autumn fruits to sample, nuts and fallen leaves to collect, small branches and twigs, torn down by recent high winds, to be used for decorating the schoolroom, or as objects for sketching in a later Art class.

It was, however, raining. The smell of damp gaberdine wafted through from the cloakroom, mingling with the aroma of warm rubbery footwear and wet hair that did not, to Miss Seeton's surprise, appear to trouble those underneath it. Country life, of course, must accustom them from their earliest years to the vagaries of the British climate: there was no doubt that the children's pink cheeks and bright eyes bore witness to bouncing good health rather than incipient fever—but for one whose umbrella (now sedately draining in one of the cloakroom sinks) was an indispensable adjunct, no matter what the weather, it seemed odd that nobody had even thought of wearing a hat. Miss Seeton raised an automatic hand to her head, then clicked her tongue and smiled for her folly as she glanced again towards the cloakroom, where Miss Maynard's peg—for a few days, her own—held both hat and mackintosh until they should be once more required.

She sighed. It seemed highly probable that they would. She had listened last night to the forecast on the wireless, and had hoped that, for once, Felton Butler of the London Weather Centre had been wrong to predict heavy rain for most of the morning. Be required, she meant. But now she very much feared that he had been absolutely right. Until it was time to go home. No nature ramble, then . . .

Her glance drifted to the cupboard in the corner. There were, she knew, wall charts, and posters: one might question the advisability of using so much adhesive tape, where drawing-pins would be inappropriate—she had never managed to work out how her fingers almost invariably became trapped when sticking, or unsticking, anything, but had long ago accepted it as a fact of life . . . yet one could not deny that letting the children *see* what they were being taught, rather than merely reading about it from (one had to admit) perhaps rather old-fashioned textbooks, with their illustrations mostly in black and white . . .

A stifled giggle from the back row roused Miss Seeton from the Old Movie daydream into which she found herself in danger of lapsing. She blinked, and shook herself. One was supposed to be teaching a class, not thinking of television.

A waving hand from the front row caught her attention. "Yes, Rachel?"

"Please, Miss, are *you* going to be on the telly?"

Good gracious. Miss Seeton blinked again, then blushed: she hadn't realised she'd spoken her final thoughts aloud. What a deplorable example to be setting the children: small wonder they were, as one had already observed, so restless. And so very discourteous. They had, after all, taken the trouble—and it was still raining—to come to school to learn: they deserved one's fullest attention and encouragement, not a teacher unable to keep her mind on the matter in hand. Discourteous . . .

Miss Seeton promptly compensated for her lack of courtesy by giving Rachel's question—in the circumstances, when one prided oneself on the modest privacy of one's life, so very surprising—due consideration before replying.

She smiled: considering, she had recalled Martha's chatter of the previous night. "I think not," she said. "I am, after all, a teacher of art, not cookery." Or history, she might have added, but refrained, believing this would be bad for discipline when one remembered that History came next on the timetable. Besides, since one's retirement, although one kept gratifyingly busy, there had been a pleasing amount of time for reading, for increasing one's store of general knowledge on a variety of topics . . .

"And I hardly think," she added, "that costume drama, as I believe it is called, could ever be a suitable activity for one such as myself."

This remark would have much amused, had they heard it, a great many of Miss Seeton's acquaintance. Unsuited to a costume drama? Why, her whole life, balanced as she is on a tightrope between the orthodox and the outré, is nothing less than a full-scale dramatic production. Costume? While from the neck downwards Miss Seeton always appears the epitome of an English gentlewoman, her hats—which, whether trimmed or not when she buys them, are almost always retrimmed by herself—would, worn by anyone else, seem not so much Costume as Fancy Dress. Indeed, an onlooker with an interest in psychology might suggest that Miss Seeton, in her attire, is subconsciously expressing the dichotomy of her nature. Take her clothes: the discreet tweeds, sensible shoes, and pastel linens are those of the conventionally costumed gentlewoman she remains convinced, all evidence to the contrary notwithstanding, she is. Take her hats, however, and one finds the Drama. *Unique* is no understatement of their character: they have been described as godawful, unmistakeable, ill-chosen: but they are Miss Seeton's deliberate choice, her one (presumably unwitting) concession to the bizarre, the unexpected, the picturesque nature of the adventures in which she is so often, despite herself, embroiled—a concession to the Drama which is her all-too-frequent companion, and which she so resolutely contrives to ignore.

"Miss, you mean you really don't want never to be on the telly?" Wide-eyed Rachel was not the only Tiddler to be astonished at their preceptress's evident disinclination for fame and glory. While village parents might be divided as to the wisdom of the entire experience, their children were united. Everyone wished to be a star. The thrilling bombshell dropped by Maureen in the post office yesterday afternoon had ricocheted, with suitable embellishments, around the village for the whole of the subsequent evening (and was likely to continue on its travels, with further embellishments, at least for the remainder of the week). Half the wives and mothers of Plummergen, reluctant to leave their sleeping children, had for the first time in living memory actively encouraged husbands and fathers to pop along to the George: and if so be they should happen to come across that Jeremy Froste, well, t'wouldn't do no harm to be friendly to the man, would it? Seeing as how he was said to have an interest in gardens, which digging, at least, was mostly the men's business, and gardens in Plummergen, especially since the Best Kept Village Competition, being well worth a visit . . . weren't they?

The Plummergen men, compared to their womenfolk mere ciphers in local affairs, meekly followed orders and forced themselves down to the pub, where (they took care to remind their wives when they returned, long after official closing time, home) it stood to reason they'd had to take a drink or two—just to be sociable, o'course. Threatened by rolling-pins and shrill voices, they sobered sufficiently to report that Jeremy Froste'd had plenty to say, and a journalist bloke taking notes, and a girl, too, taking notes—a pretty young wench as spent a fair time being chatted up by Nigel Colveden. Which weren't (grumbled the wives) hardly right, somehow, him and his father without an apple tree to their names, Rytham Hall being mostly arable and sheep, and everyone knowing Sir George was one of them as didn't want nothing to do with it . . .

The wives were still grumbling over breakfast next day;

and Plummergen's little pitchers have genetically long ears, all the better for the assimilation of gossip, scandal, and surmise once their owners have matured sufficiently to take their places in the adult world. Miss Seeton might innocently suppose that the rosy cheeks and general liveliness of her charges denoted good health: Miss Seeton was wrong. Excitement, pure and simple, had occasioned the flurry of whispers, the giggles, the sparkling eyes . . .

"I'd like to dress up and be on the telly," Rachel said, "and dance. I could be an apple blossom. I could have a pretty pink dress with white frills, and green petals on my head for a hat . . ."

" 'S wrong time of year for apple blossom," scoffed young Lizzie, as thoughts of Monica Mary, the Brettenden milliner, flashed unbidden across Miss Seeton's mind. Across the mind of Lizzie, however, had flashed thoughts of yesterday's conker skirmish in the playground, and how her champion twenty-oncer had fallen victim to Rachel's seventeener. The chance for revenge now was sweet. "Don't have blossom in October, you great stupid dummy!"

Miss Seeton, mentally shaking herself, seized her opportunity. "You are correct, Elizabeth, we don't, though there are rather more courteous ways of advising someone of this. Maybe we should try instead to name what we *do* have in October—a little competition, something different from each of you, if you can think of it, but if you can't, it doesn't matter. Rachel may go first. I'm sure she knows very well that apple trees blossom in the spring, and when she spoke of them just now she was simply using her imagination—though perhaps at not quite the most suitable time, Rachel," she added gently. "And now, can you name something that we have in October?"

Rachel, who had scowled at Lizzie's insult, brightened, and there was a note of triumph in her voice as she almost shouted: "Apples, Miss!"

At which even Lizzie had to giggle, while the other Tiddlers laughed aloud and Miss Seeton, smiling, nodded to the next child to continue.

Most suggestions were of things which had been drawn

yesterday, in Miss Maynard's art lesson. The more crafty pupils sneaked backward looks at the picture-pinned wall before volunteering the various nuts, berries, flowers, or fruits; Miss Seeton marked all correct, and chided none for cheating.

"About conkers, however," she said, "I am not entirely sure." Her eyes twinkled. "Miss Maynard, after all, did not see fit to add them to her display of Harvest Flowers and Foods, did she?"

The Tiddlers twinkled back, sharing the joke: weren't nobody as could put one over on Miss, was there? Didn't seem to mind they'd peeked, though, knowing it'd been just a bit o' fun first thing in the morning . . . The earlier metaphysical speculation as to the nature of squirrels and birds was renewed by one or two children whose parents belonged to Brettenden's Holdfast Brethren, but Miss Seeton coped with her usual pedagogic calm as matters looked likely to become fraught. Conkers, she decreed, would, for the purposes of today's discussion, be regarded not as a food—although it was her understanding that, in times of famine, people had indeed been known to eat the fruit of the horse chestnut tree, and some European countries fed them to cattle and horses—but as an Autumn Sport.

"And you will no doubt recall," she continued, above a doubtful murmuring, "that I asked you to list what we have in autumn. I did not, I believe, specify that the list had to include everything from yesterday's lesson . . . " Another twinkle, returned with delight by the brighter children, who had begun to guess how this might end.

" . . . nor," she went on, "did I specify that it should *not* include such things. I think none of you would deny that we—or rather you—have conker contests in autumn, would you? Especially when the weather," she added, above a chorus of giggles, "is so frequently wet, as it is today. For which reason, perhaps we should add conkers to our list—but, since this period is not for Games, but for Nature Study, what else can we say about the horse chestnut tree?"

"Sticky-buds, Miss," suggested someone, with a sideways look for Lizzie. "In the spring!"

The words were an inspiration for Miss Seeton. Sticky? Spring? She had always marvelled that so many children each year so enjoyed picking the red-brown buds and covering their fingers with resin; it was even more marvellous that this annual amusement should this morning have provided her with the answer to her problem. She smiled . . .

There was a brisk burst of activity as Miss Seeton requested wall charts and posters to be fetched from the cupboard, while she searched the desk for the bulldog clips she remembered having left behind on a previous occasion when acting as a substitute teacher. There was one anxious moment in case Miss Maynard—though it seemed unlikely, for she was a thrifty soul—might have disposed of them; but then, to her relief, Miss Seeton unearthed the clips from a tin in the bottom drawer. She received the first poster with thanks and fastened it neatly—no more sticky fingers—to the blackboard with the strong spring-clips.

"The horse chestnut tree," she said, using the wooden pointer to direct attention to the Latin name beneath. She blinked as she read the translation, then took a deep breath and prepared to admit her bewilderment with the best. "*Aesculus hippocastanum* . . ."

"Please, Miss," someone objected, "why does it say it's an oak tree, too? Oaks is acorns, not conkers."

"I really don't know," Miss Seeton confessed. "*Aesculus* means an Italian oak—which is perhaps different from our English variety, which could explain it. And *hippos*," she went on quickly, "is, I believe, the Greek for horse, which is why hippopotamus means river horse—because," she added as the question trembled on curious lips, "*potamos* is Greek for river. The Romans," she hurried on, before more objections could be raised, "borrowed and adapted many words from the Greeks—as we have borrowed from both, in English. So, if *castana* is a chestnut tree . . ."

She pointed again to the Latin components, one by one. The class nodded gravely. "The horse chestnut," she continued, "originally comes from Greece, as it says here." More nods. "It now grows widely throughout Europe, which is probably why so many of the poorer countries are glad of its nuts as food for their animals—and how are those nuts formed? Who can tell me?''

Not a titter greeted Miss Seeton's innocent repetition of that four-lettered word with its double meaning. In Miss Maynard's presence they might share the joke; but Miss Seeton's reputation permitted no such frivolity.

"Flowers, Miss," came the chorus. A more observant Tiddler than his peers added primly: "Panicles, Miss!" before Miss Seeton's pointer had quite reached its goal.

Miss Seeton led her class, chart by chart, through the natural cycle of, in turn, the horse chestnut—digressing briefly to cover the red-flowered ornamental cross between the white original and the American red buckeye, or *Aesculus carnea,* which produced (the Tiddlers were able to inform their teacher) conkers of very poor quality—and the hazel, or *Corylus avellana;* the walnut, or *Juglans regia;* the sweet chestnut, or *Castanea sativa;* and the English oak, *Quercus robur,* otherwise known as the pedunculate or common oak.

"Pedunculate," announced Miss Seeton, having thumbed through the classroom dictionary at her pupils' request, "means that the stalk hangs down—as one may see, from the illustrations, that it does, in the case of the leaves and the acorns."

"Then why aren't conkers called that?" demanded Lizzie, on whom the loss of her twenty-oncer still weighed heavily. "I mean—they hang down too, don't they, Miss?"

Miss Seeton, once again, had to admit her ignorance. Conkers did, undoubtedly, hang downwards: gravity would have its way; but as to why the name should only be applied to the oak . . .

"Them ole Latins and Greeks," suggested someone, as she ran out of ideas. "Talked foreign, didn't they? Stands to reason it'd not make sense in English!"

This remark, to Miss Seeton's surprise, pleased everyone save herself. While she made a mental note to check later in one of the larger dictionaries kept in Mr. Jessyp's classroom, the Tiddlers turned to more pressing topics.

"Them Latins and Greeks, Miss—"

"*Romans* and Greeks," the prim one corrected, even more primly.

"Them Romans," came the amended query, accompanied by a glare for the prim one. "Did they play conkers, Miss?"

And, as the bell rang outside for the end of the lesson, the class erupted into a burst of challenges for playground fights, accompanied by ritual expressions of enmity towards, not only the Tiddlers' friends, but also their age-old foes in Murreystone, against whom the Grand Conker Contest was yet to come.

"You know what, Miss?" rose a voice above the rest, as Miss Seeton supervised the rolling up of the posters. "They won't know what's hit 'em—my dad says we'll teach that Murreystone lot a lesson . . ."

"We'll smash 'em to bits," said someone else. "You wait and see, Miss—we'll murder 'em!"

CHAPTER 13

"Murder," said Superintendent Brinton heavily, as he stood with Foxon in the spacious—more spacious now than usual—sitting-room. "I've been afraid of this all along . . ."

Together, they stared at the sinister outline chalked on the floor. The preliminaries were over: the photographers and forensic people had played their part; the investigation proper was about to begin.

"Murder," said Brinton again, rousing himself from his gloomy thoughts. "Poor old chap!" He glanced at his silent subordinate, whose face wore an unusually wooden look. "I'm sorry, lad, I was forgetting—and sorry for your grandmother, as well. She's taking it hard, I should think, a shock like this at her time of life."

Foxon nodded. His voice sounded strained. "They were good friends, all three of 'em. Gran was at school with old Mrs. Easter—Gertie Good, she was then, bright as a button and bound to get on in the world, Gran always used to say. And Gramps was his batman in the army—Uncle Reg, I mean," he added, blushing slightly as Brinton favoured him with a quizzical look. "Er—that's what I used to call him as a kid, sir. I've known 'em for years, you see, and with him and Gertie not having kids of their own, they used to enjoy making a fuss of us lot when we came visiting. There was never any side to old Reg, for all he'd been an officer and Gramps hadn't—upset as anyone when he died, and so was Gertie, of course, being such a friend to Gran. I sometimes wonder,'' he went on, as his superior said nothing, ''if they didn't feel it more than Gran when he died—Gertie and Reg, I mean, because at least she had the rest of us, which has got to be better than nothing—which is pretty much what the Easters had.''

He sighed. ''Poor Gertie died a month or so back, which made things even worse, with Reg left alone in this great house, and not in the best of health. Mind you, he's kept— he kept,'' Foxon corrected himself, ''pretty active, despite the wheelchair—wouldn't have Meals on Wheels because he'd taught himself to cook when Gertie was first taken ill, and he could still go shopping—he even managed a bit of gardening, though I know he'd been paying the bloke across the road to do the heavy work for some time now. And Gran popped in almost every day—but it's not the same, is it, sir? As having someone of your own—but Gran's a lovely person, and—and I wish she hadn't,'' he muttered, remembering again the anguished sound of his grandmother's voice as she telephoned, in tears, to tell him what she had found, and to ask what she should do. She'd been too upset to think of dialling nine-nine-nine, to think of anything but that her old friend's house had been broken into and burgled, that he had been brutally attacked, and killed.

''Like I said, lad, I'm sorry.'' For once, Brinton couldn't find it in his heart to groan, curse, or bellow as was his wont in his dealings with his sidekick. Brinton's vocabulary, he'd have been the first to admit, wasn't up to the standard of his friend Chief Superintendent Delphick—but if anyone had asked him to define ebullient, effervescent, or irrepressible, he would have jerked a thumb in Foxon's direction and considered this answer enough. The younger man was normally so bouncing and bright that Brinton had wondered aloud, more than once, whether there were any rubber-planters in his ancestry . . .

''If you'd rather not be on this case, you've only got to say,'' he said. ''If you want compassionate leave—spend a few days with your grandmother or anything—''

"No," Foxon broke in, grim-faced, forgetful of official courtesies. "Sorry, sir, and thanks for the offer—but no. I was fond of Gertie and Reg—I know he'd looked forward to seeing her again—but it shouldn't have happened so soon, and I want to catch the blighters who made it happen. And Gran'll say the same thing, I know, when you get round to—to taking her statement," he concluded, stumbling over the final words.

Brinton said: "Reginald Easter—that name's been ringing a bell ever since we got the message, Foxon. Where've I heard of him? Quite recently, too. And I knew his face before we saw him . . ."

This was an unfortunate remark. He kicked himself, as Foxon shuddered. The old man's face had been barely recogniseable, so heavy had been the blows which had fallen on his head and shoulders: so heavy, indeed, that they had sent him tumbling from his wheelchair and sprawling to the floor, from which—the final indignity—those who struck him had already removed the carpet, so that his life ebbed away in a sluggish, red-brown stain soaking into cold, bare boards.

"On television? Surely not," said Brinton, "but I can't help thinking . . . it was black and white, I'm almost sure." He shot a wary look at Foxon. Good, the lad was starting to *think* again, to act like a copper the way he'd act with any ordinary victim—if there were such a person—to investigate. "Black and white—I can see him still," the superintendent went on, frowning quite as much as Foxon. "But for the life of me I can't . . ."

"The local paper, sir, probably." The detective constable was back on form after his—understandable—lapse. "There was a piece about their golden wedding not so long back, with a photograph, and a nice write-up about his army service. The *Beacon* really did 'em both proud . . ."

His voice faltered again. He cleared his throat. "They had an enlargement made of the snap, sir, and Gertie kept it in a silver frame on the sideboard . . ."

Brinton grunted. There was no sign of a sideboard—of any furniture of any size, or quality—in the late Reginald Easter's sitting-room. "Damned Swipers," growled Brinton, and was cheered to observe the glint in Foxon's eye.

"We'll get them, sir. If it *is* the Swipers"—even now, Foxon was unable to forego completely his customary role as Devil's Advocate—"this isn't the first time, after all. Never mind the West Country and the Midlands—what about the Whempstead bloke the other day, not to mention that poor old girl still stuck in hospital? They're on our patch now, sir—and they've made it personal, because they've stopped being just cocky they'll always get away with it—they've turned nasty. They're cocky enough not to bother waiting to make absolutely sure the house'll be empty when they go in—they've started taking risks, getting careless, giving people time to come back unexpectedly and catch 'em in the act the way that poor old girl says she did: realised she'd forgotten her shopping list and ... Uncle Reg too, for all I know." His voice was hard. "Cocky, careless, and nasty with it—we don't want chummies like that taking off to be caught on anyone else's patch, sir, do we? We want to nobble the blighters ourselves."

"If," Brinton found himself echoing his subordinate's earlier sentiments, "it really is them. I grant you the method's the same, as far as we can make out—and I still say we'd stand a better chance of nobbling them if we knew exactly what it was—and granted the *smell* of the thing is identical—but we don't know for sure. Like you said with Miss Whatsername the charity bird, could be someone pinched the basic idea and it's gone wrong because the blighters haven't done their homework, whatever it is, as well as the original lot do theirs. We don't want to waste time chasing the wrong lot of chummies when—"

"Oh, it's them, sir." Once more, Foxon forgot official courtesy in the tension of the moment. "You're always on about a good copper knowing when something isn't right without being able to say why it isn't. Well . . . "

He shrugged in as expressive a style as any detective can affect when, in accordance with investigative policy, his hands are thrust deep in his trouser pockets.

Brinton heroically refrained from questioning his side-kick's claim to being a good copper, and grunted. "Swipers—damned silly name. If the press hadn't worked 'em up into something fancy, we'd never have thought about anyone pinching the basic idea because we'd've known there was nothing for 'em to pinch in the first place. Your Uncle Reg and millions like him went through hell in two world wars for''—Brinton reddened, but spoke out bravely—''for the cause of freedom—and I can't think of a better reason. But believe me, laddie, there are times, like now, when I can't help wishing the freedom of the press could be cut back a bit—they'll be down like vultures on this little lot, and there's not a blind thing we can do to stop them. There'll be headlines—can't you just see 'em? *Sideboard Swipers Strike Again! Old Soldier Slain!*'' He was so carried away by his own oratory that he failed to observe Foxon's smothered wince. ''Gentlemen of the Press,'' groaned Brinton, exasperated before he'd seen a solitary notebook. ''Reporters—I hate 'em . . . ''

''Reporters,'' sighed Chief Superintendent Delphick, dusting down his jacket and checking that his tie was still tidy. ''I hate them—en masse, at any rate, although as individuals''—a vision of Amelita Forby floated before his inward eye—''there are those who have undoubted charm. One cannot, however, ignore the request of a desperate colleague. Duty, Sergeant Ranger, is duty.''

''Yes, sir,'' came the dutiful response, in a tone rather less than dutiful. While the Oracle was to be downstairs riding shotgun for Inspector Terling, helping him to brief Fleet Street's finest on the latest Ram Raiding incident, Detective Sergeant Ranger had been sternly advised by his superior that the paperwork mountain should on no account be allowed to increase in height—even by the thickness of a single folder.

''Continental Drift,'' said Delphick, ''be damned for a theory. There may well, I am prepared to concede, be something inevitable and unavoidable about the way chasms gape and mountains correspondingly grow around the entire surface of the planet—it is, however, the surface of my desk, and yours, which must be the sole business of this office. From the world-wide view to the particular . . . ''

He frowned, and shook his head. Something he'd just said had rung a warning bell, though he couldn't think why; and he shook his head again.

"Your tie, sir," said Bob helpfully. "You've twisted the knot under your ear."

Delphick sighed. "Would that I might come to work in casual clothes, Sergeant Ranger, with no need to knot either ties or cravats." Pensively, he made the adjustment, turning to Bob for approval of the new symmetry. "Immolation on the sacred altar of the Public's Right to Know is a terrible matter, Sergeant Ranger . . ."

Bob, who would happily have gone to ten press briefings rather than clear one in-tray of its backlog, had no sympathy with the Oracle's griping. "You could have a word with Foxon down in Ashford, sir. He's a pretty snappy dresser—though I'm not sure you'd look as good in flares and flowered shirts as he does. The, er, generation gap, I mean," he added hastily, as the look in his superior's eye hinted that he'd been on the brink of insubordination.

"Foxon!" exclaimed Delphick, snapping his fingers at the sudden realisation.

Bob sat up: surely the Oracle hadn't taken him seriously? At his age, it'd be downright daft to go prancing about in platform shoes and kipper ties—specially some of the ties he'd seen Foxon wear—never mind that the villains, who had a healthy respect for the old man, 'd laugh in his face next time he tried to arrest one of 'em, and his reputation'd be shot to ribbons for years to come, if it ever recovered at all.

"Sir," he said desperately, "I didn't—"

"Foxon," Delphick repeated, with a sigh. "Ashford, and Brinton . . . You *had* to summon up the other local Presence, didn't you? This strikes me as paltry revenge, Ranger, for being asked to do no more than clear a few files out of the way. In the War," he went on, while Bob stared at him in amazement, "which you are, there is no need to remind me, too young to recall, we were warned that Careless Talk Costs Lives; one might amend this nowadays to Careless Talk Tempts Fate. I had hoped, after yesterday, that there would be no further risk—and there's no need for you to

find it all so funny, Sergeant,'' sternly, as Bob, beginning
to understand the reasons for his superior's anguish, chuckled. ''Adopted nephew as you are . . . ''

''Sorry, sir,'' said Bob, as Delphick gave up, and absent-
mindedly began knotting his tie again.

''Plummergen, on the Ashford beat, and Miss Seeton,
and,'' said Delphick, with one fabric-tangled hand overlapping the other, ''as the icing on the cake—World Wide
Press, if I'm not very much mistaken. Did I speak just now
of immolation, Detective Sergeant Ranger? We must consider this the understatement of the year. If rumours as to
his absence abroad prove unreliable, I confidently expect to
see Thrudd Banner—and, by association, Mel Forby—
among the throng of journalists—no,'' with a sudden
chuckle, because he'd waited a long time to use it and now
the chance had at last come, ''make that *column* of journalists . . . '' He frowned. ''For heaven's sake—what was
I saying?''

''That Mel and Thrudd,'' supplied Bob, as Delphick
wrenched suddenly at the knot of his tie and unravelled the
whole thing to start again from the beginning, ''are going
to guess Miss Seeton has been called into the case—at
least, that's what I *think* you were saying, or rather were
about to say—only you, er, got carried away, sir. And you
were probably also going to say,'' as Delphick closed his
eyes and sighed, ''that if those two work it out, the others
will as well. Sir. Weren't you?''

''I fear,'' said Delphick, ''that I was.'' He reopened his
eyes, and attacked his tie with confidence. ''I was indeed—
for reasons which are, clearly, all too evident to you, Bob,
since you have so admirably extrapolated and summarised
my feelings from the few vain burblings which escaped me
before the situation utterly overwhelmed me.''

Noticeably underwhelmed, he put the finishing touches
to his tie. ''You may, if you wish,'' he said over his shoulder, ''accompany me into the lions' den. I have, as Oracles
may be permitted to do, changed my mind—there are more
important matters than paperwork in this uncertain world.
Self-preservation, for one, when Mel Forby is on the warpath . . . ''

Bob, glad of any excuse to abandon the files, did not dream of asking Delphick why he wanted—as it seemed he did—a bodyguard: he, like his boss, knew Mel Forby of old.

Mel was as yet too young to be a Fleet Street legend, though the day, everyone was confident, would come. Originally a fashion reporter, noted for her aggressive manner, assertive mode of speech, and abrasive mid-Atlantic accent, Mel had some years before successfully slip-streamed her way into one of Miss Seeton's earliest cases; and, in the process, had mellowed. Her beautiful eyes and exquisite bone structure had emerged, encouraged by unwitting comments from the little art teacher, from beneath the excess of makeup with which she had previously attempted to conceal her innately pleasant self from her professional colleagues and competitors; the acid of her tongue had given way to honey, and the accent had begun to drift more honestly eastwards, in the direction of Liverpool, city of her birth.

The recent influence of Thrudd Banner—hardened hack, cosmopolitan lover, ruthless rival in the matter of scoops—had somewhat slowed Mel's mellowing. The makeup remained soft; the accent, nourished by a diet of black-and-white movies in retrospective series in Chelsea cinemas, reverted to an echo of the former toughness—not that she was embarrassed by her ongoing relationship with the

World Wide ace, but a little protective camouflage made her feel a whole lot better about beating him, as she so often tried to do, to the next big story in Town.

But if the rumours about Thrudd's absence were right—and as Scotland Yard had called a news conference about the Ram Raids—and if the Oracle was there, and if Mel could flutter her eyelashes to remind him that they went back a long way together . . .

"She can twist us—you—round her little finger, sir," warned Bob, following his chief out to the lift and practising a menacing expression while they waited. "That's the trouble with Mel Forby—she's good, and she knows it, and she knows *we* know—that we can trust her, I mean, where with an awful lot of the others we can't—and she just sits there radiating her blessed trustworthiness in all directions, and you—we—fall for it every time, sir."

Delphick acknowledged the accusation with a wry chuckle. Mel might, on occasion, annoy him immensely, but she'd never let him down. Indeed, several times he'd positively relied on her—and, with her, on Thrudd—when a complicated case had grown even more complicated, and a little judicious juggling of the facts had been required.

"One cannot but admire," he agreed, "the success of her tactics. Yet we are both, I would remind you, married men, Sergeant Ranger; and Mel, moreover," as Bob uttered a startled protest, "is, all too obviously, spoken for—even if," with a smile, "it could be argued that the, ah, claim has not, so far as we know, been legally staked. We may well, in due course of this investigation, weaken and fall—indeed, knowing Mel, I've no doubt that we will." He chuckled. "We must, however, for the sake of constabulary confidentiality"—he permitted himself a discreet smirk—"and dignity, resist the temptation for as long as possible."

The lift arrived with a thud. The doors clanked open. Delphick ushered his sergeant inside, and pressed the button. "Temptation," he went on, as the lift began its stomach-turning descent, "must of course be succumbed to, when it is, with considerable circumspection in every aspect of the case. One should not exceed the bounds of moderation and decorum, Sergeant Ranger, even if in your particular instance you are undoubtedly able to make mincemeat of Thrudd should he object to your—our—understandable admiration of his lady . . .''

He chuckled again as his gigantic sidekick spluttered. ''Make mincemeat of anyone, come to that, should the mood take you—which I trust it won't, though there's no need, of course, to allow, ah, our audience to harbour even the least suspicion that it might. Continue to loom in that express manner, Sergeant Ranger,'' as Bob, suppressing a reluctant laugh, hunched his shoulders and scowled, ''and all—Miss Forby and Mr. Banner, should he be present, permitting—will be well . . .''

The lift came to a sudden stop, and Delphick led the way out through the clanking double doors, addressing Bob over his shoulder as he did so. ''Now Anne, I feel sure, would do far more than make mincemeat of you. A medically-trained spouse must be a copper-bottomed, to coin a phrase, guarantee of marital fidelity, I imagine . . .''

Bob sighed audibly as he trod in Delphick's wake down the corridor towards the briefing room. Maybe it was only the relief of getting away from the paperwork that'd scrambled the Oracle's brains, or had turned them—Bob managed a faint grin—to mincemeat—maybe. Granted, the old man might unbend once in a while and talk nonsense to his subordinate, but he didn't normally do it in public. Not that there'd been anyone with them in the lift, any more than there seemed to be anyone in the corridor now (and he'd be prepared to risk a small bet there'd be nobody, or at least no Inspector Terling, in the briefing room once they got there) . . . but it was the principle of the thing. More than likely—Bob's next sigh was even louder—*much* more than likely, it was the cock-eyed influence of that visit yesterday afternoon from little Guess Who. Talk about delayed reaction. Unless the Ritz'd started blending psychedelic tea, or filling the sandwiches with magic mushrooms, MissEss was up to her old tricks again, putting a topspin on everything without even bothering to try. All it took was a joke about Foxon's kipper ties and a quick mention of her journalist pals . . .

Journalists! Judging by the racket as he and Delphick

drew near, the briefing room must be full of them, and all impatient . . . No Inspector Terling? No bet. Bob Ranger grinned as, from behind—surely not from inside?—a sudden cupboard near the briefing room door, Terling's trembling sidekick cautiously appeared. He thrust a typewritten sheet into Delphick's startled hands, muttered something, and bolted back towards the lift with an air of immense relief.

The chief superintendent opened the door. Out thundered a wave of sound from what only logic insisted couldn't possibly be a thousand journalistic throats. Television, radio, newspaper, and magazine reporters perched on uncomfortable wooden chairs or on the edges of rickety tables, loading films into their cameras, finding empty pages in their notebooks, waving tape recorders and microphones in the direction of the door as soon as they spotted a likely victim.

"Chief Superintendent, can you—?"

"Mr. Delphick, what's the latest—?"

"Is it your oracular opinion that—?"

Delphick surveyed the scene with an austere smile, and murmured, just loud enough for Bob to hear, that he'd feared as much. Without Inspector Terling, the media maniacs were understandably on the warpath at having been kept waiting. Indeed, he hardly expected to escape with his life unless Bob managed to repel boarders by sheer force of personality. There seemed to be not a sympathetic soul among the lot of them . . .

His grey eyes searched the excited throng for the one or two sympathetic souls he hoped to see. Mel Forby, slipping gracefully through the tumult as her colleagues surged past her to the foot of the low platform, caught that searching look as she turned, and smiled a quick greeting, though she couldn't help frowning when, miming discreet surprise, Delphick raised an eyebrow on observing her unescorted state. As she seated herself in almost the farthest corner of the room, she tried not to glare. The Oracle thought she was as helpless without Banner as Banner himself liked to think, did he? Cookery classes, indeed! But then she remembered, and smiled again. A different occasion might have seen her seething with justifiable wrath; but now, re-markably restrained, calmly opening the notebook she'd taken from her jacket pocket—for once, former fashion ace Forby wasn't bothered about ruining the line—Mel settled herself quietly on the end seat of the row and prepared to take down whatever revelation might be vouchsafed her in the next few minutes, while the other reporters clustered in a babbling riot of questions as close to that tall figure as they could crowd.

"Ladies and gentlemen—please!" Perhaps it wasn't the noisiest press conference Delphick had ever attended, but it wasn't one of the quietest, either. "Please!" He raised a hand in admonition, and drew himself up to his full height. Beside him, in accordance with instructions, Bob loomed, lurked, and scowled as menacingly as he could.

"Thank you." The riot had faded to a mere hubbub, and was still weakening. Delphick lowered his hand, and raised his voice instead. "I know you're all anxious to put your questions, but no useful purpose can possibly be served by everyone shouting at once. Maybe you'll allow me first to give you details of today's . . . occurrence, and then we'll take in turn such questions as I've left unanswered . . . "

Muttering, the reporters retreated to the wooden chairs, watched with some interest by Mel, demure in her dark jacket, almost invisible at the back. The Oracle, grateful for her unwonted restraint, found his eye drawn briefly towards her before, bracing himself, he sent up a silent curse for the perfidy of Inspector Terling, consulted the typewritten sheet, and launched into his explanation.

"The latest in the recent series of Ram Raids," he read, enunciating every syllable with great care, "took place at around five-twenty this morning. A stolen car was reversed into the window of the Opal Art and Antiques Emporium in Curzon Street, and a quantity of goods, including a matching pair of Chinese vases worth seventy thousand pounds, was illegally removed from the premises by per-son, or persons, unknown, in the same vehicle."

He coughed. "Miss Opal Winter, proprietor of the Em-porium, who was staying overnight in the flat above the premises, during the course of the robbery interrupted the raiders, and received from them injuries which resulted in her admittance to hospital. She is, however, fortunately in no great danger.''

Delphick, drawing a deep breath, thrust the folded paper into the pocket of his tweed jacket and prepared for the onslaught. The jargon of the prepared statement had covered the basics, but naturally the journalists needed more than the basics to embellish their stories and turn them into scoops. They knew he knew more than that; he knew they knew he knew. And now that the proprieties had been observed, media speculation was about to run utterly riot in pursuit of headlines . . .

''Is it true the stolen car was a Rolls-Royce?''

''Was it really the property of the Stentorian chargé d'affaires?''

''How did the Raiders manage to overcome emba: ;y security? Did they attack the official driver?''

''Was he bribed?''

''Was he drugged?''

''Is there any suggestion that the Stentorian Embassy is a clearing-house for the drugs traffic?''

''Chief Superintendent, if the gallery owner wasn't seriously hurt, is the reason you're on the case instead of the Art Squad inspector because it's turning into a major diplomatic incident?''

''Will the Stentorian Ambassador be summoned to the Foreign Office?''

''Will the FO ask His Excellency to expel any of his staff from this country?''

''Do we have an extradition treaty with Stentoria?''

''Is there any drugs connection?''

''Do you suspect that the Ram Raid profits are being used to support foreign terrorist activity?''

''Have you any knowledge of terrorist cells currently in operation in this country?''

''Do you suspect a communist plot?''

''Did they use a Rolls-Royce to strike a symbolic blow against the capitalist system?''

Bob, still dutifully looming as Delphick attempted to deal with the barrage of questions, found his head whirling as

he listened to the wild theories being piled one upon another with enthusiasm almost as great as that with which
the shoppers of Plummergen, according to Anne and her
mother, were wont to theorise about whatever Miss Seeton
might be doing now . . .

Miss Seeton! Could her influence be to blame for the
apparent lunacy which had gripped Fleet Street? Bob didn't
need to ponder the matter for more than a moment: he knew
very well that it could—and was. One wave of her umbrella, a couple of quick sketches, and England, according
to Fleet Street, was under starter's orders for all-out war
with the People's Republic of Stentoria . . .

And he wouldn't be in the Oracle's shoes for a thousand
pounds a week.

CHAPTER 15

Delphick had talked himself nearly hoarse trying to give sensible answers to questions which weren't the least bit sensible, as well as to a few which did contain the odd glimmer of journalistic merit. He promised himself a long, bitter session with his Art Squad colleague once this was over, and wondered if by any chance there was a packet of throat lozenges buried anywhere in his desk: his frequent sips of water from the waiting jug were barely helping him to hold his own.

Amid the frantic flurry of multiple interrogation, the silence of Amelita Forby, busy with her notebook, passed almost unnoticed by her peers, while Delphick, normally observant, didn't notice it at all. He was too engrossed in the verbal thrust and parry of the inquisition to which Inspector Terling's pusillanimity had perforce subjected him to do more than register vaguely that the thrusting could have been a good deal sharper than in fact it was . . .

His larynx began hinting that enough was enough. Good public relations with the press were one thing: masochism such as this was above and beyond the call of duty. Delphick, in a not-so-exaggerated croak, informed the ravening Fleet Street hordes that any further queries should be directed to Inspector Terling; slammed his empty glass on the table with a defiant air; and bade everyone a firm, though husky, good afternoon. Bob, recognising his cue, lumbered round to the front of the little dais and in silence loomed pointedly at the reporters until they got the point.

"Alone at last, thank the Lord," gasped Delphick, as the door of the briefing room finally closed. While Bob looked on with some interest, the chief superintendent seized the almost empty jug, tipped into his glass the dregs of the official water, and drained every drop without stopping. He coughed; he wheezed; he coughed again.

"There is much," he remarked, in a voice slightly stronger than before, "to be said for the habit of carrying a flask of brandy in one's hip pocket for emergencies. Ahem. Ahem! Failing brandy, perhaps a cup of coffee—but not," fading again, "in the canteen, I think. The smoke . . ."

"Shall I stop off on the way, sir?" enquired Bob, as the two headed back to the lift. "Or should we try asking them to send something up? Like a good gargle," he added, grinning, as Delphick *ahemmed* twice more, loudly, and thumped himself on the chest. "Some of the cough medicine the doctors in Anne's surgery prescribe's pretty potent stuff, she says." And he pressed the button with a cheerful finger.

"Or embrocation," groaned Delphick, entering into the spirit of the thing as the memory of the press conference began to fade. "Ahem! Not, however, inhalation. Friars' balsam is hardly palatable in the way a good brandy—"

"Mr. Delphick! Chief Superintendent! Excuse me, sir!" The call came at just the same time as the lift. As the doors thudded open, Delphick held back, glancing round to see which of his colleagues—a junior one, from her mode of address—had hailed him.

She came hurrying down the corridor, crisp and efficient in her uniform, a notebook in her hand. Someone with news to impart, obviously . . .

News? Her uniform? Dark jacket—neat skirt—no handbag to make her look like a visitor . . .

Delphick's mouth dropped open. Bob spluttered. "Going up, of course," she said sweetly, stepping into the lift and holding the doors open as she motioned the two men inside. "Okay, boys?"

"You know very well," protested Delphick, his breath

returning as she pressed the button, "that it isn't." The emphasis he tried for on the last word made him cough again, though the sound was lost beneath the thud of the doors and the whine of the motor. Nobody, however, could call Mel Forby unobservant. She thumped him kindly on the back, and grinned.

"Not okay? I should have thought you'd be only too glad of the chance to thank me privately for not having given you a hard time in front of those ignorant clowns—sir," she added, jumping to attention as the lift stopped unexpectedly and a tall, distinguished man stepped in.

"Ah, Delphick. Your encounter with the denizens of Grub Street is successfully concluded?"

Delphick, his eyes grimly averted from Mel's illicit presence, frantically sought a suitably oracular and ambiguous reply. "Er," he said, and groped for the knot of his tie, gasping. "Lost my voice," he mouthed, trusting to fortune to help him out. All he could trust Mel for was not to give herself away, though he wouldn't put it past her to carry her impersonation of a Woman Police Constable to such lengths she'd start saluting once she realised who it was in the lift beside her.

Bob couldn't help it: he held his breath, he gritted his teeth, he bit his tongue—but nothing was any use. He gave up the uneven struggle. The lift trembled on its steel hawsers as he turned in desperation to face the corner, and collapsed, gurgling horribly, with his head against the wall.

Sir Hubert Everleigh, Assistant Commissioner (Crime), raised an eyebrow as he surveyed those broad, shaking shoulders. "Your sergeant would appear to be somewhat overcome. Surely you did not, Chief Superintendent, even in your state of acute aphonia, insist that he should be the one to stand up to the, ah, importunities of the press? Delegation, Delphick, is all very well in its place, but, when it is likely to have so dramatic an effect on one's subordinates, should be employed with considerable circumspection."

Delphick, coughing, managed to speak the name of Terling with sufficient force as to render the rest of the sentence unnecessary.

"Another example," said Sir Hubert, sighing, "of the

perils of delegation. When an inspector can induce a chief superintendent to take on his appointed duties—but we are at your floor. I will hold the doors while you and your junior colleague assist the good sergeant to a place of succour and safety . . .''

The lift carried on upwards, bearing Sir Heavily to the heights. Mel marched at Bob's side, two paces to Delphick's rear, looking more like a police officer than either of her speechless companions. In a near silence—Bob was still stifling gleeful guffaws, Delphick's breath rasped in his frozen throat—the little group made for the chief superintendent's office.

Delphick slammed the door and rounded on the reporter, his eyes bleak, his voice, though hoarse, stern. ''Miss Forby, you have a considerable amount of explaining to do. I ought to have you thrown out on your ear for this. Of all the—the . . . ''

''Confounded cheek?'' supplied Mel, as he wheezed to a husky halt. ''Brazen nerve? Brass neck?''

''How typical,'' came the automatic retort of the purist. ''Weak tautology rather than literacy. Not that one expects the telling phrase or verbal witticism from a rag like the *Daily Negative*, of course—but—''

He recollected himself, and glared again: but it was too late. Mel, with her sweetest smile, was sitting in his visitors' chair, picking up the telephone. She held out the receiver.

''Coffee, I think you were saying? Sounds great. Sorry I don't know the canteen number, but . . . ''

''Mel!'' Delphick noted with surprise that his voice was now almost back to normal, even if it was the combination of exasperation and shock which had effected this remarkable cure. Amelita Forby was irrepressible, as he knew only too well . . . And then the witty verbal possibilities of *irrepressible* and *press* made his lips twitch. He turned away. ''Sergeant Ranger,'' came the strangled instruction. ''Do something!'' And the chief superintendent choked.

''Sir,'' said Bob, willing enough, but himself weakened by memories of that awkward ascent in the lift. ''Er . . . ''

With only the anguished verso view of his superior for

guidance, Sergeant Ranger knew he must use his initiative. He sighed, took the telephone from Miss Forby's outstretched hand, dialled the canteen, and requested coffee and biscuits for three to be sent up as soon as possible. There seemed little else, with Mel's eyes on him, to be done.

"You boys have a good view from here," said Mel, ambling to the window and looking out on London. "All the sights—and then some," she added, turning back and gazing thoughtfully at the opposite wall. "Now, that rings a bell or two in this"—she looked at Delphick—"illiterate brain."

There was a glass case screwed to the wall: a case such as those in which anglers, with justifiable pride—assisted where necessary by plaster of Paris—display the ones that didn't get away. In Delphick's case, however, there was no record-breaking bream, pike, perch, or trout to be admired, but rather a battered, broken umbrella, a memento of the occasion on which Miss Seeton's path had first crossed that of the constabulary after the Covent Garden killing.

"Yes, I've heard about that." Mel moved across for a closer look. "Did she mention it when she was up here yesterday, or was she too polite to say anything?"

"How did—?" Delphick caught himself up. "Mel, you're rambling. *She?* Do you suggest that it is a woman's hand behind the Ram Raids?" As she was about to speak, he allowed himself to reconsider. "On the other hand, the female of the species, as we know, is more deadly than the male—but nevertheless I—"

"*But* be damned!" Mel's eyes were sparkling. "*Nevertheless,* nerts! Miss Seeton's who I'm *suggesting* as well you know. C'mon, Oracle, we go back a long way, remember? My spies tell me you had her along to doodle a few of her specials, and my guess is they weren't for any bigwig's private collection . . ."

She raised her eyes to the ceiling, and adopted an attitude of deep concentration. "Some of the wigs in the offices up there are pretty big, I'm told. Wouldn't have been one of them I met just now, by any chance? If you can call it *meeting* someone when nobody bothered with introductions, that is—but I'm not one to take offence. If people feel like making amends, I'm perfectly happy to pop along another few floors and make myself known . . . ''

Delphick threw up his hands, and sighed. ''Blackmail, my dear Mel, is unworthy of you—and besides,'' as she did her best to look ruthless, ''I don't believe you—though I'm intrigued by your operating methods. How did you contrive to effect your—your illicit intrusion at a time almost exactly coincidental with Sir Hubert's appearance?''

''Sir Hubert? Not many of those around, except—hey, not Everleigh? You mean I've just ridden in the same lift as the Assistant Commissioner? Wow! They'll never believe this, at the *Negative*. Wish I'd taken a snap or two for souvenirs. The way they tell me Sir Heavily likes to do with Miss S.'s doodles, if he gets the chance . . . ''

''Unworthy,'' said Delphick again, in a reproachful tone, and sighed. Mel stifled a giggle. Bob cleared his throat with unnecessary force, and without invitation dropped weakly down on the nearest chair. Such springs as there were shuddered. Mel, wincing at the noise, seated herself daintily on the other chair, and regarded Delphick in an expectant silence.

It was broken by a tap on the door, and by Delphick's command for the tapper to come in. Now, with the appearance of a burly uniformed bobby bearing a tray, was his chance to have Amelita Forby summarily ejected from the hallowed premises of New Scotland Yard . . .

He missed his chance—as Mel had gambled, as Bob had guessed, that he would: as she'd said, they went back a long way. As the bright-buttoned Ganymede made his exit, Delphick shook his head in self-reproach. ''Do help yourself to sugar,'' he invited. ''None for me, thank you: nor for Sergeant Ranger, on whose waistline the, ah, sweetness of married life has already wreaked havoc enough. Speaking of which,'' above Bob's indignant splutter, ''where is your own particular sweet wreaker at the moment?''

''Abroad without me, the rat.'' Mel, handing cups, omitted sugar from all three. ''Switzerland,'' she enlarged, sipping. ''Some drugs-and-corruption case that's going to bust a few admirals in the Swiss Navy back to able-seamen, if the leads he's chasing are right, which knowing Banner they most likely are. Which means he's all set for another scoop, and I . . . wait for mine like a good little girl. Because virtue always gets its due reward, right?''

''Wrong.'' Delphick did his best to frown: a quick look at his in-tray made it easy. ''There is too much evidence— as witness these bulging files—which I do *not,* incidentally, propose allowing you to study—to the contrary, Miss Forby. Crime, at least in the short term, does seem to reap considerable rewards, and with the police overworked as we undoubtedly are . . . ''

''You're never averse to calling in a spot of outside help, right? Hence Miss S.'s visit yesterday.'' Mel ignored Delphick's loud, weary, protesting sigh. ''Came up with the goods as usual, did she? Except—no, I guess she can't have done, or you'd have been there on the Stentorian embassy doorstep warning them to keep the official garage well and truly padlocked. Though she'll have managed to work in a few references to snow or something, won't she?''

''Will she?'' Delphick raised an eyebrow. ''Why should she? According to yourself, Thrudd's visit to Switzerland is in pursuit of a major scoop, which means he's unlikely to have spread the word around that he was involved in drugs in case someone else scooped him. Which—''

''Banner be blowed! There's snow and there's snow, Oracle, and you know darn well I'm not talking about the other sort. Apart from anything else, cocaine's not what Thrudd's after, though you'll have to wait until you read the story in one of his World Wide rags for the details. I mean wet, white, and fluffy. Falls out of the sky, blocks the roads—and freezes pipes, because it's so darned cold. In winter.'' Mel sat up, and set her empty cup on the tray. ''Guess nobody but me's noticed the coincidence—the name of the gallery the Rammers raided today—the owner's name, I mean.'' Delphick stared. Bob gaped. Mel smiled.

''A chilly sort of female, I should think, though I've never met her. Any more than I or anyone else has ever met Chrysander Bullian . . . ''

Delphick blinked. He drew a deep breath. ''Mel, that's—

that would be—fantastic. The suggestion's been made before, in a—a half-hearted fashion, but . . . No, it's too much
of a coincidence.''

"Like me and Sir Heavily in the lift? Coincidences happen, Oracle, you know they do. The way I know you're
holding out on me about Miss S's sketches. Did she, or
didn't she? There isn't another newshound who's nosed it
out . . . *yet*—and that's the way I'll keep it, if you'll only
play ball. If you don't . . . well, it's not such a long trip to
Plummergen, and if any of my pals from the Street spotted
me catching the train at Charing Cross, they'd soon put two
and two together . . . ''

Delphick forced a laugh. "You won't persuade me in a
million years that you'd ever go shares in a scoop—if it is
a scoop, Mel, and I'm not sure why you're so keen to insist
that it is, apart from your natural wish to best Thrudd in
the matter of front-page headlines. But the idea of descend-
ing on an elderly woman, perhaps browbeating her, in order
to achieve those headlines, should be repugnant even to a
Daily Negative reporter . . . ''

''Then do the Sir Galahad bit,'' said Mel, trying to look
like someone capable of severe browbeating, ''and show
me the sketches, and I promise I'll try not to do an Oliver
Twist. Except—well, I'm kind of curious, I admit. I wonder
what Miss Seeton's doing right now.''

CHAPTER 16

What Miss Seeton was doing was pouring tea from a sprigged china teapot into dainty porcelain cups, while the teapot's owner sat watching with her arm in a sling.

Miss Wicks, despite her bandages and straps, was excited enough by the after-school visit of her friend Miss Seeton to treat it, as far as possible, as an Occasion, with sandwiches and scones and two sorts of preserve. Advanced in years as she was, lavish entertainment of that kind offered by her parents in earlier days was, sadly, out of the question; but a little tea-party from time to time was quite another matter, and something she could manage easily, in normal circumstances. She owed, she knew, a great deal of hospitality—people in the village were always so sociable and kind—but somehow the idea of vast numbers of persons in her little cottage . . .

Miss Wicks had no idea that people positively preferred her not to invite them to tea. It was far more embarrassing going to her house than having her come to theirs: in their own, they had other rooms to which, on one excuse or another, they could briefly escape when her oppressive sibilance was in serious danger of imposing itself upon their modes of speech. Miss Wicks had false teeth of a decidedly squirrel-like appearance, and, while these may have fitted perfectly in the past, the evidence strongly suggested that this had been several decades past. Miss Wicks, in short, whistled when she spoke; and, as a yawn is infectious, so is a severe case of hissing when one converses with somebody insistent, for some unknown reason—quite unconsciously, Plummergen was sure—to use more than her fair share of esses.

Miss Seeton, obviously, suffered in this respect more than most, but, being of that class and generation which uses Christian names only after long acquaintance, had no real remedy beyond self-control. Her seven years' residence in Plummergen must be seen as a matter of minutes only on the clock-face of familiarity, and it would take at least an hour before she could feel at her ease being addressed by the older woman as Emily—and two hours or more before she could ever hope to bring herself to call Miss Wicks . . .

Miss Seeton, passing the old lady her cup, realised that she had no idea what Miss Wicks's Christian name might be. She would hazard a guess, however, that it would be nothing so convenient as Winifred, Hilda, or Maude.

"So kind," whistled Miss Wicks, accepting her cup with a smile. "So careless of me, to slip on the steps and sprain my wrist in such a fashion."

"I imagine," said Miss Seeton, sipping tea, "that it is easily done, in an absent-minded moment—and it could have been very much worse."

"Indeed, yes. Dr. Knight has given me a severe scold for having gone outside in my new shoes. The soles were still smooth, and there were damp leaves on the top step— but as I slipped, luckily, I caught at the balustrade, which stopped my falling any farther. And I was most fortunate, so Dr. Knight says, not to have dislocated my shoulder, instead of a simple sprain . . ."

The old lady brandished her bandaged arm in a manner which, in someone less Victorian, might have denoted pride. "I had expected," said Miss Wicks, with a twinkle, "a plaster cast, so that I was agreeably surprised only to have a sling, except, of course, that one cannot ask one's friends to scribble amusing messages on a sling. When my brother broke his arm—dear me." She twinkled again. "Such a coincidence. It was at precisely the same season of the year, as I recall, for he fell out of a horse chestnut tree, which he had climbed in search of conkers.''

Miss Seeton nodded, twinkling in turn. ''Murreystone,'' she murmured. ''The children are very restless at present—the coming contest, you see.''

Miss Wicks, gazing back to her long-distant youth, gave a little chuckle. ''Dear me, such rascals we were, poor Sebastian and I—my twin brother, you know. Always up to mischief, of one sort or another . . . '' She sighed. ''It seems only yesterday we were scampering round the estate without a care in the world . . . '' She sighed again. ''He died in the Great War: he was a Sapper.''

As Miss Seeton expressed quiet sympathy, the old lady's sad eyes brightened. ''I have such happy memories, Miss Seeton. When we were youngsters . . . We went everywhere together, and shared everything. Bows and arrows—except that I was strictly forbidden to use a sharpened point . . . We used to play Robin Hood—I, of course, was Maid Marian. Sebastian and his friends would hold a contest for the Silver Arrow . . . And sometimes we played King Arthur and his Knights of the Round Table, with catapults and stones for besieging the Castle of the Black Knight . . . Dear me!''

The old lady smiled. ''I fear I must have been something of a tomboy, Miss Seeton. Disgracefully unladylike, my governess told me, more than once, for I played truant from my lessons many times. Still, I feel sure my dear mother was only ever teasing when she said her Cecelia was a sad piece, so I'm sorry to say I took little notice of poor Miss Scott. But they were such happy days—playing at Sir Lancelot, Sir Gaheris, Sir Bors de Gannis . . . ''

She sat up. ''Have I ever shown you the photograph of my childhood home? In the silver frame on the mantelpiece.''

Miss Seeton, with a smile, hopped up from her chair to follow the old lady's pointing finger. One had, of course, on many previous occasions observed the proud display of sepia and fading hand-washed colour prints on the overmantel, but naturally one had never cared to pry. Since her hostess—and how right she'd been not to think of her as

Winifred, Hilda, or Maude—since her hostess was, however, minded to reminisce, Miss Seeton must be the perfect
guest and fall in with her mood—which suited the guest
very well. Miss Seeton smiled, stood on tiptoe, and reached
between the ormolu clock and what she realised, now that
she was close to it for the first time, was a piece of genuine
Meissen. Holding her breath as she thought of the orna-
ment's likely value, with great care she lifted down the
small, rectangular picture of a gracious country house.

The artist's eye is all-noticing. Miss Seeton's glance was
caught by a nearby studio portrait of a handsome young
man in army uniform. "This would no doubt be your
brother, Miss Wicks?" she ventured to enquire, recognising
the identical cheekbones and jawline which the passage of
more than sixty years had not altered. "He is very handsome."

Then she blushed, fearing that her artist's appreciation
of Sebastian Wicks's distinctive facial structure might be
thought rather too personal; but she need not have worried.
Sebastian's sister beamed with pleasure. She had been, in
the manner of twins, extremely close to her brother: there
were no other children in the family, and few cousins of
similar age. Cecelia Wicks was delighted to have the
chance to talk about the old days with her friend Miss Seeton, to remember her dead twin and their vanished youth,
and to show some of her most treasured souvenirs. So many
had been . . . lost, over the years (Miss Seeton nodded in
sympathy, guessing that the old lady had been forced to
sell them to help make ends meet) but there remained more
than enough memories to fill a very happy hour for Miss
Wicks. Miss Seeton admired glittering glass candlestick
lustres, a cheerful pair of china dogs, a lockable double tea-
caddy lined with lead, a tiered cake-stand with four plates,
a large blue-and-white domed cheese-dish, and an unusual
tantalus of three silver barrels with a rollicking satyr astride
the topmost, brandishing in tipsy fashion a brimming
flagon.

Each of these treasures had its own story, which Miss
Wicks narrated with sibilant relish. Sebastian and she,
running illicit races round the dining room, had knocked

the cake-stand off the table and broken the smallest plate beyond repair: if Miss Seeton looked closely, she would see that it didn't quite match the rest. Polishing the silver barrels had been their favourite task on rainy Sundays; the cheese-dish had been their dear mother's wedding-present from a much-loved aunt. Dear Sebastian had kept his champion conkers in one compartment of the tea-caddy, supposing that the lead fumes would make them even stronger . . .

When Miss Seeton at last—having cleared away the tea things and had her offer of doing the washing-up refused—said goodbye, she prepared to leave the little cottage in a comfortable glow, conscious that she had done a good deed in cheering Miss Wicks's housebound solitude for a while.

"No, really, there is no need at all for you to trouble yourself coming to the door." Miss Seeton gathered up her bag and umbrella, and patted her hat straight with an automatic hand. "Do forgive the impertinence, dear Miss Wicks, but as Dr. Knight has told you to rest, then I am sure he knows exactly what is best for you—such a good doctor, and so very wise. A sprain can be awkward, as well as painful, and it is bound to affect your sense of balance—the sling, I mean. If you were to slip again—after all, it has been raining while I have been with you—and I would feel dreadfully to blame should you perhaps hurt yourself even more."

"So considerate," whistled Miss Wicks, smiling: not that she had intended to do more than go to the top of the steps, but since dear Miss Seeton had advised against it, she would stay in the sitting-room and save herself the slightest risk of stumbling. "The sense of balance," she said, "is something of which I must suppose you to have a considerable understanding, Miss Seeton, so I will follow your advice . . . "

Miss Seeton blushed again, though this time for a different reason. While she was not in the least embarrassed by having, seven years ago, taken up the practice of yoga to the great benefit of her knees, she could never help but be embarrassed when people chose to regard her—entirely without encouragement from herself—as an expert.

"Years," she murmured, blushing again. "If not a lifetime, according to *Yoga and Younger Every Day*—for one to become expert, that is. Such strict mental and dietary regimes, not to mention the, er, rigorous and rather excessive cleansing techniques, which are hardly . . . "

She recollected herself with a start, blushed once more, and bade her hostess farewell with a further warning to take the utmost care when walking up and down stairs. And were there any errands, was there any shopping Miss Wicks wanted doing? It would be no particular hardship to carry a few additional items back from the post office . . .

The rain had almost stopped by the time Miss Seeton came out of the cottage, to pause on the top step and gauge with an expert eye the likely slipperiness of the drifted, soggy leaves which had caused the downfall of Miss Wicks. With a cautious hand on the wrought-iron chill of the balustrade, Miss Seeton, her handbag and brolly over the other arm, trod warily down the steps, pausing again at the bottom to unfurl and open her umbrella. She did not notice, as she turned back to Miss Wicks at the sitting-room window, that her actions had been the cause of some curiosity just across the road, in a window of the George and Dragon; nor did she notice when, making up her mind that the rain would very soon, in all probability, stop, instead of hurrying the thirty yards to Sweetbriars she turned in quite the opposite direction and headed up the Street in the direction of the post office . . . with those curious eyes following her from the George before they drifted to Miss Wicks, alone in her cottage, waving her bandaged arm in valediction.

"Can't say I'm too keen myself, Colveden. In fact, I couldn't agree with you more. Seems to me half the village have lost their heads over this television nonsense."

Rear Admiral Bernard "Buzzard" Leighton, leaning comfortably on his front gate, was chatting with his friend Sir George—whose car, on its way back from Brettenden, had drifted to a coincidental halt right outside Ararat Cottage, landfall of the retired Sea Lord. The drifting (Sir George would insist, should anyone be so bold as to en-

quire) was clearly coincidental, common knowledge in
Plummergen though it might be that at any time (and on
any excuse) after five in the evening, the admiral spliced
the mainbrace with considerable enthusiasm, and welcomed
with open arms and unstoppered bottle any of his acquaintance who just happened to be passing—as Sir George had
innocently been doing when, glancing across the Street as
dusk began to fall, he'd caught sight of the Buzzard's ginger beard bobbing among the flower-beds at the front as
shrubs were pruned and weeds plucked out . . .

It had (the major-general silently rehearsed for Lady Colveden's eventual benefit) been no more than common courtesy to pop out of the car and across the Street to pass the
time of day with a chap who, after all, was (in a manner
of speaking, he being Royal Navy and the baronet Army)
a former comrade in arms. "One of the best, the Buzzard,"
Sir George was wont to tell his family, in tones rather more
slurred than usual, after one of the admiral's little get-
togethers.

"Bowls a mean googly," his son would agree, referring
to Admiral Leighton's renowned hat-trick with his first
three balls in the recent Murreystone match. A chap who
was good at cricket couldn't be such a bad influence, could
he?

Her ladyship, much as she liked Rear Admiral Leighton,
rather suspected he could. She inclined to the view that she
would like the admiral even better if he served black coffee
instead of pink gin when he was entertaining. She had,
however, sense enough to know that boys, and for that matter grown men, would be boys, once in a while, and that
her wisest course was to adopt a philosophical attitude, and
to stop Nigel teasing his father too much when Sir George
complained about the terrible racket made by his son's toast
when crunched in quantity at breakfast time.

"Of course," the Buzzard continued, "I know about the
Best Kept Village Competition. Well, there's nothing wrong
with that—always like to see a place looking shipshape.
Self-respect in the community, and so on. Can't be bad. But
that was more a—a local affair, as far as I can make out:
Kent, Sussex, and people who read guidebooks. Whereas all

this popping in and out of people's houses and gardens, putting them on display for the whole country to goggle at once the blasted programme's been broadcast . . . ''

"Quite right," said Sir George, as ever impressed by the good sense of his friend. "Shouldn't be able to move around the place without tripping over charabancs, coming from Lord knows where. But if that's what people want . . . Up to them, of course, if they ask the blighters in or not—and Froste does a reasonable job, I suppose. Quite interesting, some of the programmes—so Meg tells me," he added, for he was an honest man, and had dozed on and off through several editions of *Not All Roast Beef* as his wife watched with keen attention, telling him afterwards of the bits she had most enjoyed. "Educational. But if it means turning Plummergen into a—a bally peepshow . . . ''

"You never know," agreed the admiral, "what might happen, with hordes of strangers running here, there, and everywhere taking photographs, writing pieces for the newspapers and so forth. Appreciate they've a job to do, but it's a free country, Colveden. People want 'em, they can have 'em—just as if people don't like the idea, they're entitled to say so. They've already come knocking at my door asking if they can *take a few shots* of my bees—ha!" The Buzzard's eyes glittered, and Sir George stiffened: he and the admiral planned to go into melliferous partnership next spring, and the major-general already felt a proprietorial interest in the golden throng.

"Soon set them straight about that," the Buzzard briskly reassured him. "Thanks, but no thanks, I said—and they certainly got the message in the end, though it took rather too long, for my liking. Didn't see why I should encourage the blighters, because it won't stop there, you can be sure of that—and there's such a thing as being too popular for your own good. Crowds, litter, vandalism . . . Plummergen's not that large, and I can't help thinking of the old saying about quarts into pint pots—which reminds me," glancing over his shoulder at the crimson west, "sun's well over the yardarm now, talking of pints. No beer in the wardroom at the moment, but if you fancy a spot of something . . .''

And Sir George, as he'd known all along he would, thanked Admiral Leighton, and said that he did.

CHAPTER 17

At the very hub of Plummergen society, as has already been shown, is the post office. Mr. Stillman and his wife Elsie do more than supply the village with provender, pensions, and postal services; they do more than provide a clearing-house for gossip. Their establishment has a far greater value, even if its benefits are basically intangible: the Stillmans see themselves, with justification, as playing an essential part in maintaining the true community spirit in an age when these words are too often mocked, their sentiment scorned.

While the post office counter keeps strictly to the letter of Royal Mail regulations, the shopping area opens at eight in the morning, is the only shop to stay open during the lunch hour, and does not close until six. These extended hours mean that people can pop in before going to work—when slipping out for a breather—and after work is done. Mr. Stillman does not bother staying open past six, for the national television and wireless networks broadcast the News at six o'clock, and everyone is always anxious to find out whether anyone they know—which tends to mean Miss Seeton—has done anything worthy of remark in the past twenty-four hours since the daily papers were printed. And if it turns out that anyone has . . . then who knows what additional attention their exploits may bring to the village?

"Television," sighed Emmy Putts, slicing bacon.

"Could be the Chance of a Lifetime, with them filming and on the lookout for Discoveries . . . " The wheel spun to a halt as the thought of Discovery distracted the spinner. She sighed again. "He was in here, you know, that Jeremy Froste. Ever so handsome he is, close to, lovely thick hair and all—real distinguished. Bought two pound of apples, so he did, and he winked at me!"

"You needn't suppose, Emmeline," said Mrs. Henderson, who had suddenly realised that Emmy's raptures had resulted in rashers twice as thick as she'd wanted them, "that he meant anything by it. Them telly types, they're allus all over the girls, it's part o' the—the image."

"Brought one down from Lunnon with him, remember," cautioned young Mrs. Newport, whose mother-of-four status made her inclined to condescend to her single contemporaries. "That Bethan Broomfield. Researcher, she calls herself, but you'll not tell me there's no more to it than that."

"Your ma'd have a fit," agreed Mrs. Scillicough, for once in sympathy with her sister, "if she thought you was running after another girl's bloke, wink or no."

"Maureen says they got separate rooms." Emmy, tossing her head, was busy with grease-proof paper. "And everyone knows Nigel Colveden's bin chatting her up summat rotten, which he'd never do if he thought she was bespoke . . ."

Mrs. Flax said, "Gentry's different to the likes o' you, young Emmy, and don't you never forget it."

" 'Sides," someone pointed out, "Nigel's never that lucky for long, is he? The number o' girls he's gone out with, yet no nearer the altar than when he was a babby. Most like she were only trying to make him jealous, Jeremy Froste—same as he'll have bin trying with her and you, Em." The speaker turned to Mrs. Flax. "But if they'd only ask you, now, Mrs. Flax, things'd mebbe work out well for all concerned, wouldn't they?"

The village's faith in her love-potions was great, and Mrs. Flax was too shrewd to risk the slightest loss of face. She nodded, slowly, and spoke in a voice throbbing with portent. "There's none that can't be helped, if they've a mind to ask—and if I'm so minded to help them,'' as she saw the request bubbling up to Emmy's eager lips. ''But gentry-folk have never any faith in the old ways. I'll not offer meself to their scorn, for there's none rightly cares to be shown disrespect, and I've a sense of my worth above such demeaning. And as for you, Emmeline, there's folly in the belief that a man's only to light his eye upon you and he's promised—but my skills go beyond the brewing of such philtres and charms as would make it so, if 'twas the right thing to be done.'' She drew a deep breath and allowed her eyes to gaze into unseen worlds.

''There's an insight,'' she intoned, as everyone shuddered, recognising the mood of prophecy, ''as warns me 'twould be wilful meddling in the fated path, even for powers such as mine, to make him look favourable on you, Emmeline Putts, and take you from here. For your destiny's plain enough, to them with eyes to see, never to be linked with such a furriner, in chains it'd be unwise to sever . . .''

Her audience was suitably impressed by this performance, as Mrs. Flax had known they would be. Her histrionic skills had been refined over many years: it was almost automatic for her to conjure up an atmosphere of menace and mystery on the slightest provocation; and since All Hallows Eve wasn't that far away, it would do no harm to remind a few folk that the Wise Woman was best kept the right side of. Mrs. Flax saw no reason why she need ever dig her garden for vegetables, tend her fruit-trees, or keep chickens, geese, or turkeys, when credulous villagers were prepared to leave on her doorstep their silent requests for her goodwill, their pleas for her to remove the ill-luck she took no trouble to advise them she hadn't wished on them in the first place . . .

The dark presence of a pagan past shadowed the post office as Mrs. Flax put her chappy finger to her lips and hinted at matters beyond the understanding of all save herself. Whereupon all save herself—even Mrs. Scillicough, whose opinion of the powers of Mrs. Flax was hardly high—shuddered again . . .

And then there came the welcome tinkle of the bell above

the door, and in walked the twentieth century. The Nuts had come to the rescue.

"It's simply too bad, Eric," Mrs. Blaine was saying, as Miss Nuttel, looking disillusioned, closed the door, glancing back across The Street and shaking her head. "You have to admit—and too unfair, as well. I mean—one knows the Royal Navy is supposed to have tradition, and authority, and—and that sort of thing, but I'm sure I can't see why they had to pay *quite so much attention* to what the admiral told them, when goodness knows there are plenty of other people in this village who wouldn't mind *at all* helping with the research. And if," said Mrs. Blaine bravely, "the sort of help required meant that one had to *nerve oneself* to appear before the cameras—well, I should think that anyone with the very least *hint* of community spirit would be only too glad to volunteer."

Mrs. Blaine—whose indignation had impelled her into speech without giving her time to check her audience— could have been on shaky ground here: it was already accepted that not everyone welcomed the idea of helping Jeremy Froste with his research, or volunteering to nerve themselves to appear before the cameras. The numbing effects of Mrs. Flax's performance, however, had not yet worn off, and before anyone could start to feel aggrieved, Miss Nuttel—who'd had time to glance about her as Mrs. Blaine was speaking—hurried to extricate Bunny from committing further indiscretions.

"Said he didn't approve, Bunny—fair enough, of course, not everyone does—but it was the way he said it. Seems a sight too keen to keep them out of his garden, if you ask me. More than just bothered he'd be putting on a poor show. Suspicious. Can't help wondering why."

"You certainly can't." Mrs. Blaine elected to wonder at full volume, though there had never been any previous indication that Miss Nuttel might be hard of hearing. "Especially when *everyone* must know by now that the television people are looking for old apples—and the Dawkins never did anything in their garden from one year to the next, which means when that Manuden man cut down all the brambles it was just in time for the admiral to come along and put his beehives down among simply dozens of trees"—the exaggeration went unchallenged as her eager listeners crowded closer—"and all of them different varieties, I heard him say so myself." Norah Blaine primmed her plump mouth and looked disapproving. She saw no need to enlarge on the manner in which she had chanced to hear the admiral explaining to a visiting Sir George the theory of cross-pollination and the benefits of a choice of blossom. It was nobody's business but hers and Eric's if she chose to polish the outside upper windows by leaning out with an elastic rope around her waist in case she slipped in the evening gloom . . .

"Anxious to find one, by all accounts." Miss Nuttel was absently twirling the circular book-stand, staring at titles such as *Master Pot-Throwing in Thirty Minutes* as if nothing else were currently on her mind. "Peculier."

"*And* suspicious," said Mrs. Blaine; then she tittered. "Oh, Eric, of course, too silly of me! You didn't mean *peculiar*, you meant *Peculier*—the Plummergen Peculier! At least, you meant both, because you said it was suspicious, and I must say I agree with you—that he was so *adamant* about not letting the television people into his garden, I mean, when I'm sure everyone else is only too happy to co-operate, and if they're not, at least they've been *polite* about it—to look for the Plummergen Peculier, I mean. Which it is—too peculiar." She tittered once more, then became serious.

"Too strange, I can't help thinking, with Sir George involved as well, trying to drive these television people out of the village"—somehow, she managed to remain deaf to the chorus of gasps which greeted this announcement—"when really they have as much right to be here as anyone else, I should have thought. All that talk about disturbing the bees, when they're bound to be hibernating at this time of year, aren't they? Or as good as, so I'm sure I don't see that it would upset them in the least. You're so right, Eric, it's suspicious, to say the least of it—but with Sir George positively in collusion with the admiral, I don't see there's anything to be done. These forces types," said Mrs. Blaine, with a sniff—Humphrey, her flat-footed former husband, had not been allowed to take the King's Shilling in World War II, emerging from the time of trial with neither decoration nor commendation to his name—"always stick together, of course."

"Gin pennants," said Miss Nuttel, with a look that spoke volumes—slanderous volumes, for Sir George, while always happy to accept the ready invitation of Admiral Leighton's favourite green-and-white flag, was ever mindful of his position in the village. Seldom indeed was Plummergen's squire to be seen in public under the influence of alcohol, no matter that the Buzzard poured a pinker gin, a stiffer whisky, a more muscular Horse's Neck than any of his fellow drinkers had experienced before.

"You don't suppose"—this from Mrs. Blaine, still oblivious of the eager ears flapping around her—"it's anything to do with that business about the air raid bunker, do you? Too sinister, I always thought, that there was nothing inside after all, when the Manudens were making such a tremendous fuss about raffle-tickets to open it." Betsy and Dennis Manuden, the previous occupants of Ararat Cottage, had discovered, while tidying their garden, a disused air raid bunker. In an apparent attempt to curry favour with Plummergen, the pair had proposed a Grand Raffle for the chance to open the bunker's long-locked door: but the raffle, in reality, had been no more than a cover for the Manudens' various criminal activities in and around the neighbourhood, and the bunker had eventually proved as empty as the Manudens' original favour-currying gesture. Mrs. Blaine had been talked—against the advice of Miss Nuttel—into buying three tickets, at ten pence each. The loss of six shillings in old money continued to rankle, despite repeated assurances from Miss Treeves that it had all been for the benefit of the church roof fund.

Miss Nuttel shook a regretful head for innocent Bunny's lack of logic. "Plenty of time to shift any evidence after they were arrested, remember. Influence, old girl. Said yourself, these types always stick together."

Mrs. Blaine's horrified gasp was drowned out by a chorus of *surely not Sir George* from an audience of which only now did Eric and Bunny appear to become aware, as its members crowded ever closer. Tongues were clicked, eyes sparkled, voices throbbed with indignation and dismay as the spiteful seeds prepared to shoot—though even spite has its limits. Sir George's position—magistrate as well as squire—meant that prudence must quickly absolve him of all crimes save companionable collusion before the admiral, a virtual stranger, could come under full-scale attack.

It was Mrs. Spice who reminded everyone that the Colvedens had not come to the village until after the war. "And nothing to do with the Dawkins," she went on, in tones which hinted at some slight regret for scandal lost, "on account of Queer Albie so set against joining up. He'll be obliging a friend, no more—Sir George, I mean."

"But there's never no smoke without fire," said Mrs. Henderson at once.

"And the rest of us knowing we've nothing to hide . . . "

The ground shook again a little here. Until now, the reasons for those refusing to cooperate with Jeremy Froste had been considered, by those who had no intention of refusing, strange, to say the least. It was suspected that—as Miss Nuttel had said earlier—the refusers simply feared to allow outsiders to enter their property in case they found that all was not as well as public boasts suggested: neither Mrs. Skinner nor Mrs. Henderson, for instance—in agreement for the first time in years—was prepared to invite Bethan and her notebook to view her garden, in case the researcher should accept one, and reject the other. This argument, in a village so given to feuding as Plummergen, was acceptable, though open to misinterpretation; a strong preference for personal privacy was not.

But the pleasures of slanderous speculation now outweighed all other considerations; the torrent of wild surmise roared on regardless.

"Them telly folk've bin in half the gardens in Plummergen, and never refused till now . . . "

"Chose the Dawkin place special, so he did, as everyone knows . . . "

Indeed the admiral had, deeming anywhere called "Ararat Cottage" the ideal landfall for a sailor home from the sea, but to congenitally-suspicious Plummergen there had to be more to this choice than the results of a sense of humour coupled with a knowledge of Holy Writ. Village minds—most of whose owners had, during the last war, worked in reserved occupations on the land—would find it hard to credit just how many of the signals exchanged between ships of the Royal Navy, even while on active service, were on public record as having a strongly scriptural slant.

"Psalm 17 verse 4," came the cryptic message from a submarine returning after a week's patrol, followed by a smug silence as the flotilla captain thumbed rapidly through his Bible, to read: *Concerning the works of men by the word of thy lips, I have kept me from the paths of the destroyers.* "Hebrews 12 verse 8, repeat final word," signalled an irritable commander to his squadron, whose ability to follow instructions had left something to be desired: *If ye be without chastisement whereof all are partakers, then are ye bastards.* Or, in a brief moment of congratulation and response as an officer's promotion was confirmed, "Psalm 140, second half verse 5." *They have set gins for me . . .*

The signalling method best understood by most of Plummergen was the admiral's gin pennant, herald of officerial jollification in the former Dawkin sitting-room every time it was hoisted up his purpose-built flagpole. While acknowledging the validity of the long, green-and-white triangular flag and its hospitable message, the Nuts were nevertheless always ready to leap to conclusions undreamed-of even by their fellow villagers, for, when Admiral Leighton had first moved into his new home, their curiosity had been aroused by the quaint structures quickly erected in his back garden among the flowers and fruit trees. A few anxious days had been spent, by Mrs. Blaine in particular, waiting for broomstick-mounted flyers—Miss Seeton's name went unspoken, but unforgotten—to answer the summons and swoop from the skies to join the Buzzard warlock in his sorcerous celebrations. The eventual arrival of four beehives from distant heather moors to stand atop the brick-and-timber rectangles had been an anticlimax, to say the least; and the hives' next-door neighbours were still not entirely sure whether or not to afford Sir George's new friend the benefit of the doubt. This business with the Dawkin air raid bunker and the body which everyone had thought would be inside, but wasn't—and now the television people being refused access in so very forceful a manner by a man with such a bogus-looking ginger beard . . .

"No community spirit," said Miss Nuttel. "If you ask me," she added, as everyone turned to stare. "Buying the Dawkin place," she enlarged, "and then not letting anyone in. Can't help wondering," she repeated, which was enough for everyone else.

"With all them fruit trees . . ."

"Not," protested someone, "as that's to say there's no Plummergen Peculier in someone else's garden as well, and Jeremy Froste and that girl of his sure to find it before much longer . . ."

"I'm sure," said someone else, virtuous, "it's only for the good of the village we've let 'em poke about our places and take photos and measure and make notes as they've wanted. And newspapers bound to be interested as well— stands to reason there's summat *odd* about them as'll not let 'em take so much's a peep to make certain . . ."

"Simply too strange," said Mrs. Blaine.

And, as everyone paused to contemplate the strangeness of certain Plummergen inhabitants, there came a sudden tinkle at the post office door—and a collective shudder ran around the assembled company as, with a quiet smile, Miss Seeton—strangest of the strange—walked in.

CHAPTER 18

Miss Seeton's quiet smile was hardly the pregnant, gloating leer its recipients—rendered uneasy by the coincidence of her sudden appearance—supposed. It was simply a gentlewoman's acknowledgement of her acquaintance on entering commercial premises in which they, the early arrivals, must have a prior claim for attention. Miss Seeton, observing so many of the post office regulars in attendance, looked for the end of the queue, and, failing to find it in the throng of clustering gossips, smiled again, in an enquiring manner. She meant by her smile to suggest nothing more than that no deliberate discourtesy was being shown should she inadvertently intrude upon someone else's turn to be served ...

"Oh," said Mrs. Skinner, as Miss Seeton, having been waved on by Mrs. Flax, Mrs. Scillicough, Miss Nuttel, and Mrs. Blaine, paused beside her. "Oh—that's all right, Miss Seeton, you go ahead—I'm in no hurry."

"Same here," said Mrs. Henderson hastily, as Miss Seeton—nobody in Plummergen could remain unaware of the Flower Rota Feud—glanced politely in her direction before moving forwards through a crowd which parted with some alacrity to let her pass. Miss Seeton nodded, smiled her thanks, murmured of such kindness ...

And arrived at the counter over which presided Mrs. Elsie Stillman, queen of the cotton-wool, antiseptic mouthwashes, and sticking plaster she did not trust Emmy Putts to purvey in a manner sufficiently serious. Mrs. Stillman, who liked Miss Seeton, returned her smile with interest.

"And are the kiddies behaving theirselves, Miss Seeton? And what's the latest on poor Miss Maynard? A nasty fall, and slow to mend, even at her young age. You'll be buying something for her backache, perhaps."

Miss Seeton shook her head as she fumbled in her bag for her list, shifting the handle of her umbrella farther up her arm. "Dear Martha has been running Miss Maynard's few errands and filling her hot-water bottle, and Dr. Knight has prescribed strict bed-rest with aspirin every four hours, of which I know she has an ample supply. It would be most unwise for anyone without medical knowledge to suggest adding other drugs or medicines to those she is already taking. There are certain combinations, as I understand, which can prove dangerous, if not fatal, even when one is in perfect health . . ."

Miss Seeton's voice fell to an absent babble of whisky, and paracetamol, and proprietary cold cures as she managed at last to unfold the page from her notebook; blinked; and then nodded. She cleared her throat, hoping her informant's memory had not let her down.

"I should like two ounces of—of saltpetre, Mrs. Stillman, please. And two ounces of salt prunella—and a large bottle of white vinegar, if you have it, although I expect malt would do, at a pinch—oh, and bay-salt," as she remembered another ingredient previously mentioned as possible, not as essential. "If you have it," she said again, "and if you have none, I dare say common salt would do. But we really cannot do without the saltpetre and the salt prunella, or so Miss Wicks assures me."

An intake of breath behind her. Miss Seeton, entirely at her ease, was—as ever—oblivious of the stir her words had caused. Mrs. Stillman, at first, was likewise oblivious, too surprised by her customer's remarkable requirements to notice the way the rest of her customers, crossing nervous fingers behind their backs, casting pleading glances in the direction of Mrs. Flax, were edging as close to the counter as they dared, the better to hear the exact nature of Miss Seeton's purchases . . .

And when—no longer oblivious—Mrs. Stillman recovered herself sufficiently to notice this strange behaviour, she primmed her lips in disapproval, and frowned. Now it was Miss Seeton's turn to be surprised. She blushed, ventured a timid smile, failed to catch Mrs. Stillman's eye, and blushed again as, staunchly refusing to stoop to the majority level, Elsie Stillman in stern silence weighed and measured and packaged as she had been requested—while Miss Seeton, wondering what she might have said to cause offence, looked on without further utterance, and the nervous crowd nudged one another, and whispered, and watched, wide-eyed, the postmaster's wife busying herself with metal spoons, and scales, and green glass jars of powdery crystals, and brown paper bags . . .

"Would there be anything else, Miss Seeton?" Mrs. Stillman had retrieved a dusty bottle of white vinegar from a high, distant shelf, and set it now on the counter beside the paper bags. Miss Seeton, relieved she had not, after all, offended, thoughtfully smiled.

Mrs. Stillman smiled back. "Pickling spice?" No harm, Elsie told herself, in just a smidgen of curiosity, with everyone knowing Stan Bloomer's onions were sure to be among the best in Plummergen, if the flies didn't sneak over from Murreystone and do their worst—fit to win a ribbon at the Show, by all accounts, if he'd not been so keen to make a fine display in church for Harvest Festival. It'd be some new recipe Martha had found somewhere, and—Mrs. Bloomer being a noted cook—worth trying, if the secret could only be got. "Ginger? Peppercorns? A spot of turmeric, maybe?"

Miss Seeton, suppressing another smile at this kindly—if unorthodox—suggestion, considered it, with a slight, puzzled frown of her own. "Er—thank you, I think not," she said, after some moments during which the nearby eavesdroppers held their breath. They, like Elsie, had been inspired to wonder whether Miss Seeton might not, for once, have been going to behave more like normal folk than she generally did, even if 'twas more likely Martha

Bloomer they would've expected to be dealing with Stan's onions, not her employer, share to sell after the household needs were done or not.

"That is," Miss Seeton made haste to correct herself, "yes, thank you, there is. How foolish of me to forget, when I was only just now saying to Miss Wicks . . . A birch besom, please."

A thrill of pure horror ran round the post office at her words. Fear's ice-cold fingers reached out to stroke shuddering spines, to fasten about suddenly-constricted throats. On the grocery counter Emmy Putts, dropping her cheese-wire, snatched up a steel-bladed knife and began muttering through pale lips, her eyes closed in fright. Mrs. Flax essayed a disbelieving sniff for the boasts of this foreign witch, but choked and spluttered instead as envy gnawed at her vitals. Mrs. Blaine squeaked, gasped, and clasped her hands, trying to remember prayers. Miss Nuttel's face turned green, her legs to jelly, as she staggered and slumped against the book-stand, setting it in a spin . . .

Master Church Architecture flew off, falling to the floor at Miss Seeton's feet as she made her contented way out with her replacement besom under one arm, her brolly under the other, her brown paper bundles in her bag, and her bottle of white vinegar in her hand.

The flight and providential fall was seen as an omen: as protection against the powers of darkness as personified by the little art teacher. That umbrella—a witch's wand, a sorceress's staff, disguised? Knees knocking, hands shaking, Miss Nuttel stooped with a groan to pick the paperback from the floor, and gripped it in a white-knuckled grasp. Mrs. Blaine, quivering, groaned in sympathy.

"Oh, Eric, too dreadful—I shall faint, I know I shall! The simply *brazen* way she came right out with it—talking about *dangerous drugs,* and medicines—*potions,* she meant, anyone could see that—and asking for those *peculiar chemicals*—and then to buy a—a *broomstick*! It's too, too awful—we're none of us safe in our beds!"

Before Mrs. Stillman, Miss Seeton's champion, could utter one syllable of protest, Plummergen's official witch cleared her throat. All heads turned towards her; all breaths were bated until she should pronounce.

"Aah—there's Halloween, not two weeks away," said Mrs. Flax, rolling her eyes with relish: the doorstep of the Wise Woman was always laden with boxes and baskets on the night of October the thirty-first. Generations of Plummergenites took pains to run no risks. "The night of All Hallows, when spirits fly abroad," gloated Mrs. Flax, her gaze sweeping over the trembling assembly, her voice low, throbbing with mystery. "But then, who's to say what manner o' spirits they may be as take to the skies—for good, or for evil? And who's to say," the mystery deepening with her voice, "what spells they'll choose to weave, in their heathen, devilish pride, and us in ignorance below?"

She wagged her skinny finger and looked stern. "Devilish I said, and devil I meant—powers of darkness, there's no mistaking. For what's more devilish than hell-fire and brimstone?" Her audience, hypnotised and dumb with terror, meekly nodded. Mrs. Flax glowered. She'd best put on a good show now, or there'd be an end to her influence if once that foreign witch was let get away with spells and enchantments as were the rightful business in the village of none but those born to it. She took a deep breath and narrowed her eyes.

"Which brimstone," she pointed out, "is no more nor less than another name for *gunpowder*—so if that's not what Miss Seeton's bin and bought these five minutes since—"

She need go no further. She'd acted well enough—and more than well, to judge by the gratifying confusion that resulted from those final words. Mrs. Stillman, unable to make herself heard above the horrified hubbub, threw up her hands in defeat and marched out to the back of the shop, where she rattled tins, bottles, and cardboard boxes in a cacophony of—useless, she knew—indignation on Miss Seeton's innocent behalf.

Mrs. Blaine had stopped babbling prayers, and posed, frozen with fright, in the middle of the floor; Miss Nuttel fanned herself desperately with the flimsy pages of *Master Church Architecture in Thirty Minutes*. Mrs. Newport, for all Mrs. Scillicough's vaunted scorn for the abilities of Mrs. Flax, edged close to her sister and tried to coax her (blood being thicker than water, in moments of crisis) towards the Wise Woman for the benefit of her protection and advice. Mrs. Henderson found herself beside Mrs. Spice, both quivering and breathing hard, their eyes on Mrs. Flax, waiting . . .

Mrs. Flax savoured her moment. ''O'course, with skills such as mine I'm protected, but the rest of you—ah, you've a deal to fear and more, I reckon. And it's doubtful if even I'm strong enough in knowledge to weaken her powers on a night like Halloween . . . ''

A collective whimper bubbled in fearful throats. Even Mrs. Scillicough, overwhelmed by majority opinion, found it difficult to speak, producing at her second attempt only a dry croak; whereupon her sister, anxious to conform, gasped out the ghastly revelation that had that instant been visited upon her.

''And Miss Wicks, indoors with her wrist broke— but . . . but did anybody see her tumble?''

A quavering chorus confirmed that nobody had. Mrs. Newport, satisfied with the effect of her words, yet could not bring herself to utter the next, awful piece of the grim equation. She glanced at her sister. Mrs. Scillicough duly obliged, in a trembling voice:

''So nobody knows for sure how . . . how she did it . . . ''

The silence which followed her remark was pregnant with terrified realisation. Miss Seeton, on this evidence, might well not be the only witch to ride the midnight skies above the sleeping, helpless heads of Plummergen: where there was one, there could be a whole coven. But what could anyone do about it? All eyes turned to Mrs. Flax, who was frowning awfully. If it weren't enough for this foreign witch to buy broomsticks for her own use, now she'd gone and started teaching other folk to set up in competition . . .

But Mrs. Flax's frown was not recognised as the jealous manifestation it in truth was. She was thought to be weighing up the merits of various villagers, deciding who should be offered her cabbalistic protection, who should not . . .

But the Wise Woman waited too long before condescending to pronounce judgement. Mrs. Blaine panted into the breach in characteristic fashion.

"Oh," moaned Mrs. Blaine, "where will it all end? It's too, too dreadful—it's unnatural—it's blasphemous! Oh, Eric—what on earth will happen next?"

CHAPTER 19

Martha, whisking her impatient duster over the newly-closed lid of Miss Seeton's bureau, said, "Oh, and that reminds me—you did know that reporter's here, didn't you, dear? Not here *here*," as Miss Seeton, setting down the portfolio she'd just picked up, looked at first bemused, then delighted, starting along the hall towards the front door.

"I mean here, in the village," elaborated Mrs. Bloomer, "staying. So you'd best be careful going up The Street, knowing the way things will *happen* when you're around, and not wanting to put ideas in anyone's head about"—ominously—"Front Pages. Stan's seen him in the George a few times when he's dropped in for a couple of pints and his dominoes, not to mention," smiling despite herself, "getting in some practice with the conkers, knowing the way Murreystone can play dirty when they've a mind, which after the cricket Stan says it'd never surprise him if they did."

Miss Seeton sighed her regret for the frailties of human nature, shook her head, and then forgot all about the feud as she once more picked up her portfolio, checked the contents of her handbag, turned a deaf ear to Martha's warnings about front-page news—why should anyone from the papers be interested in her quiet doings?—and continued to radiate pleasure at the thought of seeing Mel again.

Martha realised her mistake. "Oh—no, dear—sorry, it's

not that Miss Forby I meant. No more it's Mr. Banner, neither, though sometimes,'' with the hint of a sniff, ''I reckon those two might as well book rooms here permanent, the number of times you get up to your tricks and down they come from Town to write you up all over the place.'' Which was unfair of Mrs. Bloomer, for there was a marked conspiracy, capably headed by Mel and Thrudd, to keep Miss Seeton's name—if not her adventures—out of the papers as far as possible; and, given the pair's growing influence in Fleet Street, ''possible'' went farther than even their sternest critics might expect.

Miss Seeton, still busy assembling her paraphernalia before setting off to school, murmured an acknowledgement of Martha's remark, but said nothing more. It seemed the safest response: for—as she had found on previous occasions—should she venture to speak in defence of dear Mel and Mr. Banner—who were after all only doing the job for which they were paid—then Martha, for some reason her employer could never quite make out, would be—it was an impression, but, she was fairly certain, a correct impression—upset. In anyone less sensible than Martha (and if she herself had not been so modest as to the strength of the affection she aroused in others) Miss Seeton might have wondered whether jealousy played some part in this curious reaction: but she knew Martha to be undoubtedly sensible, a most kind, devoted friend, the nearest to family Miss Seeton now possessed: surely Martha must know she could have no reason to be jealous? And to disapprove of the reporters on one's own behalf when, naturally, they caused little, if any, disturbance in one's quiet, uneventful life— well, it was kindly meant, of course—but there was no need . . .

''And, surely, so very *tiring*,'' murmured Miss Seeton, whose emotions were seldom raised from that same quiet, uneventful level, so that she could only ever attempt to imagine—Miss Seeton's imagination being peculiarly limited—what the experience of strong emotion might be like.

''Tired, dear?'' Martha eyed her sternly over the duster. ''You're sure those kids aren't too much for you? We all know you're a blooming marvel with them, but Miss Maynard'll worry herself to death if she thinks you've been overdoing it, not that I'd be one to tell her so, but you know how some people love to bring bad news—there now!'' above Miss Seeton's hasty assurance that she was not tired in the least. ''*News*—forget my own name, next. That reporter I was telling you about, he's the one going to write up the telly man for the papers, that Jeremy Froste. Roy Roydon, his name is—not that I'd expect you to have heard of him, dear, with only reading your *Times* once in a while, and the *Beacon*, but it doesn't ring any bells with us neither, so if he comes up to you and starts chatting, you make sure you don't talk to him, won't you? We wouldn't,'' warned Martha again, ''want people to go getting the Wrong Idea . . .''

Meekly, Miss Seeton promised that she would allow herself to fall into conversation on the way to school with none but persons already known to her. She had to hide a smile. Martha put her so much in mind of her dear mother, cautioning the young Emily not to accept sweets from strange men—not, of course, that a gentlewoman, of whatever age, would accept gifts of any kind from anyone not already among her acquaintance, but . . .

''Oh, you can smile,'' scolded Martha, ''but it don't do no harm to watch out what you're doing, and who you're talking to when you're doing it, whatever it is—and there's another thing, dear, that smell in the kitchen. Awful's not the word for it. If you've been pickling eggs, they're addled ones and no mistake, which seeing they're fresh every day I'm sure I don't know where you've got them from.''

Miss Seeton stared, then smiled again, as Martha hurried on: ''And if it's paint-stripper you've been making on the cheap, I'd've thought buying a bottle of turps would do as well, not to mention you should have told me or Stan and he'd have popped across with ours for your brushes and no bother, because if you can't ask your friends, then who can you?''

''How careless, I almost forgot.'' Miss Seeton deposited her belongings on the table and trotted out to the kitchen, with Martha, suspiciously sniffing, at her heels. ''Thank you so much for jogging my memory, Martha dear. Miss

Wicks would have been very disappointed, for I promised to go in after school to tell her what the children said, because I cannot carry the bowl at the same time, and they will have, I fear, to wait until after lunch. The young are sometimes so impatient,'' she enlarged, regarding a large bottle of murky liquid with some pride. ''So eager for life—such intense enjoyment . . . And the competitive spirit—in moderation, that is, and properly channelled— helps to strengthen their characters for the future. Team-work . . . ,'' mused Miss Seeton, unscrewing the bottle-top, then wrinkling her nose and gasping, while Martha sneezed, and pointed an accusing finger.

''See what I mean? I'd've thought you'd had gassing enough with Mrs. Venning that time, touch and go for you it was, if you remember, and now mixing up lord-knows-what and smelling to high heaven . . . ''

''Vinegar,'' Miss Seeton informed her horrified friend, screwing the top firmly back on the bottle. ''White, not malt, with saltpetre, and salt prunella, and ordinary table salt—because Mrs. Stillman had no bay-salt, and Miss Wicks said it wouldn't matter too much—dissolved and left overnight . . . '' She gazed at the bottle, cloudy and of distinctly sinister appearance, and shook it gently. The screw-cap fizzed, and she set the bottle down again on the table.

''One soaks them, for as long as possible,'' she went on, recalling the detailed instructions of Miss Wicks as she hunted out a sturdy carrier bag. ''After having drilled the central holes, of course. This is mainly, as I understand, to toughen the skins, although it is unfortunate that, with the contest only a few days away, it will probably not be long enough to affect the insides, which is why they should be baked afterwards in a slow oven to harden them properly— but there is no harm, is there, in trying? Particularly,'' with a twinkle, ''as you say dear Stan warns of likely cheating on the part of Murreystone, and while one cannot in any circumstances condone cheating, the hardening of conkers by various—various acceptable means has always gone on, has it not? Or at least Miss Wicks assures me her brother and his friends always did so, and even at Mrs. Benn's school, when one would suppose girls to have little interest in such matters . . . ''

As she slid the bottle carefully into the carrier, Miss Seeton heard Martha snort with laughter. "Conkers!" cried Mrs. Bloomer, laughing again. "Well, I never thought I'd see the day anyone'd make me believe Miss Wicks wasn't born with rheumatics and a stick, but you could just have done that, dear—though it's hard to credit, I must say."

Miss Seeton, sighing, agreed that perhaps it was, but they must remember that even the oldest among them had once been young. Miss Wicks had lost her only brother in the Great War, and naturally cherished memories of their youth together . . .

"Well, so long as it's not eggs gone bad, I dare say it can't hurt," Martha said, opening the window with a flourish. "But if the kiddies ask for gas masks, talking of the war, don't say I didn't warn you."

Miss Seeton smiled as she slipped the carrier on her arm, and promised she wouldn't. Once more she collected her handbag and portfolio, then paused by the hall table to take an umbrella from the rack, and said goodbye to Mrs. Bloomer, who was still laughing as she waved her on her way. The sound of Martha's amusement stayed with Miss Seeton as she walked steadily up The Street towards the school, holding the precious bottle of conker-cure so that it would not clank against anyone's wall or gatepost, against any inconvenient telegraph pole or flagpole . . .

Flagpole. Miss Seeton paused, smiling at the thought, and glanced across the road into the garden of Ararat Cottage. Not, of course, that the bag could possibly have bumped, the bottle been broken, on the admiral's flagpole—it was set safely back from the public path, on his private property, well behind the fence. Even walking up his path to the front door one would need to swing it with some considerable effort to make it go anywhere near.

"Good gracious." Miss Seeton's glance had made her blink. Her pause became a definite halt. "It must," she concluded, "be a celebration of some sort. The admiral's birthday, perhaps, though as a single gentleman it would be perhaps a little over-familiar to enquire. The Colvedens, no doubt, would know. October the twenty-first . . . ''

October the twenty-first always saw the Buzzard out of bed well before the nearest lark, breaking his fast as the first hint of sunrise glimmered on the horizon. By half-past six he was out in his garden at the foot of the flagpole, the halyards in his hands, ready to hoist a six-flag signal with as much ceremony as he felt his neighbours—none of them early risers—could bear. There were no bugle calls, no fanfares, no salutes from rifle or (had he thought to borrow it from headmaster Martin Jessyp) starting pistol . . .

''Eric!'' Mrs. Blaine banged once on Miss Nuttel's bedroom door and galloped in without waiting for a reply. ''Eric, do wake up—after yesterday, and Miss Seeton buying all those dreadful poisons, it's too much! He's signalling again, and in full view of everyone this time!''

Miss Nuttel groped for her dressing-gown, and teetered sleepily on slippered feet to the window, which was still curtained. Mrs. Blaine, wide awake, was there before her, her nose already poking warily through the central crack, her eyes fixed on the hostile world outside. Miss Nuttel grunted as Bunny showed no sign of moving and she, perforce, must peer round the edge, which was far more inconvenient. Her own window, as well!

''You see?'' crowed Mrs. Blaine, as a sharp intake of horrified breath from the curtain's edge confirmed that the dreadful sight was no trick of the imagination. ''You see? I heard him open his door, you know what a light sleeper I am at the best of times, and after the upset yesterday I'm sure nobody could say this was—and I couldn't help wondering if something was wrong, for him to be up and about so early—and you have to admit I was right! All those flags—what on earth can it mean?''

''Trafalgar Day, of course,'' said Admiral Leighton, astounded that anyone—especially anyone calling himself a reporter—should need to ask.

Roy Roydon (his real name was Rodney, but this, he suspected, would not look well as a byline) stood on the

Buzzard's doorstep, and stared. "Trafalgar Day? Er—oh, yes. Of course."

He did not fool the admiral, who sighed. Were the English still an island race with salt water in their veins? There were times when he had his doubts. "The Napoleonic Wars," he said. "Eighteen hundred and five—the Royal Navy against the combined fleets of France and Spain. Nelson's greatest victory—a glorious victory! Lost his life in the thick of battle, but he'll have died a happy man. Kismet, Hardy . . ."

With a muttered cough, the admiral cleared his throat, blinking in the direction of the flagpole as he tugged at his beard and tried to look stern. Rodney, failing to recognise the Buzzard's correct quoting of the "Kiss me, Hardy," deathbed utterance attributed to Horatio, Lord Nelson, looked merely bewildered.

"His signal," said the admiral, recovering himself and indicating the flagpole with a proud finger. "Of course, I can't manage all thirty-two flags. No room, more's the pity—still, there's room enough for those six. The first two words: *England expects*. Old Horatio meant to say *confides*, but Pasco—his signals officer—told him it'd be quicker not having to spell it out letter by letter. Popham system, of course. Had to spell *duty*, oddly enough, but . . . *England expects that every man will do his duty*." He cleared his throat again. "Didn't need to say it at all, mind you, dealing with the Senior Service—you can't say better than that."

"Oh," said Roy Roydon again; and again the admiral sighed. Sometimes he wondered what the younger generation was coming to.

"None of this going into committee and gabbing for hours telling everyone what they knew already, wasting time—he got on with the job, and a damned fine job, too. Three signals for the entire operation—*Prepare to anchor after the close of day*; *England expects*; and *Close action*. Said it all, really. Well, the navy has a reputation for efficiency." And the admiral tugged at his beard once more, an efficient gleam in his eye.

Dangerously efficient? Roy took two prudent steps backwards as he framed his next question. Something about Admiral Leighton suggested that it might not be as easy as he hoped to get the answer he required—but he had to take the risk.

"Very interesting," he said. "I'd, er, like to write this up, if I may, and take some photos—for the feature, you know, the one I'm doing on Jeremy Froste—"

"Ha!" And the admiral turned upon the hapless Rodney a look similar to that with which he would have regarded a weevil in the ship's biscuit.

"Oh, yes," babbled Roy Roydon, feature-writer to the stars. "This is just the sort of thing he's interested in. Picturesque—historical—the navy—rum—"

"Nelson's blood," said the admiral automatically, referring to the tradition that his lordship's body had been preserved in a keg of rum in order to bring it safely back to England for burial with all due ceremony.

Then he recollected himself. "Jeremy Froste? The television blighter? Now look here, Nazeing, or whatever your name is—"

"Roydon," bleated Rodney, but the admiral was too irritated to hear him.

"—I've already had that chap and his young woman round here asking to film my bees, upsetting them when they're settling in for winter. I hoped I'd made myself abundantly clear about wanting nothing to do with such nonsense. Plenty of others who don't mind a bit, I told him. Go and bother them instead! Tried to argue with me then, and I had to fire a warning shot hard across his bows—but I thought he got the message in the end." He tugged at his beard, and Rodney took another backward step. "Now," said the admiral grimly, "it seems he didn't—or didn't choose to. Deaf or daft, though, makes no difference—the answer's still the same. And it doesn't impress me, tell him, sending somebody else to do his dirty work. I like a good, clean fight face to face, none of this skulking in corners, hiding behind a woman's skirts—"

"Here, I say!" cried Rodney. The Buzzard had the grace to look slightly abashed.

"Well, no offence—but the man seems incapable of standing up for himself. We didn't take Wrens to sea in the

War—and most men wouldn't run around the countryside with a posse of researchers to bat their eyelashes and try to talk people into doing things they don't want to do. Or,'' giving Rodney the weevil-glower again, ''sending so-called journalists, who've never heard of Nelson and talk bilge about signal flags being—being *picturesque*, like some blasted postcard . . . ''

As the Buzzard drew furious breath, Roy Roydon, accepting that Ararat Cottage was one house he was destined never to enter, wisely—though metaphorically—hoisted the white flag of surrender. ''Sorry to have troubled you,'' he gasped; and, turning tail, he fled.

CHAPTER 20

The Nuts had been taking sentry-duty on the admiral's sinister signal turn and turn about, without pause, since a quarter to seven. Breakfast from a knee-balanced tray, with the attendant indigestion—Mrs. Blaine, blackcurrant eyes bright with martyrdom, was heroically silent on the charcoal quality of Miss Nuttel's toast—seemed a small price to pay for peace of mind.

As the morning slowly advanced, however, the top landing of the Lilikot stairs, once trays were returned to the kitchen and dishes put to soak in the sink, became rather less peaceful than the sentries would have liked. Despite all their hopes—that is, their fears—nothing seemed to be happening outside to justify the inconvenience of keeping watch. Assorted passers-by, children going to school, early shoppers at the post office were all observed to observe the six fluttering flags—and *only* to observe them. Nobody (brooded the Nuts) *did* anything. Smiles, expressions of surprise and amusement, nudges and nods to fellow observers hinted at no more than general tolerance of this latest eccentricity on the part of the owner of Ararat Cottage. Children saluted, and giggled. There was no sign of panic, no look of guilt, no suggestion that the fluttered message had been understood and that Action Would Soon Be Taken . . .

Frustration at what both sentries secretly began to suspect

might be their wasted effort turned gradually to indignation—which made Miss Nuttel gruff, Mrs. Blaine inclined
to sulk. Cricks developed in necks, duly massaged with
sighs indicative of silent suffering, nobly borne. Weary eyes
were rubbed, cramped knees stretched, in continued silence,
for neither Nut must be the first to crack. They were determined to out-do each other in strength of purpose and
of will. Let will but once weaken, and who knew what dark
and dreadful deed might not be perpetrated, unobserved, by
Admiral Leighton? It was becoming only too evident that
he had succeeded in fooling the rest of the village, but his
next-door neighbours were not so easily fooled . . .

Still nothing happened. The effects of two hours' lino-
leum on sentinel kneecaps became, by degrees, more pressing. Mrs. Blaine, for all her plumpness less stoic than Miss
Nuttel, started to feel that face might justifiably be saved if
she voiced her long-suppressed complaint about the after-
taste of soot-flavoured marmalade, with the subsequent ne-
cessity for fresh air . . . and, even as she opened her mouth,
a sudden elbow was poked into her ribs.

"Bunny, look—down The Street! Coming this way."

Bunny looked. Her mouth dropped open. She squeaked,
thrilling, all thought of abandoning her post forgotten. She
trembled. "Oh, Eric! That bag—it looks so heavy, and the
way she's carrying it I'm sure there's something breakable
inside . . ."

Miss Nuttel bent sharply forward, her nose bumping the
window. "Ugh! Glass, probably," she said, rubbing hard.
"Bottle. Mixed the stuff last night, of course."

"The potion," corrected Mrs. Blaine. "And now she's
seen That Man's instructions, telling her when to administer
it—oh, Eric, I shall faint, I know I shall!"

Unconscious of the havoc being wrought across the road,
in the house beside that of the admiral, Miss Seeton, smiling, paused to contemplate the brightly-fluttering signal
flags and to wonder at their meaning. Then, with a gentle
shake of the head to reproach herself for curiosity—as no
gentlewoman cares to reveal her age, so courtesy would
suggest that a gentleman must feel the same way—she
passed on her way up The Street, watched until she was

out of sight by four desperate eyes.

Desperation turned once more to frustration as the Nuts failed to agree on the Buzzard's exact purpose in issuing his coded instructions to Miss Seeton. Mrs. Blaine, insistent on speaking first, inclined to the idea of sorcery, the casting of diabolical spells in preparation for Halloween. Miss Nuttel, whose grasp of the calendar—she being a keen gardener—was rather more accurate than her friend's, held that, even egged on by the admiral, Miss Seeton was unlikely to start casting her spells quite so soon before the fatal night. Ten days would surely give her victims—alerted to their danger by so public a purchase of the ingredients as yesterday's had been—time and to spare to arrange a counter-charm. No, her intention was clearly to poison Plummergen's complement of Junior Mixed Infants—

"Oh, Eric—of course!" Only pins and needles prevented Mrs. Blaine from bounding to her feet and rushing to the immediate rescue now the truth was realised. "Ugh—oh, too painful . . . " Fire-crackers exploded in her knees as she straightened. "I'm sure you must be right, and—ouch . . . " She stamped—yelped—stamped again. Agonising tingles zigzagged up her shins. Moaning, Mrs. Blaine slumped to the floor, the top of her head on the bottom of the window sill; Miss Nuttel, more prudent, eased herself upright, and leaned against the wall.

"Soon as we can get to the phone," she vowed, ignoring whimpers of pain from near her kneecaps. "PC Potter?"

The whimpers ceased. "Not Potter, Eric, you know he's in league with You Know Who." Mrs. Blaine again attempted to rise, grimaced, and gave up the attempt. "And Mr. Jessyp's no better, forever inviting her to take Miss Maynard's class—and she never says she won't, does she? I think it's too suspicious, the way she or her mother or some aunt or other always seems to fall ill just when it's most convenient for Miss Seeton to—to have an alibi," gabbled Mrs. Blaine in conclusion, trampling illogicality underfoot in the rush. "The evil eye . . . I mean, when *your* back aches, you don't ask me to dig the garden, do you?"

This time it was Miss Nuttel's turn to grimace. There

was a long, thoughtful, pain-filled pause. Warily, slowly, Miss Nuttel moved away from the wall and prepared to make for the stairs . . .

"Bunny!" Bending, she clutched Mrs. Blaine's shoulder. "Never mind—quick—look!"

For a second time, Mrs. Blaine forgot her woes in the excitement of the moment. Together, holding their breath, the Nuts watched Rodney "Roy" Roydon hold colloquy with the admiral—with what they assumed, the angle of an overlapping eave blocking the complete view, to be the admiral—on the doorstep of the house next door. They saw the reporter take a backward step—take two—remonstrate, or at least attempt to do so, with whoever-it-was who had refused him admittance—heard a naval bellow, a squeak of fright, a slammed door. Saw Rodney rush down the path and make his escape, not even stopping to close the gate behind him . . .

"Well!" said Mrs. Blaine.

"Exactly," said Miss Nuttel.

There was a further thoughtful pause. The dilemma was obvious: to maintain the watch, or to summon immediate succour for Plummergen's poisoned youth?

"She won't be able to do anything," said Mrs. Blaine at last, "until break, when they have their milk. Nobody can make people drink something they're not expecting, can they? And unless she's caught in the act, you know nobody's going to believe us . . ."

"Never have before," agreed Miss Nuttel glumly.

Mrs. Blaine creaked to her feet. "I still say some fresh air would do me good, Eric—and there's no need to look like that, you can't say your toast wasn't *far* more indigestible than mine ever is—but if," speaking louder above Miss Nuttel's splutters of annoyance, "I went out and helped you with the garden . . ."

After a moment, Miss Nuttel nodded. "Good thinking, old girl. Er—sorry."

And in perfect amity the pair struggled together down the stairs, and headed for their coats and outdoor shoes.

The mid-morning squeals of obviously healthy children, borne on an autumn breeze from the playground a quarter of a mile away, considerably dampened the enthusiasm of the Nuts for telephoning the authorities, even if between them they could decide which authorities should be telephoned—which (perfect amity being a sensitive plant, short-lived) they couldn't. By tacit agreement, the matter was dropped, or at least put in abeyance, while Miss Nuttel pruned, mulched, dug, and deadheaded, bossing Mrs. Blaine—whose horticultural abilities were as unorthodox as the culinary skills of Miss Nuttel—unmercifully until Bunny threw down her dibber in a sulk and flounced indoors to prepare dandelion-root coffee, double strength, for one.

Jeremy Froste and Bethan Broomfield, late risers, drove up The Street from the George and Dragon, pausing to gaze at the admiral's flagpole before continuing northwards out of the village. They were followed by Rodney Roydon in his own vehicle. It seemed that the search for photogenic locations in general, and the Plummergen Peculier in particular, had widened; it also—to Miss Nuttel's regret—seemed that reporter Roy could have suffered no lasting harm at Admiral Leighton's hands . . .

The admiral remained indoors until almost lunchtime: as, peeping through her kitchen window every five minutes, did Mrs. Blaine. The kitchen window was open: the tempting fragrances of vegetarian cuisine began to waft gardenwards. Could Bunny, still sulking, be doing this to annoy? Just as hunger was gnawing with sufficient force at the vitals of Miss Nuttel for her to consider capitulation, there came the click of an opening door . . .

Another click came hard upon the first. As the admiral strode jauntily down his front path, Mrs. Blaine waddled urgently down hers. Her eyes met those of Miss Nuttel, fearful above a straightened spine, the secateurs in her hand, prepared to go down fighting.

"Miss Nuttel!" The admiral nodded to his neighbour, and waved. "Mrs. Blaine!"

"Shopping." Miss Nuttel, who'd now had time to note the canvas bag in the Buzzard's other hand, jerked an expressive thumb.

"I'll get the list," hissed Mrs. Blaine, and rushed back to the kitchen.

They arrived in the post office less than a minute after the admiral, who was being gallant in a bluff naval manner to Emmy Putts at the bacon slicer.

" . . . two pounds of best Cheddar, my dear, and a dozen eggs—brown, if you have them. Mustn't forget the old pork pie either, of course."

The squabble forgotten, Miss Nuttel nudged Mrs. Blaine. Mrs. Blaine nodded. *Pork pie* was all the hint they needed—unless, of course, it was a cunning double-bluff.

"Large Melton Mowbray." Emmy plonked the crusty, jelly-rich pie down on the counter beside bacon, cheese, and eggs. "Your birthday, is it, Admiral? I mean—all them flags, and everything."

The admiral had been baffled once already by the ignorance of the younger generation: he would not risk further disappointment. "A special celebration, true, but hardly my birthday. My, er, private tribute to—to a splendid historical episode, Miss Putts, that's all." Miss Putts preened at the courtesy; the Nuts glared. "I'll come back later for the grog, if you'll be kind enough to pack my order in the meantime—give me a good excuse to see you again, eh?" Emmy preened still more. The Nuts glowered. "Settle up now, shall I?"

The Buzzard was gone, leaving Emmy to simper for a moment or two before turning, with reluctance, to Mrs. Blaine and her tinned tomatoes. Somehow it just wasn't the same.

The Nuts, determined to miss out on nothing, stationed themselves in clear view of Ararat Cottage, intent on lingering in the post office, on spreading the purchase of fewer than six items until such time as some of the younger Plummergen mothers should appear . . . either to set their minds at rest—or to confirm their very worst suspicions.

Suspicions were confirmed as Miss Seeton came in sight, walking briskly—cheerfully?—in a southerly direction down The Street, holding an empty shopping bag, heading home with who knew what horror and destruction to her discredit behind her at the school. Should they follow, to forestall further horrors? Summon help? Head north, to render such immediate aid as they could?

A lengthy, whispered—and acrimonious—discussion now ensued. Miss Nuttel, ever squeamish, was once more voicing her veto on the final First Aid option when Mrs. Scillicough (of the notorious triplets) and Mrs. Newport (of their angelic cousins) popped providentially in for sliced bread, fizzy lemonade, and jam. For savoury, they reported that every child who normally went home for dinner had bolted said dinner and gone haring back to school with its pockets full of conkers; this (Mrs. Scillicough added) at Miss Seeton's urging, according to the kiddies.

"*And* Miss Wicks," added Mrs. Newport, "though lord knows how, seeing she's not bin out of her house all week."

Mrs. Blaine essayed a shiver, but curiosity was greater than her conviction that spells might be wrought with the fruit of the horse chestnut tree. "They're . . . all right?" she enquired, following the sisters to the grocery counter to catch the slightest hint of a hidden truth behind what they were willing to say aloud. "Nobody's—nobody's, well . . . ill?"

"Bright as bloomin' buttons, the whole boilin' lot." Mrs. Scillicough's tone implied that there were occasions on which she might prefer her offspring to shine with a little less brightness.

Mrs. Blaine tried not to display disappointment; Miss Nuttel, anxious to resume a closer watch on Ararat Cottage, announced that it was time to be getting back.

"You be careful at the window, Miss Nuttel," said Mrs. Newport. "Don't want glass all over you if the Ram Raiders has a go, do you?"

Mrs. Blaine jumped. "You mean there's been another Ram Raid? Eric, for goodness' sake come away—only think of what could happen!"

Miss Nuttel envisaged the aftermath of splinters, and turned green. Mrs. Scillicough said:

"Yes, on the News at dinner-time, but miles from here—though nearer than previous, I suppose. But," with a scornful look for her sister, "everyone knows they Ram antique shops, never groceries or stamps. Don't you go paying no heed to *her*.''

With which sterling example of sibling rivalry ringing in their ears, the Nuts hurried from the post office and returned to the relative safety of their house, next door to Ararat Cottage—on which they prepared to maintain a patient watch for the rest of the afternoon.

Patience was rewarded in several ways. At the end of her lunch hour, Miss Seeton was seen walking north again, with what looked like one of Mrs. Bloomer's mixing bowls in her carrier bag. Mrs. Blaine spoke hopefully of mass poisoning and hallucinogenic potions; Miss Nuttel agreed, but reminded her there was little to be done while Mr. Jessyp and the education authorities chose to Ignore the Evidence and insisted on Trusting Certain People. The admiral popped across to the post office, returning with bottles of what he cheerfully referred to as grog; the Nuts guessed he and Miss Seeton together would soon put this to some sinister purpose. The sound of the end-of-school bell ringing its merry message on the breeze at four o'clock was almost disheartening; even more disheartening was the sight of schoolchildren, in the best of health, scampering past Lilikot's gate, hurling challenges for conker matches *as soon as Miss says they're pickled proper*. Miss Seeton walked home again, without her bowl—evidently leaving the dread potions to work their ominous magic in an empty building . . .

And Admiral Leighton emerged at five o'clock, hauling down his six-flag signal to fumble with the halyards and, with a flourish, to replace it with the green-and-white Gin Pennant, proud in the light from his sitting-room window.

CHAPTER 21

The trouble—such as it was—might be said to have begun, indirectly, with Colonel Windup.

Colonel Windup lived in a small house next to the George and Dragon, and had done so for many years, though village wags (of which Plummergen had more than its share) contended that Colonel Windup lived in the George and Dragon, next to a small house. Few could realistically dispute this interpretation of the facts: the colonel did, indeed, spend most of his waking hours in the bar of the George, speaking to nobody except to ask for the same again, please—*the same* being neat whisky, in double measure—just as nobody (apart from the professional *Your change, Colonel* from barmaid Doris, her assistant Maureen, or landlord Charley Mountfitchet) spoke to Colonel Windup—which suited the colonel very well. His sole means of communication appeared to be the cryptic letters he would unleash upon an unsuspecting public at the slightest provocation, demanding of those in even feeble authority that Something Must Be Done, while never specifying at any time what that something should be. Those same village wags maintained that, if Colonel Windup ceased his perpetual letter-writing, Mr. Stillman's revenue from stamps and stationery would be reduced by half, and postman Bert's regular round could be prosecuted by bicycle instead of in his official van.

Plummergen, in its own way, was rather proud of Colonel Windup. A few purists might have called his behaviour antisocial. While valid, this was very much a minority view, for there was undoubted merit in the colonel's ability to mind his own business—an ability, in Plummergen, so rare as to be almost unique. The fact that the business in question was the voluntary slow pickling of the colonel's liver by regular applications of neat scotch was neither here nor there. It was (Plummergen held) his own business, deliberately chosen, inflicted upon nobody else; and, in return, nobody else inflicted themselves or their business on the colonel . . .

Until Jeremy Froste and Bethan Broomfield made the mistake of trying to do so.

The television people had been unsurprised by reactions, both favourable and unfavourable, to their arrival in Plummergen. They were used to both after the past few months, during which they had travelled the country preparing for the second series of that unlikely smash hit *Not All Roast Beef*. Jeremy Froste recognised the predatory gaze of bored housewives contemplating the surrender of their virtue for the chance to appear, demonstrating long-secret ancestral recipes, on the nation's domestic screens—to the fluttered eyelashes of giggling schoolgirls with similar surrender on their hopeful, undomesticated minds. Bethan Broomfield knew well the nods and smiles, the coaxing cups of tea from pensioners prepared to share with the public their version of great-grandmother's meeting with Mrs. Beeton, great-grandfather's inadvertent sale of the patent for keeping the fizz in ginger beer . . .

"Oh, I'm enjoying myself tremendously: I'm sure I'm going to like it here. Everyone seems so *very* friendly," said Miss Broomfield, in reply to Nigel Colveden's inane conversational gambit on the occasion of their first meeting. "And they seem awfully helpful, too. I've made dozens of notes, and we've heard all sorts of things—"

"I believe you," muttered Nigel, not so smitten with the newcomer that he could ignore the irony of the situation. Given the mystical sway held by the media over a large proportion of the Plummergen populace, he was amazed the poor girl hadn't been deafened with information . . . whereas if she and the man Froste had simply turned up as private individuals to ask the same questions, it would have been the crash of silence—even from that large proportion—which deafened them, and they would have gone away next day, defeated by deliberate village dumbness: at which Plummergen, when necessary, excelled.

"—and we've only been in the place five minutes." She fixed him with a dazzling smile of what could well have been genuine pleasure. Bethan Broomfield might not, it seemed, have worked so long in television that she'd become disillusioned with its effect on those outside the charmed circle. "Well, a bit longer than that, of course, but not so *very* long"—Nigel thought her giggle quite enchanting—"and yet everyone's been so, well, helpful, talking to us, not a bit the way you sometimes hear villages are—you know, so busy arguing with each other they don't want to bother talking to strangers. I think it's wonderful—such a surprise . . ."

Nigel choked discreetly as Bethan babbled on about the surprising co-operation she'd already received, how tremendously friendly everyone was, how she was sure it was all due to the reputation of Jeremy Froste as a producer of marvellous programmes that people were so very willing to tell her things . . . though actually she had to admit (in a coy whisper) that some of what they'd been told they hadn't really needed—though all very interesting (she added hastily, blushing), she supposed. Just, well, not really what they'd been looking for.

Nigel choked again, then hastily smothered his mirth by asking what she and Jeremy Froste *had* been looking for. Of her subsequent eager recital of the rare apple varieties for which the pair were searching, he had, next morning, retained enough to be able to impress his parents; that evening, his obvious interest had apparently been more than enough to impress Miss Broomfield.

"Lots of notes," she repeated, to his further prompting. "And Jeremy—Mr. Froste—has taken dozens of photographs. We have large-scale maps of the area, and we'll—he'll—be able to work out the best angles for the shots—the sun, and that sort of thing—when he's decided where exactly he's going to film, if we can find enough photogenic places, though I'm sure we shall, because he's so very talented. And this is such a marvellous place, of course. We saw the plaque about the Best Kept Village Competition in the bus shelter. You must have been awfully pleased. I suppose you've lived here all your life? You're very lucky.''

Nigel agreed that he had been born in Plummergen, and (the village being east of the Medway) was a true Man of Kent. "As opposed," he explained, "to a Kentishman, that's a man of West Kent." He paused. Was he telling her things she didn't really need to know?

It appeared not. Bethan surveyed him with wide, wondering eyes. "Deadly rivals, I suppose?" she enquired. "Is there programme potential there? Perhaps Jeremy would be interested—he plans to do so much more than *Not All Roast Beef*, and everyone knows he'll go far."

Nigel did not follow her gaze to the nearby table where Jeremy Froste held court, surrounded by a throng of wife-nagged husbands who'd never known young Maureen so eager to bring their drinks across from the bar rather than insist, as she usually did, that they come to fetch them. "I could tell you about it first," he suggested, feeling pleased with his quick thinking, "then you could decide if it was worth bothering him with. I mean—an expert like you . . ." He observed her modest blush, and thought it as enchanting as her giggle; then blushed in his turn as she directed those wondering eyes full upon himself, and said that she was sure *he* was the expert, and she'd love to hear him tell her all about it.

"Oh, gosh." Nigel grimaced. "I remember something from school, but . . . well, er, when William the Conqueror turned up in 1066 our lot went out and welcomed him— waved green branches at him, the crawlers—and he said they could hang on to, er, whatever rights and privileges they'd had before. The other lot—well, they didn't crawl, so . . ."

"No privileges," said Bethan, smiling. "And you've been deadly rivals ever since?"

Nigel chuckled. "Our most deadly rivals live about five miles away, over the marsh in Murreystone—to the east," he added, "which must make them even more Men of Kent than we are, and I bet they crawled twice as hard. Probably waved flags as well as greenery, knowing them."

"Talking of flags," said Bethan, before he could enlarge on the dark doings at the time of the Best Kept Village Competition, "we couldn't help noticing the little house opposite the post office when we drove in, the one with the flagpole. Someone said an admiral lives there. And your father's a general, isn't he? Aren't there a lot of retired— I mean, in a little village like this . . ."

She was blushing again. Nigel said quickly, "A fair selection, yes. Our local nursing home's run by a former army major—our vicar was in the Home Guard—oh, and we've a colonel, too. As a matter of fact, he's here this evening— in that corner, if you can manage to look without making it too obvious. Colonel Windup," said Nigel, as Bethan slipped round in her seat and glanced casually over her shoulder in a manner that won his approval. "Never been known to speak a word to a soul," Nigel said, as she turned back again; and he proceeded to amuse Miss Broomfield with an assortment of anecdotes starring Major Matilda "The Howitzer" Howett, the Reverend Arthur Treeves, Major-General Sir George Colveden, and Admiral Leighton, expounding at some length on the latter's propensity for flying the gin pennant on every conceivable occasion, and on some of the consequences (these carefully censored) arising for those who should avail themselves of his hospitality.

"But," objected Bethan, who had chuckled and smiled in a most gratifying manner at each and every punch-line, "you haven't told me anything at all about Colonel Windup. Doesn't he keep bees or organise burglar-catching teams or play cricket or—or anything? I should have thought he would at least have helped your father run the Village Watch."

Nigel, grinning, shook his head. His imagination boggled at the very idea of Colonel Windup acting as anyone's second-in-command, and he explained that Major-General Sir

George, leader of the Night Watch Men, was most ably supported, when necessary, by Martin Jessyp. Since Colonel Windup's preference for privacy was so strong, that preference, as far as possible, was respected.

All of which made Colonel Windup an object of interest to Bethan Broomfield. Her curiosity was considerably piqued by anyone able to maintain such staunch seclusion in a place as friendly as Plummergen . . .

So that when, driving Jeremy back from the next day's excursion with the inevitable Rodney Roydon close behind, Bethan saw in her headlights the colonel striding north—in the opposite direction from the George and Dragon—up The Street, she slowed the car, pulled in to the side, and stayed there with the engine idling, on watch.

Jeremy Froste's journalistic shadow did the same, though he slumped as low as he could in the driver's seat, trying to make use of the mirrors in case, twilight or not, Admiral Leighton glanced across and spotted him. Rodney's nerves were still shaky after the morning's events, about which he had held forth to his idol at some length.

His idol now addressed Bethan without troubling to open his eyes. "Home already? I could do with a drink." He stretched, and blinked. His eyes opened wide as he saw where she had parked. "Oh. Forgotten something? If they shut at six, you'd better look sharp about it."

Through the windows of the post office, Emmy Putts and Mrs. Stillman could be observed, cashing up at the end of the day. Bethan said:

"No, I don't want anything—I'd just like to know where the colonel's going. Nigel told me he spends all his time in the pub, when they're open, and in the house writing letters when they're shut, so—"

"So if," scoffed Jeremy, "you avert your gaze from the approaching figure in front of you to the letter-box in the wall at your side, you may possibly—I repeat, possibly—infer the purpose of the colonel's oh-so-remarkable excursion; and, having drawn the inference, you may also infer that there is no reason to postpone our journey drink-wards."

Bethan turned pink. "He isn't carrying any letters—at

least, I don't think so. And he can't be buying stamps, because the post office part of the shop shuts at five . . . ''

"Nigel told you that, too, did he?" Jeremy's tone was even more scornful, since her younger eyes had noticed what his had not, and he didn't want to let her feel uppity. "Quite a fund of information, our Nigel."

"Well—yes." Miss Broomfield blushed again. "I was only thinking . . . perhaps for another programme, even if the admiral wouldn't let us film his bees, I mean, because he—Nigel—told me about the gin pennant, as well, *and* what it looks like. All those flags he flew for Trafalgar Day—and I couldn't help noticing there's a different one now, so I just thought—if he's throwing a party . . . ''

Even as she spoke, Colonel Windup stepped sideways off the pavement and, without stopping to check for traffic—fortunately, there was none—marched diagonally across The Street, still heading north. Bethan said:

"After all, we do tell people we want to film anything of interest, don't we? I don't just mean what Rodney said about Trafalgar Day—but this gin pennant, if that's what it is, which does seem likely from what Nigel said—"

Jeremy snorted, then sat up straight as the colonel's northerly march continued at a slower pace and he came to a halt outside the open gate of Ararat Cottage. "You could be right," said Jeremy Froste, watching Colonel Windup tramp up Admiral Leighton's front path and in through the lighted rectangle of his open door. "You could be right— a gin pennant party for Trafalgar Day sounds just the sort of quaint tradition a television show like ours could use, some time or other. Make a note of it, Bethan—and well done. Er—didn't Nigel tell you it's as good as saying *everyone welcome*, or *the more, the merrier*, when you see it?"

"I—well, yes, I think so—but . . . ''

"But nothing. And never mind Roy back there—he's out of this particular adventure, but that admiral doesn't scare Yours Truly. Switch off the engine and grab your notebook. You and I are going," said Jeremy Froste, "to a party!"

CHAPTER 22

Miss Nuttel and Mrs. Blaine, having found (just in case) a large torch, had probably the best view of the contretemps which eventually ensued. Bethan, for once standing up for herself, insisted on driving down to the George before returning to Ararat Cottage on foot. By the time she and Jeremy—neither of them country-folk, and missing, in the dusk, streetlamps far more than did the natives—were back, with Roy Roydon lurking warily in the rear, two more ex-officers had accepted the admiral's unspoken invitation, and the Trafalgar Day party was almost full steam ahead.

"Any other time, I'd have hoisted Colours at nine," the Buzzard was explaining as he poured drinks of triple measure into every glass within reach. "Navy regulations, y'know, once the equinox is past—but Trafalgar Day, that's quite another matter. As soon as it was light, I—ah," as foot-steps could be heard in the hall, "here comes the Padre, God bless him. Last, but not—good God!"

"Good evening," said Jeremy Froste. Beside him, Bethan giggled nervously at the expression on Admiral Leighton's face, and the angry twitch of his beard. Major Howett and Major-General Sir George stared, and exclaimed; Colonel Windup merely stared, his empty glass in his outstretched hand as he waited for his second refill.

"Evening," came the admiral's automatic response, and he nodded to Bethan—was not the Navy's traditional Sat-

urday-night toast *Sweethearts and wives*?—before coming
to his senses. In his turn he stared, then blinked, and set
down the bottle of whisky with a thump which quite dismayed the gallant colonel, who emitted a startled groan.

"Evening," said the Buzzard again, gruffly. "Don't believe I heard you ring the bell—or knock, come to that.
You'll excuse me if I ask what the devil you're doing in
my house—though I hardly think I need to. Trespassing,
I'd say. Wouldn't you, Colveden?"

He turned to Justice of the Peace Sir George, who rubbed
his chin as he also blinked at the intruders. The law of
trespass was one of the trickier statutes on the book, trespass itself being a tort (for which a civil action on the part
of the person having suffered the trespass was necessary)
rather than a crime directly punishable by the state. Unless
identifiable damage should be done, or a theft or other
crime committed, during the trespass, *Trespassers will be
Prosecuted,* as land owners knew to their occasional cost,
was no more than legal bluff.

"Trespass—yes. Er—ask 'em to leave, if you don't want
'em here," came the magistrate's advice at last.

"Want them here? No, I don't. I never have!" The admiral squared his shoulders, then shot a quick look at Bethan. "No offence, my dear—but I thought I'd already
made it pretty plain I'm having nothing to do with your
television nonsense. Barging into a chap's house without
an invitation—no, no, it won't do, I'm afraid. This is a
private party, and—"

"No invitation?" broke in Jeremy Froste, seizing Bethan
by the upper arm as she seemed about to blush her apologies and make her way back down the hall. "But what
about the gin pennant? Open house, we understood it to
mean, and—"

"For officers only," interjected the admiral, but Jeremy
was too busy enthusing to pay any attention.

"—and exactly the sort of thing—traditional, picturesque—we could use in our programme, which is why
we've dropped in to see what it's all about. Work up the
Nelson connection, Trafalgar and so on—it's quaint, it's
got character, we could make a real period piece out of it

with the right actors—we might even be able to fit you in as an extra, looking the way you do. Of course,'' hurriedly, above the admiral's splutter, above Sir George's muted rumble of wrath, ''you'd have to stage the whole occasion again later for the cameras—but we'd pay you for your time and trouble, no question, and the drinks would be on us. How about if we—?''

''*Quaint?*'' cried the admiral, his beard bristling. ''Period piece? What with that chap this morning, and now—*actors*? Stage the whole thing again for your blasted cameras? I've never heard such an outrageous suggestion in my life!''

''Damned cheek,'' chimed in Sir George, while the Howitzer nodded beside him, her eyes grim below her iron-grey curls, her forehead resolute as she faced the intruders. The colonel helped himself, unobserved, to whisky, and retreated to a corner to watch the coming battle in comfort.

Battle duly came. ''I'll thank you to leave,'' said the admiral, regaining himself with a visible effort. ''Leave this minute, if you'd be so good. And I don't want to see you here again, thank you—begging your pardon, my dear,'' automatically to Bethan. ''But an Englishman's home is his castle, and on Trafalgar Day, of all days . . .''

Words failed him. Unfortunately, they did not fail Jeremy Froste, whose eyes darted about the sitting-room—presumably for further evidence of the quaint, the traditional, and the picturesque—as he said, ''Aren't you being a little hasty about this, Admiral Leighton? I'm sure if you only thought things over calmly, you'd see—''

''Hasty?'' Admiral Leighton took two furious steps in the direction of the television producer: who took three swift steps sideways, moving closer to Bethan Broomfield than he'd ever been in his life. ''Young man,'' said the admiral, dangerously quiet, ''believe me, *I'm* not being hasty. Neither, more's the pity, are you. I've asked you to leave my house, and you haven't. I give you fair warning— if you and your young lady don't make haste to clear the decks, I'll have to throw you out—so are you going, or do you mean to stand there gaping like a lunatic making idiotic speeches until I clap you both in irons?''

Before Sir George could warn his friend that the threat of violence, if carried out, rendered the sufferer of the trespass more guilty, in the eyes of the law, than the trespasser, Bethan seized her hero by the sleeve, and tugged.

"I'm so sorry, Admiral Leighton," she said quickly. "*We* are sorry," she amended, as Jeremy stared at this unexpected turning of the meek researcher worm. "We didn't really mean to upset you—it's just that—well, I suppose we just didn't understand properly, so we'll go away now and not bother you again." She tugged again at Jeremy's sleeve as she began, blushing and unhappy, to retreat.

The admiral looked almost as unhappy as she: officers of the Royal Navy are rightly renowned for their gallantry towards the fair sex; but, while he might have been willing to stretch a point on Bethan's behalf, Jeremy Froste—with his floral cravat, his flared trousers (entirely different in concept and style from a naval rating's bell-bottoms), and, worst of all, his corduroy jacket—was more than several points too far for Rear Admiral Leighton.

"See you on your way," he muttered, as Bethan continued to move slowly backwards, her eyes as restless under his scrutiny as ever Jeremy's could be. Major Howett and Major-General Sir George looked on in silence. Colonel Windup wandered out of his corner to fill his own glass.

The explosion occurred just as everyone was starting to think the incident safely over. Rodney Roydon, having lurked for a while on the far side of The Street, had at last ventured across it to hover, with bated breath, at the very gate of Ararat Cottage, peering up the path towards the open door through which the television team had disappeared.

He was concentrating so hard on the likely response of the admiral to his unexpected visitors that he did not hear, until they were close behind him, the footsteps of an impending vicar. The Reverend Arthur Treeves, finding his way blocked by Rodney's rear end, cleared his throat; and Rodney—whose conscience at the best of times was tender—jumped several inches into the air.

"Dear, dear—I do most sincerely beg your pardon," said the Reverend Arthur, before the reporter's teeth had stopped chattering. "Startling a fellow guest—though we have not, I believe, been introduced—my, er, name is Treeves." He was never at his best with strangers: Molly was always the one to handle these awkwardnesses—but Molly Treeves (whose wartime service had been on the land rather than with His Majesty's Forces) was, to her brother's regret, more than a quarter of a mile away. He drew a deep breath: the situation demanded more than the normal courtesies: he must explain himself further. "I was in the Home Guard, you know, though I have also played my part as an air raid warden." Rodney blinked. The Reverend Arthur smiled a nervous smile. "But you will, I trust, not take it amiss if I say"—looking closely at Mr. Roydon for the first time—"that *your* experience must surely have been in far happier times, times of peace. Peace on earth," enthused the Reverend Arthur, forgetting his original drift. "Goodwill to all men—friends, so very important . . ."

While Rodney gaped, the vicar recollected himself. "Er—talking of friends, have you know him long? You will not mind if I accompany you up the path? Crowds, you see," putting the stranger at his ease. Molly Treeves would know that her brother was seeking protection rather than offering it, although why the thought of meeting three persons, long known to him, in the house of a fourth should make him nervous, she could never hope to understand.

"Er," said Rodney, uneasily echoing the vicar's words, unable to find any of his own. "Well, I . . ."

But the Reverend Arthur was sturdy of build as well as (occasionally) firm of purpose. It was his plain duty, having startled this fellow guest, to make amends by accompanying him to the Admiral's door. Accordingly he bowed, took the reporter by the arm, and steered him through the gate of Ararat Cottage in the direction of the front steps . . .

On the topmost of which now appeared the rear-to-sideways views of Bethan Broomfield and Jeremy Froste . . .

Followed, as the pair presented a more frontal aspect as they made their way together down the steps, by the Admiral.

"Good God!" The roar could be heard halfway down

The Street. Inhabitants of nearby houses dropped whatever they were doing and hurried out to their front gardens, peering through the gloom to find out what was going on.

"You again! Hell's bells, I thought I'd told you to—sorry, Padre." In his rage, the Buzzard had failed to notice the vicar until now. "Didn't realise this . . . this chap was with you." He gritted his teeth, and remembered that England expected every man to do his duty. "Better come on in, the pair of you, and—and join the party. Any friend of yours, Padre . . . "

He was unable to continue: he felt as demoralised as any of Her Majesty's officers has a right to feel—and puzzled, as well. Why hadn't the miserable landlubber said this morning that he'd be coming to the party later on? There might just have been some excuse for his nonsensical questions—

"A friend? Of mine?" The vicar blinked. "One's fellow man, of course, but . . . " Shaking his head, he dropped the stranger's arm and took a step backwards in order to gaze from Rodney to the Admiral, then back again. "I thought—that is, there appears to have been some . . . I understood him to say . . . I may, of course, have been mistaken, but—I thought he was a friend of *yours*, Admiral."

Miss Nuttel and Mrs. Blaine, discussing the subsequent chase later with their less conveniently situated (and torchless) cronies, agreed that it was remarkable how much faster the reporter had run down the path in the evening than he had in the morning. They would have expected him to be tired after the day's outing (about which the entire village had managed to inform itself the previous afternoon) with Jeremy Froste and Bethan Broomfield, but he'd put on an amazing turn of speed, and the television people hadn't been much slower . . .

Admiral Leighton, crying aloud for a cutlass to repel boarders, for a cannon to blast them from the face of the earth—this time, he didn't even try to beg the vicar's pardon—pursued the intrusive trio to his very gate, and only dropped his reluctant anchor there with Sir George's warning shout from the doorstep. He contented himself then with slamming the gate behind the fugitive guests, and shaking his fist as they hurried towards the post office . . .

To a chorus of further warning shouts and cries from all who recognised the dull amber headlights and wheezing roar of the aged, smoke-exhausted motor chugging its southerly way down The Street—who knew the likely condition of its brakes: which screamed in an agony of asbestos and steel and panic pressure as old Mr. Baxter stamped, just in time, on the pedal, and the taxi squealed to a halt.

The passenger window was wound down. "You certainly," said a well-known voice of the female gender, in clearly audible tones, "see life in this place, don't you? Nobody hurt? Okay, then—let's get on to the George and Dragon!" Amelita Forby was back in town.

"I'd love a cup, if you're offering," Mel told Miss Seeton, five minutes later. The young reporter had popped her head around the George's front door and caught the eye of Doris, head waitress-cum-receptionist, to let her know she'd arrived safely on the train she'd hoped to catch when she rang from Town to make the booking. Would Doris take it as read she'd check in properly in about an hour, and book a table for half-past seven? Doris was a doll, and Mel was really grateful!

"Told her I'd see her later," Miss Forby now explained, "at dinner—for two, with luck. Have you eaten yet?"

Miss Seeton, taking biscuits from a tin while she waited for the kettle to boil, said that she had not, but there was plenty to choose from in the larder. She supposed dear Mel must be hungry after her journey from London and the lengthy—she sighed, but there was really no other word for it—the lengthy wait for Mr. Baxter's car, since this was one of the days the bus didn't run. Would Mel care for some of Martha's cake as well? Or—

"Or nothing, Miss S., thanks. Nothing for me apart from the tea—nor for you, if you can hold out another hour or so, because I'd like you to join me at the George for a bite to eat and a glass or two of something."

"Me?" Miss Seeton blinked. "Why, Mel, dear, when you spoke of dinner for two, I thought that you and Mr. Banner—" She broke off, a delicate blush pinkening her cheeks. They always seemed so happy together, yet here was dear Mel, and no sign of—one would not wish to be tactless, but—

"Don't worry, honey." Mel patted her on the shoulder and chuckled. "Banner and I still loathe each other as much as we ever did—that's why he's gone scurrying off to Switzerland without me, the rat."

Miss Seeton recognised the customary note of affection, and knew all was indeed well. Smiling, relieved, she poured tea as Mel went on:

"He says he'll give your regards to the highest Alp he sees. Bring back happy memories, he said—isn't that where the two of you first met?"

"Indeed it was." Miss Seeton arranged cups beside the biscuits and picked up the tray before Mel could beat her to it. "Such an enjoyable holiday, and most interesting. I had never flown before, you see, and . . . "

There was a brief pause, while Miss Seeton recalled the somewhat unusual circumstances which had led to her landing in Genoa, Italy, some hours before she'd arrived, as had originally been intended, in Geneva, Switzerland. She'd never quite understood how the mistake had come to be made, but since everyone had assured her afterwards that it had all worked out for the best . . .

"Let me have that." Mel took the tray before embarrassment sent crockery sideways to the floor. "We'll go through to the sitting-room," decreed Miss Forby. "And we'll take a seat not too far from your bureau—that's still where you keep your sketching gear, isn't it? Because I plan to make you sing for your supper, Miss S., even if it *is* only dinner at the George and not a swanky afternoon tea."

Miss Seeton, who had forgotten Mel's invitation to dine in the distraction of memory, blinked, and stared.

Mel laughed. "Think I don't know the way you've been gadding about Town escorted by eligible bachelors with Bond Street galleries, and married men from Scotland Yard? You must've had a whale of a time—but, *Negative* expenses or not, I'm afraid it's the George for us tonight, not the Ritz—and not even the George until you've done me one of your Seeton Specials, Miss S., or, better still, two.'' She looked urgently at her hostess from her undoubtedly beautiful eyes, their makeup so much softer, more expressive since one of Miss Seeton's sketches had shown her there was no real need for the harsh lines she'd affected along with her accent and her abrasive personality.

"Miss S.,'' said Mel, "I could do with your help. There's been another Ram Raid—and I'm relying on you to give me a scoop before anyone else thinks of asking you. Do you think you can do it?''

Miss Seeton continued to stare. Mel, after a moment, laughed again. "I'm sorry, honey. I shouldn't have sprung it on you like that. Suppose we have our tea and biscuits while I tell you all about it, and then we take it from there?"

They sat on easy chairs, with the tray on a low table to one side of them. Miss Seeton, the puzzled pucker fading from between her brows, reverted to the role with which she was most happy, and poured. "Did you have a good journey?" enquired the kindly hostess, handing Mel her cup. "London in the rush hour, I always think, can be very tiring—so many people, in such a great hurry. Do help yourself to a biscuit, unless"—the pucker returned—"that is, one would not wish to spoil your appetite for dinner, but . . ."

"The invitation stands," said Mel quickly, as Miss Seeton blushed for her forwardness in reminding her guest of her earlier remarks. "Whether or not," went on Mel, "you come up with the goods—though I don't see why you shouldn't, because you've never let anyone down before. That sketch you drew for the Oracle the other day was right on target."

Miss Seeton's brow cleared. "You've seen dear Mr. Delphick? I enjoyed myself so much that afternoon, and of course for Mr. Szabo to join us was an unexpected pleasure.''

"I've seen him," said Mel, "Delphick, I mean, though he didn't say anything about Szabo." She grinned. "Didn't say anything about anything much, come to that. The poor man had lost his voice after a press conference about—er, diplomatic relations with Stentoria—and before you ask," as Miss Seeton's eyebrows expressed mild surprise, "no, for once it wasn't me who kept firing awkward questions at him, it was the other reporters, honest." She giggled. "I was so busy taking notes, I never said a word. You wouldn't have known me—any more than the Oracle did afterwards," she added, aside. "At first . . . "

She giggled again at the memory, then smiled as Miss Seeton regarded her with courteous interest. "Don't mind me, Miss S., I'm just rambling. Thinking about the Oracle, I guess—you know I've always had a soft spot for the man, though as far as I can tell the feeling's mutual. Why else do you think he let me take a look at the latest addition to the Seeton Collection?"

The results of this inspired remark pleased Mel greatly. Miss Seeton smiled, hesitated, and then nodded, intimating her willingness to draw—since dear Mel had now explained that Mr. Delphick would have no objections—another of the cartoons on which, since they paid her an annual retainer, Scotland Yard must naturally have the first claim.

"He won't object," Mel assured her. "You needn't worry I'm trying to do the dirty on him by sneaking in ahead of him—Banner, yes, any time, but the Oracle, never. The man's my personal hotline to high places—you think I'd risk blowing that, with every other journalist on The Street out to do me down?"

Miss Seeton could see the force of this argument. Her smile was sympathetic as she nodded again, before once more frowning. "I fear," she said slowly, "that I know almost nothing—if, indeed, anything at all—about the kingdom of Stentoria, though it has been much in the news of late, as I understand—except, of course, that I don't. International politics . . . " Miss Seeton sighed. "But then, as you know, I have very little interest in the papers—oh, I do beg your pardon, Mel dear.'' Miss Seeton blushed. "I meant nothing personal, for naturally I appreciate that reporters, like everyone else, have their living to earn. Perhaps I should rather say that I have little time to read them—the papers, I mean. There is always so much to do, especially when one is a householder.''

Her gaze wandered round the sitting-room, with all its mementoes—furniture, pictures, ornaments—of dear Cousin Flora, and she smiled fondly before, with a sigh, picking up the teapot; then shook her head for her absent-mindedness, and put it down again. "Another biscuit?'' she enquired, gesturing towards the plate. "After your journey from Town—which I trust was a pleasant one . . . ''

"The journey,'' said Mel, "was fine. Right up to the last part, that is, when I was practically on your doorstep. There wasn't time to phone ahead for Jack Crabbe to meet me—one minute I heard about the Raid, the next I was grabbing my overnight bag and rushing for the train—so I had to take Mr. Baxter's taxi from Brettenden, and you know what *that* means.'' Miss Seeton sighed faintly: she, in common with the rest of Plummergen, knew.

Mel grinned. "Well, it could have been worse, I guess, because the car didn't break down, or the engine blow up, or anything of the sort you locals must've been expecting for years. Nor's Mr. Baxter half as doddery as I always thought he was—nor his brakes, come to that, though I have to say it was pretty close . . . '' She shuddered expressively, and Miss Seeton gave a little anxious cry. Mel grimaced.

"A darn sight too close for comfort, believe me. We'd just about reached the post office, and I was looking over at the pennant on the admiral's flagpole, when three people just appeared, right out of the blue, and charged straight into the middle of the road slap bang in front of the taxi.'' Miss Seeton gasped. Mel said quickly:

"If any three characters were asking to be splatted for their pains—but by some miracle they weren't, they managed to keep running to the other side of The Street. And''—Mel chuckled, though it sounded rather forced—

"that cranky old car, would you believe, *still* stayed in one piece? No headlamps exploding, no brake lights going bang with the excitement, no wheels flying off, and even the seatbelts only kind of hiccupped. It was amazing. And then all Mr. Baxter did was check he hadn't hit anyone, and drive on down to the George without batting an eyelid, so of course Amelita Forby had to act calm, as well. Fleet Street expects every hack to do her duty—but you'd never think it to look at him, would you?"

"Appearances," agreed Miss Seeton, as tactfully as she could, "can certainly—impressions, that is—be deceptive. In my own case . . . "

"I'll second that." Mel supposed Miss Seeton to have meant no more than that her own impressions were often quite unlike those of everyone else, if not, indeed, unique. What Mel had meant as she seconded Miss Seeton's innocent remark was something else entirely. The little art teacher, with her grey hair and quiet demeanour, was, after all, one of the most deceptive crime-busting forces around . . .

"This Ram Raid," said Mel, now that the conversation seemed to have reached a convenient pause. "You've heard all about the others, haven't you, from the Oracle, when you drew that sketch for him? Well, this is another one, almost exactly the same as the rest—masked men, a stolen car, backwards at full speed into a shop window, help themselves to the best of the stock, and gone before anyone's had time to dial nine-nine-nine."

Miss Seeton clicked her tongue, and looked disapproving. Mel did not notice the look: she was watching, not Miss Seeton's face, but her fingers, as they rested quietly on her lap. "*Almost* the same, I said, but there's one thing that's changed. The other raids have all been during the night, or early in the morning, before anyone's in the shop to raise the alarm too soon—but now they're getting cocky, Miss S. They don't seem to be worried any longer about people spotting them—they think they've got it down to a fine art, if that's not too horrible a pun."

Mel paused to allow Miss Seeton to raise twinkling eyes from her lap—those as-yet-not-dancing fingers seemed to intrigue their owner quite as much as they intrigued her guest—and twinkled right back at her. "Sorry. Guess I couldn't resist trying out my headline on you beforehand—except that the Ram Raiders haven't actually, uh, *refined* their technique quite as well as they thought they had."

Lowering her gaze again to Miss Seeton's still-peaceful hands, Mel chuckled. "They really should've checked things out a little better this time—I told you they were getting cocky, and cocky means careless—because the car they stole was nowhere near such a bargain as the Stentorian ambassador's Rolls." She chuckled again. "Talk about appearances being deceptive! The engine was fine, nice and powerful, and the steering could turn the thing on a six-pence, *and* there was a whole tank of petrol—but when they tried to load up with the loot, they found it was about an inch too small for a couple of the pictures, so when they couldn't close the lid of the boot on them, they had to dump them back on the pavement. Seems they didn't have time," as her hostess clicked her tongue for such vandalism, "to start cutting the canvases out of the frames."

Miss Seeton's wince was almost audible—and her fingers twitched on her lap. Mel, allowing herself to notice the twitching only from a distance, went on: "But while they were busy messing about trying to make the pictures go in the boot, that gave the owner of the shop time to dial nine-nine-nine—*and* to get a look at them. This was about half-past four, you see, so it wasn't properly dark. And as far as I know," said Mel, watching Miss Seeton's digital dance as it became ever more pronounced, "this man's still at the Yard being interviewed, with a crowd of the Street's second-best hacks hanging around, waiting for someone official to tell them what's been going on. Fleet Street's *very* best," she continued, with a wink and another smile, "is right here with you, Miss S. Amelita Forby's never been one for queues and crowds and the same old story as everyone else—not when there's you and your sketchbook to help her on her way to another scoop, she hasn't! After all, with Banner out of the country, someone's got to show the rest of them how it should be done."

Miss Seeton smiled at her young friend's exuberant self-confidence, but in an absent-minded way. Her fingers were noticeably restless now, her eyes pondering invisible visions as the pucker returned between her brows. Mel held her breath as the smile faded without the one who had smiled uttering a word . . .

And Miss Seeton's eyes drifted at last to the bureau in the corner—the bureau which held her sketching gear.

Mel sighed with quiet relief. "I'll slip out to the kitchen to top up the pot," she volunteered, as Miss Seeton began to look mildly embarrassed. Mel knew that expression of old. Nobody could ever understand why Miss Seeton should be so uncomfortable about her cartoons, but uncomfortable she undoubtedly was. Seemed to think they weren't quite proper—was always surprised Scotland Yard should pay good money for them—refused to let Mel show them to the art editor of the *Daily Negative*, who would be only too glad to publish them . . .

"The teapot? Oh, dear." Miss Seeton blushed, brought back to her hostessly duty by her guest's remark. "I should really have remembered—I'm so sorry . . . ''

"Not to worry, honey." Mel, jumping from her seat to take the teapot from the table, waved her away. "If I don't know where things are in the kitchen by now—unless you've been spring cleaning, of course, like Admiral Leighton with his pennant drying high on the line."

Miss Seeton blinked, then ventured a chuckle, her embarrassment forgotten. "Spring cleaning, in October?" Mel's idea of a joke, no doubt—and yet, perhaps . . .

She coughed. "If you will forgive me, Mel dear, I think it most unlikely that the admiral can have been so—so unorthodox in his habits, even though the Royal Navy is noted for tidiness and efficiency. He might, I suppose, have felt a sudden wish . . . but I rather think," with another cough, "that the pennant is in commemoration—or rather," in the interests of accuracy, "the flags this morning, a splendid display—a celebration of Trafalgar Day, or so dear Lady Colveden led me to understand when I spoke to her on the telephone earlier this evening. The Christmas pantomime, you know—and Sir George, naturally, has been invited. She asked if I would be prepared to help with the scenery, since I fear I have few other talents, and certainly none for acting—or singing," with a sigh, "or dancing. Miss Maynard, I believe, is to arrange these matters, although naturally, I would be more than willing to do my best, if nobody more suitable could be found, but . . ."

Miss Seeton shook her head, then brightened. "Prompting, of course, once she knew that I had acted in that capacity in one or two of Mrs. Benn's little productions—following the script, and judging exactly when to speak, which can be difficult when one is unsure whether the actor has forgotten the lines or is merely pausing for emphasis. But at least one may refer to the written word, which is a great help. So many people," said Miss Seeton earnestly, "have, I fear, a tendency to—to ramble, in their everyday speech, which can make it rather difficult to know exactly what they mean."

Mel, hovering by the door, could say nothing, though the teapot lid rattled in its china neck as she quivered. Miss Seeton sighed again. "And certainly not sewing. The costumes can be so elaborate—but there is, fortunately, no need, with dear Martha such an expert, and Miss Armitage, of course—though I rather believe him to have brought them with him, rather than having asked Martha or Miss Armitage to make them once he had come to live in Plummergen."

Mel blinked; the teapot rattled again. Oblivious as she rose to her feet, Miss Seeton rambled on: "Mementoes of his old ship, one imagines. A splendid display, indeed, though I had always supposed that one brought them down—the Girl Guides, you know—except that I believe the correct term is strike—like tents. Unless the gin pennant doesn't count. At sunset—or gongs, which could be most confusing if one was not careful, though he must be accustomed to them, I imagine, from the war. Sir George, that is, not the admiral. One could hardly use them at sea without considerable difficulty, and the idea that the navy would be unable to find an easier way . . . Tents, of course. Except that the term is used by members of Her Majesty's Forces to describe medals, is it not? Gongs, I mean, which of course they have, being all most gallant and courageous gentlemen—Sir George, and the admiral, and Colonel Windup, though I confess . . .''

Miss Seeton hesitated. The colonel was a decidedly private individual, and from what Martha had said of his habits would hardly care to have one gossip about him, even in so—surely—innocuous a manner. She blushed. ''Their individual meaning, of course, was a mystery to me—the flags of the admiral's signal, I mean—but Sir George, no doubt, with his army background, must be able to understand them. Dear Nigel, you know, is rather naughty, and teases his father about it. He says that all Sir George needs to understand is the gin pennant, when there is a party as there is this evening . . .''

She blushed again. Would dear Mel take this careless remark as another reminder of that kind invitation to dinner? In confusion, Miss Seeton stared about her—and found that her guest, nodding and smiling, was slipping into the hall; while she herself had somehow arrived—she did not recall crossing the floor, but she must have done—had arrived at her bureau, and was on the point of opening it. Mel could have told Miss Seeton that her verbal ramblings were no more than precursors of the equally vague, trance-like state in which she would most happily Draw in her own special way . . .

Miss Seeton did not know this—had never known it. She only knew that the tingle in her fingers was uncomfortable now—and that the sooner she worked her mental turmoil out on paper, the more comfortable her fingers would be.

CHAPTER 24

As the tail-lights of aged Mr. Baxter's almost-as-aged car moved off steadily down The Street, Admiral Leighton let out a thankful sigh that there could be no blood (he believed he might assume) on the taxi's unbattered (he further reasoned) front bumper. He then squared his shoulders, stiffened his spine, and brandished his fist in the direction of the post office, against the subdued out-of-hours lights of which were silhouetted the nervous figures of Rodney Roydon, Bethan Broomfield, and television supremo Jeremy Froste.

"Let that be a lesson to you!" cried the Buzzard, and he would have concluded with a few salty oaths until he recalled, just in time, that the vicar was in the vicinity. "Full steam ahead down The Street," he commanded, "and don't let me see any of you near my house again!"

He glared across through the uneven darkness for a few moments, growled into his beard, then nodded in satisfaction as the three began to make their way south towards the safety of the George. "Good riddance," muttered the admiral—and strode back to join his guests.

The party had become somewhat muted during the previous minutes, but the host's return prompted a swift resumption of festivities. More drinks were poured, and the vicar was coaxed into having his ginger-beer shandy made at double strength, in honour of the occasion.

"Grand chap, Nelson," said Admiral Leighton, as anecdote and reminiscence became the order of the day. "Not just a fine commander, but a born leader of men—they'd have followed him anywhere because they loved him, and quite rightly. Know what he did, the day before the battle? Wrote to Lady Hamilton, of course, in case he didn't come through, if you, er, don't mind my mentioning her, Padre . . ."

The Reverend Arthur Treeves blinked, appearing untroubled by the name of the celebrated mistress. Either he had no idea who she had been, or he judged her liaison with Lord Nelson so very historical that it didn't matter now.

"Ah—yes," said the admiral, and coughed. "Everybody else was writing the same sort of thing, of course—people do." He coughed again. Major Howett and the vicar sighed; Sir George huffed into his moustache; Colonel Windup cleared his throat. "So, off went the letters in the mailboat, and then someone found out the *Victory*'s coxswain had been so busy collecting the mail and getting it bagged up, the poor chap hadn't had time to write himself. But Nelson didn't hesitate—he made 'em signal the mailboat back. He said they none of 'em knew whether they'd be alive the next day, and if a British sailor wanted to say goodbye to his wife, he had as much right as anyone to say it. Signalled back the mailboat on purpose—with all that on his mind!" And he took a hearty swig of pink gin to hide his feelings.

"A great man," agreed Major Matilda Howett, delighted with this story, while the vicar beamed. Colonel Windup signified his approval of Nelson's behaviour by emptying his glass in a silent toast, and glancing about for a refill.

"Knew how to handle his men," said Sir George, as the admiral hospitably rose to fetch the whisky. "More than you can say for some of the brass hats."

"Talking of hats," said the admiral, busily pouring, "ever noticed his effigy in Westminster Abbey? That cocked hat was made specially, y'know, with a shade for his blind right eye. Lock's, I believe."

"Should think so," said Sir George, as the other officers nodded. The establishment at Number Six, St. James's Street, was renowned throughout the world for the quality of the headgear it had supplied during the past three hundred years to royalty, the nobility, the gentry, and members of HM Forces. The baronet chuckled. "Lock's—fell out with Edward, didn't they? The Seventh, I mean—wouldn't open up after hours to let him sneak into Marlborough House the back way, without being saluted by the sentries. Adventurous sort of life, the Prince of Wales—ahem!"

He recollected the presence of Major Howett and the Reverend Arthur Treeves, and once more huffed into his moustache. The admiral said quickly, "Talk about turning a blind eye—there was a chap on Channel convoy duty who never let on till the day he was demobbed that he couldn't see a thing without contact lenses. Had to get his friends to memorise the chart for him before he went for his medical, because he didn't buy 'em until halfway through the war—some of the first in the country, I believe. Broke 'em in by wearing one at a time, a few minutes more each day. Must have been damned—sorry, Padre—uncomfortable, but it was the only way he could cover a full eight-hour watch, to begin with. Only wore both, he said, if he was going into action. Now, that's what I call a pretty brave chap."

"Suppose," enquired Major Howett, her medical curiosity aroused, "he'd been wounded, and knocked out? Even with the modern lenses you can't risk leavin' em in while you're asleep—you could end up blinded. And hardly anyone would have known about contact lenses durin' the war."

"Scratched a warning on the back of his identity disc," said the admiral, amazed that anyone—even an army officer—should doubt the resourcefulness of an officer of the Royal Navy. "He was lucky, though—came through without so much as a splinter. They used to say, begging the Padre's pardon, that when he went to sea, the Archangel Gabriel piped the duty watch to look after him." He sighed, and stroked his beard, his eyes suddenly clouded. "A good number old Gabriel couldn't seem to find time to pipe the watch for, more's the pity . . . "

There was a pause. The Reverend Arthur shifted on his chair, looking guilty. Major Howett said sadly:

"And now we're gettin' to the stage when even the ones who lived through it are finally leavin' us for good. Open the paper any day, and ten to one there's somebody you know—used to know, rather."

Sir George nodded. "Sometimes feel we'd do better tearing out the obituary page before we read it—supposed to be a sign of old age, though I must say I don't feel a day older than I did then. And reading them brings it all back, one more time. Paying your respects, you could say . . ."

The admiral drained his gin, clinked his glass on the table, and jumped to his feet. "This is a party, and we're getting down in the dumps. Now, I've a treat in store for everyone, once I've topped up the glasses—bit of a change from pork pie, but a real naval delicacy: Hammy, Eggy, Cheesy Topsides! And I don't want you shaking your head about too much fat, Major, today of all days. Many a ship's company lived on Topsides right through the war, and most of 'em are still with us thirty years on."

Major Howett chuckled. "One of my cousins was in the navy, Admiral, and our side of the family—the army side—used to tell him the reason your Cheesy Topside was so popular was that even a man could cook it. Now then, what d'you say to that?"

The admiral twinkled at her. "Heard that said myself, Major. So you won't want to pop into the galley to keep an eye on what I'm doing, will you? Perhaps you'll be kind enough to see to the drinks while I'm gone . . ."

And he made for the kitchen, leaving Major Howett to explain to the other guests that their host was about to toast a slice of bread—removing the crusts, since everyone there was an officer—and butter it before adding a slice of ham and a lightly-poached egg, in that order, with a final layer of mature Cheddar cheese, grated, and popped under the grill until it was oozing.

"Rich," concluded Major Howett, busy with the whisky, gin, and ginger beer. "Not that it'll do any of us any harm, once in a while, but we'll need somethin' to wash it down. A drop or two of the hard stuff's good for fat, the diet chaps say, so don't you go lookin' at me like that, Vicar," as the Reverend Arthur tried to refuse the offered shandy.

"I promise I won't breathe a word to your sister about how much you drink tonight—but you'd better join us and have somethin', just in case. We wouldn't want to read *your* obituary in the papers tomorrow, would we? Best take care of the old ticker . . . Just hang on a moment there, Colonel, and I'll fix you another scotch . . . ''

"Another sherry, Miss S.? Or shall we go in to dinner?"

Mel, despite the tea and—she'd weakened, with the excitement of Miss Seeton's eventual Drawing—biscuits, was starting to feel hungry. She and Miss Seeton were sitting in a quiet corner of the George's saloon bar, studying the menus Maureen had dropped off at their table with a mumbled explanation before hurrying away to flutter her eyelashes and parade her best profile in the neighbourhood of a little group of three—two men and a young woman—in the middle of the room. The young woman and the elder of the men seemed to regard the other man as a person of much importance, hanging on his every word, gazing at him (on the rare occasions when he wasn't speaking) with great attention. He so clearly expected to be the centre of attention that Mel, who had never met him but knew his reputation, took a mischievous delight in not allowing her gaze to drift, even for an instant, in his direction.

At Miss Seeton's smiling nod, Mel gathered up the menus, and rose from her chair. "We'll take these through with us, to save time," she said, "if that's okay with you— I could eat a horse, now I've got round to thinking about it, after the journey and everything." She giggled. Her schooner of sherry had been twice the size of Miss Seeton's. "Not that I'd want to, really. I know they eat horsemeat on the Continent—poor old Banner, I almost feel sorry for him—but I do hope the George hasn't gone and done a deal with Dan Eggleden!"

Miss Seeton smiled again at the jocular reference to Plummergen's blacksmith, but said nothing: she, too, was starting to feel a trifle peckish. Following Mel's lead, she unhooked her brolly—her very best gold-handled umbrella, since she was dining out with a friend—from the back of her comfortable chair, and slipped her handbag over her arm before moving out of the bar towards the restaurant.

Maureen was returning with more drinks to the table of three, her head high as she tried to emulate the gliding walk of film stars and top fashion models such as Marigold Naseby. Mel's eyes remained resolutely averted from the man she'd recognised as Jeremy Froste, whose ego was a legend among media folk. Miss Seeton, who prided herself on discretion, couldn't resist a very quick peep at the television people of whom she'd heard Martha chattering . . .

The triple collision was more of a shock than anything else. Neither bones nor, surprisingly, glasses were broken, and only the carpet received a generous libation of Campari soda, gin-and-orange, and advocaat. Nobody's clothes were splattered, nobody's shoes were splashed.

Exclamations and apologies filled the air, turning every head in the room towards the table of Jeremy Froste. He, of course, was in his element, rising graciously to the occasion, loudly assuring Maureen no harm had been done, looking on as Bethan bent to collect the fallen glasses, as Rodney picked Miss Seeton's brolly from the floor, while he himself patted shoulders in a soothing manner, and smiled on the assembled female company—and continued to smile.

"No, no, don't worry about a thing. Accidents will happen—just put it on my bill, and never mind—Bethan, make a note." He glanced sideways as he spoke, and met the beautiful eyes of Amelita Forby, which watched him with a faintly mocking air. "Now, you must allow me to buy you both a drink," he said. "I insist. I won't take no for an answer. Maureen, my dear—it *is* Maureen, isn't it?— we'll have two more chairs at this table, and if our friends would say what they'd like . . . ?"

"Thanks," said Mel, "but there's no need. As you said, no harm done—we'll just pick up our bits and bobs and be on our way in to dinner."

"If you're sure I can't persuade you," Jeremy said, "we might perhaps have an after-dinner drink together." Those eyes, in that bone structure, had made a great impression on him; besides, there was something familiar about her, though she didn't look the type to fall for the haven't-we-met-before routine. He wanted to find out more.

"Perhaps," said Mel, who had no intention of accepting; and no qualms about refusing, without the courtesy of even a silent exchange, on Miss Seeton's behalf as well. "Thanks," with a smile of genuine warmth for Rodney, as he appeared at her side and bowed an odd, jerky little bow, before handing her the gold-handled umbrella. "But that's not mine, it belongs to—uh, to my friend here."

Rodney blushed, and bowed again as he corrected his innocent mistake, holding the brolly out with a look of awe on his face. "Can this," he enquired, in a breathless voice, "be real gold? Surely not!"

Miss Seeton received her property with gratitude, and beamed in the pride of possession. "Indeed it is. Not *solid* gold, of course—the weight, you see, not to mention the expense—but yes, it is real, and I am so thankful it was undamaged. Gold, I mean—since it was a present from a gentleman who . . . "

She hesitated. Should she describe Chief Superintendent Delphick as a friend, or as a colleague? He was, of course, after so many years' acquaintance, both—or so she felt, and believed him to feel the same; but at the time of his first giving her the umbrella they had only just met—and their professional relationship, as one naturally must call it, had not developed until more than a year later . . .

"Well, it wasn't damaged," said Mel quickly, before Miss Seeton could betray an identity the reporter had no wish to let the television team discover. For a person who valued her privacy, Miss S. could sometimes be awfully casual about what she said and who she said it to. "Not even the tiniest scratch," said Mel, taking hold of the handle as if to check it, and giving it a surreptitious tug. "So we'll be on our way, and leave the three of you to it. Shall we go, uh—before the place gets too crowded?"

Miss Seeton—who, reassured as to the condition of her umbrella, had started to apologise for the accident she had come to believe must have been her fault—responded at once to her hostess's hint with a quick blush, and a murmur of penitent farewell. She stepped nimbly around the kneeling form of Maureen, scrubbing with a lamentably unglamorous dishcloth at the carpet, and hurried after Mel as she made for the relative safety of the dining-room.

"I'm so sorry," she said, as she caught up with her friend in the hall near Reception. "To have delayed you, that is, though he was most charming about it, was he not? And one has to say, I fear, that Maureen, too, was somewhat to blame, since if she had been paying proper attention to where she was going—though that is no doubt unfair, as I must confess to a little curiosity on my own behalf concerning the television gentleman—"

"Don't worry about Jeremy Froste," advised Mel, "and I wouldn't agonise too much over the spilled drinks, either. It really was just one of those things. Come to that, I was so busy looking the other way on purpose, you could say I was as much to blame as Maureen—poor kid," she added, with a grin. "If she wanted to impress our friend Froste—well, she's certainly made an impression—though I don't think it's quite what she had in mind."

Miss Seeton, still feeling guilty, blushed again, and began to murmur once more of curiosity, and ill manners. She fell silent, however, as they arrived at the door of the dining-room, and head waitress Doris came to show them to their seats; and by the time all the business of ordering was done, she was almost herself again.

Mel suggested a Beaujolais to accompany the meal, and when Doris returned with the bottle enquired: "That *was* Jeremy Froste in the bar, wasn't it? So what's he doing," as Doris intimated that it was, "in Plummergen? If he's poaching on my preserves, I'll sue him for breach of copyright!" For Mel considered Miss Seeton's village her personal territory, not to be shared with an outsider—which, after so long, she hardly thought herself to be. Those Plummergen Pieces she wrote for the *Daily Negative* must have established her claim to this particular beat, if anything could . . .

"Looking for an apple tree," said Doris, tugging at the cork. "Leastways, so he says—now, shall I pour some to taste, or will you just drink it?—and there's that Miss Broomfield busy taking notes and measuring all day long— tasty, isn't it?—and photos, too, popping in and out of folks' houses to look at their gardens—leave it here, shall I, for you to help yourselves?—and with that Roydon, he's a journalist, following 'em around asking all them questions for this article he wants to write, we've had a rare old time of it these last few days.''

She regarded Mel with approval. Miss Forby might be a reporter, but she wasn't such a Nosey Parker as some. ''He wouldn't,'' said Doris, ''be anyone you know, of course.''

Mel shook her head. ''No—though Thrudd might know him, I suppose. These freelance types,'' smugly, ''aren't in quite the same league as the Fleet Street regulars. Your Roydon's probably a stringer for one of the nationals, based on some local rag writing obituaries and weddings, hoping to break into the big time with a story on Jeremy Froste. Well, the best of luck to him—we've all had to come up the hard way. And there's room,'' said Mel, looking as smug as she sounded, ''for all sorts on the Street, once you're there. But none of them scoops Amelita Forby . . . ''

The next morning found Mel early awake, poring over one of the menus from dinner which she had smuggled upstairs without being noticed. She knew it would be no use asking Room Service, in the person of Maureen, to bring her breakfast before the restaurant opened; she also knew that she wanted black coffee and something solid inside her before she could consult the police . . .

"But not the Oracle, I think," Mel murmured, gazing at the menu—or rather, at the blank back of it—or, rather, at the back which had been blank before Miss Seeton doodled on it in pencil, said pencil having been out of Mel's bag and held across the table as soon as the reporter recognised her guest's fresh attack of twitching fingers. "Somehow, I don't believe this one's for the Yard just yet . . ."

And she decided, with reluctance, that breakfast would have to wait.

An hour later, she wished it hadn't.

"Brinton or nobody," she insisted, standing before Desk Sergeant Mutford in the police station at Ashford. She'd hoped to creep in through the back as she'd done on a previous occasion, but the sun had been shining then, the doors open. A chilly start to an October day had kept the doors firmly closed, and Mel decided to bow to the inevitable. If she asked nicely, they might give her coffee and a bun to make up for the rigours of the cross-country bus ride . . .

"You can't," said Mutford, "just go a-barging into the super's office as you please, young woman."

"I don't want to barge," said Mel. "I want you to tell him I'm here, and I'm on my way, and he needn't bother laying on an escort because I already know where I'm going—"

"You're going nowhere," she was informed. "Regulations say as *nobody*'s to be let wander willy-nilly about the station, lest their eyes light on things it's not their lawful business to see." Desk Sergeant Mutford was a staunch member of the Holdfast Brethren, a curious sect renowned for sticking as closely to the strict letter of the law as the twentieth century would permit. "Moreover," he added, as she was about to protest, "it's not fitting."

Mel's brows arched above her beautiful eyes. "Why not?"

Mutford looked scandalised. "With you a weaker vessel, and him a married man? To think I should ever hear words so brazen, with my very own ears!"

"Well, you'd hardly hear them with anyone else's—"

"Brazen," thundered Mutford, "and immodest! Besides, he isn't in yet," as Mel could contain herself no longer, and burst out laughing: hunger had made her light-headed, and if she didn't laugh, she'd explode. She'd once written up the Brethren in a tactfully-disguised Piece, but she'd forgotten just how unyielding they could be. She was surprised she could find it so amusing . . .

"What's the joke?" came a voice from behind—a voice she knew. "Sarge, that was never you laughing? Miss Forby! What are you doing here?"

Mel turned, smiling with relief. "*Trying*," she said, with emphasis, "to see your boss. But it's turned out more difficult than I'd expected."

Detective Constable Foxon, who knew very well what she meant, smiled back at her before turning to the fulminating Mutford, who was babbling that Brinton wasn't in, for one thing. And for another—

"It's okay, Sarge, I'll vouch for the lady. And wouldn't

it save bothering the super about seeing her if I talk to her first, and find out what she wants?''

"What I want," said Mel, as she followed Foxon down the corridor in the direction of Brinton's office, "is coffee—and plenty of it. Do you realise I missed my breakfast to be here early—so early I hadn't the heart to dig Jack Crabbe out of bed with his taxi? But what good's it done me? If you hadn't come along when you did—"

"But I did," said Foxon, striking an attitude before diverting towards the canteen. "The early bird catches the constabulary coffee . . . And try to look," he begged, as he threw open the canteen door, "like an informer, if you can. Sergeant Mutford's right—you're not really supposed to be here, and you'll never kid anybody you're one of us plain-clothes lot."

"Don't be too sure of that," murmured Mel, thinking of recent successful kidding. But she knew, as all good journalists must, how to be discreet, and she said nothing more—on the topic of impersonation, that is. She was, however, more than eloquent on the topic of Miss Seeton . . .

One quick coffee and a sticky bun later, she was urging Foxon back to Brinton's office to study the sketches in detail. The superintendent had still not arrived as Foxon sat Mel in his visitors' chair, dragged his own round the desk at an angle, and sat gazing at the two sketches and the menu Mel spread on the blotter before him.

"She drew this one first," said Mel. "A day or so after she got back from seeing the Oracle about the Ram Raids . . . "

Foxon spent a few moments studying the sketch, and then found he was clearing his throat with unnecessary vigour.

Mel twinkled at him. "Got you the same way, has it?"

"Well," he said slowly, "either she's gone in for a bit of weather-forecasting, and wanted to warn us about this morning's fog—it was pretty murky in patches, which must be why the super's still not in yet . . . "

"Or?" prompted Mel, as he paused to cough again.

"Or she's getting ahead of herself somehow, because

Guy Fawkes isn't until November, and these certainly look like fireworks, to me.''

"Starbursts," said Mel. "I thought so, too."

"And that flag . . . '' He jabbed a finger at the proud standard blowing in the breeze. "Don't tell me—I used to be a Boy Scout, and national flags was one of the badges . . . Stentoria," he said, remembering, as Mel applauded quietly. "Never dreamed it would come in useful again."

"I guess she got *that*," said Mel, "from something I said about the ambassador's Rolls-Royce being used for one of the Ram Raids, and then Admiral Leighton's Trafalgar Day party. Boy, does that man know how to celebrate!"

"By all accounts," Foxon said, "he does. Potter once had to warn Sir George—'' He pulled himself up sharply. "Flags, and fireworks—funny kind of star, though . . . ''

The Stentorian flag drawn by Miss Seeton was just one of many, flown not from a vertical flagpole but from a horizontal line, hanging between two stout posts: the effect was more that of a string of party bunting than a sober naval signal or a display of national flags. Only the Stentorian flag was clearly drawn, with the others mere roughed-in shapes, as roughly shaded, giving the impression of movement without detailed form, and obscured for the greater part by debris from those puzzling starbursts.

These—if starbursts they were—had been shown exploding not above the line of flags, but below it, close to the ground. Through Miss Seeton's pencilled streaks of debris, smoke, and light could be glimpsed three persons of indeterminate gender, with, in the far background, a large, powerful car. Near the rear of this car the most violent of the firework explosions seemed to have occurred. Strange shapes—oblong, square, round—of various sizes—some almost as large as a car door, some smaller than one of its headlamps—were arranged, as far as Foxon and Mel could tell, in an assortment of pyramids, clumps, and rows, most of them in the foreground, but some—the largest—near the back of the car, in less formal array.

"I only came down to ask her about the Ram Raids,"

Mel said. "I never thought about anything else, but now—well, I can't help wondering. Just take a look at the sketch she drew on the menu, and see what you think about her having muddled what I wanted to know with what she wanted to tell me . . . about those Sideboard Swipers you've had around here for the past few—sorry?"

Foxon was breathing heavily. "I said they got an old family friend the other day, damn them. Almost broke my grandmother's heart, finding him like that—so I just hope you're right, Mel. Or rather that Miss Seeton is . . ."

The menu sketch was a vivid depiction of a room with a graceful, bow-fronted sideboard—Chippendale? Sheraton? Hepplewhite?—in its exact centre, and bearing, as well as a tempting group of bottles and an indistinct photograph in a frame, a selection of plates and dishes heaped with assorted goodies such as cheeses, sweetmeats, and fruits of different kinds. To one side of the rug, towards the back of the room, stood a television inside a cabinet with similar curved lines to those of the sideboard: it was almost as if those early masters of furniture design had foreseen the twentieth century. In the foreground lurked a faceless figure in trousers and a buttoned mackintosh, with a folded newspaper under its—his?—arm, and a notebook and pencil in its other hand as if jotting down—maybe sketching—details of the scene.

"Doris at the George," said Mel, as Foxon looked up with a pucker between his brows, "can chatter away with the best of them, if she's in the mood. She was telling us last night about all the fun they've had recently with the television research people, and the reporter"—she tapped the notebook-and-pencilled figure with an emphatic finger—"who wants to make his name writing the definitive article on Jeremy Froste, for some strange reason."

She fixed the still-silent Foxon with a meaningful look. "Now, let me throw a few guesses at you, and you tell me if I'm right. The Swipers' victims—they're usually elderly people?"

"Around here they are, yes, more's the pity. And I'm pretty sure it's the same in other parts of the country."

Mel nodded. "From what I've read, it is. And these elderly people—they've all been in the papers, one way or another, not so long before they were burgled?''

Foxon nodded. ''The old girl in hospital had told 'em how she was starting some charity collection in memory of whatever-it-was her sister had just died of—and then there was poor old Reg. One minute it's his golden wedding, with 'em taking snaps of him and Gertie cutting the cake, and the next he's at her funeral. They wrote a grand obituary for her, though, and he really went to town on the entry in the *Deaths* column—I'd never have believed a stiff-upper-lip sort of bloke like him'd let everyone know how upset he was. Then what happens not five minutes later but some devil breaks into the house and . . . ''

He stopped. He looked at Mel, whose stare was still as meaningful as it had been a few moments earlier. He said:

''Let's think this through, Miss Forby of Fleet Street. You're a reporter, and a pretty famous one, as well—now.'' Mel's eyes gleamed, but she said nothing. Foxon went on: ''But you had to get started somehow, didn't you?''

Slowly, Mel nodded, her eyes still bright. Foxon said:

''Are you thinking what I'm thinking?''

''I think,'' said Mel, ''that I just might be.''

There was a pause, during which the two exchanged conspiratorial glances. In the end, Mel said:

''I guess it's pretty far-fetched, when you think about it in cold blood, but—well, coincidences happen . . . ''

''And,'' said Foxon, ''if they don't—I suppose they can always be helped along a bit, can't they?''

There was another pause. Mel, in the end, was the one who broke it.

''Of course, she's never been much of a one for—well, for playing a part for the press—and we've gone along with that, as far as we can. If we want to try this, though . . . ''

Foxon laughed. ''Playing a part? We all know she's not what you'd call an actress, but—you think she'd have to? Besides, she's gone undercover, so to speak, before—like that witchcraft business a few years back.'' Absently, he rubbed the upper arm injured by the hired thugs—Majordomes—of the sinister Nuscience cult it had been intended Miss Seeton should infiltrate.

"Of course—and in Switzerland," said Mel, still half-heartedly brooding on Thrudd's refusal to let her accompany him, though she had the feeling that a possible Seeton Scoop in the hand was worth any number of seasick Swiss sailors in the abstract. "And that gambling case, except I know she wasn't too keen on dressing up for the casino . . ."

"But she did it," said Foxon, who'd only come in at the end of the Thatcher affair, but who'd had graphic accounts of its origins from others. "Don't forget her sense of duty, Mel. Once she knew what it was all about, I'm sure she'd be the first to want to do something—and yet . . ." The tone was very serious now. "I can't help wondering—and the super'll do a damn sight more than wonder. Is it really such a good idea to let Miss Seeton loose on this?"

CHAPTER 26

Friday's final patrol of Night Watch Men, homeward bound at sunrise on Saturday, were not greatly surprised when they met PC Potter emerging from the police house with the air of one who has already broken his fast on eggs-and-bacon, sweet tea, and plenty of toast. Potter was on foot, not in his car. His buttons were bright, his regulation cap had been replaced by his trusty, hard-topped helmet, and he carried a stout, old-fashioned truncheon in his hand.

"Morning, lads," he greeted Jack Crabbe and company. "Off to your beds, eh, and leaving all well?"

"So far," replied Jack, in ominous tones, "all's well. You'll be bound for the village hall, I don't doubt."

"I am," said Potter. He tapped the side of his nose in a knowing fashion, and winked. Jack and his colleagues exchanged glances. Potter, intercepting the glances, brandished his truncheon at those who glanced.

"We'll have due respect for the forces of the law, if you please, lads—though that's not to say as I might not have to call on you later, if things get . . . lively." Chuckles and mutterings greeted this remark. Potter grinned. "But until they do—and just maybe they won't—well, we'll keep the peace, as best we can. All right?"

Reluctantly, the patrol agreed that it was—and headed bedwards as Potter had instructed, leaving him to make his way up the Street to Plummergen Village Hall, outside the front door of which—having checked fire-doors and lower windows for signs of illegal entry—he took up his station, very much on guard.

In normal circumstances, produce show organisers do not require a police presence at the scene of the event. Jars of home-made jam, bottled fruit, sponge cakes, and baskets of vegetables are hardly given to riotous assembly. Novelty displays such as *Hats Trimmed: Fruit* or *Seed-Box Gardens* sit peaceably on wooden benches until their proud designers take them, disassembled, home. The most probable excitement at a produce show is the inadvertent hatching of wrongly-dated eggs, warmed in their cotton-wool nest by the autumn sun . . .

PC Potter nodded a greeting to the first arrivals, but said nothing as he slapped the truncheon in the palm of his hand, watching further arrivals—evidently dismayed by so prompt a start to proceedings—appear almost simultaneously at the end of the path. The newcomers huddled together, suspiciously staring, before marching up the path en masse. A large key appeared from someone's pocket, the door was unlocked, and Plummergen—closely pursued by suspicious Murreystone—hurried into the hall to arrange its exhibits for the joint Produce Show.

The Judging Committee was, for safety, composed of an equal number of gardeners and gourmets from each village. The hall was cleared as judging took place: a large and interested crowd gathered on the path as PC Potter, his ear cocked for sounds of dissent from within, kept his eyes open for signs of disaffection without.

" . . . really too bad," grumbled Mrs. Blaine, "if all your hard work doesn't win a prize, Eric, because I'm sure if anyone knows how to grow leeks, it's you."

Miss Nuttel gazed modestly down her equine nose, and did her best to blush. "Luck of the game, Bunny, when all's said and done. Only a bit of fun, after all."

"Fun?" Mrs. Putts, perennially debarred from the Cakes and Pastries class on grounds of professionalism—her job in Brettenden's biscuit factory was deemed to give her an unfair advantage—was minded to strike a sour note. "Some people take it a sight too serious, if you ask me.

There's bin talk,'' with a darkling glare for the Murreystone contingent, ''of duck-eggs painted to look like chickens'— ah, and of marrows fed on sugared water, which nobody could say was good honest fertiliser, now could they?''

Murreystone pointedly ignored the insinuation, gazing in any direction but that of the frustrated pastrycook. PC Potter shifted from one side of the doorway to the other, re- minding everyone of his presence. Jeremy Froste nodded as Bethan Broomfield opened her bag to scribble something in her notebook: *Not All Roast Beef* would no doubt contain a stirring episode of Horticultural Sabotage and Dirty Tricks in its next series. For a long while, nobody spoke.

On the still October air, voices were heard from the body of the hall. The crowd began to edge forward, hoping to peer inside, yet keeping well out of truncheon-range . . .

The Show proper opened at two o'clock. PC Potter had remained on guard the entire time, asking Sir George and Nigel, as working farmers too busy to grow things for fun—Lady Colveden's eggs didn't count—to act as his deputies when the necessary aftermath of his early-morning tea took him away from his post. For Nigel in particular, this was no hardship. Miss Broomfield, soon abandoned by a bored Jeremy Froste, was taking notes in great detail, and asking questions Sir George promptly professed himself un- able to answer. Lady Colveden, arriving with her eggs, read the unspoken appeal in Nigel's eyes, and went home to return with a flask of tea, which she insisted PC Potter must share with her menfolk, and from which Nigel poured with a more than lavish hand. For his part, he could have stayed outside all morning, notwithstanding a wireless forecast of heavy rain: he hoped midday would never come . . .

Eleven o'clock came, and went. Twelve, and the sun was overhead, the promised rain as yet only a hint of high, far- away cloud. Twelve-thirty, and everyone except PC Potter popped home for something to eat. By one-forty-five, they were nearly all back again; by one-fifty-five, in a bristling silence, what seemed like the larger part of Plummergen and Murreystone was waiting outside the village hall—on pointedly opposite sides of the path—to learn the fate of their various entries in the first ever combined Produce Show.

"Miss Seeton!" Lady Colveden greeted the new arrival with a wave. "I know you wanted to walk up, but do remind me to offer you a lift on the way back—I imagine the rain won't hold off much longer."

Miss Seeton, wearing her yellow bead necklace and a new hat in honour of the occasion, patted the gold umbrella over her arm and smiled. "You are very kind, but I am well prepared, as you see, and wouldn't wish to make you wait when it is really no great distance. And I have promised to drop in afterwards to see dear Miss Wicks, to tell her about the conker contest, in which she is naturally most interested."

Listening Plummergen shuffled its feet, and hid smiles of secret understanding. Puzzled Murreystone, whose knowledge of Miss Seeton was much distorted by five miles' distance and an almost total ban on communication with its neighbouring village, wondered what point it was missing.

"And of course," continued Miss Seeton, "since dear Stan was unwilling to let me enter my eggs in the Show, there was really nothing for me to carry—or my apples, or indeed anything else, ready for church tomorrow—though I suppose it would have been in the morning. To be judged, I mean, rather than in the afternoon—to bring them, that is, as, presumably, you did, which would have been most helpful, except that I didn't . . ."

Exactly on the hour, the door swung open. From inside the hall, closed against invaders and sabotage since seven that morning, a warm, moist, gardeny, flowery, bakery aroma wafted, heavy on the autumn air.

Noses twitched, eyes brightened as people pressed closer to the entrance. At the official ticket table, postmaster Mr Stillman—impartial as only a servant of the Crown can be—sat ready to take the money.

The explosion was not loud—but it was unexpected. Up from his table leaped Mr. Stillman, scattering change from his float tin. Those who had opened the door looked at each other in horror, then at the startled crowd—and then back, into the hall . . .

"Not honest—didn't I say so?" cried Mrs. Putts, as news of Murreystone's latest perfidy filtered through the crowd. The impersonating duck-eggs, deceiving nobody, had been disqualified almost at once. The rumoured record-breaking cucumber had proved—after considerable argument—to be a rare variety of edible gourd, and thus ineligible. In all the excitement of destroying entry cards and striking names from lists, the possibility of machination among the marrows had been overlooked by the Plummergen judges, and instinctively ignored by their Murreystone counterparts. When, swollen beyond their regular growth by a diet of sugar solution, the marrows had begun to ferment in the heat of the airless hall, it was only a matter of time before the worst occurred . . .

The doors of the hall were closed against the crowd as the ensuing debate raged within. Without, PC Potter smacked his truncheon loudly in the palm of his hand, and surveyed the scene with an air of quiet menace which convinced everyone he was in command of the situation, though inside he was wishing he'd thought to ask Superintendent Brinton for any spare men going, Saturday overtime or not, because he wasn't anywhere near as confident as he'd have liked to be that there wouldn't be a punch-up before long . . .

"Thought it was Bonfire Night come early," came the general chorus. "And the smell! Talk about a brewery!"

"Beer," remarked Mrs. Skinner, to nobody in particular, "can be powerful stuff, there's no denying, though there's surely none been trying to make it in the village hall, it being difficult enough at the best of times—wouldn't you say, Mrs. Henderson?"

Mrs. Henderson's husband had once caused the destruction of their entire ground floor glazing by his insistence that his wife, for reasons of economy, should make good use of the traditional family recipe for Strong and Wholesome Barley Beer. Though the broken windows had been replaced, the cracks in the plaster had never been properly repaired; the cost of the glass alone had almost bankrupted the Henderson household.

"For my part," said Mrs. Henderson, with a sniff, "I was more reminded of the war, with doodlebugs falling, and land-mines. Lucky nobody was hurt!" She glared round at guilty Murreystone as it slunk off, sniggering, to a safe distance.

From Plummergen, a few murmurs of agreement were heard, but they were drowned out by Mrs. Skinner's no-body-in-particular remark that Some People should take care about Giving Away How Old They Were, letting on just how well they remembered the war.

"We *all*," said Mrs. Flax grimly, "remembers the war, save them as weren't yet born, o'course."

"Thirty years—why, that's nothing," said Mrs. Spice, who was of similar vintage to Mrs. Henderson.

"And when we don't remember," chimed in Miss See-ton, who had wartime memories of her own, "we have, of course, television." Miss Seeton was a keen viewer of old movies, whose black-and-whiteness did not make her regret that she had, as yet, no colour set. She so seldom watched television that the expense seemed unjustified—and as the Colvedens were so very kind when there were art or wild-life programmes she might wish to watch . . .

"There's war," muttered someone, "and then there's dirty tricks—and we all know the difference, or if we don't it's a downright disgrace—"

"And somebody," somebody said, "ought to teach them as is ignorant just what's what—"

"And before much longer, as well!"

Lady Colveden, catching PC Potter's anguished eye, felt that *noblesse* obliged her to intervene—fast. "Talking of the war," she said, "perhaps, Mr. Froste"—for Jeremy and Bethan, with Rodney as always never far from his idol, were drinking in every choleric syllable—"you might find material in Plummergen for an altogether different series, once you've finished *Not All Roast Beef*. Although my hus-band and I didn't come to live here until two or three years after VJ Day, we do know that the Hall was used by the military for something terribly hush-hush—and of course

Kent was right in the thick of things with the Battle of Britain, fighters shot down and—and that sort of thing. *A Village Remembers*—something along those lines, perhaps?''

Before Jeremy could reply, someone said that their most vivid memory of the war was Woolton Pie, which made all who could recall this curious comestible—chopped seasonal vegetables, oatmeal, and plain white sauce combined beneath a potato topping for the nutritional benefit of beleaguered Britain—chuckle. Someone else mentioned whale steaks; the name of Dr. Edith Summerskill was coupled with snoek, otherwise known as barracuda. People spoke of Spam, of dried eggs (''God bless the Yanks!''), of coupons, and of points.

''Butter, marge, lard, cheese . . . ,'' chanted Mrs. Skinner, now in a better mood.

'' . . . eggs, sugar, jam, tea,'' continued Mrs. Henderson, for once in harmony with her rival as she completed the ration-book litany familiar to so many for so long. It was not, after all, until 1954 that fourteen years of meat rationing had finally come to an end.

''Those who have the will to win,'' somebody recited, ''Eat potatoes in their skin, Knowing that the sight of peelings, Deeply hurts Lord Woolton's feelings!''

And everyone—Mrs. Henderson and Mrs. Skinner included—laughed together. Jeremy Froste, edging closer to her ladyship, smiled a winning smile.

''Lady Colveden, you could just have had the idea for my next series. Bethan—make a note. There's still a lot of interest in the war, though I don't really remember it myself, of course,'' hastily, in case anyone should think the young television Turk so old. ''If it could be done—at least one programme, anyway—from the perspective of a typical English village . . . ''

Nobody thought to disabuse him of the notion that Plummergen was anything like a typical English village, or its inhabitants anything like typical English villagers. Plummergen saw no reason why it should not star in a documentary feature about the war, and began to preen itself.

''Service reminiscences too, perhaps,'' mused Jeremy,

his eye falling on the neat ginger beard of Admiral Leighton, the moustache of Major-General Sir George. Bethan made another dutiful note, and Rodney Roydon nodded approval; but the expressions on the faces of the two old warriors, and a sudden stirring among the listening crowd, warned Mr. Froste that he might have misjudged public sentiment.

"Of course, it would be the Home Front," he said quickly, "where most of the interest would be concentrated—your talk of rationing, for instance, has certainly inspired me." He adopted an Inspired pose. "The difficulty of baking cakes without fat—we could show someone cooking Woolton Pie—make do and mend, for clothes—home-made soap . . ."

He recollected himself with an effort as Rodney Roydon coughed at his side, and Bethan's pencil slowed in its flight across the page. "Alas," sighed Jeremy Froste, "I must complete *Not All Roast Beef* first. If only I could find a Plummergen Peculier . . ."

CHAPTER 27

He turned to Miss Seeton. "I do beg your pardon, but I was unable to avoid overhearing your earlier remark to Lady Colveden about your apples, and how you aren't exhibiting any in today's show. We met," he reminded her, with a winning smile, "the other evening, you no doubt recall. And as I believe your garden is one of, er, the few we haven't yet been invited to visit . . ."

Beside him, Bethan already had her notebook open. Miss Seeton puzzled over his remarks for only a moment, then smiled. "Why, yes—the kind gentleman who picked up my umbrella. Or rather"—her eyes flicked past Jeremy to meet those of Roy Roydon—"your friend—although of course . . ." She blushed, wondering if her desire for accuracy had made her sound rude. She hoped not. She smiled again. "So very kind, even if there was no time to introduce ourselves properly. That is . . ."

Lady Colveden stepped promptly into the protocol breach. "Miss Emily Seeton—Jeremy Froste, the television producer, and his colleagues, Miss Broomfield and . . ." This was more awkward, since she couldn't recall the other's name.

"My . . . associate," supplied Jeremy, doing his own bit of breach-filling. "Roy Roydon—the reporter, you know. Roy is researching"—a smirk—"an in-depth article about me for the national press."

"A newspaper reporter?" Miss Seeton's eyes brightened at the recognition. It wasn't that she cared whether Jeremy had a dozen in-depth articles written about him, but . . . "I do beg your pardon—but you must have thought me very foolish," she said to Rodney, who was nodding still at Jeremy's elbow, saying little. "Not to have known who you were, that is—although admittedly she was in something of a hurry at the time, after the trip from Town—to go in to dinner, which would explain why she forgot—dear Mel, I mean. To explain in her turn, that is."

Rodney blinked. Jeremy frowned—though with caution: creases made him look older. Bethan and Lady Colveden tried—successfully—to hide their smiles.

"Amelita Forby," went on Miss Seeton, with affectionate pride. "She writes for the *Daily Negative*, as of course you know—but then you could hardly be expected to know, could you?" She saw Rodney's mouth fall open, and hastened to enlighten him. Lady Colveden, who could guess what manner of convoluted simplification was coming, hid another smile—of compassion for Miss Seeton's innocent audience.

"That it had been arranged, I mean—for you to interview me," said Miss Seeton, as Rodney continued to stare at her in some consternation. "At home, after your official part, if one may so describe it, in Mr. Froste's affairs was over—because of course it wasn't, when one thinks about it—that is," and she lowered her voice, belatedly mindful of the need for caution, "undercover," with a meaningful nod, "as I understand the term to be. So very expressive." Rodney's eyes had started to glaze over; Jeremy Froste was likewise blank of face; Bethan had turned pale. Oblivious, Miss Seeton babbled on.

"From the films, of course, although spies are not my favourites, generally speaking. And not exactly official, in this case, since Scotland Yard—or at least," remembering Mel's remarks about her chat with Delphick after the press conference, "not yet—but Mr. Brinton, or I suppose I should rather say Superintendent Brinton . . ."

"I believe," broke in Lady Colveden, taking pity on the bemused trio forced to suffer Miss Seeton's serpentine explanation, "that they may be about to open the hall at last. You'll find it interesting, I expect, Mr. Froste. While Miss Seeton"—with a smile of apology to her friend for having interrupted her—"may not have been, um, allowed to exhibit any of her garden produce, there are sure to be plenty of other apples for you to look at."

Her guess had been correct: with a creak and a rattle, the door swung open, and everyone shuffled their feet, hoping to be among the first inside.

"I look forward to it," said Jeremy, recovering himself more readily than either Bethan or Rodney. "Failing the Peculier, one could always fall back on hops, or cherries—the wrong time of year, I know, for cherries, but . . . "

"And for hops," said Miss Seeton, with a smile. Jeremy and his companions, who naturally knew about hop-picking and the annual autumnal invasion of the Cockneys, decided now that the old lady must really be as muddled as they had suspected. "If one plans," she went on, "to eat them, that is, rather than dry them for making beer. They can be cooked—the young shoots, with butter, in the spring. Rather like asparagus, I understand."

"And very tasty they are," agreed Lady Colveden, who had caught the quick exchange of glances among the strangers, and was indignant on her friend's behalf. "However, you'll be wanting to hurry off in search of your elusive apple, no doubt, Mr. Froste. Don't let me keep you. Miss Seeton," turning away with a cool smile from a startled Jeremy, "you must come with me and be moral support for George and the admiral—the honey, you know. George is so looking forward to next season . . . "

Chattering, curious, excited, the Plummergenites moved into the hall, followed by Murreystone in combative mood. The judges' decision in the matter of the marrows was not, Murreystone felt, likely to meet with the outsiders' total approval—but the day was not yet over. There were other surprises up the collective Murreystone sleeve . . .

"Really, it's too bad!" The decision of the judges was being questioned in other quarters, closer to home. "Eric, it's simply not fair—after all your hard work, ending up without even a Highly Commended." Mrs. Blaine waxed loyally indignant on behalf of Miss Nuttel, who kept a stiff upper lip with some success. Only Bunny's outburst had let anyone know just how disappointed she was that her leeks had won not a single ribbon.

"And to give the First Prize for preserves," moaned Mrs. Blaine, "to That Man, of all people!" Those about her who recognised the Nutty nomenclature for Admiral Leighton gathered round to listen. "Too unfair, when nobody else in the area keeps bees. And simply everyone makes jam—though it isn't sour grapes on my part, Eric"—Mrs. Blaine's marmalade had been as uncommended as Miss Nuttel's leeks—"it's just a strong feeling of community spirit, that's all, and giving first prize to someone's honey doesn't strike me as being—well, it's simply too unfair. Heaven only knows how he managed it, when he hasn't been in the village five minutes—oh, Eric!" Frightened eyes were fastened on Miss Nuttel, still stiff-upper-lipping and silent. "Eric! Too dreadful—what did I just say? *Heaven* only knows—or—or . . . ?"

Mrs. Blaine could not force her tongue to frame the fearful words. Miss Nuttel, throwing back her head, braced herself. "Not that long," she brought out, through faltering lips, "till . . . till Halloween, remember."

"Oh, Eric!" Blackcurrant eyes glittered with terrified realisation. "Eric, let's go home—too dreadful even to think about—and I don't feel well anyway, with all the noise and worry and disappointment." Her gaze swept the hall, seeing nobody. "And it makes me too uneasy, Eric, being alone and unprotected like this—well, being so far from home." Two hundred yards loomed in the general consciousness as two thousand miles. Mrs. Blaine wafted a plump hand to her brow. "Eric, I'm sure I've got one of my heads coming on . . ."

Mrs. Blaine's headaches were a Lilikot legend. Miss Nuttel, already troubled more than she cared to admit by the failure of her leeks, felt she could cope with no more just now. "Home, Bunny," she said, without hesitation. "Cup of chamomile tea, and you'll soon be better. Won't bother"—glancing at the clock—"staying for the conkers—"

"I should think not!" Mrs. Blaine shuddered artistically. "The noise—with my head . . ."

And the Nuts, without a backward look, passed slowly from the village hall through a throng of fascinated observers they still did not allow themselves to see.

Yet not everyone was fascinated by their passage. Jeremy Froste was engaged in earnest conversation with Rodney Roydon; Bethan Broomfield was making ever more notes in her book; those who had won prizes were exulting over those who had not, while those who had not voiced their displeasure, with some force, and cast numerous aspersions at the probity and likely genealogy of the judges, from either village. PC Potter stood, ever-vigilant, on the stage, clearly visible to one and all, his buttons bright with admonition, his truncheon a reminder that good behaviour was required.

The first thrilling moments over, the hubbub in the hall subsided as people began totting up whether Plummergen or Murreystone had the higher score of stickers, ribbons, and rosettes. The coveted cups waited, gleaming softly silver, on the green baize-covered table beside the watchful Potter. In such a crowd, it was not easy even to estimate which side might be ahead. Larger persons always seemed to block the view of shorter individuals, particularly if those individuals chanced to hail from the opposing village. There was a strong suspicion that Plummergen was in the lead, but this triumph—if, indeed, triumph it was—could yet become dust and ashes . . .

The general prize-giving would not take place until after the Grand Conker Contest, climax of the afternoon's activities. Watches began to be checked against the hall clock, and mutterings were heard as it was thought About Time to be Getting On with the Show, and Why Was Nobody Doing Anything?

It fell to Sir George, in conference with the leader of the Murreystone team, to announce that play would begin once a suitable space had been cleared below the stage. The Show Committee had deliberately left this part of the hall free of tables, so if everyone would kindly move to one side . . .

A coin was produced, examined for two heads, and agreed—reluctantly—as the genuine article. Jack Crabbe was the first Plummergenite into the ring, followed by his opponent, a weasel-faced little man with a leathery skin and sharp, darting eyes. There were sniggers from the Plummergen spectators as they saw that the conker dangling from the string in his hand was a cheeser, one of the awkward, wedge-shaped nuts produced when two or more horse chestnuts developed inside the same prickly husk.

The coin was tossed: the Murreystone weasel, as the visitor, called—and lost. Jack Crabbe grunted, and took up his position.

"Ibbley obbley onker, my first conker," he said, using the ritual challenge. "Ibbley obbley oh, my first go!"

The Weasel duly held up his conker, dangling from its string a foot below his hand. Jack, concentration in every inch of his body, swung his own conker around and down with a whistling motion to strike—to miss!—the other.

Plummergen sighed, but said nothing: a would-be conqueror was allowed three attempts before the turn of his opponent came. Jack swung again, and this time his aim was true. The Weasel's cheeser was struck and sent spinning, swinging on its string—but it was unbroken, without even a chip out of its shiny brown skin.

"Third strike, and last," said Sir George, as Jack shook his head over a small dent, a sliver of creamy white showing through. Frowning, the Plummergen opener prepared for his third attempt.

"Strings!" Both men cried out at almost the same time, as Jack missed his mark and his conker, speeding through the air, tangled with the Weasel's string in a spinning spiral. There was a roar of disapproval from Plummergen as the Murreystone umpire tried to suggest that the Weasel had called first: Sir George was firm that Jack's voice had—just—been heard before the other. Bowing to the majority opinion, Murreystone told the Weasel to play on . . .

Jack's free blow scored another direct hit, but still did not shatter the cheeser. With a nod to his opponent, the Plummergen player held up his conker and waited for the Weasel's attack.

Strike one: another dent in Jack's conker. Strike two: the previous split widened, though examination of the Weasel's cheeser showed a split of equal size on the rounded side. Strike three: a portion of Jack's nut broke off and fell to the ground.

First blood to Murreystone. A muted roar of triumph, an exchange of knowing looks. Jack Crabbe's turn to strike . . .

It was more than five minutes before the Weasel struck the winning blow. The sharp, wedged end of his cheeser made a lucky connection with a weakened hollow in Jack's conker, which had already lost several chunks of various sizes. Now it shattered into so many pieces that the string could no longer hold it, and what was left of it fell to the floor.

There was a yell of triumph. "Cracketts! Cracketts! First round to Murreystone!"

"A oncer!" cried the Weasel, holding up his battered nut with a grin as he made the traditional boast, then retired to join his friends so that the second bout could begin.

Each village fielded a team of eight. By a complicated process of scoring, of challenges issued by winning conkers to winners from other rounds, a clear victor would eventually emerge; and this victory was no mean achievement. Cheating and chicanery were attempted by both sides at every turn, and the umpires had a difficult task. They must do far more than keep score. A sneakily mis-aimed blow could land on an opponent's hand rather than on his conker, and force him to withdraw from the contest. Umpirical eyes must stay alert for substitution: a handkerchief produced from a careless pocket to wipe a heated brow, a new lease of life in an otherwise dilapidated weapon . . .

There were age-old ways of improving conkers long before the battle began in earnest. Certain horse chestnut trees were regularly fed throughout the year with the slops from beer-barrels, and from failed attempts at homemade wine. Frost and high winds in spring were dreaded, lest the flowery spires should fail; summer rain was welcomed as swelling the immature seed. Once fallen from their spiny husks, the conkers were eagerly appropriated for treatment. Some swore that repeated passage through the digestive tract of a pig—purists considered Gloucester Old Spots the preferred breed—hardened a nut to perfection. Others claimed that overnight baking in a low oven, coupled with prolonged soaking in pickling vinegar, would guarantee a champion . . .

It had been their children's playground success with Miss Seeton's version of Miss Wicks's formula which encouraged the men of Plummergen to perform their own experiments. Their wives might denounce it as a witch's brew; their husbands maintained that Murreystone was the devil's own place, and it took fire to fight fire. Mr. Stillman's stock of salt prunella, saltpetre, and bay salt was quickly exhausted, and those demanding the white vinegar their reluctant wives remembered Miss Seeton as having bought were informed that it must be malt, or nothing, for at least another week. Even for the sake of village pride, Mr. Stillman was unable to collect his order from the warehouse earlier than that—and telephoning it through for immediate delivery wouldn't work, because they didn't. Deliver, he meant. And they wouldn't accept an order from anyone unauthorised, so it was no use nagging him, he'd done his best . . .

And Plummergen sentiment had come to believe that indeed he had. The fearful smells in kitchens and sheds the length of The Street had faded; the butcher had received his fresh consignment of metal skewers; the draper's and the post office were well-supplied with string. Plummergen was convinced it was on the road to success . . .

So why, now, was success proving so elusive?

CHAPTER 28

It was when the gloating cry of "A niner!" went up that Plummergen began to suspect Murreystone of more than usually dastardly doings. Niners, naturally, were not unknown during the conker season; they were not unknown during a match such as today's; but for one to appear so soon . . .

The contest continued, bout by bout. Conkers shattered to cracketts, and a forfeit was added as each new nut was brought into the fray. Murreystone edged slowly ahead, each chalked-up win another blow for disillusioned Plummergen. Murreystone chuckled, and sneered at its rivals with as much emphasis as the umpires would permit.

It was Nigel Colveden, when his turn came to risk making the Murreystone niner a tenner, who solved the mystery. Nigel, Plummergen cricket team's best bat, was blessed with an excellent eye for all games. While working farmers had little time for sport, young Mr. Colveden—like most males—could not resist the lure of smooth, shining, richly brown conkers, the excuse to revert to childhood in challenging the foe to single, dramatic combat. With the eyes of Bethan Broomfield, among others, upon him, he had swung and struck at his opponent's nuts in skilful fashion, and had rejoiced to win his bouts after comparatively few strikes.

Now his conker's latest innings brought him face to face

with the hitherto victorious niner, still as smooth, shining, and richly brown as it had ever been. The Murreystone man, a noted poacher—PC Potter, among others, had been after him for years, with absolutely no success—suppressed a smirk as Nigel prepared to receive the first strike.

"Ibbley obbley onker, my first conker. Ibbley obbley oh, my first go." The poacher gabbled the challenge, and swung before Nigel could even blink, chipping a small piece out of the already-battered Plummergen nut and almost dashing the string from young Mr. Colveden's hands.

Nigel winced, but said nothing, waiting for strike the second. The poacher leered, and swung again. Again Nigel's conker was chipped—a larger piece this time. Nigel stared in some dismay, comparing the damage suffered by his nut to that of the Murreystone niner: which was none.

None at all. Nigel frowned . . .

"Third strike to come," warned the umpire, as Nigel continued to frown. He jerked out of his trance, nodded, and stood ready, arm outstretched, conker dangling.

The poacher, grinning, struck again.

"Strings!" cried Nigel, as the conkers embraced.

"Foul!" cried the poacher, at exactly the same time. "He moved!"

"A cheat! A cheat!" The cry went up from Murreystone as Sir George, unable to believe the evidence of his eyes, gazed at his son in stupefaction. Lady Colveden held her breath; Miss Seeton clicked her tongue. Bethan Broomfield was so excited that she forgot to make any notes.

Nigel's grip fastened on his string, and he yanked at it suddenly before the poacher could disentangle his own. With a yelp of surprise, the poacher watched his conker flash out of his hand and into Nigel's . . .

"A cheat," said Nigel grimly, holding up the Murreystone conker beside his own. "A cheat—I cry foul!" He had to raise his voice above the growing hubbub; he had to take a mighty backward leap as the poacher sprang towards him, bent on wresting his conker from his opponent's grasp.

"A foul!" came Nigel's breathless cry from the safety

of the stage, beside PC Potter. "A foul—this isn't a conker! This is—this is a *stone*!"

Uproar, as his words reached Plummergen ears and Murreystone attempted to deny the truth of the charge. Umpire Sir George, as grim now as his son, marched up the steps to take the disputed niner from Nigel's hand. PC Potter, with truncheon raised, stood ready to repel any attempt at rescue and disposal of the evidence ...

The evidence (announced the magistrate, after a few moments' scrutiny) was undeniable. One member—at least one, he amended in ominous tones—of the Murreystone team had brought the noble sport of conkers into disrepute by deliberately disguising a stone of suitable size—cutting, honing, painting, and polishing—as an ordinary nut, and daring to enter it as such. Disqualification (went on Sir George) was the very least penalty that could be imposed ...

The ensuing fisticuffs were (everyone afterwards agreed) far less vehement than on many previous occasions of discord and dispute between the two villages. It was not thought necessary to summon Dr. Knight and his colleagues from the nearby nursing home; nobody (not even the Murreystone poacher) was arrested by PC Potter, though there were several near misses; nothing of great value was smashed within the hall, and no real damage was done outside it. Jack Crabbe, Nigel, and the rest of the team acquitted themselves well: the power of a righteous wrath meant that they hardly needed their friends to assist them in the justifiable trouncing of the opposition. Such assistance, however, was more than freely offered, to the accompaniment of cheers from many of the female onlookers, who hurled into the fray not themselves, but assorted missiles in the form of various fruits, flowers, and vegetables from the display tables ranged about the hall.

Not everyone was so bloodthirsty, though even Lady Colveden, beating a prudent retreat with Miss Seeton, had to admit that it did serve Murreystone right. To substitute a stone for a conker was, well, was ...

"Hardly cricket," supplied Miss Seeton, who had not forgotten similar skullduggery on the occasion of the recent match. A fleeing figure hurtled past, pursued by a vengeful blur. Miss Seeton ignored both as she and her ladyship continued on their way out of the hall. "One understands, naturally, that there are what may be called *legitimate* means of ensuring victory—dear Miss Wicks, the children were so pleased—but in this particular instance, though of course one must deplore the strength"—as an agonised yell indicated further damage inflicted on the foe—"of the—the protest, or perhaps one should say of the *response*"—as a potato flew past—"it must be said that there was, unfortunately, a considerable degree of provocation."

A bunch of grapes splattered on the floor at Miss Seeton's feet, splashing stickily. Calmly, she unhooked her umbrella from her arm and opened it, inviting Lady Colveden to share its shelter. A vase of chrysanthemums shattered on the wall above their heads, spraying water in every direction. Flowers fell on the black silk of the brolly; Miss Seeton, with a practised twirl, shook them off, with the accompanying drops of water, and made her way through the door at a speedy, yet still dignified, pace.

Outside, it seemed that the weather was about to become as stormy as the atmosphere inside the hall. Thick, grey clouds loomed low overhead, and a stiff breeze had arisen. Those who had escaped the battle within huddled together under the porch, debating what to do next.

"Would it, I wonder," ventured Miss Seeton, "be thought an impertinence if one were to telephone the police? Since Mr. Potter is already present, that is, and might be annoyed if the impression should be given that one thought him incapable of controlling . . . of preventing . . ."

"I don't honestly think," said Lady Colveden, "anyone could do much, um, preventing until things have calmed down a little." Her sudden giggle was as suddenly suppressed. "Goodness, that sounds positively slanderous about poor Mr. Potter, because he's certainly more than capable—but you know what I mean, I'm sure. Quite apart from the fact it's bound to be all over by the time anyone could reach us from Ashford or wherever, if they're allowed to let most of the steam out of their systems now, it will stop it bottling up inside them and, well, boiling out later when—and where nobody's expecting it, which could be a great deal worse—though I imagine George will want to keep the Village Watch on patrol for a few nights more, to be on the safe side. As for now—well, it's not as if''— another giggle—''they aren't used to this sort of thing, is it?''

''A safety valve,'' said Miss Seeton, with a sigh, and a regretful nod. ''It is, however, hardly the sort of example one would really wish one's pupils to be set—seeing their elders incapable of controlling their emotions, and indulging in such very . . . undignified behaviour—''

She broke off with a blush. Was not Lady Colveden's son foremost among the Plummergen warriors? Did not her husband appear to be overseeing the battle from the stage, with the admiral—who had hurried to join his friend—and PC Potter at his side? She had intended no disrespect by her remark—Lady Colveden must not think—

''I'm not thinking,'' said Lady Colveden, ''anything of the sort, and even if I were, I know exactly what you mean. So please don't worry about it, Miss Seeton.''

''Miss Seeton?'' It was Jeremy Froste, one of the few males—his perpetual shadow Rodney Roydon was another—to be outside the hall rather than in. Doubtless it had been concern for the safety of Bethan, wide-eyed and breathless, which brought the pair hurrying through the door to the open air, free from flying fists, fruit, vegetables, and vases. ''Miss Seeton? I imagine you must be a very disappointed lady right now.''

''Disappointed?'' Miss Seeton blinked. ''I hardly see . . . That is, certainly, one cannot *condone* such behaviour— but, as I was saying just now, one can, to some extent, *sympathise*—and, as her ladyship has remarked, it is perhaps better for them to have a—an immediate release for their feelings rather than to bottle them up for release at a . . . an even less appropriate time. It is hardly,'' with a faint smile, ''as if this is the first occasion on which there has been a disagreement of so—so forceful a nature. Three hundred years,'' Miss Seeton pointed out, ''is a not inconsiderable period over which feelings of rivalry may develop, wouldn't you agree?''

The producer of historical docudramas brightened. "You mean they've been slugging it out around here for three centuries? Over *conkers*? Bethan—make a note!"

He had no real need to issue the instruction: his assistant was already delving into her handbag. Miss Seeton, after a quick look at Lady Colveden, hid a smile and murmured of the Civil War, adding the rider that she believed the *very* first intimation that the two villages did not see eye-to-eye on politics—a topic about which a great many people found it hard to remain . . . well, entirely rational—had occurred during the Wars of the Roses . . .

"The Red Rose and the White," said Jeremy Froste, dreaming up titles. Rodney and Bethan gazed at him with awe. Miss Seeton and Lady Colveden gazed at him with polite interest. "York and Lancaster—five hundred years of strife from then till now—oh, we could do a wonderful programme!" as the crashes and yells from inside the hall found an echo in a roll of distant thunder. "Talk about living history—these people *do*! They *are*!"

So Descartean—and so very audible—a conclusion to his raptures made some of Jeremy's more distant audience stare. Others, not necessarily out of sight, shook their heads or tapped knowing fingers against their temples. For one reason or another, various Plummergen factions had been unable to allow themselves to fall beneath the producer's spell. They freely admitted they'd never *quite* known why: well, now they did. The man was obviously mad. And the fact that Miss Seeton, of all people, was happily talking to him—Lady Colveden's presence was excused on the grounds of sharing Miss Seeton's umbrella, with it looking like rain coming on—only made it worse . . .

"We'll need," said Jeremy, "a theme—a symbol . . . ." He raised his eyes to the cloudy heavens, then clicked his fingers as inspiration struck. "Bethan, make a note—the conkers! The chivalric tradition—jousting and conquest and single combat—games of skill replace hand-to-hand fighting . . . Would they set up a replay of the match if we asked, do you think? Miss Seeton—your secret formula." Miss Seeton blinked at him. Before she could explain that it had been Miss Wicks who supplied the recipe, and that to call it *secret,* since she'd gladly shared it with an entire class of children, was perhaps something of an exaggeration, he hurried on:

"Would you let us film you mixing the stuff, or whatever you do with it? Age-old recipe, passed down through the generations—traditional costume—now, how about that for an in-depth interview!" Miss Seeton looked considerably startled. Jeremy waved a hand, dismissing what he believed her fears to be. "We'd pay for the ingredients, of course—like I said, you must be really disappointed not to have had the chance to see your side win with your help, but if we can persuade them—and I can't see why they wouldn't want to do it all again—"

There was a sudden outcry from within, which should have suggested to the meanest intelligence that whatever experience currently being undergone by the outcriers was not one they would willingly—even for the sake of a television programme—undergo again. Jeremy Froste ignored it, looking eagerly at Miss Seeton, who blinked again, and sighed.

"As to the matter of *interviews,* I had rather thought—a newspaper reporter, not television . . . " A pucker appeared between her brows. "When it is a police matter, of course, one should hardly hesitate, but—"

A louder, closer outcry, and an eruption of high-speed Murreystone, pursued by triumphant Plummergen and a selection of airborne foodstuffs. Lady Colveden, Bethan, and Rodney Roydon uttered little cries of alarm, and stepped back; Miss Seeton, her brow still puckered, stepped nimbly to one side as Jeremy jumped to the other, disappearing from his view behind a phalanx of excited bodies—and, as the phalanx moved speedily onward, behind older, slower bodies only slightly less excited.

"George!" Lady Colveden caught her husband's sleeve as he and the admiral, surveying the rout, seemed on the point of following it. "I won't ask what on earth's been going on, because I know very well, but is Nigel all right? Where is he? I didn't see him come out, although there was such a crowd I might have missed him . . . ''

But by the time Sir George had allayed his wife's understandable apprehensions, it was Miss Seeton who was missing.

They had not heard her murmured farewells above the growing confusion of explanation and coagulation—the explanation coming from Sir George, staunchly seconded by Admiral Leighton, and the coagulation being that of the crowd, as the rain began at last to fall. Everyone within range at once hastened back to huddle in the shelter of the hall doorway, and Lady Colveden, standing on the top step, saw over the tops of the approaching heads the familiar sight of a black, bobbing circle opening above a small female form trotting off southwards down The Street.

"There! When I'd promised poor Miss Seeton a lift home. It really is too bad of you, George, now it's raining—and of you, Nigel," as the Colveden son and heir came to join his parents. "Nigel!"

Nigel essayed a careless shrug and brushed raindrops from his thick, wavy brown hair. "A black eye—I've had worse, at rugger. And you should see the other chap." He spoke to his mother, but his words were for Bethan, hovering nearby. "Serves the blighters right—stones, indeed!"

Jeremy Froste, who seldom missed much, insinuated himself, with a smile, into the conversation, followed—as ever—by his faithful attendants. "Ah, yes—Mr. Colveden, you were the one who spotted the substitution, weren't you? I should think that against stones, even Miss Seeton's magic potions would have little effect."

He was so intent—as he often was—on the sound of his own voice that he failed to notice the reaction wrought by his words among openly eavesdropping Plummergen. Miss Seeton? Magic potions? Hadn't they said the man was up to no good—and didn't this just prove it? And those who had gone so far as to welcome Jeremy Froste, Bethan and—either with the others, or in their wake—Rodney Roydon into their homes, began to wish, very much, that they hadn't.

"I don't suppose," said Jeremy, with a winning smile, "you happen to know what the stuff's made of? Bethan, you might take a note of what Nigel—if I may?—says," as Mr. Colveden, conscious that Murreystone ears might just be lurking in unnoticed corners, hesitated.

Village loyalty prevailed. Nigel smiled apologetically. "Oh, all sorts," he said, trying to look as if such farming aids as chemical sprays and artificial fertilisers were utterly beyond him. "A pinch of this, a dollop of that—you know how these old recipes are handed down. Sorry not to be more helpful—but I heard someone say something about pickling spices, if that's any use. You'll have to ask Miss Seeton herself . . ."

And Nigel wished him joy of the enquiry.

Miss Seeton had been only too relieved, while listening to the proposals of Jeremy Froste, to recall her promise to Miss Wicks that she would drop in for tea, to report on the success (or otherwise) of the conker mixture against the Murreystone nuts. When dear Mel—and how strange that she had not been present at this afternoon's . . . Miss Seeton, groping for a suitable word, found herself suppressing a chuckle . . . this afternoon's *event*—which, though shocking in some ways, was sufficiently unusual, one would have supposed, to attract the interest of one who wrote a—a syndicated column about village doings, which was very popular, so one gathered, and which had contributed greatly to Mel's success . . . when Mel had explained that it would be most helpful to the police if one were to permit a reporter to conduct an interview at home, in one's sitting-room, among all dear Cousin Flora's pretty ornaments (and certainly there had been no talk whatsoever of the kitchen, which is where the mixture would naturally have to be mixed—or, far worse, of *costume:* it sounded uneasily as if one had been roped, after all, against one's will into taking an active part in the proposed Christmas pantomime, instead of designing scenery and prompting, as one would prefer) . . . when dear Mel had, as it were, set the scene, one had understood—not that one would dream of suggesting that Mel had deliberately misled, but . . . though perhaps, in the undoubted confusion, she had not so much misremembered Mel as misunderstood Mr. Froste—whose evident enthusiasm . . .

''Oh!'' Outside Ararat Cottage, Miss Seeton jumped, completely losing her train of thought as something small, brown, and squeaking shot from the admiral's hedge near her feet, hotly pursued by a huge, spitting streak of furious feline fur. ''Oh, dear—no . . . ''

It was widely known that remonstrance was seldom of any avail with little Amelia Potter's notorious tabby cat. Cat? The superstitious held that Tibs metamorphosed, at the full moon, into—a werewolf being too much even for Plummergen to credit—the tigress rumoured to play so large a part in her genetic makeup. At such times, insisted Plummergen, the tiger-cat from the police house would scorn the more usual mice, voles, or rabbits in favour of dogs, sheep, and even badgers . . .

''Stop it!'' Miss Seeton, far too sensible for superstition, brandished her umbrella in the direction of imminent bloodshed. ''Shoo!''

While Tibs had so far managed to ignore the current downpour in the excitement of the chase, it was less easy to ignore the huge, heavy drops being deliberately shaken on an already sodden coat. She glared round, growling, as the brolly loomed closer, and Miss Seeton's shrill command came again.

''Shoo! Leave that poor mouse alone this minute!''

Such was the power of a voice trained over many years in pedagogic projection that Tibs, although protesting, with a hiss and a final growl allowed herself to be shooed, whiskers dripping, away. The mouse, its tiny frame quivering, ventured to open its eyes; saw that its tormentor was gone; and bolted, with a flurry of its tail, back to the shelter of the admiral's hedge.

Miss Seeton sighed with relief as she watched it scurry to safety before herself trotting once more on her way. The poor little thing. It was, of course, a household pest; but one could not help feeling sorry—especially in the rain—for any small creature being chased by one so much larger. She sighed again and paused to contemplate a puddle, on the surface of which a pleasing pattern of interlocking rain-drop ripples was repeatedly being formed. One might almost feel sorry, indeed, for oneself, if such a sentiment did not seem a little . . . self-indulgent; exaggerated. To see oneself as the prey, as it were, of what in so many respects one could not help but regard as vulgar interest . . . And yet it was undeniably the duty of a gentlewoman—especially one who had what must be termed a professional relation-ship with the police—to assist them as far as possible . . .

An interview. In one's home. With photographs of one's possessions. To be on show, in the public eye—which was so very far removed from one's normal sphere . . . Another sigh, so gusty that ripples became waves. One would, of course, do one's duty. A hostess, no matter how reluctant, had her obligations. The best china; tea and biscuits; maybe—the ultimate sacrifice—some of Martha's fruit-cake . . .

"Tea!" exclaimed Miss Seeton. "Cake! Oh, dear—Miss Wicks . . . " And she promptly left the puddle to its own devices, holding her umbrella firmly as, having checked carefully in both directions for traffic, she crossed The Street and headed for the post office.

She did not do so unobserved. "Bunny!" Miss Nuttel raised the alarm. "Bunny—quick! That Woman . . . "

She needed to say no more. Mrs. Blaine, lying down with her headache, was off the sofa, up the stairs, and along the landing as fast as plump legs would carry her. "What is it, Eric? What's she done now? Oh, tell me the worst—don't keep me in suspense!"

"Staring," said Miss Nuttel, who for the life of her couldn't conceive why Miss Seeton—why anyone—should wish to stand in the pouring rain, umbrella or no umbrella, and gaze for so long at the ground without moving. It wasn't anything she, for one, would ever do—which opinion she offered to Mrs. Blaine, who agreed that Eric was too right, nobody but Miss Seeton would ever dream of it.

"Waved her umbrella first," said Miss Nuttel. "Then stood and *stared*. Went galloping over to Mr. Stillman's in the end," she concluded grimly. "Must have realised I'd spotted her. But . . . " Neither Nut cared to confess to ignorance, even to the other. "Bunny," Miss Nuttel said, coaxing, encouraging, "you don't suppose . . . ?"

It was encouragement enough, and to spare. Theorising on the flimsiest of evidence was a Nutty speciality. "Yes, Eric, I do," replied Mrs. Blaine, her headache forgotten. "Especially this near to Halloween. Remember, when we caught her buying that besom, and those terrible powders— too dreadful that Mr. Stillman would even think of stocking such things—but perhaps it all depends on how you mix them together, and *normal* people," with a delighted shudder, "will be perfectly safe, because they wouldn't know how. I mean—I'm sure *I* don't know . . . and neither do you."

"No," agreed Miss Nuttel, a little miffed Bunny hadn't used a more definite tone to express her vote of confidence. Mrs. Blaine went on hastily:

"If it weren't raining so hard—you know I was sneezing this morning, and it's too risky, if I catch a cold, and it goes to my chest—though perhaps, Eric," as Miss Nuttel was moved to expostulate, "I could *stretch a point,* at a time like this. Right outside our house, you said? Too sinister—she must," moaned Mrs. Blaine, "have been *casting spells.*" And Miss Nuttel heaved a sigh of relief that the mystery had been solved without her having confessed to anything. She ventured, indeed, to enlarge on the solution.

"Not *quite* outside," she said, in ominous tones; and her head jerked grimly sideways in the direction of Ararat Cottage. "Not outside *here*, I mean . . . "

"Oh, Eric!" Mrs. Blaine licked pale lips. "Those flags he was flying . . . "

"Signals," said Miss Nuttel.

Mrs. Blaine went white. "Oh, Eric—right next door to us! What shall we do?"

"Go shopping," said Miss Nuttel bravely. Mrs. Blaine, her eyes bright, after a moment's pause decided to follow her leader.

"You're right, of course, Eric. That Woman's probably in there *this minute*—"

"She is," interposed Miss Nuttel.

"—buying more gunpowder," groaned Mrs. Blaine, "and—and," as even her imagination failed, "and just let me put my mackintosh on, and my gumboots . . ."

By the time that Mrs. Blaine had wrapped her scarf twice around her neck, had found her low-brimmed rubber hat, and had in every way rendered herself proof against the weather, Miss Nuttel could have been three times across the road and back. She said so, with some force. She added that she had a very good mind to go without Bunny, and let her come after—except that she knew Bunny would never dare go into Mr. Stillman's shop unprotected—

"Protection! Herbs!" babbled Mrs. Blaine, scurrying off to the kitchen and returning with a handful of dried wither, as recommended in *Ghosts and Go-Betweens* as a safeguard against Evil Powers. "Eric—in your pocket, do!" And Miss Nuttel promptly did.

Thus rendered invulnerable, the Nuts finally made it out of their front door and down the path. Miss Nuttel pointed out that it was no longer raining. Mrs. Blaine complained of feeling stifled in this rig—of her headache returning . . .

And then they saw Miss Seeton, her furled umbrella over her arm, on the point of closing the post office door, pausing to hold it politely open for the benefit of another customer. The two exchanged words. The Nuts could not hear what was said, but Rodney Roydon—for it was he—was seen to nod, and to stare thoughtfully after Miss Seeton as she left him before, with a curious expression on his face, he hurried into the post office, leaving the door ajar.

It was a matter of seconds before the Nuts were crowding through that same door, their ears flapping. They might now be too late to find out what Miss Seeton had been buying—though it is doubtful whether even they would have regarded the purchase of a packet of Earl Grey tea and a madeira cake, which Miss Seeton had promised Miss Wicks she would bring, as being of earth-shattering importance—but it was obvious she had passed instructions to her hench-man, which would surely be proof enough. Everyone knew that the Roydon man, following him everywhere, did ex-actly what Jeremy Froste told him. Those television people were as bad as reporters, always looking to make a story out of something. The chance to film a genuine witches' sabbath on Halloween was one no producer would want to miss, but for the sake of his career, of his image, he couldn't do the dirty work himself . . .

"Calcium carbide?" Mr. Stillman was saying, as Miss Nuttel and Mrs. Blaine hurried to place themselves well within earshot, but out of sight. "Yes, we've a tidy amount of that, with everyone clearing their own moles now, in-stead of getting it done official."

This reference to the village's disgraced mole catcher, Jacob Chickney, seemed to be lost on Rodney, though the Nuts understood it well. *Poison* . . .

"A—a large tin, please," said Rodney. "And—and a small tin of—of black treacle—"

Muted sensation among those out of sight.

"—and some matches . . . and a box of wax candles."

Which sebaceous conclusion of the Roydon shopping list resulted in a further sensation that was far from muted—very far indeed.

Because Mrs. Blaine, with a squeal of horror, fainted.

The midnight sky was clear above the whole of southern England, and there was a crispness in the air which was echoed in the faint crystal powdering of frost, first of the season, faintly glittering beneath the gibbous moon.

In a sleepy Home Counties town, a police patrol car sat stationary under a streetlamp, its engine mute, its lights off. Only the agitated glimmer of a small torch, waving in front of the dashboard, proved that the panda was occupied.

"You need a screwdriver to fix that," said Police Con-stable 1234 Hatfield. It was the seventh time he had made precisely the same point.

"If you tell me that again," said Police Constable 9876 Heath, "I'll knock your ruddy block off! If you know so much about it, how come you can't fix it?"

"I didn't break it."

This was undeniable. It was also unhelpful. "Could've happened to anyone," said Heath, hopefully, as he probed yet again with his ballpoint pen in the depths of the broken radio. The vinegar-soaked chip remained stubbornly where it had landed, a silent witness of the constable's unexpected sneeze in the middle of an illicit snack.

"That the argument you're going to try out back at the station?" Hatfield chuckled maliciously. "Better practise a bit before you do—you wouldn't sell a fridge to an eskimo sounding like *that*."

"Talking of eskimos"—Heath suddenly straightened, and switched off his torch in despair—"it's getting chilly." He shivered artistically. "What say we give this up as a bad job, and get back on patrol? We could at least have the heater on, with the engine running. It's only another"—he held his wrist to the streetlamp's glow—"ten minutes or so till we clock off. It's not as if things have been all that lively tonight, is it?"

"Apart from you busting the radio, you mean."

"Apart from me busting the radio," agreed Heath, groping again for the torch, and wondering whether a brief outburst of assault and battery could be thought justified, in the circumstances. He sighed, and decided it couldn't. He put the torch down with a clatter. "Come on—let's get going," he begged. "Another ten minutes, and we can roll this lot up for the night and go home. I mean, what's going to happen round here, in the middle of the night?"

In the midnight sky above Plummergen, the gibbous moon shone down on the sleeping fields, the lampless street, the darkened houses. No wind stirred the frost-bright air, the silent, bare-branched trees; the only signs of movement were the occasional swooping owl, its prey the scuttering mouse, the frightened vole. In their frantic flight, they ran through fallen leaves, their passage marked by dry whispers echoing, echoing through the otherwise peaceful night . . .

Until that peace was disturbed by the padding of furtive feet. A shadowy form—human, muffled against the chance of recognition—came creeping between the moonlit dark towards the cottage at the southern end of The Street—the cottage on that corner where The Street narrowed to cross the canal bridge—where it turned right into Marsh Road.

The cottage where Miss Seeton lived.

Sweetbriars . . .

The muffled figure, its pockets suspiciously a-bulge, set its hand on Miss Seeton's front gate—hesitated—and lifted the latch. There came a click, clear on the frosty air. The figure held its breath . . .

In her bedroom, Miss Seeton's breath came regular and soft. She did not stir.

In her front garden, the figure began a steady progress up the path, flinching as a moth flickered before its—his? hers? impossible, through the muffling, to tell—face. The moth, made far larger by fear and the illusive silver light, flew on.

An owl hooted overhead; a fox, in a distant field, barked. A rabbit squealed.

The figure, frozen with fright, forced itself to creep onwards, round the corner of the house.

Miss Seeton still slept, in her comfortable bed . . .

And she did not even stir when the peace of the moonlit night was interrupted by the sound of breaking glass . . .

CHAPTER 30

The sound of breaking glass had come to their ears just as Hatfield had been about to start the car. His hand froze on the ignition key—but only for an instant. He turned the key, gunned the engine, switched on the lights, and was off.

"Over that way," said Heath, pointing. "That way!"

"Hard to tell, this time of night. Things . . . echo."

"Echo be damned—I'm sure it was back there. For goodness' sake, turn round!"

Hatfield drove on in a grim silence. Heath wrestled in vain with the radio, hoping against hope it would work.

It wouldn't. He cursed. He looked up as the forward movement of the panda suddenly changed.

He said, "You're cutting them off? Good thinking!" It was as near to an apology as there was time for.

"Hope so. Just us, and no chance of reinforcements, we can't afford to do the charge-right-up-to-the-beggars bit, we've got to box clever."

"How about the siren?"

"Nobody else to hear it on this patch." He turned another corner. "Unless the others came on duty early, which they won't have done till we've reported in . . . Ah!"

"There they are!"

Indeed they were. Outside the antiques shop, reversed up from the road to the pavement, was a large car which gave every appearance of having just pulled forward from the window smashed by its tail-end attack. Moonlight and streetlamp glow glittered on slivers of glass, on dented metal, on scarred, shining paint.

The lid of the boot was open. Hurrying figures moved to and fro between the window and the car, with strange shapes in their arms. Torch-beams stabbed the shadowed interior of the shop, and staggered their way to the front as people carried more strange shapes outside.

A cry went up at the panda's first approach. Torches danced and darted as those carrying them dropped what else they carried and fled back to the car. The boot was thumped shut as people passed—the driver slammed the door—the car, with a roar, leaped forward.

"Blimey!" PC Hatfield's training had prepared him for maniacs who might drive straight at, rather than round, him—but theory and practice were, he now discovered, very different. "Hold tight!"

A swerve, a skid, a screech of brakes. The stolen car— could anyone in their right mind use their own vehicle to carry out a Ram Raid?—hurtled past with an inch, at most, to spare, and headed down the high street at full speed.

"Hang on!" A twist of the wheel, a lurching turn, and PC Hatfield was off in hot pursuit . . .

In Plummergen, a gloved hand slipped through the broken pane of Miss Seeton's French window and groped for a key. There was none. The hand moved to the handle and turned it very, very slowly.

A sigh of relief. The window swung open; the intruder entered, and pulled it shut again. A listening pause . . .

Miss Seeton slumbered on, unmoving. Peaceful.

A click, as a pocket torch was switched on: no moonlight beams could reach so far indoors. A cautious step across the little room—and another. And another . . .

"He's a good driver," observed PC Heath, as the fugitive car in front continued to elude the pursuing panda. "Almost as good as you—and with a few hundred yards' start, as well."

"If what you're saying is we won't catch him," retorted Hatfield, "you're wrong. We will—in the end."

"Did I say we wouldn't?" Heath braced himself as the panda took a corner on half a wheel, brakes squealing. "You keep after him the way you're doing now, and we'll get him, all right. No question."

The Ram Raiders ignored a "No Entry" sign. PC Hatfield ignored it, too. PC Heath said:

"They're heading out of town. Once they're on the open road, you can really let her rip. What'll we do, get in front and block 'em?"

"There were four of 'em in that car, if my eyes didn't deceive me. I'm not one for heroics, even if you are—we just keep on until they lose their nerve, that's what we do. And we hope," said PC Hatfield, "they lose it soon . . . "

The door handle slipped in the gloved, nervous grasp; the latch rattled, and the door bumped against its frame. The intruder stood still, listening.

Upstairs, Miss Seeton stirred, sighed, and turned over, still asleep. The movement made a floorboard creak beneath the bed, and Miss Seeton sighed again.

Downstairs, in front of the closed door—impossible to set the deadly trap with the draught from the broken window blowing through the house—the head of the muffled figure turned from side to side, searching, following the thin beam of the torch as it probed to and fro in the almost silent darkness. Which way now?

May as well try that door . . .

"I'll catch him," muttered PC Hatfield, "if it's the last ruddy thing I do!"

A sigh of relief: right first time. Into the kitchen crept the muffled figure, the torch its only guide. One step—two—three.

A gasp—a shudder—a clatter, as the torch fell to the floor from startled fingers. That awful, looming shape—the huge blackness of its bat wings! The witch's familiar? They'd said she might have sinister powers! And—heart thumping, mouth dry, the figure could not move—had the noise of sudden terror roused the sleeper overhead?

Miss Seeton, in her cosy nest, stirred, and stretched. She turned, stretching again. Slowly, her eyes opened.

"I think we're gaining on him!" If PC Heath had been a few years younger, he would have been bouncing in his seat from excitement.

"So does he." PC Hatfield could only spare half an eye for the car in front: the other one-and-a-half were on the road. "He's up to something—"

"Oy!" Instinctively, Heath ducked as a dark shape came hurtling from the open passenger door of the car in front, scattering sparks as it hit the road, its myriad shattered pieces flying in all directions. Above the throb of the panda's engine, the scream of agonised metal was suddenly heard, and a series of ominous clunks.

"If that's buggered our brakes—!"

"Something else coming!" And PC Heath gritted his teeth as the panda barrelled on through the dark, with PC Hatfield wrenching the wheel to avoid the barrage of unknown objects from the fugitives ahead.

In Sweetbriars, silence. Miss Seeton lay gazing drowsily at the ceiling, wondering what had woken her. She was normally an excellent sleeper: she couldn't remember the last occasion when she hadn't enjoyed her full eight hours. Perhaps—she frowned—it had been the cry of a mouse, or some other small creature, caught by a passing owl, a stoat, a fox. In the country, one became, sadly, accustomed to such sounds. Or even—she sighed—Tibs. Tibs . . .

Miss Seeton yawned, and sighed again. No doubt the cat—so foolish for anyone to believe she could ever turn into a tiger—was still annoyed at having been thwarted of her prey earlier on. One could hardly suppose her to be hungry: little Amelia Potter doted on her pet, and was rumoured to give her top-of-the-milk at tea time while she and her parents had the skimmings. Tea . . .

Miss Seeton closed her eyes, pulling the covers up snug about her shoulders. Such a pleasant afternoon with dear

Miss Wicks, being shown more of her treasures, with no-body—with no reporters—to intrude . . .

Miss Seeton drifted off into a doze.

Downstairs, the fallen torch was seized in a tremulous hand; the tinkle of broken glass was a pealing alarm to the intruder's ears. A desperate thumb on the button—nothing. Nothing . . . And then eyes grown accustomed to silvery darkness brightened by an invisible moon saw the huge bat still lurking—still, and lurking—beside the kitchen sink, with faint upcast glimmers from the metal draining-board showing every rib of its hideous, hovering wings . . .

Bats can see in the dark. They hate the light. No time to waste! Before it swoops to the attack—a frantic fumble in the coat pocket—a matchbox snatched—a match struck—and snapped, falling lightless to the floor . . .

Another match. Outside, a hooting owl. The match falls on the floor—a muffled curse.

At the third attempt, a flickering flame.

An umbrella! Open, drying after rain. Why not upright in the sink—in a rack? Why that hideous hellfire, pale as death, crawling like gold about the handle and the shaft?

An icy finger stroking a shuddering spine as, step by almost hypnotised step—shake out the match, drop it on the floor, nobody will ever know—the intruder approached the umbrella. It had to be moved . . . couldn't stay there . . . hellfire and bat wings and—and . . .

A deep breath, an outstretched hand. Fingerprints on metal? No fear of leaving traces! After the explosion, there would be no identifiable remains . . . Shaking hands closed on the cold gold of the umbrella, cold turning burning hot with guilt. Move it quickly, out of reach—out of sight, out of mind—waste no time in furling, fold and prop in a cor-ner and forget, while the business of the night goes on.

"What the hell's that?"

The open door, another hurtling object—sparks, a crash—and sudden blackness on one side as the night roared in.

"Bloody headlight's gone . . ."

* * *

Safely back to the sink, the umbrella in its corner. Hands fumble for the plug—into the hole—pressed firm. Then, in the pocket, the container, cylinder-shaped—out of the pocket, the lid prised off—the contents emptied in a pile in one corner of the sink, some spilling on the draining board as hands shake still more—

A clatter, as the empty container slips and falls to the tiled floor.

Freeze! *Freeze!* Has anyone heard?

Miss Seeton, half-waking from her doze, blinked— blinked again—saw silver star-patterns and pewter moon-light filling the cloudless sky, and wondered what had woken her. Another owl, perhaps? Perhaps not. Sleepy memories vaguely recalled a faint pattering from the kitchen: once more she thought of mice. Poor things—al-though one should not, of course, encourage them—but, with winter approaching, one could well understand why they should wish to take shelter indoors . . .

She smiled drowsily at the cloudless sky. At least it had stopped raining. The mouse would no doubt be safely gone by morning . . . The vision of a small rodent wearing mack-intosh and rainhat, carrying an umbrella, floated across her inward eye as her lids began to droop. A whimsical idea, of course, but no more so than the trilby-hatted Tibs she'd sketched after her little tea party with Miss Wicks. Tibs— and, wearing a policeman's helmet, a tiger . . . Not that she believed such stories for a moment, of course, though one could not deny that the cat had a strong personality, if one could say such a thing of a domestic pet . . . Safely gone by morning. She would not—Miss Seeton yawned—have to set the trap, which always made her feel a little guilty . . . though there could be no doubt that one quick snap of a heavy spring across the spine could despatch a mouse fas-ter, and with more kindness . . . Tibs always played with the poor creatures first . . . if killing anything could be re-garded as kind . . .

Miss Seeton closed her eyes, and drifted back to sleep. Her last conscious thought was that the mouse would be glad of its mackintosh, now that the rain had started again.

The muffled figure stepped warily back from the sink as

the thin, sinister crystal of the slow-running tap—not the sound of rain, but the tank above Miss Seeton's bed filling with water—began its deadly work. Back . . . back . . . turn, walk on, leave this door open—along the hall to the front of the house, too risky to pull the bolt of the kitchen door . . . eyes darting, on the watch for unexpected furniture—feet shuffling, groping for rucks in the carpet, for uneven tiles—a fall now would be fatal . . .

The hall stand—a table with a telephone. A sigh of triumph—so far, so good. Ignore knocking knees, shivering limbs—out of the pocket again for matches, for candle. A final, long-held breath. Above a thumping heart, can anyone—any movement from upstairs—be heard?

Nothing. Miss Seeton sleeps on . . .

Strike—strike—strike—and, at last, flame. Flame to wick, the stinging smell of fire, the candle alight. A dollop of hot wax tipped on the tabletop, the base of the burning candle pressed down, left standing, burning . . .

Dynamite—or near enough.

"That was a near thing!" From the fugitive car to the road—from the road, with a lucky—unlucky?—leaping bounce to the bonnet of the panda, yet—thankfully—not up to the windscreen, but across at an angle, and back to the road. "If we don't get him soon, he'll bloody kill us . . ."

No time, now, to linger. Turn the key in the door, open, and slip through—deep, welcome breaths of the outside air . . . a backward glance at the candle, still burning. Rubber arms reach to pull the door shut. As the latch clicks, the candle gutters in the draught.

Jelly legs can carry the intruder as far as the gate, but no farther. Look back at the hall window . . .

Indoors, the candle burns more brightly still.

And still Miss Seeton slumbers . . .

"Where the hell are we?"

"Must be halfway to the coast—well, somewhere in Kent, anyway. If you ask me, they're trying to take the stuff across the Channel . . ."

*   *   *

All is quiet in Plummergen; all is calm. Nothing—nobody
moves. Jelly legs have finally collapsed, in the fortunate
shadow of the high brick wall; overwrought nerves have
given way at last. The pounding heartbeat thunders in the
brain, and the whole world spins.

Down The Street, side by side, silent in the moonlight,
came the Nuts. In crêpe-soled shoes, dark pullovers, and
even darker slacks, their pockets crammed with talismanic
herbs, they were determined to show, once and for all,
that—urged on by the television man, but none the less
culpable for that—Miss Seeton and her cronies (whose
identity, suspected but not proved, would now be revealed)
practised diabolical rites in indescribable ceremonies. What
mattered it that the candles bought had been, not ritual
black, but ordinary white? The fires of hell need little encouragement to burst into earthly flame . . .

"Eric!" Mrs. Blaine's recovery from her faint had been
followed by a lengthy bout of hysterics and an even more
devastating headache. Not until this late hour had she felt
well enough to venture forth in pursuit of the dreadful truth.
And now . . .

"Eric!" She gripped Miss Nuttel's arm. Miss Nuttel did
no more than wince, though the grip was pincer-tight. "Oh,
Eric, look! Through the hall window—I'm sure it's—it's
too dreadful! It looks just like . . . "

"Candles," croaked Miss Nuttel, licking dry lips. She
glanced across the road towards the vicarage—the church.
Would a cry for help bring succour before—dry lips, dust-
filled mouth, frozen throat—the powers of evil, made man-
ifest, overwhelmed? And—if help came too late—if
stricken throats were powerless to cry—what ghastly form
might such manifestations take?

On quaking legs, supporting one another, the Nuts crept
closer. Eyes stared, hypnotised by fear, at the flickering
glow behind the closed door. Pulses raced and roared in
terror-deafened ears. Was that low, rhythmic thunder the
sound of chanting? Was the Beast, summoned from Beyond, about to spring?

CHAPTER 31

The chanting grew louder. The snarl of the Beast told of horrors to come: of human sacrifice—of blood. Mrs. Blaine felt her legs give way. Falling, she twisted. She saw . . .

"Eric!"

Behind her, two huge, glowing eyes—the Beast already present, conjured not from the flame but—uncontainable in its fury—leaping into sacrilegious life in the open air, racing down The Street towards those who had called it into being . . .

A moan. "Eric . . ."

Behind the Beast, another, yet more terrible—one-eyed, the empty socket glowing demonic red—a speeding onslaught, a tortured scream . . .

Mrs. Blaine fainted. Miss Nuttel, seeing, closed her eyes, collapsed, and waited for the end.

A squeal of brakes as the fugitive car, misjudging in panic the width of the narrowed Street, seeing shapeless forms of unidentifiable nature right in its path, turned on a sixpence to flee along Marsh Road, first flinging the latest missile towards its dogged pursuit.

"Bloody hell!"

The spare wheel bounced—clanked against the wing of the panda as PC Hatfield tried to turn—ricocheted, with added momentum—flew, spark-trailed, up and over the fallen huddle of the Nuts in the middle of the road—soared high above the moon-shadowed brick wall . . .

And crashed, with a carillon of broken glass, through the window of Miss Seeton's bedroom . . .

To land precisely in the centre of her bed.

Before the tail-lights of the panda had vanished round the first bend of Marsh Road, other lights were coming on along both sides of the southern end of The Street. Curtains were snatched apart, windows opened, heads thrust out to ascertain what on earth was happening.

Lights appeared in every occupied room—save one—at the front of the George and Dragon. The exception was that room occupied by demon reporter Mel Forby, whose instincts told her that Miss Seeton—somehow—was At It Again. The first sounds of gunned engines and squealing brakes had her flinging back the blankets; the resonant clank of the spare wheel on the panda's wing brought a sparkle to her eyes; the smashing of Miss Seeton's window was the signal for her to spring from her bed in a single bound. She paused just long enough to grab her notebook, and to slip on the casual coat which doubled, when necessary, as a dressing gown; then she was out of her room, running down the stairs, tearing across the hall to the front door, bending to drag at the bolts . . .

The door was unbolted. Mel wasted valuable time turning the key, turning it again as the door, now locked, would not open—finally fighting her way outside, while others— landlord Charley Mountfitchet, henchwoman Doris, assorted guests—galloped after her, demanding to know what on earth was happening . . .

"Good heavens!" Mel and the rest stopped to gape at the figure in the moonlight, staggering—bleating with shock, wringing its hands—across The Street towards the hotel. Golden light from startled windows plainly revealed, despite its muffled wrappings, the identity of the figure— which goggled, bleary-eyed, at the unexpected welcoming committee. Of which Mel was the only member wide awake enough to ask:

"What on earth are *you* doing, prowling about the place at this time of night?"

Before a suitable reply could be framed, there came a babble of frantic cries from a hitherto unnoticed bundle of rags in the middle of The Street, which disassembled itself into two almost separate bundles—one dumpy and short, one tall and thin—clinging together, voices raised in fright. The shapes and the voices were instantly recognised, though the words could not be distinguished: but the sentiments were unmistakeable. Something too terrible had happened . . .

"The Nuts," gloated Mel, even as she prepared to storm to whatever rescue might be—surely must, for all Miss Seeton's silence, be—required at Sweetbriars, "have been driven crackers at last!"

Bleating, babbling—hysterics all round; Charley Mountfitchet was minded to take control, insisting that everyone must keep calm. Not as if there was a fire, was it? And if there'd bin a regular car smash, there'd be certain signs of it in The Street, the racket that'd bin going on not five minutes since—and there weren't, so there hadn't, and no need for folk to go upsetting themsel—

"Aaaah!" A terrified scream. Mrs. Blaine, all eyes at once upon her, raised a pointing hand. "Too—too horrible—a headless corpse! I mean—"

But her meaning was lost in the general outcry which now ensued. Where golden light met and mingled with moon-silver on the ground, a myriad shadows and reflections tricked the eye—made that which was small enormous—gave movement to the stillness of stone and brick—*gave life to that which was dead* . . .

A shimmering skull, eye-sockets and mouth deep hollows of eternal blackness, floated, shroud-white, down the front path of Miss Seeton's cottage. Beneath the skull, nothing—the gaping void of the tomb. Wisps of smoke—sulphur fumes from the nether world—eddied where spectral feet walked the ways of the unimaginable . . .

"Aaaah!" Another scream, yet more terrified—but not from Mrs. Blaine. Another pointing hand, raised from the muffled wrappings. "No! Stop her—keep her away from me! She wasn't meant to die until the bomb went off!''

It was late next morning when Amelita Forby tapped at Miss Seeton's door, an enormous box of chocolates in her hand.

"Hi, Miss S. For you, in exchange"—Mel's nose twitched—"for coffee, and a slice of Martha's cake, okay?"

"Oh, Mel." Miss Seeton was grateful, but embarrassed. Surely even a reporter as famous and successful as dear Mel could not afford to give such very, well, expensive presents to one who, really, although (she hoped) a friend, had done nothing to deserve such generosity . . .

"Nothing?" Mel followed her hostess down the passage to the kitchen, noting with secret amusement the umbrellas in their clips along the wall. Miss Seeton, she was willing to bet a dozen boxes of chocolates, even now probably had no idea that it was the sight of her apparently ghostly form—not a headless corpse, but a corpseless head—long white nightie discreetly covered, in the emergency of hurrying out of doors with no housecoat, by an opened brolly—which had driven her would-be killer to confess. To confess to more, to Mel's delight, than just the murder attempt. Another Seeton Scoop for Amelita Forby, and boo to Banner and his Swiss Drugs Scandal.

"Miss S., you're a marvel. I'm the editor's blue-eyed girl again, so you just enjoy your chocs without losing any sleep over them. Talking of which"—she lounged against the table as Miss Seeton busied herself with spoons, cups, and the kettle—"how did you manage in the spare room last night, or rather this morning? And have you done anything yet about getting your windows fixed?"

Miss Seeton, about to pick up the tray, nodded. "Superintendent Brinton was kind enough to arrange for someone to call. A matter of kindness, or should I say courtesy, to a—a professional colleague, as I understand it, because"—her eyes twinkled—"one does not usually expect them to be so prompt in performing what is, after all, a relatively small task. Might the apposite phrase be *pulling rank*? And especially since today is Sunday."

Mel nodded: she'd had to walk the Ashford streets for some time before finding a newsagent stocking a sufficiently lavish box of chocolates for Miss Seeton's due reward.

"Except, of course," said Miss Seeton, "that he was not a policeman. Tradesmen, that is—but he was here not half an hour ago, and did an excellent job, which is why I was unable to attend morning service, although the dear vicar, I feel sure, will understand. So very kind of him—Mr. Brinton, that is. The glazier, not Mr. Brinton—though I must confess to being a little puzzled when he insisted there was no charge. I even telephoned him to make sure—Mr. Brinton, I mean, but he said he had been quite correct in not accepting any money today, and in saying he would not be presenting his account at a later date. I do hope," said Miss Seeton, with a pucker between her brows, "that dear Mr. Brinton will not be paying for what was no more than an unfortunate accident out of his own pocket. Or do the police perhaps have some form of—of sinking fund, for such an occurrence? I would hate to think of my little mishap causing any—any financial difficulty . . ."

Mel laughed as she took the tray from Miss Seeton's anxious hands. "I told you before, Miss S., you can rest easy. One window's a very small price to pay for what you've done—believe me, Brinton and the rest of the boys in blue are mighty pleased with you right now. If I'm the *Negative*'s golden girl, that's nothing to what Old Brimstone thinks of you . . ."

Charley Mountfitchet had always entered with enthusiasm into the spirit of whatever remarkable crime the police— from whatever force—might be investigating while staying in his hotel. He would ply the visiting plainclothes officers with after-hours whisky, was always willing to provide late-night sandwiches or bar snacks, and positively revelled in being asked to identify suspects, or to volunteer theories.

And now his finest hour had come. Mel Forby's quick wits worked out just five seconds before Charley's the likely meaning of the hysterical babbling about bombs, the true reason for the terrified response to the innocent sight of Miss

Seeton walking quietly down her own front path . . .

"I'll call the cops!" she snapped, digging Charley in the ribs. "You make a citizen's arrest!"

But, though Charley's moment of glory was not snatched from him, Mel was thwarted of hers. As she was heading back into the hotel, PC Potter, alerted by the earlier sounds of mayhem, arrived in a hastily-buttoned tunic—to see Charley Mountfitchet clapping a hand on the shoulder of a shivering Rodney Roydon, and uttering in a gleeful voice the well-known words of The Usual Warning.

Mel insisted that Rodney was in such a state he couldn't be taken to Ashford without medical supervision. She had—she claimed—in far-off times been a Girl Guide: she knew about shock, and faints, and first aid. She directed the full force of her beautiful eyes upon the hapless Potter: who was as putty in her devious hands . . .

"Forby?" Superintendent Brinton was never happy at being dragged out of bed during the hours of darkness. "What the hell is that woman doing here again? Has she taken up residence?"

Potter shuffled his feet and cast an anguished eye in the direction of Detective Constable Foxon. "She, er, said she was sure you'd want her to be in on all this, sir—seeing how it was her idea in the first place, she said. Sir. She, er, said you knew all about it . . ."

"She's right, sir." Foxon rushed to the rescue of his hapless friend as Brinton buried his face in his hands, groaned, and then began tearing at his sleep-ruffled hair. "I know it doesn't seem to have worked out the way she—we—you planned it, sir, but—well, it's worked, all right. If this chap's the front man for the real Sideboard Swipers, I mean. And if Mel—Miss Forby—says he is . . ."

He glanced at what he could see of his tormented chief, and grinned. " . . . subject, of course, to confirmation from, er, Miss Seeton . . ."

"Foxon!" Brinton leaped from his chair, his eyes wild. "Potter—get out. Go home. And don't forget to wring that woman's neck on your way!"

"Sir," said Potter, beating a hasty retreat, but not so

hasty that he missed Foxon's mischievous enquiry as to whether it was Miss Forby, or Miss Seeton, who had inspired such unorthodox instructions . . .

They knew that Mel would sit and wait for her story for as long as it took; and they also knew, in fairness—once Brinton had been soothed with a cup of canteen tea and a peppermint or two—that she deserved that story, if anyone did. Indeed, the effect of the peppermints was so soothing that Brinton was prepared to let his suspects pickle quietly in their cells while he and Foxon picked Mel's brains about exactly what had been going on.

"Easy," Mel told them, yawning over the tea she couldn't believe anyone in their right minds could possibly enjoy, but more than willing, in the circumstances, to make the effort. "This reporter—so-called. *I've* never heard of Roy Roydon, and I pride myself I know a fair bit about what goes on in and around Fleet Street . . ." She gulped a mouthful of tea, made a face, and sat up straight. "Seems he's been using the excuse of writing an article on that conceited television character to pop in and out of houses up and down the country, snooping. Made quite a pest of himself on occasion, I've been told, and . . ."

She tried not to seem affronted at the look on Superintendent Brinton's face. Amelita Forby was no foot-in-door journalist, as he ought to know by now.

" . . . and the poor mugs who ended up being burgled on his say-so had naturally invited their visitors into the sitting-room—nothing but the best for the telly folk—where, of course, smack in front of them were the sideboards, all set out with knick-knacks and ornaments just asking to be pinched . . ." She hid another yawn. "Which they duly were, once the *Not All Roast Beef* caravan had moved on, and Rodney had moved on after it. So nobody made the connection . . ."

Brinton shot her a shrewd glance. "Including you, Miss Forby. The line you spun me—and a pretty convincing line it was, I have to admit—was all to do with obituary columns, and articles in local newspapers, and opportunist burglars homing in on the helpless. Get Miss Seeton to pretend she's just been bereaved, you said. Set her up to tell the local rag all about poor, dear, dead Cousin Flora, and snap her in the parlour with the deceased's bits and bobs on display behind her—''

''Ah,'' said Mel; and laughed, her eyes bright. ''Well, I got the gist of it, didn't I?'' She laughed again, and the superintendent had an uncomfortable feeling that she was keeping something from him. ''I *knew*,'' she went on, before he could voice his suspicions, ''there was a newspaper side to this story—and I *knew* Miss Seeton would come up trumps again . . . and I was right. So she did . . . er, twice over, if you count the Ram Raiders.'' She coughed. ''Which, okay, I agree I was more interested in, at the start . . . ''

''Come off it,'' said Brinton, sidetracked as Mel had meant him to be. ''How can you say it's anything to do with Miss Seeton that the Raiders ran out of petrol just outside Rytham Hall?''

''Just in time,'' she amended, ''to end up the meat in the sandwich between those two in the panda car, and a crowd of the Night Watch Men. Sure, the Plummergen Patrol'd already heard the racket from The Street and were heading back that way in any case, but if it hadn't been for the Nuts throwing a wobbly right outside Sweetbriars, the Rammers would never have turned up Marsh Road because they'd got nervous about cutting across the canal bridge. If they'd gone straight on without ditching that spare wheel, they'd have been over the canal by the time the gas ran out, and with the Night Watch Men half a mile away, the panda pair wouldn't have had a hope in hell of catching them in the dark.'' The expressive eyes fastened soulfully upon Superintendent Brinton's frowning face. ''Be fair, now. Would they?''

''Local knowledge, sir,'' chirped Foxon, as his chief shut his eyes in despair. ''If the Nuts hadn't been so sure Miss Seeton was a witch—if Sir George's gang hadn't known the best way to head off the Rammers at the pass—if—''

''All right!'' Brinton slapped a brooding hand on the desk, and sighed. ''It's the wrong time of day—or night— to start trying to work out the cockeyed logic behind whatever fairy story you're trying to sell me. I'll buy it—for the sake of peace and quiet, if nothing else. Miss Seeton's done it again—though I'm blowed if I can quite make out how.''

Mel tapped the cardboard portfolio she'd been guarding, keeping it on the table just out of the superintendent's reach. ''Here's how,'' she said, with a knowing smile. ''You think you've seen these sketches before, of course—and a couple of them you have . . . but she's done another one since, and *that* little number puts quite a different interpretation on the rest.'' She smiled again. ''The same, but different, if you see what I mean. Which you will,'' she added kindly, ''once you've taken a close look . . . ''

Brinton's features were acquiring an unusual burgundy tint. ''Don't push your luck, Miss Forby,'' he growled, as Mel began to untie the strings of the portfolio. ''And don't play games with me. Let's do all this nice and tidy, shall we? What sketches? Where did you get them? As if,'' he added in a hollow voice, ''I couldn't guess . . . ''

''These?'' Mel was casual. ''Oh, I grabbed them once things had calmed down a bit, when people were still pouring cold water over the Nuts—you know, I'm sorry I missed out there—and the awful Roydon, trying to find out what it was all about. But I went right to the heart of the mystery, to Sweetbriars''—she ignored Brinton's groan—''because Martha Bloomer—you know she lives just across the road from Miss S.—said she thought she'd heard sounds of breaking glass coming from the cottage as well as the hooha she knew must be a car crash. We went back with Miss S. to check . . . ''

She shivered, her casual pose forgotten. ''Plum in the middle,'' she said. ''If Miss Seeton hadn't been on her way downstairs . . . ''

''Yes,'' said Brinton, ''why was she? Not that I'd want her with broken glass and spare wheels all over her, but why wasn't she in bed, like anyone else at that time of night? And don't tell me,'' sourly, ''it was some sort of blasted premonition—though I suppose you will.''

''I won't,'' said Mel, ''though I think you'll like the truth—as far as I can make it out—even less. It was all thanks to, uh, her umbrella . . . ''

"Her umbrella!" Brinton closed his eyes again, and groaned. "Yes, of course—what else would it be?"

"Seems she'd been disturbed in the night," Mel went on. "Thought it must be mice charging about the kitchen with hobnailed boots on—though my guess is, it was Roydon breaking into the place and setting up his . . . his bomb." Even Mel's insouciance, professional as it was, weakened here: she was truly fond of Miss Seeton, and the realisation of how close her friend had, yet again, come to extinction worried her more than she cared to think.

She sighed. "I knew there must be *something* wrong, the way he went over the top when Miss S. appeared—but all that yelling about a bomb, well, I didn't believe a feeble type like him could have dreamed up anything quite so— so drastic. I just knew he was a wrong 'un, and whatever it was he'd been doing, he had to be stopped, and the bomb made a good excuse. In any case, he started rabbiting about the candle going out—seems when she opened the door to check on the accident, Miss S. raised a bit of a draught— and I . . . I was so keen to get the story, I suppose, I told myself whatever he *thought* he might have done, it must be safe enough to go back in and check, while Charley Mountfitchet stopped him doing a bunk. I guess I figured," with a wry grin, "Miss S.'s guardian angel would be watching out for her, same as always . . ."

"Certainly did," grunted Brinton, "getting her out of bed just in time to miss that wheel. She wouldn't've stood much of a chance—sorry," as Mel winced. She'd seen the damage done to Miss Seeton's cosy bed: Brinton hadn't. "Go on."

Mel gulped. "Yes, well . . . We didn't spot the candle on the way in, any more than Miss S. had seen it on her way out—we were in a hurry both times, of course—and then we went upstairs and saw the wheel. In all the excitement, of course, we thought *that* must be what he'd meant about a bomb—flying through the air, loud bangs, lots of mess— just like the starburst sketch, when you stop and think about it. Except when we first saw this," and Mel waved towards the drawing now in Brinton's puzzled hand, "we thought it must be something to do with my story about the admiral chasing those characters across The Street, and Mr. Baxter slamming on the brakes and his car not falling to pieces after all—but, well, we were wrong."

Mel managed a grin. "Anyway, the Nuts were burbling about Forces and Powers . . . and once we'd taken a look at the . . . the damage, Miss S. thought a nice cup of tea might not be such a bad idea." Mel gazed at her own cold, treacle-brown tea and sighed.

"And while I helped Martha make up the bed in the spare room, little innocence was down in the kitchen, running the cold tap to clear the nasty grey sludge in the corner of the sink, and wondering if it had come off her umbrella, and thinking wasn't it lucky it had rained so hard she hadn't left it in the hall rack to drain, because it would have made such a mess—and if that," said Mel, "isn't some sort of guardian angel, or a premonition, I'll eat my favourite hat. Which," she added, as Brinton seemed set to argue, "is a Monica Mary special—and they don't come cheap."

"You're dead right there," said Brinton automatically. His wife had once visited the renowned Brettenden milliner on the occasion of a family wedding. The remembrance of how much it had cost him to see two distant cousins joined in holy wedlock could still give him nightmares about his overdraft. Then he blinked. "Hats be damned! What," he demanded, as Foxon sat grinning at his side, "was in this grey sludge that's obviously the whole point of this damned rigmarole? And how could anyone make a bomb out of it?''

Mel, who'd kept a creditable hold on proceedings so far, relying on her reporter's memory as she narrated the facts and the deductions she'd drawn from them, now had, for the first time, to consult her invaluable notebook.

"Calcium carbide," she said. "Don't ask," as Brinton opened his mouth, "because I don't know—it's some sort of chemical, and you can use it to get rid of moles, so Potter told me, and I believe him. But you have to keep it dry, or it turns to, uh, acetylene, which is a gas, and—''

"I know that," growled Brinton. "Oxyacetylene torches, welders for the use of, right?"

"Right." Mel frowned at her shorthand notes: she'd told the editor of the *Negative* this bit had better be checked by the science correspondent before it went to press, and she'd passed the same warning to the Sundays who'd run her story as a Late Edition fudge. "You make it wet, it gives off gas—you set it alight, and it explodes. The more gas the merrier, of course. Rodney put the candle on the hall table so that by the time the acetylene reached the flame there'd be more than enough to—to blow Sweetbriars sky high . . . ''

"Only Miss Seeton," supplied Brinton, "opened the door to deal with whatever accident she thought there'd been in The Street, and out went the candle, and—and what happened to the acetylene? Granted it hadn't built up enough to explode by the time the candle went out, but why weren't the pair of you gassed when you went back into the house?"

"That guardian angel again, I guess." Mel shrugged. "Our Rodney had been careful to close the door behind him when he smashed a window to get in—the old burgling trick of black treacle and newspaper—and he didn't want the gas leaking out before it could build up enough to do the damage. But there was a much bigger window broken when the wheel came crashing in—and Miss Seeton left the front door open when she popped out to the accident— and if an angel worth its salt's going to do anything, it's going to set up a dandy through-draught to clear every last puff of the stuff out of the cottage before anyone goes back inside.''

As Brinton digested this, Foxon ventured to put a question. ''You never said why Miss Seeton wasn't in bed when the wheel, er, dropped in. Her umbrella, you said?''

Mel giggled. ''Or that mouse she was bothered about—or could be both, if you ask me . . . '' Which was indeed—though neither she nor anyone else ever knew this for certain—the way it had been. ''Seems Rodney took her brolly out of the sink so he could mess about in comfort, only it was dark—he dropped his torch, I found it—here, sorry, I forgot, I guess that's evidence—anyway,'' as Brinton groaned to see the handkerchief-wrapped cylinder, brooding on smudged fingerprints, ''he somehow mislaid the empty tin, after he'd unloaded the calcium carbide, and I imagine he was too nervous to want to hang around looking for it.

''And *something*—like I said, that mouse, I'll bet,'' and Mel chuckled, ''bumped into it and rolled it into the brolly, and knocked it over—which must have been the noise Miss S. heard, and she came downstairs to check. Only she hadn't reached the kitchen before there was all that rumpus in the road and she went outside, and—and, well, there you are. When Martha and I found her,'' she concluded, ''Miss S. was making tea, calm as you like, and just happened to mention she didn't remember leaving her umbrella over in the corner on the floor, she thought she'd drained it in the sink the way she always does when it's got really wet, and then opened it up to dry without too many creases. It was her gold one, you see, and she's always extra careful with that because the Oracle gave it to her. He'll be pleased,'' said Mel, ''to think he helped, in a roundabout way. Some coincidence, huh?''

''Coincidence be damned! I suppose you'll be telling me next,'' retorted Brinton, ''that it was pure *coincidence* young Foxon's Uncle Reg was done in by *another* set of thugs who just *happened* to think breaking into his house was a bright idea? He doesn't sound like the sort of chap who'd let the likes of Jeremy Froste and his crew into his house.''

"He wasn't, sir." There was no hint of doubt in Foxon's reply. "And even if he had been, my gran would've known all about it—and she never said a word."

"And Jeremy Froste didn't call on people that close to Brettenden—I asked him," said Mel, putting the clincher on the argument. "Coincidences do happen, Mr. Brinton: like the coincidence that for once it wasn't . . . a certain criminal mastermind," said Mel, hurriedly hedging her slanderous reference to Chrysander Bullian, "behind the Ram Raiding thefts, if what that crowd you've got in the cells told you was the truth."

"Probably wasn't." Brinton was disposed to be glum. He'd grown so accustomed, over the years, to having Miss Seeton pull numerous guilty rabbits out of assorted nefarious hats that he'd almost come to expect it as his right. Now it seemed she hadn't, for once, come up with one hundred per cent of the goods, he was confused . . .

"All right," he said, helping himself wearily to another peppermint, and pushing what remained of the packet across the table for Mel to help herself. "I'll buy a coincidence—a whole string of the blasted things, if you insist—but just where does that leave me? Us, I mean—with a murder to investigate''—Foxon frowned—"and an old lady in hospital, not to mention the burglaries . . . and with the lot your pal Roydon's been fronting for not the same lot at all, according to you!"

Mel, about to open the portfolio, hesitated. Then she glanced at Foxon; and grinned. "Guess it leaves you still chasing the theory we handed you yesterday," she said, producing Miss Seeton's sketches with a flourish. "Remember these? Well, take a look at the latest addition."

Triumphantly, she handed Brinton a swift, vivid drawing of a fierce-looking tiger in a policeman's helmet, with an equally ferocious tabby cat, in a trilby hat, beside it. Each animal had an open notebook in one paw, a pencil in the other; their poses of intense concentration were identical in every respect—save one. They were exact opposites . . .

"Mirror images, okay?" Mel saw Brinton's bewildered

eyes raised in disbelief and said cheerfully, "Coincidences do happen, I'll say that again, but this was no coincidence, it was a deliberate imitation—what we've simply got to call a *copycat* crime—of the original Sideboard Swipers. Except that your copycats never worked out how Rodney and his crowd chose their victims, and had to come up with a method of their own." And she pondered the first of Miss Seeton's sketches, the one Delphick had been coerced into showing her: the sleek cat reflected in the mirror, with the ram—the ram from the wrong, confusing case—beneath it on the bonnet of the Rolls-Royce in which Ferencz Szabo, of the Stentorian voice, rode so proudly.

"Copycats—but we'll catch them," she said. "I mean, you will, thanks to Miss S., because according to her what you're after is a gang with the brains to make use of the local newspapers. If that cat's not wearing a reporter's trilby, my name isn't Amelita Forby . . . And what you're going to do is bait a trap, I hope, and wait for them to bite. Be a sport, Mr. Brinton. After all the trouble I went to yesterday, I'd say the least you could do is carry on the way we originally planned. Do you realise"—she did her very best to look aggrieved—"that I passed up the chance for an eye-witness Piece on the Produce Show and the Conker Contest, just so I could do a proper job of sweet-talking the editor of the *Brettenden Beacon* into playing ball?"

Memories of a highly sociable afternoon and evening in the company of one who'd turned out, to Mel's delight, to be an old friend—a former Fleet Street hack who'd retired to the country to give his liver a long-overdue rest—sparkled in Mel's eyes, had Brinton taken the trouble to notice them. He, however, was still brooding on her original suggestion.

"You still want Miss Seeton," he said, "to act as a—a decoy for these blighters? After all that's happened?"

Mel shrugged. "So what's happened? A couple of queer coincidences, as you said yourself—but pretty lucky ones, for you police types." She pointed to the helmeted tiger, dwarfing the journalist Tibs. "My guess is, you've got the Ram Raiders and the front man for the Swipers tucked away in the cells, judging by this. And Rodney Roydon's no hero, take it from me—he'll spill the beans on the rest of his gang the minute you ask him, I'll bet you dinner at the George any time you want.''

She giggled: she was starting to feel light-headed. ''Come on,'' she said, ''enjoy yourself for once, Mr. Brinton. You know I'm right about Rodney, and you know they're the Ram Raiders—though please don't take my word for it.'' She favoured him with a wide-eyed Forby Special Stare. ''Ask the Oracle. I've seen Miss Seeton's sketch, and you haven't.'' Wide-eyed innocence turned into a grin. ''Just you phone him at a Christian hour and tell him all about it. He'll agree with me, bet you anything you like—''

''I'm not arguing with that,'' said Brinton, who'd have argued about it until dawn, if Mel hadn't called his bluff first. ''I'm just—well, knowing Miss Seeton . . . ''

''Knowing Miss Seeton,'' supplied Mel, ''you know she'll be only too willing to do her duty by the forces of law and order. Be fair—if she hadn't been, she'd never have got so muddled when Roydon was chatting with her outside the village hall—and you know how muddled she can get, Mr. Brinton. That's why he was so positive she'd sussed him as a crook, and thought he had to—to get rid of her . . . before she could tell anyone else.''

Mel lifted her cup with shaking hands, and took an absent-minded swallow. ''Yuck! This,'' she said, wagging an admonitory finger as she set the cup hastily down, ''ought to be the best champagne, Superintendent, not dishwater. Save it for Miss S., though,'' as he seemed about to protest. ''If it takes as long as a week, once the story's been published, for the crooks to see her as an easy touch, I really will eat my Monica Mary special . . . ''

Mel's hat, of course, was in absolutely no danger. It took exactly four days.

CHAPTER 33

It would take just four days from the appearance of the
Brettenden Beacon before the Obituary Opportunists
made the mistake of testing the accuracy of the newspaper article in which a grief-stricken, though courageous,
Miss Seeton told the world that, despite her sad loss,
nothing could stop her travelling by bus to her usual
weekly flower-arranging class in the nearby market town.
Cousin Flora would have expected her to put a brave face
on things—to soldier on regardless—to resume her normal life as soon as possible . . .

It was inconvenient, of course, that the ability of Miss
Seeton to act was almost nil. If Mel hadn't known that an
obituary by an outsider—especially one from Fleet Street—
would generate far more local comment than was wise for
the success of the scheme, she would have done the job
herself. As it was, she briefed her trusty editorial friend to
supply the most sympathetic reporter on the books, and this
he duly did. Any awkwardness or embarrassment in Miss
Seeton's manner was attributed to the strain on a gentlewoman of concealing her undoubted grief. Making every
allowance for her emotion, the reporter produced a piece
of purple prose which needed only a little judicious em-
bellishment to make it completely irresistible, as Mel and
Brinton had hoped, to the Obituary Opportunists.

Lady Colveden, sworn to secrecy, whisked Miss Seeton

away for tea at Rytham Hall. Foxon, at his own insistence, hid in Miss Seeton's under-stairs cupboard with a walkie-talkie radio; and there was an unmarked car parked (to the delight of Charley Mountfitchet) in front of the George, with uniformed officers lurking in the after-hours bar. The trap was set—and, as the Opportunists broke into Miss Seeton's empty cottage, was sprung. Foxon insisted that he had used no more than reasonable force to apprehend the startled burglars: it was three to one, and he'd hardly had time to call for support before they'd realised he was there, and had tried to make a break for it. Brinton wisely chose to ignore the gleeful expression on his subordinate's face as he contemplated his bruised knuckles. Reginald Easter—Foxon's Uncle Reg—had been avenged . . .

But these stirring events were still in the future when Mel appeared, that Sunday morning, on Miss Seeton's doorstep with the box of chocolates in her hand, and an invitation to lunch on her lips. Fresh coffee, coupled with generous slices of Martha Bloomer's fruit-cake, did much to expunge from Mel's memory the nightmare recollection of Ashford police station's horribly stewed tea, and the interrupted sleep she'd suffered during the past twelve hours. There were, however, far less advantageous tribulations in a journalist's life, and Amelita Forby was not complaining. She'd been able to file her story—two of them; she'd roughed out an Obituary Opportunists article, ready to roll once Miss Seeton's undercover exploits cracked yet another case; and she'd been offered a reduction in her bill by a gratified Charley Mountfitchet, still basking in his moment of glory.

"So I'm taking you out to lunch," Mel informed Miss Seeton, "and I won't take no for an answer. Give that umbrella of yours a first-class polish, and let's go!"

They did not, of course, go at once. Mel had first to deal with Miss Seeton's modest reluctance to put her friend to any cost or inconvenience; only jocular references to tea at the Ritz managed to convince her that it would not be self-indulgent to accept an invitation which came (said Mel, in a moment of inspiration) not just courtesy of Charley Mountfitchet and the editor of the *Daily Negative,* but with more than good wishes from Superintendent Brinton and Chief Superintendent Delphick—not to mention Inspector Terling of the Art Squad—as well. Miss Seeton, with a blush of pleasure and only a moment's anxiety for the small piece of beef in her refrigerator, smiled, and said thank you.

"Afterwards," promised Mel, as they emerged from Miss Seeton's front gate and prepared to cross The Street to the George, "we'll pop into the church to admire the Harvest Festival decorations. Hope the vicar had a good turnout," she added, catching sight of the tyre-marks burned into the surface of the road. "Guess half the village must've slept as late as I did—but then," as Miss Seeton looked vaguely guilty, "I guess they didn't, because I saw quite a few familiar faces trotting to church while I was still waking up." She giggled. "Charley offered me breakfast in bed, but I told him not to bother. Catch young Maureen slogging upstairs with a tray—and even if she did, you bet she'd drop it before I got it!"

Miss Seeton, acknowledging the truth of this remark, had to sigh, though she said nothing: dear Mel, so quick and lively. People in the country were often so much more . . . relaxed about things. Everyone had different talents, of course, and it must be conceded that Maureen . . . Doris, one had to admit, was far more—alert, perhaps was the word, though there had been a certain degree of animation in poor Maureen over recent days which . . .

"The television, of course," murmured Miss Seeton, following Mel across the George's forecourt.

"Him, too, would you believe?" Mel had heard the murmur without understanding it. "*And* young Make-a-Note Bethan, off to church with their tonsils all present and correct. That pair probably went straight back to bed and slept the sleep of the just the minute all the, uh, fuss was over."

Miss Seeton sighed again; Mel could have kicked herself. "They'd better not," she said quickly, "try to horn in on my territory—not that I'd get much of a Piece out of Harvest Festival, of course. The Produce Show and the Conkers are more my line—I'll be staying on a few days to interview everyone who was there, so I can work out my story." It was good cover for the Obituary Opportunists scoop. Nobody would be surprised that a Fleet Street reporter, known to be an expert on Plummergen, was staying in the village when there was no ostensible reason for her to do so.

The hotel bar and public lounge were far from empty as Mel and Miss Seeton arrived: indeed, the volume of sound and the number of people made Mel's every journalistic sense start to quiver. She could not, however, abandon her guest before they'd even ordered drinks; and, since Miss Seeton seemed slightly overwhelmed by the barrage of sound reaching her ears from every direction, all Mel could do was find a relatively quiet corner in which to seat herself and her friend, then go in search of someone who knew what on earth was going on.

She giggled at the thought: it was almost becoming a cliché, when Miss Seeton was around. She cleared her throat as Miss Seeton regarded her with polite interest, and said:

"Hang on there, Miss S., and I'll go rustle up a sherry, or something. And the menus," she added, as Miss Seeton was obviously about to say she couldn't possibly. For her own part, Mel knew she not only possibly, but positively, could: she had a feeling there was something about this brouhaha she'd need a stiff drink to help her digest . . .

Above a tumultuous sea of heads, she spotted Doris, holding indignant court behind the bar. She managed at last to catch the waitress's eye, waved, indicated the corner, mimed acute thirst, and, after a few moments, departed, to wait in hopes of the rest of the story whose fundamentals she had finally acquired.

"Seems Jeremy Froste's gone and upset *everyone* now," she told Miss Seeton, as she sat down. "Seems yesterday, before all the, uh, upset at the show, he spotted two entries in the apple class he thought were Plummergen Peculiers—and one was from Mrs. Skinner's garden, and one was from Mrs. Henderson's. You know—well, no, I suppose you don't," remembering the village innocence of her audience, "but apparently they wouldn't let him look round before, either of them, because neither of 'em wanted to risk having the other one scoring over her. It would have been," said Mel, chuckling, "the final straw if he'd found one garden worth putting on film, and not the other, wouldn't it?''

Miss Seeton, not always quite as innocent as her friends believed, was discreetly amused before remarking, ''But if Mr. Froste has found two of the apples, would not an acceptable compromise be to use both in the programme? For myself I would hardly care for such a—but others, I know,'' with a hasty blush, ''feel very differently, and . . . ''

''I gather,'' said Mel, ''he was going to. He told both of them he'd be round to discuss it with them first thing this morning, when he'd had time to think it over. Well, he didn't make it first thing—but he didn't,'' as Miss Seeton yet again looked guilty, ''even hang around after church to catch them then, which is what's upset everyone on both sides of the quarrel—even if they're trying their best to make out they're upset on the vicar's behalf. Though it doesn't,'' said Mel, ''sound that irreverent to me, and to be honest I can't see Mr. Treeves taking offence so easily— but then, you know what this place can be like.''

Miss Seeton, who was fond of the vicar and friends with his sister, said that she did. Mel grinned.

''I only got the gist of it, but it was something to do with the church decorations—what was that, honey?'' as Miss Seeton suddenly turned pink, and coughed.

''Oh, dear, poor Stan—though it must be said that one would have hoped for—that is, it is surprising he allowed himself . . . '' Miss Seeton blushed. Even to think of criticising one who was almost a member of one's family—yet dear Martha had been so much more than critical . . .

''It was, I fear, all because of the conkers,'' began Martha's employer, who had received an unexpected visit from her henchwoman on Saturday evening, once she had returned from afternoon tea with Miss Wicks. ''It is no doubt foolish to say so now, but . . . '' She sighed. ''Had I but known, you see, I could perhaps have persuaded him to enter them in the Show after all, rather than . . . not, of course, that it is a—a competition so much as decoration of the church, even if displays from—from both villages are used. Decani,'' said Miss Seeton, sighing again, ''and cantoris,'' referring to the two sides of the church on which, for important services of the Christian year, the two congregations, enforcedly amalgamated, would sit doggedly apart.

"But," she continued, with another sigh, "in all the . . . the regrettable confusion at the Show, poor Stan received a black eye, and became—understandably, one has to say— annoyed about it. And, so Martha told me, lost his temper completely. He was justifiably proud of his year's work," lamented Miss Seeton. "And such events do a great deal to foster the community spirit, which is so very important— except, of course, that in the case of Murreystone one has to concede . . . and he refused . . . "

"Say no more," said Mel, grinning. "I get the picture: no Seeton-Bloomer produce on display, right? Which means at least it isn't Stan's fault, or yours, that Jeremy Froste got ants in his pants in the middle of the service. Hardly sang a note, they're saying, just sat and goggled— and then he didn't wait to shake the vicar's hand before doing a bunk with young Bethan, which I admit's a bit off, but I wouldn't call it downright insulting. Last seen heading over the canal bridge at top speed, I gather, and that flash car of theirs should be able to speed pretty well. Leaving Mrs. Skinner and Mrs. Henderson rather peeved, and of course it's all backfired on their husbands, and their friends, and . . . "

"And it's too much!" came an explosion from over their heads, which made them both jump. They looked up. There, pink-cheeked and rumple-haired, was Doris, with menus in her hand and a sparkle in her eye. "A downright disgrace, that's what it is, and I don't care who knows it!"

Without waiting to enquire whether they wanted pre-prandial drinks, she thrust the menus under their astonished noses. "An insult," said Doris, fuming. "That Murreystone lot—done it on purpose, that's what they've done!"

"Done what?" demanded Mel. Miss Seeton looked puzzled, but did not say anything, though even if she'd wanted to, there would hardly have been time.

"Apples!" said Doris, fuming still more. "What did they devils do on Saturday, but sneak some precious apple nobody had ever even heard of into church with the decorations—sneaky enough not to put it in the Show, that's

Murreystone for you, first the conkers and now this . . . ''

As she paused to draw breath, Mel slipped in a question. ''Another Plummergen Peculier?''

''A Murreystone Marvel,'' moaned Doris. ''Just the one! Stuck it right under his nose, that Jeremy Froste—how they knew where he'd be sitting beats me, but they did—and off he went to look at it, and there's only one tree left, while Mrs. Skinner and Mrs. Henderson makes a pair, and everyone knows he wants 'em as—as rare as can be, so when it's two of ours or one of theirs, guess which he thinks is rarest?''

They made all the right noises, but Doris would not be easily appeased. She favoured her audience with a scathing denunciation of the character of Murreystone, a withering description of its Marvel, and a slanderous accusation of its ancestry. Not to mention (she went on) all the upset to Mrs. Henderson and Mrs. Skinner, there was Maureen, in floods of tears behind the baize door because now she didn't stand a hope of being on the telly . . .

At last, having let off at least some steam, overworked Doris stormed off to deliver trayloads of drinks without giving Mel or Miss Seeton time to order any for themselves.

There was a thoughtful pause, during which, for want of anything better to do, the two perused their menus. Mel, having made her choice, looked up—and saw Miss Seeton, a pucker between her brows, gazing sadly into space.

''What's wrong, Miss S.? Nothing you fancy?''

Miss Seeton started. ''Oh, dear, no—it all looks most delicious, and I must thank you again, Mel dear, for having invited me. But I was thinking—remembering, rather. The apple which Doris described with such—such force,'' said Miss Seeton, rejecting *venom* as rather an exaggeration, then wondering if, after all, it wasn't.

''What about it?'' Mel shrugged. ''An apple's an apple, to the likes of me, but if you insist . . . Green, flecks of russet—acid taste, pinky-orange flesh, cook or eat—pure white blossom, stores well—that's more or less what she said he said, isn't it?''

Miss Seeton nodded. ''And you know, Mel, it made me

wonder . . . I could not help but be reminded . . . '' She nerved herself to confession. ''There is a—a tree in my garden, you see, which bears fruit very similar indeed to the apple Doris mentioned. And I was wondering—if it should prove to be a Murreystone Marvel . . . '' She drew a deep breath. ''I was wondering whether—in the interests of the village—with everyone evidently so disappointed . . . whether I ought . . . since I am, in any case, to be interviewed,'' with a sorrowful sigh, ''which might somehow not make it seem quite so—so . . . ''

As she struggled for the tactful word, Mel rushed to intercept the dread suggestion before it could be made. A Murreystone Marvel in—of all places—Plummergen? In— of all gardens—Miss Seeton's? She'd bet her next three scoops there wouldn't be another in the entire village . . .

Mel looked at Miss Seeton, and saw Duty to Plummergen visibly contending with Distaste for Publicity on her old friend's unhappy features. She looked to the future, and saw Murreystone, incensed at having their glory stolen from them, in combative mood—saw dastardly deeds of every kind, mischief and mayhem and malevolent machination . . .

She made up her mind. She leaned forward, and lowered her voice so that only Miss Seeton could hear.

''A bargain, Miss S. You don't say anything about this apple of yours to anyone—and neither, I promise, will I.''

ABOUT THE AUTHOR

Hamilton Crane is the pseudonym of Sarah J(ill) Mason, who was born in England (Bishop's Stortford), went to university in Scotland (St. Andrews), and lived for a year in New Zealand (Rotorua) before returning to settle only twelve miles from where she started. She now lives about twenty miles outside London with a tame welding engineer husband and two (reasonably) tame Schipperke dogs. She is a fully-paid-up, though non-participating, member of the British Lawn Mower Racing Association. Under her real name, she writes the new mystery series starring Detective Superintendent Trewley and Detective Sergeant Stone of the Allingham police.